# THE
# MULtitUDE

# J. M. FRASER

# A Modern-Day Resurrection

*April 12, 2020*

WARDEN SPENCER, FLANKED BY two guards, gaped at a boulder a short distance from the Subway Killer's cell. Scrapes in the floor suggested this eight-foot ball of granite had somehow been dragged from directly in front of the cell door to its current resting place. A boulder having no reason to be anywhere near the prison compound, let alone inside of it.

And the thin, bearded prisoner who'd pushed a woman to her death seven or eight years ago?

Gone.

# PART I:

# GENESIS

# CHAPTER ONE

*Far western Virtus, twenty days after harvest moon, 3414*
*(September 29, 2013, in our universe)*

QUINTUS LASKARIS PEERED THROUGH his spyglass at a smoking beast in the distance. White steam poured from the cylindrical metal chimney of the huge, barrel-shaped machine. The wheels beneath gripped two endless strips of metal stretching in parallel lines all the way to the shimmering horizon. The enemy's clever inventors had come up with a way to neutralize the uneven terrain.

If the rumors were true, ten thousand slaves had worked the project, spiking those metal strips to wooden slats every few feet over an incredible distance, beginning in this scrubby desert where Nirvana's frontier settlements encroached upon Virtus's rightful land and traveling west to the distant mountains and then to the sea. Many had frozen to death in the highest passes when the winter blizzards set in, but slaves were replaceable. The job got finished at that terrible price.

Quintus shuddered. The Nirvana nation was renowned for its violence and heartlessness. Worse than his own countrymen. And they'd soon be coming in force. Several carts waited behind the beast, strung together like beads on a chain. They'd be used to transport goods, weapons, *and soldiers* faster than a horse and without ever tiring.

Somewhere behind him a twig snapped, jolting him with enough adrenaline to bring a metallic taste to his tongue. He shifted from his prone position to a crouch and whipped a dagger from the sheath at his ankle.

"Steady now." A heavy-set, bearded soldier stepped from behind one of the scattered boulders Quintus had been using for cover. "We're on the same side, last I checked."

Quintus relaxed. He and the lieutenant had a good history. "Maybe we should reconsider our loyalties, Bertramus. We'll be outmuscled soon." He handed over his spyglass.

The lieutenant squinted into it and let out a low whistle. "What is it?"

"They call it a locomotive."

"And you're here to steal the plans?"

"We're a little late for that." Quintus looked his dusty companion up and down, then shifted his attention to a small group of soldiers waiting on horseback just beyond the boulders. "Since when do we exiled scouts get reinforcements?"

"That's not why I'm here," Bertramus said. "The king sent for you."

An old wound on Quintus's thigh throbbed as it always did when the weather changed or his nerves frayed or his brother tracked him down. "What could Albus possibly want with me?"

"Come east and find out." The lieutenant delivered the line with a chuckle in his voice, diminishing any concern the king might be up to worse than his typical random foolishness.

"Leave my post and journey for a week? Just tell me now."

"He wants to surprise you." Bertramus crossed his arms. "I'm under strict orders to keep my damned mouth shut."

"Wonderful." Quintus looked to the heavens for escape. If only he could fly like a bird to a land so distant Albus would never find him. Soar to the recent comet so bright in the evening sky he could almost see a smudge of it now, *there,* twenty degrees to the right of the midday sun. He pointed.

Bertramus followed his gaze and grunted. "Another day without a cloud. Will rain never come?"

"Let's not dwell on the weather. Aren't daytime stars bad omens? This might be the beginning of a story we won't like."

The lieutenant clapped him on the shoulder with a heavy hand. "Who can say where a story begins? Are you a scribe or a soldier?"

*The story began here, lieutenant, sixty-eight years earlier.*
*Hiroshima, August 6, 1945*

The angel Gabriella likened Asura Ito to a delicate porcelain doll. Beautiful. Vulnerable. Adored. The twelve-year-old prodigy sat on the opposite bench, across the flagstone path, with hands folded, colorful pins in her hair, the girl's blue-and-white kimono interpreting the sky.

While Asura seemed like an ornament stolen from the Japanese garden on the other side of the wall, Gabriella strived to be no more remarkable than a stepping stone. She'd assumed her preferred appearance as a child, darkening her otherwise blonde hair and reshaping her eyes to blend in. She wore a plain kimono. Her hairstyle didn't sport a single pin—a simple strategy to fool the pilgrims into underestimating her as an ordinary friend, perhaps the girl's poorer cousin, if they noticed her at all. Otherwise, they might have been unsettled by her timeless eyes. Angels, even those as amazing as she knew herself to be, were most effective when whispering their suggestions from the shadows.

The pilgrims had already started forming a ragged line a few yards away, but Asura didn't seem ready for them. The girl brushed nonexistent wrinkles from her kimono, traced a fingertip across the butterfly tattoo on the underside of her wrist, then moved her hands to her head and fussed with some loose strands of hair. Nerves, probably. Too many visitors seeking miracles day after day.

7

"Asura." Gabriella motioned beyond the pilgrims, farther down the path, where stone blocks had been fashioned into a circular entrance in the center of the garden wall. A great eye one might pass through, or a clock, without hands. This gateway framed the fairyland of rocks, shrubs, and blossoming flowers on the other side. Koi darted after insects at the surface of a pond, creating ripples with each thrust. The scent of lilacs wafted in the breeze. "Look into the garden to calm yourself."

"I did, but the weight of the world's secrets still crushes my serenity." Although Asura delivered her odd comment with a tremble in her voice, she managed a half smile as the first pilgrim approached her.

An old woman came forward, dropped an apple into Asura's basket, and touched the girl's hair. The woman moved on in deference to the others, but Asura held up a hand to stop the next from approaching.

Gabriella probed Asura's mind and beheld a wondrous sight, a treasure chest overflowing with impossible information—the precise locations of the world's oil deposits, as well as its gold, silver, diamonds, and uranium. "How did you learn these things?"

Asura shrugged as if the priceless knowledge she'd gained were no more important than an old coin found in the street. "A girl told me about them in a dream."

Only someone from the distant future could share such knowledge. Perhaps an angel who learned these things *after* mankind had fully mapped the world. An angel traveling backward through the vast, timeless World of Mortal Dreams to visit Asura in her sleep. And yet, "We messengers are forbidden from allowing our secrets to escape the deepest realm of slumber. You shouldn't have remembered them."

Asura's smile widened. Mischief sparkled in her eyes. "Is this rule carved in stone?"

From the mouths of children! Gabriella probed deeper into the girl's mind but reached an impenetrable wall. "What are you hiding from me?"

"Perhaps the rules for a game." Asura motioned another visitor forward. The line of pilgrims curved out of the wall's shadows into the glow of the early-morning sun. An air-raid siren blared, but no one looked up. Bombings happened in places other than this.

A gray-haired man approached and bowed his head. "I have pain in these old bones. Heal me."

"I am not a miracle worker. Rise above your handicap."

Something didn't seem right with Asura. She *was* a miracle worker in the sense she knew how to trick people with remarkable illusions. Why undermine her potential dominance by claiming to be ordinary?

A chilly wind swept out of the garden, spurring dead leaves into broken flight. Something wasn't right at all.

The man moved on, and a woman came forward. Asura held up a hand to again slow the homage any messiah worth her salt should have hungered to receive. "I have a ball in the garden, Gabriella. We could chalk the path for our game."

"You'll disappoint these visitors. They're your friends."

"No, they aren't."

Gabriella had been planning to broach the subject of an alliance, but too many questions now hung in the air. "Asura, tell me about this girl you dreamed about."

Asura reached into the basket for the apple, pulled it out, took a bite, chewed. The gleam in her eyes intensified. "She told me I should ask you a question."

"Yes?"

"What would happen if we dropped a pebble into the garden pond?"

"Nothing. A ripple would form but fade away."

Asura leaned across the path and offered the apple.

"Thank you." Gabriella bit where the girl had bitten. Perhaps her sense of foreboding had been misplaced. She plunged ahead with her proposal. "I want to work with you, Asura. You can't imagine how strong we could be together."

"Strong?" Asura met Gabriella's eye with the unsettling

expression of one who truly did know all the secrets. The breeze sharpened, stirring a murmur among the pilgrims, some of whom had to chase their hats. Asura's face remained a mask of innocence despite the unsettling show of power she'd just unleashed. The breeze hadn't strengthened to these gusts on its own.

Gabriella swallowed. "I'm suggesting we could do more than stir the weather."

"Tell me," the girl said.

No. The morning had turned unlucky. A day earlier, ten minutes earlier, Gabriella might have revealed her desire to subjugate the dithering masses. After two horrible wars within forty years of each other, who couldn't read God's message that mankind needed better leadership? But Asura had let down her mask, revealing wisdom and strength far beyond the simple, frail saint she pretended to be. The girl couldn't be manipulated.

Feigned altruism was best for now. "We might save mankind, Asura."

A monarch butterfly landed on Asura's knee. She puffed her cheeks and blew the insect back into flight. "My dream visitor said your pride is too great."

This damnable dream visitor was far too perceptive. Gabriella groped for the best response. "Perhaps it is, but a girl who can remain humble despite learning the world's secrets might help me overcome this flaw."

"The question I asked has two parts."

Gabriella cringed but kept the smile pasted on her face. "Ask the other."

"What would happen if we dropped a boulder into the pond?"

Dozens of fluttering butterflies grabbed Gabriella's attention. They'd abandoned their randomness to form a V in the circular gateway, becoming the missing hands of the clock she imagined earlier. They followed a remarkable choreography, rotating from right to left, the long hand moving so fast it lapped the shorter one, mimicking a clock spinning backwards.

Gabriella couldn't imagine mindless insects flocking in such a manner by chance.

*Had God spoken to her at last?* Her heart pounded.

She'd never heard His voice. Or if she had, He'd spoken too long ago for her to remember. But she wouldn't give up. She'd been searching the shadows for heavenly signs all her life. Anything out of the ordinary could be a message, anything mathematics failed to explain.

A flash incinerated the butterflies, the garden, and the amazing Asura, bright and alive one moment only to melt into a shadow on her stone bench the next.

"Nooooooo!" The blast overwhelmed even Gabriella, its flames scorching her lungs and its winds twirling her into their mighty vortex.

Other screams lifted above the roar. Ninety thousand strong. A collective wail surely piercing the collective subconscious of every living thing.

Then silence.

Gabriella gasped for breath from the top of the mushroom cloud.

This couldn't be happening. She shut her eyes tight, reopened them...closed them again.

How to reconcile such a horror? Yes, mankind's long, twisting road out of Eden had been pitted by war and brutality. But she'd seen it repaved numerous times, through inventions, brilliant works of art, the births of major religions, the spread of civilization around the planet.

All leading to this?

Impossible.

Hiroshima lay in burning ruins far below. An entire city. What had been the point of Abraham? Or Noah, Moses, Jesus? Why had prophet after prophet, and even a messiah, failed to steer man from the gates of Armageddon?

*Because they'd been false prophets?*

She tried to think past the rage boiling in her veins. Those incredible butterflies had delivered a message. God had spoken through them. He wanted her to set a new course.

Or...

Inspiration flashed through her, brighter than the atomic bomb.

God wanted Gabriella to reset the old course. She'd travel back in time to create a butterfly effect so far-reaching the modern world wouldn't bear the slightest resemblance to the one burning below.

Gabriella stormed away to do what needed doing.

# CHAPTER TWO

*Whoosh! From Hiroshima to the Judean Desert,*
*two weeks after the birth of Christ*

GABRIELLA GAZED ACROSS THE sunburned plains from her position atop a cliff. Behind her lurked the castle of King Herod. A leader reviled by history.

Gabriella gazed across the sunburned plains from her position atop a cliff. Behind her lurked the castle of King Herod. A leader reviled by history.

Heat rose from the desert in shimmering waves, interrupted only rarely by reluctant wisps of a breeze. The Dead Sea teased her by scenting the air with the illusion of rain, but when she lifted her head, she found only dry sun. No blessed showers to wash away the stains of her angry tears.

Enough with the crying. She needed to focus on her mission. Hiroshima wouldn't happen for almost two thousand years. She'd left that horror behind for the moment. Or ahead?

No. Not anymore.

She'd traveled backward through the World of Mortal Dreams—the shared, timeless dimension all humans visit in their sleep. A place where dreams linger even after their hosts have awakened. She'd skipped from one such dream to another, leaping from place to place, era to era, until she found a dreamer at the proper coordinates, in Herod's front yard. Gabriella had stepped back into the waking world at that point.

Only a few gifted mortals had the ability to use the World of Mortal Dreams like a cosmic subway ride, but angels could do it with ease. Of course, they weren't allowed to change the past. Gabriella knew such an act to be a mortal sin. Yet, God had spoken to her, had he not? She'd seen and heard *His Word* through the choreographed butterfly dance in the garden gateway and Asura's odd question about a boulder falling into the pond.

Gabriella knew just which boulder might work, but she trembled at the implications. Suppose she'd misinterpreted, allowing her rage, her grief, *and the image of Asura's burnt shadow* to cloud her judgment?

No way.

The magnificent burst of logic bringing her to Judea had been inspired by the heavens above, not from any turmoil within her soul. God had sent her to reverse many centuries of madness.

The world's greatest religions had long been magnets for violence. If she could nip one in the bud by eliminating its founder, perhaps the clock would spin in a peaceful direction, avoiding crusades, jihads, inquisitions, pogroms, the development of advanced weaponry...*the destruction of Hiroshima.* She choked back a sob.

Enough! She'd left her emotions behind. The path she now followed was a righteous one. And if she'd turned at the wrong fork here in Judea, she could travel further back, to Moses. Or perhaps forward a bit. She'd try over and over again, because she was...

Playing God?

No. No. No. No. *No.*

Following God's direction.

She turned to the scene behind her.

Deep within a mighty palace, King Herod the Great rolled over and continued his nap in the peace and contentment of a protected man. The mile-long wall protecting his palace stood tall enough to discourage the fiercest army. The masonry rose twenty feet above the ground, and sentry towers soared three times as high.

Fiercest army be damned. Breaching the fortification would be mere child's play.

Gabriella hypnotized the guards into opening the gate and then rendered them asleep, along with everyone in the palace who hadn't already settled down for a midafternoon nap.

She stepped into Herod's dream.

History and legend tell many tales about kings heeding messages received in their sleep, but Herod had an inkling of his madness and never trusted his dreams. Therefore, Gabriella settled on a different strategy for communicating with the man. Since he claimed to be a Jew but hedged his bets by harboring a secret belief in mythology, best to have him perceive her as a goddess visiting his *waking life* from the heavens. He didn't need to know he was sleeping, now did he?

She set the king into a sleep walk.

Herod slipped into a white tunic and threw a silk robe over his shoulders. He fitted an emerald-studded leather band around his head. Then he stepped to a marble table and preened in the reflection of a washbasin. Advancing years and desert sun had bleached the man's beard, sideburns, and hair but spared his brows their darkness. They enhanced the brooding madness in his eyes.

Gabriella led the king out of his bedchamber, across the decorative marble tiles of a hallway, and into a lounge where servants, guests, and soldiers lay scattered about, all having been rendered fast asleep. She and Herod stepped around those who'd collapsed to the bare floor. Upon reaching a glistening pool in the center of the room, she awakened him.

While the king splashed water on his face, Gabriella admired the great artwork surrounding them. Intricate clusters of circles, squares, and curlicues adorned the floor and walls. An Egyptian fresco had been painted across the high ceiling to please the eyes of guests awakening from their naps. The eastern décor reflected the influence of Cleopatra, the lover of Herod's best friend, Marcus Antonius.

Eventually, the king turned from the pool and gasped at the sight of those lying senseless at his feet.

The time had come for the game to begin. Gabriella came up behind him. "They say you are the king of the Jews."

Herod spun around, reaching for the dagger sheathed beneath the folds of his robe. But the panic in his face evaporated at the sight of her.

Gabriella had arrived wearing a 1940s skirt and blouse—a wildly provocative outfit for this biblical time. And the king loved young flesh. His second wife, Miriamne, had been but fourteen when they married.

If Herod's bulging eyes were any indication, Gabriella had his rapt attention. But could she hold it? History remembered the king as a madman for good reason. She found only chaos and bursts of uncontrolled laughter echoing within his head. There would be no reading his mind.

"What maiden dares address a king?"

She folded her arms, pressed her lips together, and glared. When playing the role of goddess, one must show a king who is boss. She strolled to a cushion and settled onto it.

"My name is Gabriella, and I come from on high. Perhaps you know my homeland as Olympus." While she couldn't tell a direct lie and refer to an actual goddess's name—the inability to fib is a cross all angels had to bear—she'd always been able to misdirect with ease. Roman and Greek mythology included countless gods and goddesses. The king couldn't have kept up with every one of them.

"Gabriella, you say." Herod moved his hand to his chin.

She nodded.

"I know of no such goddess."

She shrugged.

After a long staring match, he motioned across the room. "You struck down these others?"

"Only you are worthy to cast eyes on me, Herod. They'll awaken after I depart." She patted the cushion beside her.

The king sat and wasted no time petting the flesh above her knee.

Gabriella brushed his grubby fingers away. "I've come from the future."

"What manner of goddess can do such a thing?"

"Think of me as a messenger, if goddess doesn't suit you. Where I come from, we have a revered book called the New Testament, and within that treasure, the scribe Matthew tells of you."

"Ah, history remembers me."

"Not fondly, I'm afraid."

Herod gripped her leg.

She swatted his hand. "Matthew spoke of a plot you uncovered."

"A plot?"

"Yes, involving a pretender to the throne. The locals claimed a new king of the Jews had been born, and according to Matthew, you sent three trusted men to determine the infant's location."

Herod returned his hand to his chin and looked past her with cunning in his sharpened eyes. "Tell the rest of this Matthew's story. Do I succeed in killing the child?"

"His reference to the three Magi was accurate?"

"A *goddess* from the future should know."

The king would have been shocked by Gabriella's limited store of firsthand knowledge. During Christ's years on earth, she had lived in Ethiopia, oblivious to the events unfolding in Judea. But she did know the Bible. "According to Matthew, someone advised the three Magi to remain silent. You haven't heard from them, have you?"

Herod burst off the cushions. He paced in front of her, muttering to himself. Back and forth, back and forth, hands clasped behind his back. "I'll send my soldiers to hunt the pretender down!"

"You won't find him."

"I've heard he was born in Bethlehem. We'll kill every infant in the village."

"Herod."

"We'll search Jerusalem, too!"

"Please sit with me. I've come to help." She patted the cushion again.

The king returned. Muttered some more. Quieted. He kept his hands to himself, the threat to his throne having trumped his lechery.

Gabriella met his simmering eyes. "The Magi were warned in a dream. Only an angel could have provided such a signal. Angels are God's messengers."

"Which god?"

"The only God. In any event, I no longer believe the angel acted on His behalf. Perhaps she misinterpreted His intentions." Gabriella suppressed an involuntary shudder. That particular knife could cut both ways.

Herod caressed his beard with spindly fingers. "The gods want *me* to be king."

"We can right this wrong."

"How?"

If she answered his question, she'd be denying the world its messiah.

But the dancing butterflies had pantomimed a clock spinning backward, and Asura had spoken of boulders.

*God wanted this.*

Didn't He?

What was she doing? What was she doing? What was she doing?

Gabriella took a deep breath. "Send your soldiers to Egypt. I'll draw a map of the region where Joseph, Mary, and the young pretender are hiding."

*Next stop: New York City, August 6, 1945*

Gabriella again used the World of Mortal Dreams for passage, returning to the proper date on the calendar. What would she find in the Americas? Would the region even be settled yet? Her heart thumped in her ears.

Perhaps God would reward her. Maybe she'd find the gates of heaven within the forested island, which might not be known now as Manhattan. He might favor her with a seat at His right side. Oh, what a joyous blessing that would be. She'd whisper counsel to him. So many ideas floated in her head. She might even—

Wait.

The World of Mortal Dreams waystation at the end of her trip back from Judea, the sleeping mind she now stepped out of, belonged to a vagrant on a bench within a well-known but completely impossible and desperately unwelcome financial district.

She stood in the middle of Wall Street! The towering Chrysler and Empire State buildings still pierced the northern sky, despite the boulder she'd tossed into Herod's pond.

She blinked.

Taxi cabs honked their horns.

How could this be? Without Christianity, the dominoes should have fallen in a different direction. The Crusades would have been avoided, other wars waged, alliances formed, treaties broken, different babies born, Columbus never conceived.

Gabriella hurried to a specific address, Seventy-nine Broadway. One of the city's oldest architectural monuments.

Trinity Church still pointed its spire to the heavens.

She caught her breath.

That insane fool of a king hadn't used the information she provided.

Unless...

Perhaps God had spoken again, this time in anger, using a flick of an almighty hand to deflect her feeble attempt at changing the past.

Gabriella lowered her head, awaiting the inevitable lightning bolt to strike her down.

An airplane buzzed high above. Two children laughed as they played marbles in an alleyway.

*Come to me.*

God's anger couldn't have been clearer. He snapped His consonants and elongated His vowels. The voice she'd waited a thousand lifetimes to hear now seared her heart to blackened coal. She choked back a sob.

*Come to me.*

He spoke from the direction of the Hudson River. She trudged forward, an ineffective, outcast angel, summoned by a Creator who no doubt despised her now.

Legions of women rushed by, hurrying to offices where they'd been filling the shoes of their overseas men. Vendors hawked their wares. Traffic clogged the streets. Apparently, news about Hiroshima hadn't reached across the ocean to plunge these people into a mood as dark as hers. But given the lack of proof she'd changed anything, the bomb surely had fallen. Ninety thousand people had perished. Asura was gone.

*Come to me.*

Perhaps God planned to aim the lightning bolt at the water's edge so no one else would be hurt when He struck her down.

The crowd thinned in Battery Park. A few sailors loitered with their girlfriends. Two young women pushed buggies side by side, chatting, giggling, unaware a shocking event in Japan surely portended a time of despair for their unborn children. Mankind would never stop with a single bomb. Apocalypse beckoned civilization like a moth to the flame, and her act had done nothing to stop it.

Gabriella reached the shore and waited. Slow minutes passed. Nothing happened.

She gazed across the brackish waters at the Statue of Liberty in the distance. "How do I even begin to ask forgiveness?"

The statue held her tongue, but a tugboat hauling a battered warship to a repair yard tooted a laugh, and the river stank of fish. These were not favorable signs. She turned away.

A rumble sent her spinning back.

The water bubbled, steamed, and lifted in reaction to something pushing up from below. Only an object of great mass could create such a disturbance—an impossible event, such as a meteor returning to the cosmos as explosively as it had arrived eons earlier.

Although the turbulence roared like a waterfall, no one seemed to notice. Longshoremen used pulleys to load a ship with containers from a nearby dock. Taxicabs beeped their way around Wall Street traffic. The voice of a boy hawking newspapers rose above the clamor.

A shadowy shape far less massive than befit the initial ruckus lifted out of the water. Soon, a mere sheet of smoke hovered a few feet above the surface, rushing from bottom to top with dizzying fury, each end curling into itself like a scroll.

Gabriella trembled.

"Hiroshima!" the newspaper boy hawked.

A tugboat blasted its horn again.

The smoke drifted toward her.

The hand of God?

# CHAPTER THREE

*Tense moments later, still in Manhattan, August 6, 1945*

NO SULFUROUS HELL FIRES.

Gabriella savored the aroma of fish in the Hudson, car exhaust, factory smoke, hot dogs, and a hundred other city smells. God hadn't struck her down with an angry hand.

She turned her back on the roiling curtain of smoke and headed uptown, if not walking with a spring in her step, at least enjoying a strong measure of relief. But anguish over the day's earlier events soon closed in on her again, tightening her throat and watering her eyes. She walked faster. To where, she didn't have a clue. *Away.*

The smoke tagged after her like a lonely puppy. Just as before, nobody noticed an impossible, three-foot-high column softly murmuring like a distant waterfall. Not the sailors on leave in their smart white uniforms, the women hurrying this way and that in a city whose young men were still mopping up the war overseas, the shoe-shine boy beckoning customers, or the street vendor lording over a steaming cartful of hot dogs. In the chaos of New York, was almost *anything* taken in stride?

No. More than likely, she was dealing with somebody's idea of a joke meant only for her. In Gabriella's worries over retribution for a failed blow against Christianity, she'd mistaken simple illusions for a heaven-sent message. A prankster toyed with her.

Henry Stoddard came to mind.

Like those few others of his kind, Stoddard spent most of his time living as a hermit in the World of Mortal Dreams. His breed of wise men—some might say sorcerers, but she knew better—possessed three gifts that set them apart from ordinary mortals. And these were grand gifts, indeed. Each of these men knew how to freely travel back and forth between the waking world and the World of Mortal Dreams without losing awareness of one side while visiting the other. Each enjoyed an excessively long lifespan. And each had the ability to draw on the collective imagination stored in mankind's infinite collection of dreams to create staggering illusions.

Gabriella had a destination now. Not Uptown or Midtown or across the river to the next borough. Not inside or outside or up or down. *Within.* She closed her eyes, freed her mind, and crossed from the waking realm to the World of Mortal Dreams.

Henry Stoddard kept his castle where most dreamers didn't tread. Gabriella trudged across a forbidding fantasy of badlands and cliffs, her unwelcome smoke cloud in tow, until she caught sight of the white tower rising above the rocky hills.

She hesitated. The wise man hadn't welcomed her into his castle since the days of the Puritans. Although the Salem witch trials had ended over three hundred years ago, he still harbored a grudge over her small role in the matter—a few whispered suggestions gone awry. Why was an angel always to blame? People made their own choices. She hadn't forced anyone to follow her wishes.

But perhaps the smoke breathing down her neck was Henry's awkward attempt at extending an olive branch after all these years. What better time than this? After losing Asura, she surely needed a friend.

Gabriella found him puttering in a garden outside the castle walls. The man stood as tall as ever and still cut a handsome profile in a rugged sort of way, despite the toll of centuries. He'd shaved his beard and trimmed his dark mop of hair to a civilized length since the last time she'd seen him. Now he looked like just another ordinary, suntanned fellow who happened to rival Moses, Abraham, or Noah in lifespan.

Henry glanced up from a bush he'd been pruning and stared at her for a long moment. "Well, look who the wind blew in." Not smiling, exactly, but not frowning, either. He set his shears on a worktable beside an assortment of roses.

The flowers might have been meant for Sarah. He'd been visiting his wife's grave for centuries. Or perhaps he'd found a new love interest at last. Gabriella would have probed Stoddard's mind, but the man had a sixth sense for detecting such an invasion, and he always got grumpy over it. He'd extended an olive branch. Improper behavior on her part could set their relationship back another three hundred years.

"What have you got following you?" Henry had humor in his voice. A fine start.

"You tell me."

He stepped up to the smoke, held a hand near it as if testing it for heat, then plunged inside, up to the wrist. He pulled out, none the worse for wear. "How would I know?"

"I thought you conjured it."

Stoddard glanced from her to the smoke and back again with hand on chin, lips pursed. "To what end?"

He had to be bluffing. Maybe if she just stole a quick peek inside his—

"Are you rooting around in my head, Gabriella?"

Slogging through a morass of irritation would have been a more apt description. She almost tripped over his scowl on the way out. "I'm having a bad day."

"That's no excuse." Whatever friendliness might have been evident in his expression at the start of this conversation had now turned to ice.

Gabriella almost melted into a puddle of tears. She fought them back and shook her fist at the smoke curling from bottom to top in its never-ending rush. "This *thing* rose out of the Hudson River and decided to shadow me wherever I go."

"Move along, then." Henry took up the shears and bent to a bush.

"But I came to see you."

"Go away. You're a *maloika*."

The scent of flowers brought too sharp an image—a Japanese girl, the shared bite of an apple. The tears were getting harder to hold back. "A what?"

"A *maloika*. Trouble. The evil eye. You bring bad luck wherever you go."

She couldn't stop her shoulders from trembling.

Henry took a step back. "Oh no, you're not going to—"

The well of tears burst, bringing racking sobs, helpless sobs, lonely sobs.

He wrapped his arms around her. "We all have bad days. Wait for tomorrow."

"But what will I do tomorrow?"

They sat at a table in the middle of Henry's kitchen. Every time Gabriella looked up, his disapproving expression sent her scurrying for cover. She told most of her tale to the steam rising from her mug of hot chocolate.

Fire roared in the hearth on her left, but her column of smoke had positioned itself in the way, diminishing her view in that direction to glowing shadows. A few blackened pots hung from pegs on the opposite wall, a sink with a water pump stood against the third, and an old wooden cutting table rested at the fourth. Henry could browbeat her all he wanted. He had his own set of issues. Rather than let go of Sarah, he still lived centuries in the past.

On the positive side, the wise man did keep a crucifix on the wall above the cutting table. And she'd seen him kneel before it for morning prayers. Despite his magnificent gifts, Henry knew who was mortal and who was God.

Too late for her to follow *that* example. Having finished her story about miracle workers and bombs and failed suggestions to insane kings, Gabriella dared look into Henry's scolding eyes. "Can you blame me for what I did?"

"Let me get this straight. You took it upon yourself to change history by trying to kill the most influential figure in two thousand years—someone *I* happen to believe was the Son of God—and you don't think you should be blamed for it?"

"You had to be there, Henry. In Hiroshima."

"You better hope God doesn't take this personally."

"He shouldn't. I was interpreting His will."

The mop-haired, self-righteous, scowling curmudgeon spread his arms and looked heavenward. "Did you hear that? She didn't think you'd mind!"

"Go ahead. Twist the knife." What had she been thinking? Why hadn't she talked to someone like Henry before heading to Judea? The signs she'd read in Japan had been ambiguous at best. Fury must have clouded her judgment, even though she'd imagined herself calm when she met with Herod. She'd been as crazy as the king!

Henry lowered his arms and stared into her soul again, sending her running for cover, back to the warm steam of her drink. "I know you have a moral code, Gabriella, warped though it may be. You must have had a guiding hand at some point."

"Not really. I figured things out on my own."

"Heaven help us."

"I did hear voices when I was very young, but they weren't useful."

"What did they say?"

"No, no, no, no, no, no, NO!"

Henry burst into guffaws. "You should have listened."

"Do you enjoy making fun of me?" She stole a sip of her burnt drink. The old fool had tried roasting a pot of hot chocolate over the flames of his hearth instead of doing something modern such as conjuring a stove with controllable burners. Nevertheless, she didn't complain, and she didn't use her magic to improve the flavor. Henry had hugged her. She'd respect his ways. She'd even endure a scolding.

"I'm thinking there's a reason you shape yourself in the image of a child," he said.

"I like the look."

"You angels live forever. Maybe your emotional adolescence lasts thousands of years."

"Maybe you should be more respectful of an angel."

Henry scowled. "Try acting like one. Do any of your little friends have a user's manual for metaphysics? You might want to bone up on the topic next time you get a notion in your head to mess with history."

He had her there, on two counts. She'd love to get her hands on such a book, and, "I don't have any *little friends.*"

"How do you know? Would you recognize another angel if you saw one?"

Probably not. Nor was she good at pegging messiahs. Her thoughts strayed to the image of a human shadow burned into a marble bench. She shuddered.

"Perhaps your brethren are shunning you," he said.

"Careful. I might not be done crying yet."

Henry took up his mug, sipped, grimaced, and set it back down. The browbeater wasn't perfect. He couldn't even make a good cup of hot chocolate.

Gabriella stifled a smile.

"Here's a lesson," he said. "A small change to the past won't have any more effect than dropping a stone into the ocean."

Or a pebble into a pond. "Are you quoting your elusive book of metaphysics?"

He rubbed his hands together. "We'd make a pretty penny selling one, wouldn't we?"

"You have no answers, do you?"

"I know of a theory."

"Yours?"

"I've heard it bandied about."

"Do share."

"The past already happened. You can't change it."

"Thanks for the news flash," she said.

He leaned forward and eyeballed her, glanced at the smoke, then back again. "Wait, there's more. The theory goes like this. You can't *change* the past, but if you create a big enough wave in it, a new version will spring alive in another dimension."

She blinked.

He nodded.

By telling a mere secret, had she duplicated the world, along with all two hundred fifty million of its inhabitants at the time? She'd have set them on a new course while leaving the original universe intact. One civilization for her and one for God.

Hers might be the better one! She'd spend so much time with this combination of dollhouse and chessboard, guiding mortals away from the violence in their souls.

And yet, all she'd seen while in Manhattan had been... Manhattan. "How would we know if I created a new world?"

"There's talk of portals." Henry directed his attention to the smoke again. "Did you have that thing on your heels *before* your little trip to Judea?"

The pebble of insight nearly flattened her. She couldn't find her voice.

"Step through it and see what you find," he said.

Gabriella pushed her chair back and turned to the possible doorway of a magical new dimension. But playing God might be heavy work, relentless. When would she rest? And mightn't a dimension without Christ's own influence be a dark place—even worse than the one she'd tried to fix?

Suppose her role was to trudge across this other earth now like Diogenes, searching for an honest man to replace *the son of man*. How many centuries might *that* take?

"I need to think about this. Thanks for the hot chocolate. And the hug."

"Come any time." Henry spread his hands. *"Mi casa es su casa."*

"What if I never step through the smoke. Will it go away eventually?"

The spark of humor returned to his eyes. "Ah, the ostrich approach."

"Mocking me. Always mocking me." She headed toward the door, with the gray curtain nipping at her heels. "I just might dropkick this thing back into the Hudson River and walk away."

"It's all the same to me," Henry said. "I can control *my* curiosity."

Ha ha. Gabriella had a notion to fashion the smoke into a club and beat him with it. And yet, he did hug her. "Do we have each other's back, Henry?"

"Are you asking whether I'll fish you out of there when you get stuck inside?"

"I can control my curiosity, thank you very much."

She left the castle.

*Back in Manhattan*

At the banks of the Hudson River, Gabriella turned to her unwanted pet. "Scoot! I don't want you."

The smoke's waterfall-murmur grew as loud as thunder.

"Go," she said.

Nothing happened.

"I'm not stepping through you."

Still nothing.

"I'm not."

The smoke had all day.

She lasted nearly an hour before curiosity overcame her.

*And on the other side? Sanctimonia:*
*Forty days before harvest moon, 3346*
*(still August 6, 1945, in our world)*

Gabriella staggered out of a small log cabin located within a meadow surrounded by thick forest. A summer breeze warmed her face, but dusk would soon settle, judging by the position of the sun. She hesitated, considered bolting, and glanced back. The portal of smoke, this ridiculous doorway from one place to the other, hadn't abandoned her. She could leave whenever she wanted.

She moved away from the cabin then, in slow, measured steps. Ten paces. Twenty. She stopped again, looked back at the portal, blessedly unwavering, then resumed. Thirty. The grass softened her footfalls like a plush rug. Thirty-five.

"Umphhh."

An invisible barrier with the elastic texture of a balloon bent inward but refused to let her through. She tried to walk around but bumped into it again. And again. Gabriella headed in the opposite direction, back to the portal and beyond. Ten paces, twenty, thirty, thirty-five. Again she hit a barrier. A swarm of butterflies teased her by flying right through it, but when she pushed, the wall held fast.

She returned to the portal and tried another direction but couldn't break free. She came back, tried another, failed again. More butterflies danced back and forth, unimpeded by the invisible wall. The wind scattered leaves through the barrier. A chipmunk scampered from one side to the other.

Enough. She headed back to the portal. If God wanted to be the only creator, why hadn't he just told her so? A simple no would have been far clearer than His ridiculous signs.

"Ho!" A man's voice came at her from the trees to the south. His green outfit blended so well with the forest, she didn't see him until he stepped into the meadow. He carried a crossbow in his right hand and looked as though he'd leapt from the pages of Robin Hood. "*Exspectata ut Sanctimonia*," he said.

Welcome to Sanctimonia.

Gabriella hadn't heard Latin spoken outside a church or rectory in fifteen hundred years.

# CHAPTER FOUR

*The village of Aricia in western Virtus*
*Twenty-one days after harvest moon, 3414*
*(September 30, 2013, in our world)*

QUINTUS TROTTED ACROSS A stretch of cobblestone marking the entrance to a dusty village. Several yards ahead, a golden-haired beauty in peasant dress hurried onto the road and threw an armful of palm leaves in his path. He reared his horse, nearly pitching himself off the saddle to avoid running her down.

His friend and escort, Bertramus, along with their small company of soldiers came up from behind with a clamor of hoofs on stone and shouts of *"Whoa," "Steady, girl."*

The beauty, a maiden of perhaps nineteen, offered a shy smile. She shaded her eyes against the sun. "Welcome, sire."

"Sire?" What manner of foolishness was this?

The pretty young woman held her ground in his path like a siren luring her prey to an exquisite death. She offered no explanation for littering the road or addressing him as king.

Quintus averted his gaze from her ample bosom and focused his attention on her face. He had as much desire for women as any man, but he'd lately decided to deny himself a pleasure that always proved fleeting at best. *Love and honor the woman first, do her right by marrying her, and then enjoy the fruits. A* laughable motto in this savage land, but one he believed would bring greater happiness in the long run.

He kept that bit of wisdom to himself. Why open himself to ridicule by others, such as the men accompanying him who had already started chuckling over something? He ignored them and addressed the woman. "Your offering almost killed me. And for what? You can't possibly think me a king."

She bowed her head. "Oh, yes, I do, King Albus."

The soldiers' chuckles exploded into laughter.

*Of course.* The men had ridden through this village earlier on the way to retrieve him from his post. They must have spread the false news among the local populace. Quintus turned to their lieutenant, Bertramus.

The red-bearded scoundrel winked and laughed.

The woman reddened. An unintended victim of the prank, she now seemed ready to burst into tears.

Quintus dismounted and draped an arm over her shoulders. He summoned as regal a tone as he could invent. "You've honored me greatly, dear lady. Ignore these laughing fools. They're jesters in training."

She glanced up at them, then back down at the road. "Jesters in…?"

"*Training.* For a performance in the capital." He led her away from the chuckling fools. "Enough about them. Let's talk about you."

"About *me,* sire?" She spoke to the cobblestone at her feet.

"Tell me your name."

"Livilla," she whispered.

Quintus lifted her chin with a finger. "Livilla, your blue eyes remind me of the great saint Gabriella. And your golden hair is ever more beautiful than hers. You've heard of Gabriella, yes?"

Livilla beamed. "The saint the of woods? Yes, sire, but Gabriella is a myth. No one in these lands has ever set eyes on the girl."

"Oh, she's real, all right. One must travel to Sanctimonia to find her, for she never leaves her cabin grounds. But why would anyone hazard such a journey when the proud village of Aricia boasts a woman as special as you?"

Livilla graced him with a smile.

Quintus helped her gather the palms from the road.

*Twenty-eight years earlier, in Peace Memorial Park, Hiroshima, in our world, August 6, 1985*

For the fortieth time in as many years, Gabriella planted a vibrant yellow flower at the approximate point where a circular gateway once hosted a swarm of butterflies. The memory of Asura's demise brought fresh tears to her eyes.

A crew of groundskeepers lurked nearby. They'd pounce when they found the tulip in their azalea patch, just as others had done each previous year—rooting the flower out and bringing a fresh stab of pain to an angel's heart. This emotional ritual of birth and death surely served as suitable penance for Gabriella's misguided message to Herod, but did God even notice? His voice remained silent.

She trudged from the garden to the cenotaph, a white monument resembling a horseshoe standing on its legs. As always, she focused on the spot where Asura's name should have been carved with the others, but the child's death had gone unnoticed by the sculptors.

Not for the first time, hope stirred her heart. Perhaps the girl who knew all the secrets had survived the blast. Maybe she'd been an angel disguised as a human. But if so, why hadn't Gabriella sensed the girl's nature? And why had Asura never returned?

Oh, to block the fruitless meanderings of a lonely mind! Other victims had been left off the official record as well, their hopes, dreams, loves, and conquests vaporized into nothingness, just like Asura—a forgotten miracle worker who'd left only a burnt shadow on a marble bench.

Gabriella turned to the skeletal remains of the Industrial Promotion Hall in the near distance. The cylindrical portion of the crumbling stone complex remained intact, but the beautiful green dome it originally supported had melted in the blast. Only a metal frame remained to hint at the structure's former grandeur.

How to reconcile the majesty of man's architecture with the destruction caused by his darkest weapons? She'd once thought religion had been the principal cause of violence. Now she knew better. She'd inadvertently duplicated the universe when she whispered to the mad king, cloning a copy of earth without Christianity. Within that alternate world, the brutal fiefdom of Virtus now thrived. A land with a long history of mayhem and bloodshed, and religion had nothing to do with that.

Gabriella glanced over her shoulder at a curtain of smoke still following her after so many years. She'd rendered it invisible to avoid embarrassing questions by onlookers, but she still knew what lurked where others saw only shadow—not just a portal to another dimension but a constant reminder of the hard lesson she'd learned. Wars, murders, rape, and treachery had all been on the increase in both dimensions since 1945. If anything, the world needed more messiahs, not fewer.

Hiroshima day. She'd had enough of her annual pilgrimage. She found an elderly man dozing on a nearby bench and escaped into his dream.

"I've seen you before," he said.

"I visit on this date every year."

"But for such a young girl to come without her parents, always *alone...*"

The word bit hard enough to bring more tears. An all-too-brief friendship with Asura had eased the ache of loneliness for a while. After that, solitude. She turned away to hide her face.

"Crying won't shame you," the man said.

She fled to a woman's dream in Tokyo and then to a boy's in Hong Kong. She leapt from there into Europe, dashed across the ocean, bounced through New York, Pennsylvania, Arkansas, and finally emerged from the World of Mortal Dreams into a region of northeast Texas where the hilly Ozarks fade into thinning forest.

On the other side of the portal lay a different place despite its perfect correlation with these geographic coordinates in the southern U.S. During one of her earliest forays through the smoke, she'd matched the two areas by studying the stars, but the solution to that little mystery only led to more questions. Why had God opened a gateway to one particular location—Sanctimonia, a peaceful wooded region bordered by the hostile and violent fiefdom of Virtus? Did a messiah live in the immediate area? Thus far, her search for one had proven fruitless.

Yet she still couldn't shake the notion a savior in Sanctimonia might be a step in God's grand plan. The original world remained deeply troubled despite once having been blessed by the birth of Christ. Perhaps a second, newer messiah would emerge in Sanctimonia, travel to Virtus, where he'd show the barbarians the light, and then march across the portal of smoke to try saving God's original children again.

Hence the butterflies dancing in Asura's garden just before the atomic bomb exploded.

Surely God had given a sign to her in 1945 Hiroshima. To believe otherwise would be to admit she'd committed perhaps the most heinous act of defiance against Him since Adam and Eve bit the apple.

But could mankind be saved? And what could she accomplish from a distance? Whenever she stepped through the smoke, the barrier circling the cabin grounds held her captive. God hadn't hinted at a solution yet, or if He had, she'd never noticed. His signs remained maddeningly ambiguous.

Cold rain pouring down through the trees sizzled behind her.

She turned to the smoke. "What do you hold in store for me today, old friend?"

Her dogged shadow never provided any answers.

*Sanctimonia: A moment later*

Gabriella crossed from chilly, damp weather to summer warmth, witnessing again the spectacular repercussions of her simple conversation with a biblical king. On Sanctimonia's side of the portal, her erasure of Christianity's birth had caused different patterns of settlement, a delayed beginning of the industrial revolution, less deforestation in critical areas, and many other factors leading to a radical climate difference.

The sun-drenched meadow before her led to a nearby forest. As always, the trees teased her with a scent of pine she'd never been able to savor up close. But she always tried. Gabriella took a deep breath and started walking until the barrier announced its presence thirty-five paces later. The invisible bubble held fast against her probing hands.

What a fool she'd been to expect anything different! She'd risen in the morning with a rare hint of optimism, believing this day might hold something special in store. Forty years had passed since her act, and that number carried biblical significance. Now, her failure to break through the barrier spoke volumes about God's anger with her. Misguided hopefulness wouldn't change the situation.

A mild breeze brought the lilting voice of a woman lurking somewhere near the garden. Gabriella headed back toward the smoke and around the cabin, admonishing herself for her recklessness. The sunshine must have addled her mind!

The local Mystic tribe had no way of knowing about the bubble unless some fool of an angel flailed against it in broad daylight. These natives passed through the barrier unimpeded, as did the birds, the butterflies, the squirrels, the leaves blowing in the wind. Anything and anyone except Gabriella. The invisible wall existed for her alone, and not by some freak of nature. She'd taken it upon herself to redesign God's grand plan, and this clearly represented His punishment—a taste of the world she'd created, but access to only an acre of it.

The Mystics were a cynical people likely to reach the worst possible conclusion if they learned about her imprisonment. They couldn't be expected to straggle into a *sinner's* garden for the blessings, dream interpretations, marital advice, biblical teaching, and the many other charitable acts she'd been performing to regain God's favor. Thus, she'd taken great care to cultivate the image of an eccentric priestess who restricted her wanderings to the cabin grounds by choice rather than heavenly edict.

Luckily, the dark-haired young woman waiting on a bench kept her gaze fixed on the garden and seemed lost in the melody of the ballad she sang. In fact, Gabriella came all the way over and settled onto the facing bench before attracting any notice at all. The woman had been twisting her long braid of hair in the lap of her weathered dress. Now she released it, clearly startled.

"*Abyssus.*" Gabriella used the Latin word of greeting.

Latin still thrived on this side of the portal. From what she'd been able to piece together after thousands of conversations with these locals and various travelers, the world she'd created was, in many respects, a biblical reflection of the original one across the smoke. Yet despite the Roman Empire's survival here, a four-thousand-mile distance defeated the emperor's attempts at authoritarian rule over the vast regions his armies had settled. Thus, Latin amounted to no more than the ineffective shadow cast by a toothless empire. A common language hadn't been enough to prevent the colonists from splintering into tribes. Some, such as the barbarians across the border in Virtus, allowed themselves to be ruled from afar by proxy. Others, including these Mystics, proved impossible to control.

Gabriella likened these loveable people to the Judeans of Herod's era and found significance in the similarity, grasping at this straw as evidence a new messiah would wander onto her cabin grounds sooner or later.

"*Abyssus*." The woman's initial wide-eyed reaction reverted to the stoic expression typically exhibited by members of her tribe. These hardy people preferred to reveal emotion only when it suited them. Otherwise, they favored the blank slate— maddening for an angel who couldn't read minds on this side of the portal—another of the curses God had rained down on Gabriella's head. She had no greater power here in Sanctimonia than the meekest of mortals.

"I'm Gabriella," she said.

"I am Carmella." They stared at each other for a long moment until the woman added, "What they say about you is true."

"And that is…?"

"Goddess, you have the body of a fawn but the eyes of a lioness!"

"Don't call me goddess. I am only a prophet!" Gabriella relished the love these people had for her, but good lord! If she allowed them to feed her vanity by worshipping her, she'd probably *lose* grace with God rather than regain his favor. The road to forgiveness had so many forks.

She had only herself to blame for her deification. She'd let the Mystics watch her pass through a portal that never admitted any of them, she'd stubbornly clung to her youthful appearance despite the passage of forty years, and she'd worked "miracles" by curing their illnesses. The medicines she brought through the portal always went flat and the food stale, but she knew how to make penicillin from bread mold and aspirin from the bark of a willow tree.

A cynical inner voice reminded her she craved adoration. Asura had been right about her vanity. For that reason, Gabriella had tried doubly hard to please God by helping these people, teaching such subjects as advanced navigation techniques, the use of cover crops to avoid erosion, and on a spiritual level, lessons from the Old Testament. Perhaps this visitor had come to hear a Bible story. Mystics took delight in hearing Gabriella verify their ancient myths about Abraham, Noah, and Moses. Her promises of a messiah thrilled them.

If only God would allow *her* to assume the role of savior! But the barrier had its own ideas.

The woman gestured toward the circular stone entranceway in the center of the wall. "You created a beautiful garden."

"Your people lifted and set the stones at my direction, but yes, I planted every seed and dug the pond with my own hands." Gabriella couldn't hide the pride from her voice.

They gazed through the entranceway together. The replica of Asura's garden seemed to captivate the young woman, just as it had enchanted legions of Mystics before her. After obtaining medicine or a hint of magic or whatever else Gabriella came up with, they'd linger on the bench and soak in the flowers, the shrubs, the stones, and the koi in the pond. They'd tell their stories.

Perhaps Carmella would add to the treasure trove of fact and folklore the others had already shared. Gabriella loved learning new details about their beliefs, ambitions, value systems, traditions, motivations, and dreams. But God hadn't brought her here to serve as local historian. A messiah would come to her doorstep one day, and she needed to absorb enough local culture to bond with that person with ease.

Meanwhile, the timing of this visit was decidedly odd. The Mystics lived in constant danger from their hostile neighbors in Virtus. This woman had risked her freedom to visit during a period of border unrest. "You shouldn't have traveled here alone," Gabriella said.

The admonishment won a fleeting glance, but Carmella returned her attention to the garden. "I do what I must."

"Virtus lies less than a mile southwest of here."

"I'm familiar with the local geography."

Although Carmella seemed distracted, Gabriella pressed on. "Five women have been stolen in the past week. Perhaps you'll write to me about the geography after you've been dragged across the border and sold as a bride."

Smoke rose from deep within the forest. The barbarians of Virtus might have been sacking a Mystic outpost even as Gabriella spoke.

Carmella swept an arm toward a thicker forest on the opposite side of the meadow. "If this region is so dangerous, why didn't you settle farther away in a different clearing?"

Why indeed? Gabriella looked to the heavens. This cabin location certainly hadn't been *her* choice.

"Because a goddess fears nothing! Nor does a Mystic." Carmella delivered the answer to her own question with fierce pride shining in her eyes. "Woe betide the hapless raider who tries dragging *me* across the border." She hiked her dress to reveal a curved dagger hidden against her calf.

"Good luck with that. We both know the raiders carry far more weaponry than a butter knife."

"I'll take my chances."

"You don't want to be captured by the barbarians of Virtus, Carmella. They stone adulteresses and crucify thieves. They slaughter innocents to thrill the crowds in the arena." A persistent throb in Gabriella's temples reminded her who had inadvertently created such a people.

"All right, then. Let's speak of innocents." Carmella leaned toward the garden. "Stop hiding, Maynya! Come greet our hostess."

A girl's giggle rose above the white noise of crickets from the other side of the stone wall.

"Good heavens, Carmella! You traveled alone with a child?"

"My daughter is the reason for this visit."

A lovely, dark-haired girl of perhaps three appeared within the circle of the gateway. She flashed a wonderful smile, but the dancing butterflies above her head stole the show. They circled *counterclockwise* before breaking away and scattering into the garden.

Gabriella gasped. What were the odds a migration of butterflies would swarm into a stone entranceway and dance this way yet again, forty years to the day after Hiroshima?

Carmella's voice came at her through a fog. "Can a prophet stop my child from speaking in tongues?"

The air became harder to breathe. Words spoken in tongues

came directly from God, did they not? Gabriella gazed into the girl's eyes. "You are Maynya?"

The child nodded.

"And you speak in tongues."

"No."

"Come here, Maynya, and sit beside me."

The child scurried over to the opposite bench, climbed onto it, and buried her face in her mother's shoulder.

Carmella picked thistles out of the girl's hair. "If the elders label my daughter a witch—"

"Hush. She's no such thing."

"Maynya," Carmella said. "Say one of the words."

The girl kept her face buried and said nothing.

"Maynya, please."

"You said I shouldn't." The girl muffled her words into her mother's arm.

Carmella lifted Maynya onto her lap. Gabriella leaned forward, reached across the narrow path, and ran her fingers through the child's hair. "Your mother has nothing to worry about. I see a perfectly normal child."

The perfectly normal child stiffened. She stared past Gabriella with thousand-mile eyes. "My mommy takes me to Burnet Park every day." She spoke the words in perfect English.

The rushing in Gabriella's ears rose above the crickets, the squawk of a crow, and the rustle of a breeze through the garden. Gravity lost its grip on her. She grabbed the bench with both hands to keep from floating away.

Carmella took a braid in her hands again and twisted it into a nervous tangle.

Meanwhile Maynya came out of her trance, squirmed off her mother's lap, and ran to a patch of dandelions sprouting from beneath the garden wall.

"You warn about raiders," Carmella said, "but we both know the elders cast witches *and their mothers* across the border to be rid of them. You speak of crucifixions. Do you know what the barbarians would do to *us*?"

"Maynya, come back for a moment." Gabriella struggled to keep her voice from trembling.

The girl ambled over and offered a yellow flower.

"Thank you, dear. Tell me now, where did you hear those words?"

"They live in my head." She had reverted back to Latin.

"Always?"

"Mostly when I dream."

"And you dream about...?"

Maynya picked another dandelion, this one gone fuzzy. She puffed her cheeks and blew the parachutes apart. "My other mommy," she said, in English.

# CHAPTER FIVE

*Burnet Park, Syracuse, New York (in our world), the next day*

A V-SHAPED SHADOW DIVERTED Gabriella's gaze from the children on the playground to a flock of geese overheard. Forty of them—no more, no less—and who wouldn't find God's voice in the sum?

The Bible used forty as a period of testing—the duration of the great flood, the Israelites' years of enslavement, the days Jesus spent in the desert. Gabriella had endured her own long trial, waiting, wondering, searching for answers, until Maynya appeared in her Sanctimonia garden on the *fortieth* anniversary of Hiroshima.

Carmella's daughter mentioned regular visits to Burnet Park with her "other mommy." Gabriella hadn't found any sign of the mother and daughter yet, but with forty geese honking encouragement from above, something fantastic was bound to happen.

She glanced over her shoulder at the portal lurking behind her. Although she always cloaked the roiling curtain invisible and silent to everyone else, the murmur of rushing smoke still rose in *her* ears above the white noise of nearby traffic. "I'm hoping you'll soon be obsolete, old friend."

Yes, superseded, because a possible second portal between the two worlds had been revealed. How else could Maynya have learned English, visited this park, and referred to a different mother? The child had most likely found a World of Mortal Dreams passageway into the dreams of an American girl.

Extrasensory links often moved in both directions, offering the breathtaking possibility that if Gabriella located the American kid, she could access the same dream channel and travel in the other direction to any part of Sanctimonia and beyond, not just to a stale old cabin surrounded by an invisible barrier. She could widen her search for a messiah, or *perhaps play the role of one* and tame the barbarians in Virtus. Her heart beat fast, but she chided herself for putting too much stock in a possible pipe dream. The long, heretofore fruitless wait had bred a measure of cynicism even in her.

After all, she'd already searched the children's spray fountain and the zoo, places where *other mommies* brought their kids every day. This playground had been the next logical stop, but the boys and girls on the swings didn't provide any clues...only the meandering thoughts of young children. *Parents, siblings, toys, pets, backyards, Hot Wheels, ice-cream cones, churches, schools, day care, and goldfish swimming laps in a bowl.*

Gabriella clenched her fists. Suppose the dream visits had been one-sided? If the American girl had never reciprocated by traveling into Maynya's dreams, she wouldn't carry a single hint of Sanctimonia in her head. No words of Latin, no images of forest, no memories of peasant women who braided their hair or men who brandished crossbows when heading off to work. Without such a marker to distinguish the child, Gabriella wouldn't find the right girl if she searched every young mind in the country! She'd never get to explore Sanctimonia and Virtus.

She couldn't even be sure she had the right location. Maynya might have meant Burnett Park in Jacksonville or some other park with a different name entirely. A young child schooled in Latin couldn't be expected to pronounce an English name correctly.

"Excuse me." The voice of a woman approaching from behind almost startled her off the bench. "Are you one of my friends' daughters? I'm sure we've met."

"She's Gabriella!" a girl cried.

Gabriella shot off the bench. Nobody should have known her name. She took pains to stay ordinary, anonymous, just another child in the crowd.

She spun around…and caught her breath.

Carmella and Maynya had stepped through the portal.

No, such a notion was preposterous. The smoke had been adamant for forty years, granting passage only to confused angels—in fact, just one in particular.

Besides, these two weren't dressed as Mystics. They came wearing ordinary, American skirt-and-blouse combinations—pink and blue for the girl, white and floral for the mother. Dark, *unbraided* hair ran straight down their shoulders. The mother highlighted hers with streaks of auburn, and her daughter sported pink ribbons.

Yet these touches did little to mask the similarity of features, facial expressions, and gestures with…whom? Their cousins on the other side? The mother played with the bottom of her blouse where she'd tied it closed, approximating Carmella's signature nervous tic with her braid. And the girl bent to pick a dandelion, just as Maynya had done.

The woman extended her hand. "I'm Bethany. Were you in the scout camp at Cayuga Lake last summer?"

"No."

"Well, you've met Carla *somewhere* before."

"Carla?"

The little girl beamed, clearly pleased to be acknowledged.

"*Quando autem—*" Gabriella flinched. Finding the mystery girl had flustered her into speaking Latin! She tried probing Carla's mind to find hints of any connection with Maynya, but the three-year old's thoughts were fixated on playgrounds and ice-cream cones. "The two of you do look familiar, but I'm sure we've never met."

"I suppose all of us might have known each other in a previous life," Bethany offered.

Gabriella flinched. How much did this woman know about

Sanctimonia? How could she know anything? Gabriella raced into Bethany's head, but she didn't find any hidden meanings behind the old cliché she'd spoken.

Carla tugged on her mother's hand. "I wanna play!"

"Go ahead," Bethany said, "but stay near the swings where I can see you."

Before the child ran off, Gabriella stole one more peek inside her mind. She fought her way past a blast of joie de vivre and discovered a hidden gem in the quieter area where reality and dreams sometimes converge. She saw butterflies and a patch of dandelions in the Japanese garden outside Gabriella's cabin. Gabriella blinked.

The butterflies took flight.

She leapt into Bethany's head, searched the same somnolent region, and found enough vague images of forestland—and a crossbow leaning against a tree—to suggest the woman might have visited the other side of the portal, as well. Gabriella collapsed onto the bench.

"Do you mind if I share that?" Bethany asked.

Did she mind? Gabriella slid over. "Please do."

The woman settled beside her. "You seemed preoccupied when we came along. I didn't mean to startle you."

"I'm a little off today."

"Are you worried about a test?"

"Yes. No. A what?"

"In school."

"School?" Gabriella's mind swirled into a maelstrom. How could anyone on one side of the portal still have a clone on the other? Yes, the world split into equal parts when Herod's soldiers killed the baby Jesus on the Sanctimonia side, duplicating every man, woman, and child. Yet two thousand years had come and gone! Surely the butterfly effect would have been too extreme for a mother and daughter in one world to still have a match in the other. "Christianity completely changed history, didn't it? Take the Crusades, for example."

"So it's a history test you're worried about."

"No, I—"

Bethany cupped her hands to her mouth. "Stay where I can see you, Carla!"

No point counting the children in the playground. They had to be forty in number.

"I'm a history buff, and you're right about the Crusades. They did change everything." Bethany's babble seemed muted, as if she spoke from a great distance.

Great indeed! Gabriella's mind had wandered two thousand years away. Crusades, inquisitions, pogroms, deaths, marriages, births—all would have been different on one side of the portal than the other. The elimination of Christianity in her dark, parallel world should have swept through the genealogy lines like an avalanche. She couldn't fathom how a single mother-daughter pair there could have mirror images *here*. "This must be the hand of God."

"The Crusades? The Muslims would argue against *that* idea."

"What?"

"Are you religious? So few teenagers are anymore."

"I've struggled with my faith at times, but I'm coming around." Gabriella needed greater focus to get the conversation back on track, but a new question pushed her ever deeper into thought. Even if a line of identical clones *had* survived on both sides of the portal, how were a mother and daughter able to pass memories from one world to the other? They shouldn't have had any connection.

Unless...

Her conversation with Herod might have triggered the birth of a new *physical* world, but perhaps only God could create the unique form of self-awareness known as a soul. In that case, she hadn't duplicated every soul alive two thousand years ago. She'd cleaved them in half!

Each half soul would have split its awareness between two bodies—compartmentalized, awake on one side while asleep on the other, or perhaps flitting back and forth from moment to moment. Reality waxes and wanes. A person could spend a full day in one head over the course of a three-minute catnap in the other. *And perhaps some memories seeped across whatever firewall separated the two*—apparently the case with Maynya and Carla.

But how could half souls still exist two millennia after her act?

Through choreographed butterflies, the number forty, and all things holy.

*Through the hand of God.* Gabriella forgot how to breathe.

Carla raced over, all flushed cheeks and shiny eyes. "Let's go swimming!" She grabbed her mother's hand, and the two of them headed away.

"Good luck with summer school," Bethany called over her shoulder.

"Thank you." Before they got out of range, Gabriella picked a home address out of the woman's head.

*Midnight*

Gabriella crept through the ground level of a raised ranch while Bethany and Carla slept upstairs. She deciphered notes scrawled on calendars, lingered before crucifixes on two walls, riffled through a few bills strewn across the top of an antique secretary, and opened a side door to examine the many carpentry tools in the attached garage. A family's trappings can provide a more reliable picture than the distorted perceptions carried in their minds.

She had a handle on these people by the time she climbed to the second floor. *Happy, hard-working, middle class, Christians.* A likeable family.

Upstairs in the bathroom, fluffy blue towels hung from racks. The ceramic floor was handsomely arranged in a herringbone pattern and the walls were papered with seahorses and coral.

Everything gleamed—the basin, the tub, the faucets. These trappings added color to the portrait she'd sketched downstairs. The man of the house was a carpenter who kept up his castle. The woman was tidy. Nothing in the room suggested anything but a modern American family. Nor had she seen hints of other worlds in the living area downstairs.

The woman, Bethany, tossed and turned alone in the bedroom to the left. Gabriella probed her mind and found trouble. A new construction project in Buffalo kept Bethany's husband away for days at a time. Alone at night with her worries, she focused on his health. The doctors had been reassuring about his cancer remission, but she stressed over whether he'd live to see their daughter grow up.

Gabriella made a mental note to do something, perhaps leave a prayer card for her. Prayer was the best solace during hard days.

She headed to the bedroom on the right.

"Oh my," she whispered.

Bethany must have been influenced by hazy Sanctimonia memories when decorating her daughter's room. A forest-green quilt covered her sleeping daughter. The wallpaper displayed woods and log cabins and Hansel and Gretel wandering where they didn't belong. On the top of a bookshelf, where one might expect to find a Pinocchio figurine or a wax Snow White, an Amazon warrior stood guard with a spear in her hand.

Carla stirred. "I want to sleep with my mommy." She looked up with drowsy eyes, unfazed by the unexpected appearance of a visitor standing just outside her bedroom.

Gabriella didn't need to look inside the girl's mind to realize the world of any three-year-old presented a steady stream of surprises. Small ones such as the random appearance of a vaguely remembered ponytailed friend didn't necessarily evoke a response.

She approached the bed and ran her fingers through the child's hair. "Your mommy's proud of a girl so brave she sleeps alone in her own room."

"Is she proud of Cassy, too?" Carla held up the typical, well-worn child's doll. A stuffed deer.

"She's mostly proud of you. Now close your eyes and take me for a ride."

"Where?"

"The forest would be nice."

Carla snuggled tighter into her stuffed deer and drifted off. Gabriella stole into her mind.

*Minutes later*

From her prone position on a cot, Gabriella looked down at a dirt floor and across a small room to a rough wooden table and two chairs. Embers glowed in a stone hearth off to the left, the remnants of a fire that had burned three logs to dark chalk. Blackened pots hung above the mantel. On the right, a crescent moon and stars shined through an unfamiliar half-open window—not the one in her cabin and not the window in Carla's bedroom.

She could have burst into song. Not only had the dream portal worked, leading her into Maynya's head, she now beheld a place beyond the boundaries of her Sanctimonia cabin grounds.

Gabriella gathered her essence and prepared to leap from a dream to reality, just as she'd done countless times before.

But she couldn't move.

"Pssst. Maynya."

The girl offered no response.

"Maynya, let me out!" As much as Gabriella hated to admit a mistake, she couldn't deny overlooking a critical supposition. Since she'd never had any powers on the Sanctimonia side of the portal, why had she expected to play the supernatural angel and leap from Maynya's dreams into the waking world?

Gabriella gasped for breath. She'd gotten stuck inside the head of a young child.

The room went black.

Was this how the inside of a closed coffin felt? For the first time in her life, Gabriella knew claustrophobia. She trembled at the thought of the worst-case scenario. After forty years of purgatory, God had banished her to Hell for her sin. Perhaps He let Maynya die in her sleep, trapping a wayward angel in her lifeless head. They'd turn to dust together.

But no. Wait. What was that?

A snore?

Maynya's breathing steadied. She hadn't died. She'd closed her eyes and fallen asleep.

"Wake up!" Gabriella tried to calm herself and *think*. "Carla?"

Two eyelids fluttered open, revealing a beautiful sight—a modern American bedroom once again. She couldn't scramble out of the girl's head fast enough.

"Can I have a drink of water?" Carla gazed at her with sleepy eyes.

"Give me a second."

"Why are you crying?"

"I had a bad dream."

"Monsters?"

"Worse." Gabriella escaped to the bathroom and buried her face in a towel. After a long moment, she gathered enough strength to fill a Cookie Monster cup with water and bring it into the bedroom.

The girl accepted the offering with two small hands, stole a sip, and shifted her gaze to her stuffed animal. "Cassy's thirsty, too."

"We don't want a mess. Let me help her drink it." Gabriella took the cup and made a show of holding it to the deer's mouth before setting it onto the bedside table.

By then, Carla had closed her eyes again.

The courage to plunge back into the girl's mind didn't come easily. Many minutes passed before she took the leap.

Maynya must have gotten up, for Gabriella now stared out the window through the eyes of a girl whose nose pressed against the glass. The child stood peering into the darkness alone but with no sign of fear. Odd for one so young. Then a hint of motion in the gray light of early dawn provided the reason for such fortitude. Maynya's mother, Carmella, held a position outside, guarding the girl from twenty yards away.

More likely than not, the woman protected an entire village. She stood with a spear in one hand and a crossbow slung across the opposite shoulder, sporting the leather tunic and high boots of a warrior. This woman was far more than the simple peasant she'd seemed when she brought her daughter to the cabin. No wonder she'd been so self-assured about traveling alone. *Guardians* were widely acclaimed for their fearlessness.

Gabriella had heard numerous tales of valor about these warriors. They'd been stationed in scattered outposts along the edge of a thick forest separating Sanctimonia from Virtus. Many a barbarian raider had stolen through these woods in the past, usually during the dead of night. The guardians watched for them.

A woman such as Carmella held a revered position in the Mystic tribe, one inherited, perhaps from a husband who'd been killed. The job would pass to Maynya one day.

Carmella looked toward the window at Maynya and shook her head. She began creeping sideways, shooting glances at the woods while closing the distance to the cabin. When she reached the window, she glared with such ferocity a timid girl would have scampered away in terror.

Instead, Maynya raised an insistent voice through the open window. "*Ego sum siccus.*" I am thirsty.

Her mother's expression darkened further. "*Servo vestri own postulo!*"

No help would be coming from that quarter any time soon.

Maynya headed to the table on her own. She hauled herself onto one of the chairs, stood upright, managed to keep her balance, and scooped water out of a basin with a tin cup. After she drank her fill, she scrambled back down and returned to her cot.

The girl closed her eyes again.

Gabriella fought off a new onslaught of claustrophobia. If she wanted to travel beyond her cabin grounds, blindness would be the price she'd have to pay whenever Maynya slept. She calmed herself with the rhythm of the girl's heartbeat, the chirp of crickets out the window, the whisper of wind against the cabin walls. To pass the time, she put her mind to work on the puzzle of God's recent signs, but pieces still seemed to be missing. Best to be patient and let Him play His hand.

Eventually, *Carla* awakened, cracking her eyes open.

Gabriella gasped at what could only be described as Dali's version of the Syracuse bedroom. A half-opened dresser drawer melted to the floor. Cassy the deer floated toward the ceiling. The room brightened. The ceiling turned from off-white to lavender.

An eye-blink later, everything reverted to normal.

She probed Carla's mind for the reason and beheld something so rare and beautiful she could scarcely believe her eyes. The fleeting illusions had been caused by an extra brain lobe—the type found among only a few blessed mortals, such as Henry Stoddard. Though microscopic in size, these lobes gave their hosts the ability to project massive illusions...a gift or curse, depending on the local reaction. Although some societies revered those gifted by God with extrasensory abilities, history held many examples of illusion casters persecuted as witches...or sorcerers. Henry spent most of his time as a hermit for a reason.

Spiritualist or demon? Carla wouldn't likely be regarded as either. She had the lobe but lacked the sharpened cognizance required for casting illusions. Not that she was a dull girl. She simply didn't know she possessed her gift. And telling her would do no good. She had to feel the power within.

Gabriella blamed herself. Two thousand years earlier, she'd split every soul in existence. Suppose she'd weakened those with special powers to the point they didn't know they had any? In that case, those descendants still divided would cast only the dimmest of psychic glows, like too many lamps plugged into the same socket. Only if merged together might Maynya serve as the switch and Carla the light.

Then she considered the opposite possibility. What if Carla were the switch and Maynya the light? Gabriella collapsed onto the edge of the bed.

Oh, what a light show Maynya might be! The ramifications exploded like multicolored fireworks in Gabriella's head. They tasted like chocolate, smelled like perfume, and warmed like crackling logs in a fire.

Within the woods of the Mystics, or better yet, the much darker desert home of the Virtus barbarians, an illusion caster might be regarded as a miracle worker. Maynya could mesmerize a following, inspiring them to look upon her as a true messiah, *if* she harnessed her power. Thrust into a leadership role by this circumstance, she could preach a message of love and altruism guaranteed to etch itself into her followers' minds.

God had lifted His elusive whispers to a roar when He sent the girl to Gabriella, providing—at last!—a solution to a forty-year-old riddle. Why had the Sanctimonia cabin been placed where it was?

For Maynya to find.

Gabriella needed to bring the two half souls back together, igniting their lamp to warm the cold universe across the portal. She glanced over her shoulder at the smoke. Suppose she snatched Carla out of bed and carried her to her twin, where the two girls might merge into a single messiah?

No. She could never steal a woman's child.

Could she?

Well, maybe, but the portal had never admitted a mortal before. The Mystics had always flinched away from its heat.

Besides, she needed to bring the girls' souls together, not their bodies.

A hint of an idea tickled the back of her mind but darted like a dust mote each time she tried to grab hold of it.

A scream rose from the other bedroom.

Gabriella hurried across the hall.

# CHAPTER SIX

*A moment later, in the bedroom across from young Carla*

THE GIRL'S MOTHER, BETHANY, leaned against the headboard of her bed, still fast asleep but with eyes wide open. She stared sightlessly through the tangle of dark hair hanging down her face. "Make them stop!" she rasped.

Gabriella touched the woman's wrist. "Shh. You're just having a bad dream."

Bethany slumped down to her pillow. Her breathing slowed. "Visions," she muttered.

*Visions?* Gabriella's heart beat faster. Visions could be messages from God!

She dove into Bethany's subconscious.

Gabriella squinted at the glare of a bright, sunny day. She and Bethany stood on an unusually empty Manhattan sidewalk. In the near distance, flashing emergency lights and blaring sirens diverted the normal crowd of people. Whatever the reason—a traffic accident, a fire, a mugging—the two of them were left alone, at the head of a stairway leading down to a subway station.

The immediate cityscape had undergone a surreal transformation from 1980s Manhattan. Porn shops and strip clubs had been whisked away, the storefronts modernized, the entire skyline updated, all like a Hollywood set for a science fiction movie.

Buildings gleamed. Cars on the street were sleeker than Gabriella knew them to be.

She swallowed. Bethany's vision had pulled them into the future.

Gabriella found confirmation in a newspaper discarded on the sidewalk. The tabloid's headline spouted nonsense about an inconsequential presidential debate, but smaller font in the upper corner whispered earth-shaking news—*October 23, 2012.*

Bethany groaned beside her. She'd gone pale. Terror hollowed her eyes.

Gabriella took her hand. "We're fine. I'll protect you." But how could she protect anyone in a future she didn't know? She tightened her grip.

Bethany stared down the subway stairs as if she'd seen a ghost. "She...she..."

"Who?" The stairs were empty.

"*My Carla.* She'll die down there. I've seen it three times!"

*Three*, the biblical symbol for completeness. Gabriella's stomach fluttered. Was God ready at last to reveal the tapestry He'd been weaving since Hiroshima? "Slow down. Your toddler died?"

"Not my baby. She's grown." Bethany paused, sobbed, gathered herself. "I followed her down the stairs three times. She jumped, she fell, a man pushed her onto the tracks."

A sandy-haired young man swept past them and shouted down the stairs. "Carla!"

"He's the man!" Bethany lurched forward.

"No." Gabriella held fast to her hand. "Let me do this." She leapt into the man's mind.

*Save Carla. Die with Carla.* The man's panicked thoughts were diametrically opposed. Gabriella dove past the chaos of his stressed-out, unreliable awareness and examined his memory. She found Brewster DeLay, an American who sometimes dreamed *in Latin* about another world. But unlike Bethany and Carla, he didn't have a duplicate self in Sanctimonia. His other half lived in the kingdom of Virtus—*among the fallen people Gabriella wanted to save.*

She caught her breath. God had blessed her with two possible messiahs, each with a half soul in either world. First Maynya/Carla. Now Brewster and some mystery man on the other side.

Gabriella waded back into Brewster's conscious mind and picked out whatever lucid thoughts she could find. Brewster knew Gabriella. *She'd sent him on the run.* But why?

No intelligible answer.

She glimpsed a date and gasped. The sands of time had formed dunes that collapsed in on themselves. She and Bethany had come forward twenty-seven years, but Brewster was traveling *backward* by one. God in His puzzling wisdom had pulled from both directions in bringing them to this time and place.

Damn her pounding heart. She'd lost the thread of the man's thoughts!

Gabriella released Bethany's hand and raced down the subway stairs after him, out of the daylight and into the gloom. She paused at the first landing and glanced around. An empty cashier's cage. Advertisements plastered to the wall. Toothpaste, perfume, a men's cologne. An expired movie poster—*Exodus, return engagement, coming October 4.*

A swarm of butterflies burst past the turnstiles. She hurried through them and started down gloomy stairs toward the tracks.

Darker. Darker still. Five steps down, only the dimmest rays of a withering sun shone at her back. Lower, nothing but a black void. She stopped short and stared into an infinity of nothingness, the far edge of Bethany's vision.

*Or her own?* Perhaps this glimpse at the future was the road God had paved for *Gabriella* to follow.

She hurried back up the stairs. "I lost him."

Bethany had picked up the newspaper by then. She looked up from it with an expression of fierce resolve. "None of this has happened yet. I can keep Carla from ever coming near this place. Not now. Not when she's ten. Not when she's twenty…" She returned her gaze to the paper and its telltale date. "Or *thirty.*"

*Thirty.* A tingle ran down Gabriella's spine. Perhaps the dunes of time had shifted for a reason. *Luke 3:23. Now Jesus himself was about thirty years old when he began his ministry.* She'd stolen a glimpse of a birthdate when perusing Brewster's memory. Carla would be thirty in 2012, but he'd only be twenty-nine. Did God pull him back from a year in his future so he and Carla would each be the same blessed age at this climactic moment?

The idea tickling Gabriella's mind earlier in young Carla's bedroom now flared like a thousand candles. In the case of two people sharing a single soul, the death of one should make the other stronger. The premise had such dizzying implications Gabriella had to grab a lamppost to keep from falling. Maybe Carla's accident or suicide or murder in the subway station would merge two half souls together within Maynya. Might the rare brain lobe then come alive, igniting the power of illusion?

In that case, on October 23, 2012, the *thirty-year-old* daughter of a Mystic guardian could begin her ministry, ready and able to use miracles in convincing a doubting people of God's glory.

And Brewster's alter ego in Virtus?

A co-messiah perhaps. Or Maynya's protector.

Except one lived in Virtus and the other in Sanctimonia. Clearly, God wanted Gabriella to bridge the gap.

But how?

Step one would be to let some things play out as intended. Carla would have to die at age thirty.

Gabriella pressed a silver coin into Bethany's hand. A *quatrant* used as currency in Virtus.

Bethany looked down at it, turned it over, ran a fingertip across the symbols. "What is this?"

"Payment for your daughter, but I owe you twenty-nine more." She pulled Bethany back to Syracuse, erased the vision from the woman's mind, and left.

Gabriella had hard thinking to do.

Carla, Brewster, Maynya, and a Virtus mystery man. The hazy outlines of a plan began taking shape in her mind.

# PART II:

# WATER INTO WINE

# Chapter Seven

*The town of Dubris in Western Virtus*
*Twenty-two days after harvest moon 3414*
*(October 1, 2013, in our universe)*

QUINTUS ROSE EARLIER THAN his companions and crept out of camp without waking them, moving on foot in the gray light of early dawn. He followed a maze of narrow streets past the still-sleeping marketplace, around weathered dwellings ranging in quality from mud hovel to adobe splendor, and up to a place of worship nestled just inside the town's sweeping walls.

He'd found this place three years earlier when moving in the opposite direction, *away from* his brother, Albus, and the circle of debauched followers who clung to the man like a dirty cloak.

This crude temple had been referred to as a *church* by a group of pilgrims loitering on its steps that day. They claimed to be the designers of the steep-roofed structure and the large, wooden cross hanging above the entryway. But upon further questioning, he learned they'd gotten the plans from legendary Saint Gabriella in Sanctimonia. She'd taught them all she knew about the *one true God,* as well.

Quintus had been impressed by the humble devotion exhibited by those pilgrims and by the logic of their beliefs, for the most part, not counting their fantastic claims about a girl who never aged. But mostly, he'd been drawn in by the ethereal calm that came over him when he entered this church and sat on one of its wooden benches.

Today, he didn't find calm. Or any of the pilgrims. Instead, grubby moneylenders had already set up their stations at the base of the stairs, sitting on wooden crates before small tables, eagerly waiting for the most vulnerable borrowers—those who had such urgent needs they'd come at the earliest opportunity and pay the highest rates.

These thieves or their kind had removed the cross and scrawled crass messages on the church's adobe walls. *The cost of money. The price of wine. The rates charged by local whores.*

And the pilgrims? He'd heard the tale. They'd been caught in the wide net of a pogrom. Some had been enslaved. Others crucified.

Quintus shuddered. Why return to this desecrated site? What did he hope to find?

"Ho there! Have you come in need of coin?" A cloaked lender hurried out from behind his table, approaching close enough for Quintus to smell his sour breath.

"I've come to remember what was lost," Quintus said.

Yet how to recall such a thing? Virtus had never been a benevolent kingdom in his lifetime. Nor had he heard it to be one at any point in its long, violent history. Overwhelming sadness almost made him sob. He turned his back.

The lender persisted, grabbing Quintus's sleeve. "You've no money at hand? Perhaps you left your purse at home? Come, we'll set down your name and strike a deal for later."

*His name?* He'd lost it in the clouds of gloom now choking him from throat to heart.

*Who am I?*

The clouds parted. *I am Quintus, Quintus, Quintus...no...*

*I am—*

Dut-dut-dut DAH!

The opening of *Beethoven's Fifth* buckled his knees.

Brewster shot up in bed and groped for his bearings in the mental shadows between dreams and reality. Static electricity must have triggered the doorbell. Or wind. Either way, he remembered his name now.

He was Brewster DeLay, a businessman and part-time writer living in Northbrook, Illinois, a place where smart phones, Twitter, Facebook, and Roku ruled the land. He hadn't been summoned from the front to journey across a desert nation where angry mobs crucified pilgrims.

He didn't live in a world where everyone spoke Latin.

He'd first had these nighttime episodes as a boy, but his dad, a professor of language studies, explained them away at the time. *You've heard my lesson rehearsals, and they've gotten stuck in your head,* the old man had said.

What would he say now, some twenty years later?

He'd say, *you are Brewster, Brewster, Brewster—*

Dut-dut-dut DAH!

The blasted musical chime sent him sliding back down beneath the covers. The list of midnight visitors a man hoped to find on his doorstep was short.

A supercharged storm must have pressed its angry thumb on his doorbell. Gusts still buffeted the house, humming through every crack in the frame. Thunder rumbled in the distance and flashes illuminated the window shade, but halfheartedly now and at decreasing intervals. After pausing to punk him, nature had moved on.

But what if somebody real rang the doorbell twice?

Brewster manned up and got out of bed. He padded on bare feet into the hallway and peered over the railing into the foyer. He couldn't see anyone through the little panel of glass near the top of the front door.

He shifted his attention to the living room and stared straight out the picture window behind the couch. A streetlamp at the edge of the driveway cast enough light to provide a shadowy portrait of his lawn, the cul-de-sac, and the neighbors' lawns across the street. At first, no doorbell-ringing soldiers of the night marred his view, but as he started turning toward his bedroom, he caught a hint of motion.

Someone approached from a few houses down—coming not going, and therefore not guilty of ringing his doorbell, but out there all the same. A woman just visible in the dim lighting ambled across a neighbor's lawn, stepped over the curb onto the pavement of the cul-de-sac, and looked up at his house.

Brewster shrugged off a baffling stab of foreboding. An unexpected stranger could seem creepy in the dead of night, but *come on*. The recurrence of the Virtus dream must have set his nerves on edge.

*Virtus*, Latin for power. What an odd name for a nation, even in one's dream. What was his subconscious trying to tell him? Probably that he longed for those pre-recession days when a man didn't fear losing his job, doorbells didn't ring on their own, and mysterious women didn't come calling in the dead of night. And yet, that last item wasn't necessarily undesirable.

He headed into the bedroom, stripped off his pajamas, and hurried into jeans and a shirt. Then he grabbed a pair of sandals from a shoe rack and rushed back to the hallway.

By the time he returned to the railing and glanced out the window, the woman had settled into a sitting position in the middle of the street. Her dress formed a circular pool of dark fabric beneath her, not quite touching the puddles on either side but close enough to suggest she didn't care.

She could join the club of stressed-out middle-class recession victims. Brewster counted himself a member. He'd earlier handled a flurry of emails and phone calls about yet another unsolvable problem at his failing day job. The office had been following him home with increasing frequency lately. A home in need of repairs he could barely afford. Was it any wonder his subconscious had fled the known universe yet again this night?

Still, problems of his own or not, he'd always been a sucker for damsels in distress. He got his sorry ass in gear, headed downstairs and out the front door.

Heavy summer air hadn't headed south yet despite a turn of

the calendar into early October. The thick atmosphere could have fogged a mirror and provided every indication the evening's pyrotechnics hadn't ended. The rain had stopped for the moment, but its damp odor lingered in the heavy air. A second storm flashed strobe-light glows in the western sky, accompanied by so many individual rolls of thunder they combined into a single low growl.

He hesitated. A seemingly helpless woman might have an accomplice waiting in the shadows. Together they could take him down, break into his house and...what? Handle some of those annoying emails from his workaholic office manager? His priceless art collection amounted to a few cheap prints he'd picked up at local fairs, and the strongbox in his bedroom closet—an oversized flowerpot full of loose change—weighed in at about a hundred bucks.

He gazed beyond the cul-de-sac down a winding street lit here and there by driveway lamps. Nothing about the scene struck him as suspicious. He left his porch, followed the short sidewalk cutting across his lawn to the curb, and stepped around a puddle into the street. "Are you okay?"

The woman looked up at him with a foggy expression at first but returned to planet earth with remarkable speed. She scrambled to her feet and brushed her hands down a dress as dark as her hair. "I'm fine."

She could have leapt from the pages of a failed Brewster DeLay novel—a quirky heroine dressed for a cocktail party but wandering the rain-slick streets after some misfortunate event cast her into the midnight shadows. Her spicy perfume intoxicated him. He lost himself in her shaggy hair, gray-green eyes, high cheekbones, half smile, then drifted his gaze down a longish black dress tight enough to reveal all the right curves. He plunged lower still and discovered wildly impractical three-inch heels.

Then came the inevitable fit of insecurity. How would he measure up under *her* scrutiny? He kept himself reasonably fit, although halfheartedly, but he didn't dress well, and he seldom bothered to use a brush or comb. Hopefully she'd agree light hair looked best in a state of mild disarray. He'd been getting away with the excuse for years.

Brewster dragged his gaze back up her figure. She'd arched her brows by then, evidently having recovered sufficiently to notice him undressing her with his eyes. He tried to feign innocence with a shrug. "Sorry, I'm not all the way awake yet."

Her smile widened to full amusement. "That's one of the better excuses for leering I've ever heard."

She had him there.

"You need to be more gentlemanly on our first date," she added.

"Is that what this is?"

She glanced down at herself. "I am *dressed* for a date, but we'd probably know each other's names if we were on one, wouldn't we?"

"I'm Brewster DeLay."

"Carla Summers."

"How'd you keep from getting drenched in the storm that blew through here?"

She motioned toward a house with a wraparound front deck. "Those people have an old-fashioned porch swing. I might have been tempted to spend a little time on it even in good weather." The thunder in the distance grew louder, closing in on them, although she didn't seem hurried by it.

"I'm always looking for ways to slow the world down, too," he said.

"You're fine. I'm the one who was sitting in the puddles." She looked down at her dress again and ran a hand across a damp patch by her hip.

"Yeah, what's with that, anyway?"

"I got lost taking a walk. Your streets are twisty." She shifted her gaze to the wet pavement. "I decided to sit there until I evaporated with the steam of leftover rain."

He couldn't write a line that good if his life depended on it.

"You've got a *she's crazy* look in your eyes," Carla said.

"I'm clumsy on first dates."

"How are you with directions? Can you tell me which way Sanders is?"

"The road?" He pointed west. "It's miles from here."

"That's where I live."

"You sure took a hike."

"Tell me about it."

Lightning flashed. A sharp crack of thunder soon followed, and a fat, chilly raindrop struck the back of his neck. "We need to get you out of this weather. Come on, I'll give you a ride home."

"Thanks, but I'm meant to be alone tonight." She turned away and headed back across the street.

Carla had wandered into his cul-de-sac, probably without any ID—she didn't have a purse—and wearing shoes that didn't fit her story of having walked three or four miles. A scam of some sort was certainly possible. Maybe the most sensible action would be for him to head back into his house, grab his cell phone, and call the cops. They'd hustle her out of his life, taking her drop-dead looks, her easy humor, her air of mystery... "Wait."

She stopped and turned. Another splat of rain came down, and another. The skies threatened to open at any moment.

"Come on in and wait out the storm."

"You won't try to…"

"Believe me, the most I'll do is offer you a drink."

"That's a slippery slope," she said.

"Just coffee then."

"I don't drink coffee."

"How about tea?"

# Chapter Eight

*While midnight rain soaked the neighborhood*

**BREWSTER SWIRLED A GLASS** of vegetable juice in his hand, trying to reshape it into something more appealing. He glanced across the kitchen table at the dark-haired beauty who'd wandered into his cul-de-sac like an offering from the god of thunder. *Behold Carla, and happy birthday.*

"I knew you'd never drink that." She'd teased him into trying the juice earlier when she discovered the can in the fridge next to a six-pack of beer.

"I'm saying a little prayer over it first."

"More like a novena." The hint of humor in Carla's expression defeated a comic, crossed-arm attempt to come across as a stern schoolmarm type. A plunging neckline also betrayed her intended image, although he supposed if she wore glasses and kept a straight face, she could play a stern, naughty librarian like a champ.

He hated to back down from a challenge. Maybe if he closed his eyes and gulped this slop down, he could get on with his life and never shop healthy again. But what about the aftertaste? Carrots? Beets? Probably not beets. Otherwise the drink would be red. Cauliflower? He shuddered.

She reached across and patted his hand. "I won't torture you anymore."

"Whew."

"Why did you buy the stuff? You look slim enough already."

"Yeah, for now, but I hit a bad age milestone."

"Thirty?"

He nodded.

"And that's when it all goes to hell?"

Hmm. That brought him back to the immediate issue. Judging by Carla's earlier behavior—wandering into the neighborhood on foot during a thunderstorm, settling onto the wet pavement as if for a midnight picnic in the rain—maybe she'd been trying to escape a far worse version of Hell than a damned glass of vegetable juice. What pushed her off the ledge? "Can I ask you something?"

She closed her hands around her mug and hunched over it.

Clearly, that was a no. Women who melted into puddles had no use for probing questions. But he was a businessman, trained to inquire, probe, engage, learn, and then form plans around the ambiguous bits of information gleaned whenever the opportunity for interrogation presented itself. The truth could always be found by asking seven questions.

Carla had fallen out of the sky and into his life wearing a tight black dress and spiked heels. What did it mean? How could he help her? Had she come to help him? He was beyond help. He couldn't even think of seven questions. "You look like you're dressed for a party that didn't happen. Are you okay?"

She hid behind her coffee steam. "I don't want to think about what brought me here, let alone discuss it. Hopefully, that doesn't seem—"

"No, I shouldn't have brought it up."

"Let's change the subject." She reached for his glass, sipped some of the stuff, grimaced, and slid it back to him. "I'll stick with tea."

"Wait till you're thirty."

"Shh. I'm there already."

They shared an easy laugh. Carla's smile brought a welcome glimmer to those gray-green eyes, but a loud gust of wind broke the spell. "Your house hums," she said.

"Stick around long enough, and the doorbell will blast you out of your chair."

"Who's coming?"

"It goes off on its own."

She glanced around, leaned forward, and moved a finger to her lips as if sharing a secret. "Brewster," she whispered. "Maybe you have a poltergeist."

"And here I was groping for a scientific explanation."

"My mother's into the occult."

"And you?"

"Hah!" She shook her head, dizzying him with a swirl of black hair. "Why invent the supernatural when we still have the mystery of our dreams to explore?"

Dreams. She sure struck a chord with that one. "Hey, now that you mention it, just before you came along, I was locked into a rerun of this repetitive, Latin—"

Dut-dut-dut DAH!

That crazy doorbell. Brewster nearly had to reach down and pick Carla off the floor. "Well, I did warn you about that."

She stared out of the kitchen toward the front door across the foyer, hopefully not measuring her escape route. "You're sure we aren't dealing with poltergeists?"

"I'm thinking thunderstorms. Static electricity. *Beethoven's Fifth* blasted me out of bed during the last one."

"Try lowering the sound."

The doorbell box loomed high up a wall near the entryway. He'd thought many times about pushing a chair over there or grabbing the stepladder out of the garage, climbing up, doing something about it.

Plans. Whenever he was lucky enough not to be dealing with the spreadsheets and calendars of his regimented office life, he shunned all attempts at enterprise. Work was one compartment, home quite another. Carefree novelists didn't make plans. They let their doorbells run wild.

The wind hummed louder. Carla kept her focus on the door, and Brewster took the opportunity to sneak his attention down the front of her dress. What was the thing about women in black? His sex-crazed subconscious always latched on to the color choice as a suggestion of availability or, even better, a willingness to walk the wild side.

He settled his gaze on the swell of her breasts and the impressions of nipples beneath. That bra had to be flimsy if she wore one at all.

But he'd been busted earlier when looking her up and down a little too lasciviously on the street. Besides, what the hell was wrong with him? This poor woman had entered his home seeking sanctuary from whatever had been haunting her, and all he could think about was burying his face in her breasts, running his hands through her midnight-black hair, moving them lower, down her arms, along her hips...

He scurried back to neutral territory just in time to meet her eyes as she turned her attention back to him. "What do you do when you aren't getting lost at night on twisty streets?" he asked.

"My shop keeps me busy." Carla reached into her sleeve, came out with a card like a magician, and slid it across the table.

The placeholder displayed the image of a woven basket overflowing with handmade dolls. *Rag Thyme*—her clever play on words had been shaped into a crescent of rainbow-colored, cursive font beneath the sketch. "Craft store, huh?"

"Mmm-hmm."

"Cute name."

"Thank you." She smiled at him through the steam of her tea. "Nine eighteen Church Street. Stop by and browse sometime."

"What do you sell?"

"Handmade dolls mostly, and teddy bears, eggshell ornaments, herbs."

That had about as much appeal as a chick flick. "I like creative people," he offered.

Carla slumped. Surely she'd pegged his comment as a patronizing come-on, which it had been, mostly.

He needed to elevate his game. This woman was interesting and likeable. Yes, somewhat sensitive, too—probably understandable given whatever circumstances had driven her here—but mysterious and appealing in a *must know her better* sort of way. Not someone to hit on as if they were beginning a mating ritual beneath the strobe lights of some club.

Unfortunately, they'd strayed into his danger zone. He'd never been good at the basic human intercourse known as small talk. He often pushed too hard and turned clumsy, saying something misconstrued, rushing things along, or not moving quick enough. The main crisis still loomed ahead when they'd run out of things to say.

He tried to rally. "I do some writing."

That got her attention. She clasped her hands together. "Tell me more."

"Do you like modern-day fairy tales?"

"You're a romantic?" Carla's obvious delight curved her lips into the perfect shape.

"I guess so." He'd brought a smile to her face, and the entire universe brightened in response. This was how the world was supposed to turn. The cosmos demanded he make the woman happy. She was *not* an object of possible conquest.

"Are you published?" she asked.

"No, but honestly, that doesn't matter to me as much as it should."

"Why?"

"I look at writing as an escape from the here and now."

"I suppose that beats midnight walks in the rain."

"Wait here." With the pounding heart of a schoolboy—because he'd never shared his writing dream with a stranger? Because she bedazzled him? Because her eyes revealed the hint of attraction? Because she cast an aura that could only be described as two parts saint and one part sinner?—he left a table spilling over with questions and rummaged through the drawer of a small counter by the stove. His rubber-banded packet of business cards peeked out from beneath a tangle of pens, paper clips, and forgotten notes scribbled on crinkled Post-its. A more important but hitherto unshared message had been printed on the cards: *Brewster DeLay, writer. Words escape me.*

He brought the offering to his goddess of the night. "I had these made a few weeks ago when I got a new phone number, but the poor things have to live alone in a drawer until I get published."

She took the pack and cradled it in cupped hands as if protecting a delicate flower. "Try pulling them out and talking to them every day so they don't feel lonely."

"I don't have any experience at parenting."

"No problem. I can adopt one and take better care of it." Carla slid a card out and slipped it into her pocket.

Oh, to join it in there.

She sipped her tea and regarded him in silence for a few moments before perking up again and sweeping her arm. "This is a nice place for a starving writer."

"I've got a day job."

"Doing what?"

"Lending money that never comes back. Every month we're still in business is a gift from the usury gods."

She laughed but turned somber a moment later, staring down at her tea. "I've been struggling with my business, too."

"Times are tough."

"But we're not starving."

"That's the spirit."

They settled into comfortable silence. Brewster tried to talk himself into another sip of liquefied carrots, tomatoes, frog eyes, and whatever other secret ingredients lurked inside his juice glass. He glanced at Carla for reassurance.

For the briefest moment, the fridge showed through her, as if she'd faded as translucent as a ghost.

He blinked.

She returned to normal.

"Wow," he said.

"What?"

"I guess I'm not awake all the way yet."

She set her cup aside. "I'm boring you."

"Impossible." He blinked again.

"How would the opening chapters of a Brewster DeLay novel go?"

He tried to snap out of the fog before it dissolved the mood completely. He needed to say the right thing. Yet words truly did escape him, and he could only stare into her bottomless eyes.

"Would things move quickly between your hero and heroine at the start of the story?" She settled a hand on his forearm.

The timing of this exquisite physical contact suggested a double meaning in her words. "Huh?" Great response. He was on a roll.

She removed her hand. "Or do you prefer dragging things out for the reader to savor?"

"And the writer." Those vibrant lips, so kissable.

"I should leave then." She pushed her chair back.

"Wait, I—"

Carla was already halfway out of the kitchen.

He raced after her and almost bowled the woman over when she stopped within an arm's reach of the front door.

"Thanks for the shelter, and the company," she said.

"At least let me drive you home."

"No. That slope would be slipperier than the one we just traveled."

She opened the door and stepped outside. The rain had stopped and a hint of moon peeked out between fast-moving streaks of clouds. "Let's trust fate to bring us together for a second date, Brewster. I look forward to the next chapter."

"Can we settle on something more concrete?"

"I'm afraid not. My dreams take me where they will. You were quite the pleasant surprise tonight."

Now the street showed through her. What the hell was happening with his eyes? He groped for her arm but came up empty.

Carla had disappeared altogether.

Brewster lost his balance. He slapped a hand on the doorframe, gripping the molded wood for dear life until the world stopped swaying.

He waited. Endlessly. Fruitlessly. The universe failed to right itself and bring Carla back.

He reached into his shirt pocket where he'd slipped her placeholder, the only proof he hadn't gone insane and imagined the entire encounter. The only lifeline to a midnight vampire who'd nibbled a bite of his heart.

*Rag Thyme.*

# CHAPTER NINE

*Syracuse, New York,*
*The morning after dreaming she met a man named Brewster*

"**LET THE DRAMA BEGIN.**" Carla marched into Dr. Elaine Larsson's office but steered clear of a fiendish recliner guilty of lulling her into submission during previous sessions. The therapist had coaxed her eccentricities, fears, *and dreams* into the light of day far too easily.

The lingering echo of Carla's most recent nocturnal adventure had the markings of true insanity, and she had no intention of falling into Elaine's cozy trap again. The facing chairs in the middle of the room offered sanctuary. She picked one, settled onto blessedly uncomfortable wood, crossed one leg over the other, and waited for her therapist to get ready.

"Good to see you, Carla. Give me a moment." Elaine grabbed the free chair, opened her laptop, and switched it on. As usual, the woman projected the aura of a professional but the haggardness of one whose hours were too long. She hid her attractiveness, no doubt deliberately, by fixing her blonde hair in a bun, wearing a dark business suit, and hiding her eyes behind studious glasses. The bags beneath those eyes suggested too little sleep and probably too much reading, judging by the floor-to-ceiling shelves crammed with books and scholarly journals on two walls of the office.

Initially, all of that stuff, along with the diplomas and plaques, had intimidated Carla, but she'd come to consider Elaine something of a friend, if not in a social context, then in a secret-sharing arrangement, albeit one-sided. She hadn't learned much about her therapist. The game didn't work that way.

She glanced around the office and settled her gaze on a painting she couldn't remember from previous visits. Colorful sailboats skimmed frosty waves, and a couple stood watching, hand-in-hand, from a pier. They'd dressed in summer whites and blues, ready for a day of sailing. Elaine had probably selected the scene to soothe troubled souls. It almost succeeded, until Carla glanced at a thriving palm bursting out of its pot in a corner of the office. Once again, she'd forgotten to water her own green pet, a spider plant drooping with thirst in the window of her apartment. Journeys back and forth between one reality and another had been muddling her mind lately. That and the worry her eventual diagnosis would be schizophrenia.

She shifted her attention to Elaine's dancing fingers. The log-on process was taking forever.

Elaine had begun using a computer during their last session, complaining of carpal tunnel syndrome from constant writing on a pad. Carla wanted to be sympathetic, but this brutally permanent method of recording her mental wanderings could lead to…what? She didn't know. She set her hands on her legs in an effort to stop twisting them.

At last, Elaine finished pecking her keyboard and looked up with a smile. "Alrighty! What would you like to talk about today, Carla?"

"Ending my sessions? God knows I could use the money I'd be saving."

The shot across the bow spurred Elaine to type a flurry of notes. "You came seeking answers. Have you found them?"

"Who does?"

"I'm guessing the dreams haven't ended, then."

"What's the point of digging so deeply?"

"You're edgy today."

Carla couldn't think of a suitably cutting answer.

Elaine motioned to a couch and coffee table positioned a safe distance from the lurking recliner. "I made tea." A white ceramic pot and two matching cups had been set out.

"You're trying to seduce me into sharing more secrets," Carla said.

"That's an interesting choice of words. Just mentioning the dreams triggers sexual associations. You see that, don't you?"

"You think it turns me on to dream about offing myself?"

"What do *you* think?"

Elaine's black-framed glasses made her seem overly studious to the point of being unapproachable with any secrets on this particular day. Carla held fast to her resolve and looked away. "I think you make me feel uncomfortable. Maybe it's that laptop, recording my every thought."

The therapist stood, set her computer on the chair, went to the coffee table, and poured tea. "I won't record anything. We'll just talk."

"Or I will. Stick with the game plan, Elaine."

"Did something happen to set you off?"

"I'll say." She gave up the chair for the couch but perched on the edge of it, keeping her back a safe distance from the comfortable cushions and letting the coffee table foil her desire to cross her legs again. Discomfort seemed the best strategy for staying mum. She talked too much when relaxed.

The therapist stared at her during a stretch of silence. Carla grabbed her teacup and looked into it.

"You seem frightened," Elaine said.

"Don't tell me how I seem. You know how I hate that." She lifted the cup to steal a sip, but a brief tremor in her hand stirred a tiny leaf to the surface. "This tea is off."

Elaine made a show of sipping her tea with relish. "Consider yourself lucky. My coffee would kill you."

The humor in those overworked eyes weakened Carla into melting backward and becoming one with the cushions.

"You dreamed something, didn't you?" Elaine said.

Carla kept her gaze fixed on the steam rising out of her cup.

"Tell me the setting," Elaine coaxed.

"One setting led me to the next."

"Let's talk about the first one, then."

"I asked somebody to push me in front of a subway. Satisfied?" She fought her way back to a fully upright position and bumped a knee against the table in the process.

"Suicide again?"

"Contrived death has a nicer ring to it." She rubbed her knee and closed her eyes, skipping to the memory of a far more bearable dream, the one in a man's kitchen—Brewster's kitchen—a scene she could picture as clearly as if it had happened. But it hadn't and she'd only sink deeper into malaise by pretending otherwise. She needed to stick with the fantasies she knew all too well.

She'd been having a recurring dream about life in a primitive forest for so long she regarded it as her midnight pastime. She'd initially sought counseling because of a bizarre element to the fantasy—when her dreams included dialogue, the language spoken seemed to be Latin. Yet she'd never had any waking experience with the language, or so she thought. But Elaine had suggested she'd probably heard snippets of Latin here and there in various movies or perhaps from other venues such as an Easter high mass during her early childhood. Maybe her subconscious had shaped them into a church language to poke fun at the ritualized nature of her recurring dream. The subconscious can be quite a trickster.

But a far more disturbing element had burst onto the scene recently, providing plenty of fodder for additional therapy sessions. Her forest dreams now included a macabre opening act on a subway platform where a man shoved her in front of a train at her request, or she twisted away and leapt on her own. What did it matter?

"You fell onto the tracks again."

Carla nodded.

"And into the next dream."

"The good one."

"Your home away from home."

The continuing kindness in Elaine's smile eased Carla into the cushions again. "I fell into Sanctimonia."

"To watch for barbarians?"

"One can't be too careful."

"Or too virtuous. That's what Sanctimonia means in Latin, isn't it?"

They'd covered this ground already—more subconscious teasing, this time her brain assigning a happy name to her happy place. She shifted in her chair. These sessions were becoming redundant.

"So once again, your suicide dream—"

"Contrived death."

"Your dream about contrived death acted as a passageway to this other world of yours."

"Sanctimonia can't only be mine. These dreams seem far too real."

"A contrived death and then this other world of *ours*."

Carla had to admit the woman had a gift for understated humor.

"Did I just notice the hint of a smile?"

"You coddle me like a child, Elaine." The tea had a pleasant aroma, despite a loose leaf or two. She gave in and brought the cup to her lips, and the lemony taste pulled her back to the man's kitchen. "I'll tell you what happened, but I don't want to hear a word about me being crazy."

"You know I'd never say such a thing."

"I was swept out of Sanctimonia to a different place."

Elaine's fascinated expression was priceless. They hadn't had a new insane fantasy to discuss since the subway nightmares began.

"One minute I was in the forest and the next in my own neighborhood. Except I wandered down a street I didn't recognize.

The day turned to night. Then a thunderstorm blew through and melted me into the pavement."

"Go on."

"A man invited me into his house."

"Sounds risky."

"Not really. He had kindness in his eyes. Besides, I knew I was dreaming." Or had she been? Doubts loomed large in the light of day. She moved her fingers to her temples.

"What's the matter?"

"Nothing." She groped to recapture her train of thought. *Train*...bad choice of words. She closed her hands around her cup to stop another tremble. "We sat in his kitchen and enjoyed each other's company."

"You liked him."

"I wished I didn't have to leave."

"Where did you need to go?"

"Anywhere but there." Carla glanced at the lucky couple on the pier. *She'd* been physically and emotionally attracted to a man who didn't exist. "He was only a figment."

"A dream."

"So why do I have this?" The tremor in her hand intensified. She fumbled in her purse and found the business card Brewster had given her.

Elaine examined the card with pursed lips, flipping it from side to side before handing it back. "You dreamed about someone you'd already met."

"No, you aren't following. Brewster is a complete stranger. He gave his card to me during the dream and I awakened with it in my hand!"

Elaine glanced across the room at her PC still resting on the chair. No doubt she was dying to log into an online thesaurus and find the kindest synonym for crazy.

"I looked for him this morning," Carla pressed, "but I couldn't find the right street."

"Let's think about this."

She'd thought about it far too much already. "My mother

would claim something supernatural happened, but you're thinking I'm nuts."

"I'm not leaning that way."

"You're just stroking me again."

Elaine fixed her with her signature expression of reassurance— a pleasant, crinkle-eyed smile. "I'm sure there might be a dozen sane explanations for what happened, but let's just explore one, okay?"

"Whatever."

"You don't think you ever met this man before?"

She shook her head.

"Do you collect customers' business cards in your shop?"

"I'm not following."

"Many storekeepers keep little boxes or bowls at the counter where a customer might drop a card in the hope of winning a drawing. Do you have anything like that?"

Ah, the magic of *what if.* Elaine's bag of tricks was bottomless! Carla did collect business cards, and she sometimes brought the bowl home. Perhaps one of the cards spilled into the clutter of her apartment until it found its way to her bed, along with the lingerie, toiletries, books, and other random articles she had to clear away when carving out some sleeping space each night. She might have registered the man's name in her mind before casting the card aside. Then she dreamed about him and later awakened with his card still in the bed, near her hand.

Elaine continued boring that soothing gaze into her soul. "Feeling less crazy?"

No. The last time the fishbowl had come home with her was a month ago when she blasted a bunch of emails out for her Labor Day sale. Why would a random name stick in her head that long? But any more conversation about an imaginary man whose card was somehow real would drive her straight to the recliner, where she'd talk crazier and crazier until doctors in white jackets came to drag her away. "Relieved is the better word." She tried to fake a smile.

# Chapter Ten

*Brewster's Chicago office, the morning after Carla's visit*

**BREWSTER GAVE UP ON** the paperwork littering his desk and studied a floral print on the wall. Would anyone else examining the picture perceive the identical image? Perhaps his blue flowers were everyone else's purple. He took the notion further and considered whether his viewpoint was so unique nobody's sight, sound, taste, touch, or smell was the same as his.

The next step brought him to the end of the path, a scary question teetering over the edge of a bottomless pit. The only perception he could be sure of was his own, and even that had been proven unreliable. Suppose everything and everyone were figments of his imagination in a fantasy world suddenly flipped upside down? He stared into the abyss and watched with his mind's eye as Carla vanished from his porch again.

He scrabbled back to the reassuring reality of his workplace, a relatively reliable environment where midnight visitors didn't disappear into thin air. Only money did.

Brewster grabbed a loan application from his in basket and tried to focus. The monthly payment was too high. He scribbled a note on the cover page, instructing one of his deal processors to reduce the interest rate.

Before the market crash, he'd kept a plaque on his desk proclaiming greed as good—a proclamation by false gods, as things turned out. He'd recently replaced this with a more practical framed cliché. *Never calculate your yield before recovering your principal.* A loan structured with unaffordable payments would eventually morph into a problem. In fact, the cabinets just outside his office overflowed with defaults.

He tossed the application into his out basket, noticed a day-old coffee stain on his desk, and grabbed a tissue to wipe it away. He'd recently axed the after-hours janitorial service in yet another round of budget slashing.

Crestview Finance's losses had taken a heavy toll on what had once been a gleaming building full of carefree, prospering employees. Earlier cutbacks during the prolonged recession had already left the place with outdated phones, clunky laptops, and an Internet service often blinking out at the most inopportune times. Fading decorative plants pined for the care of a florist who no longer came at night to prune and water them. The kitchen fell short of condiments and plastic utensils, daily delivery of the local newspaper bit the dust, 401(k) matching contributions disappeared, and health plan premiums and deductibles spiked upward.

Frantic employees had done their best to embrace cost consciousness, but their attempts to keep the mother ship from listing typically proved more annoying than effective. Brewster had to grope his way out of the john recently when somebody switched the lights off to save power, unaware of his presence in one of the stalls.

He flicked a tiny red mite from his keyboard and looked up at the probable culprit. The dying leaves of a potted palm draped over the edge of his desk. The miniscule spider must have abandoned that happy home in search of a hot spot, spurred by a poorly maintained air conditioning system locked into ice-cube mode for the day. He brushed another mite from his screen but took care not to smash the thing, knowing from past experience the red smear would look just like blood.

With loan processing and pest control out of the way, he grabbed the placeholder card for Rag Thyme from his shirt pocket—proof he hadn't imagined Carla's visit. Yet the card didn't have a phone number, and he'd failed to find any reference to her shop on the Internet.

He reached for the phone to try directory assistance, but it rang before he could lift the receiver from its cradle.

"Brewster!" The front-desk receptionist had lowered her normally perky voice to a hush.

"What's up, Ronda?"

"There's a customer here to see you. Igor Tesfaye. He's waiting on the couch."

"Very funny." The employees of Crestview Finance and their customers never set eyes on each other. The company financed over-the-road truckers looking to buy big rigs, and like many lenders in the industry, they conducted their business behind a veil of anonymity, relying on the selling truck dealers to act as intermediaries. Applications came in over the computer, Brewster's coordinators communicated approvals and declines by email, his loan processors overnighted closing documents to dealer locations for execution, and the truckers had their monthly payments automatically pulled from their bank accounts. Collectors closed the loop by hounding customers over the phone—the one's whose payments bounced.

Crestview never included a street address in its documents or allowed one to be published in any directory. Borrowers could grow angry for any number of reasons in the lending industry— perceived overcharges, imagined insults by phone collectors, fear over pending repossession—and angry customers sometimes became dangerous. A shooting had been reported at a Joliet consumer-finance company only a few weeks earlier.

A customer such as Igor Tesfaye shouldn't have had a clue how to find the place without some determined, creepy stalking. He was probably mad as hell about something.

"I'm not joking," Ronda said. "This guy is waiting for you, and he doesn't look happy."

"Um, okay, look. Why don't you offer coffee and slip into the kitchen to get it? That'll give you an excuse for getting away from him."

"What if he doesn't want any?"

"Then tell him you're getting some for yourself."

"Okay...and...?"

"Take your time fixing the coffee until the police get here."

"Oh. My. God!"

"Don't get all panicky, Ronda. Just walk away."

"Fine."

Brewster called the cops. After being assured by a dispatcher a squad car was on the way, he went looking for Heather, the chain-smoking mother of two he'd hired a year earlier. Always a sucker for the hint of corrupted innocence, he'd lost all objectivity during her job interview when he noticed the sexy tattoo on the side of her neck. A butterfly. She'd proven to be a capable office manager despite being hired for all the wrong reasons, and Brewster had finally reached the point where he could talk to her without stammering.

He found Heather in her office. "We've got a visitor," he said.

She fixed him with a blank look.

"A *customer*!"

"Oh!" Heather left her desk and hurried past him into the bullpen, emerging from the cluster of cubicles a few moments later with a straggling line of employees in tow. Brewster joined a step behind the company's beleaguered staff and headed out a side door to wait for the cops.

A dozen of Crestview's finest soon stood along the side corner of the building and lit up their cigarettes, out of sight and about a hundred yards from the front entrance lobby, where Igor Tesfaye cooled his heels. Heather took a long drag, exhaled a cloud of smoke, and turned to Brewster. "Is this the guy who called you last week to complain about his loan?"

"Yeah. He doesn't understand why he owes thirty-two thousand for a truck he supposedly bought for thirty. I asked why he signed a contract without reading it."

She took another drag. "You're assuming our customers can read."

"I'm guessing his wife or girlfriend can. She probably gave him hell when he brought the contract home. Anyway, I explained that a finance charge is no different than points on a mortgage, but he didn't grasp the concept."

"I'm not sure I do."

"You need to think outside the box, Heather." The time for feeling guilty over Crestview's fees had long since passed. The company barely covered its overhead anymore, let alone turn a profit, despite its hefty fees.

Long, smoky minutes passed. Chatter and occasional laughter about sports, movies, dinners, and maniacal office intruders grew louder, probably noisy enough to alert Igor Tesfaye to their hiding place—if he truly did have a gun and wanted to take them all out. Brewster peeked around the corner of the building and motioned them to keep it down.

A few employees edged toward the door. The undusted, drooping-plant work area waiting inside still had some appeal. Those not tasked with harassing deadbeat customers for payments could sit and relax, working at three-quarters speed in the undemanding business environment—not many truckers had been buying rigs lately—or jump online and surf any interesting websites that had survived the company's relentless, fun-blocking software.

Brewster stole another look beyond the double row of cars in the company parking lot into a street still lacking any squad car cavalry. More than likely, the cops had been reluctant to leave their lucrative speed traps up the road. He decided to call them again if they didn't arrive by the time Heather's second cigarette burned out.

The sound of a lawnmower wafted from the distance and hustled his wanderlust down a winding path of associations. Mowing equaled grass equaled nature, hills, countryside, distant mountains, shining seas...escape. The job wasn't fun anymore. Maybe it never had been.

"You've had a dreamy look on your face all day," Heather said.

He flinched. The distraction of a workplace emergency had served as a temporary but welcome barrier, holding an impossible memory of Carla's vanishing act at bay. Heather's comment created a hint of turbulence, threatening to collapse the wall, but he manned up, turned to her, and managed a noncommittal shrug.

"I don't think it's the job," she added. "Things aren't any worse than they were a year ago, right?"

"Right."

"Crash and burn is our normal now."

"Guess so."

"Then what is it? Did your dog die?"

"I don't have a dog."

"A kid got sick?"

"I'm single, remember?"

Her eyes lit up. "Maybe you met someone!"

The wall collapsed, tumbling its bricks through his stomach. Brewster couldn't go it alone. He needed someone who could share a similar experience and team up with him to solve the mystery of shadows. "Heather, have you ever seen a ghost?"

"No, but I saw a UFO once."

"Yeah?" He leaned toward her.

She flicked some ashes to the ground and grinned. "Well, maybe not. After I switched from beer to wine, the hallucinations went away."

"Very funny."

"Are you saying *you* saw a ghost?"

He regretted having said anything. The Carla incident would have seemed surreal enough if brought up after a couple drinks at a bar. In a completely out-of-context work setting, he doubted Heather could even register the words he might speak. He pictured a bubble of language attached to his cartoon head and watched as it mixed with her smoke rings and drifted away.

A squad car barreled down the street and bailed him out before she could press him further.

The cop arriving on the scene seemed the hard-nosed, no-nonsense type capable of handling any insanely angry trucker who happened by. Brewster and Heather fell in step behind the man. He led them back into the office building with an aura of authority, but the nemesis they found inside didn't seem much of a threat.

Igor Tesfaye rose from the lobby couch to stand no more than about five foot eight, slump-shouldered and rumpled, from his wavy, unkempt hair to a faded shirt, worn jeans, and dusty shoes. Nevertheless, he carried the sharp-eyed, pressed-lips look of a determined man. The recession had been tough on truckers. Many now stood only a fuel-price hike away from bankruptcy, an engine failure from homelessness. A two-thousand-dollar finance charge was a big deal to a guy like Tesfaye. The extra fifty bucks per month took food off his table.

The trucker opened his mouth to speak, but Brewster cut him off before he could spit out a word. "Why are you here?"

"I called, but you wouldn't answer my questions. Last night a girl comes to my door and—"

"We don't want you coming back."

The trucker plowed on. "You'll take care of me, she says."

"What?" Heather had slipped off to the side in an apparent attempt to blend into the wallpaper, no doubt embarrassed the cops had been summoned to ward off a harmless-looking deadbeat, but this revelation drew her back into the thick of things. "Are you saying someone from this office came to your home?"

"No, I don't think so."

"Then what *are* you saying?"

The cop didn't wait for an answer. He folded his beefy arms and stepped between Brewster and the trucker. "Mr. Tesfaye, these people don't want you in their office. If you come back, I'll arrest you."

The driver took a backward step toward the door but paused and fixed his gaze on Brewster. "You overcharged two thousand dollars. Who needs the money more?"

Rather than try to explain a standard, if somewhat high, finance charge, Brewster went for the sympathy vote. "We haven't made a profit here in three years."

They stared each other down until Tesfaye gave up the fight and turned to Heather. "A girl comes along at midnight and shows me a problem with the paperwork. She tells me to go see Brewster DeLay at Crestview. I ask why. She says he'll have my money. Then, poof, she disappears."

Brewster's stomach took a roller-coaster dip. He couldn't have heard him right.

"Too much vodka," the trucker added.

"What did you just say?" Brewster asked.

"Vodka."

"No, before that."

The trucker spread his hands. "Poof."

Brewster had trouble thinking over the sound of his pounding heart. "Poof as in Carla?"

Heather edged closer. "What's the problem?"

He ignored her. "Help me out here, Tesfaye. Was her name Carla?"

"She didn't say."

"Are you talking about a woman with black hair? About five foot six, gray-green eyes—"

Igor furrowed his forehead and looked back and forth between Brewster and Heather as if *they* were the crazy ones. "Not a woman, a young girl, twelve or thirteen, blonde hair, blue eyes. American as apple pie is the saying, no?" He moved a hand to the back of his head. "She had what you call a ponytail?"

The trucker had the look of a man on a bender, but Brewster couldn't ignore the coincidence of this guy bringing up a disappearing midnight visitor. He'd granted refunds for reasons far flimsier than the fact he might be helping a fellow victim of cosmic jokes. Yeah, this was crazy, but...he turned to the cop.

"I think we've made a mistake with this guy. We'll pay him the money he's asking for."

"Mr. DeLay, if you folks are being stalked, we can—"

"No, that's not it. Sorry to bother you."

After a long, hard stare and scolding shake of his head, the cop mumbled halfheartedly about the call not being a bother at all, one couldn't be too careful anymore, and so on. Then he turned on his heel and left.

Heather grabbed Brewster's arm. "Can I speak to you for a minute?" She looked ready to rip his head off.

"Wait here, Igor." He followed Heather into the hallway leading back to the offices.

"What's this about a girl?" she asked.

Good question. Now how to respond without coming across as nuts?

"We have fifteen hundred other customers just like this guy," she added.

"Heather, this man came to our door. It's a good idea to keep the stalking types relatively happy."

Besides, squeezing a profit from the ill-fated occupational choices of others wasn't what he had in mind when he graduated business school. Maybe chucking his career and pursuing the life of a starving writer wouldn't be such a bad idea. He turned away from her and headed back to the trucker in the lobby. "Poof?"

Igor flashed a sheepish grin. "Too much vodka, no?"

That was the rub. How could he assign this clown any credibility? "Around midnight?"

"Or later."

"Didn't you think it odd for somebody so young to be wandering the streets ringing doorbells and—"

"She knocked."

"Did you ever meet her before?"

"One time in a dream."

Brewster cringed. He looked past Igor, the cop, Heather. He stared out the window at a world he thought he understood. A world without disappearing midnight visitors and young girls who knocked on doors in the dead of night when they weren't visiting truckers in their dreams.

*Too much vodka.* A hard-partying Russian fixating on a perceived overcharge might have imagined the girl's visit and promise of settlement. A man's subconscious worked in mysterious ways. On the other hand... Brewster fished a business card out of his pocket. "Would you mind calling my cell number if the girl comes around again?"

The trucker took the card and slipped it into his pocket. "This girl. She's a magician, eh?"

"Maybe she's part of a troupe." And it was high time to track down the performer he'd seen with his own eyes.

# CHAPTER ELEVEN

*A few minutes later*

BREWSTER HELD LITTLE HOPE Igor Tesfaye would get back to him with more information about midnight callers. Heavy-drinking, potentially hallucinating truckers couldn't be counted on to solve life's mysteries. That's what Google Maps was for.

He did find a Rag Thyme listing, but weirdly located in New York State, not Northbrook.

Carla copied another store's name? No. More than likely she considered the name so unique and clever, she didn't check to see whether anyone else had come up with it already.

That left him with a far more old-fashioned search mechanism, and one he wasn't sure even existed anymore. He left the office building, escaped to the privacy of his car, and called 411.

"Operator."

"Do you have a listing for a Rag Thyme in the 847 area code?"

"Is that a newspaper?"

"Craft store. T-H-Y-M-E." He closed his eyes and succeeded in conjuring Carla's image, sitting her at his kitchen table again. The memory was so vivid he could have reached across to sweep a stray bang of hair from her forehead, but a click on the line yanked him back to the lonely present.

"I'm sorry, sir. We don't have a listing for a Rag Thyme."

He groped in his shirt pocket for Carla's card. The universe could recklessly attempt to rewrite history all it wanted, but Brewster had proof of his wild adventure. He'd found someone so uninhibited she'd sit in the middle of the street for a time-out when the twisty streets conspired against her, so enthusiastic her eyes sparkled when she talked about her store, and so compassionate she adopted one of his business cards just to make him feel good about his writing. Carla was bright, creative, interesting, beautiful, perceptive. She probably ran off when she realized he'd spent their whole time together trying to undress her with his eyes like some sex-crazed idiot.

She didn't run off. She faded into the night.

Maybe his parents forgot to tell him about a family history of epileptic blackouts?

Based on the street names she mentioned, the store had to be in the Northbrook vicinity. "Try the 773 area code."

Long pause…then, "I can't find a listing there, either. Should I try 312?"

"Chicago's too far."

Maybe Carla only recently opened Rag Thyme? A brand-new shop might not be on the grid yet.

No way had he imagined her.

She'd told him the address, *918 Church Street,* so he still had that going for him. Sure, a thousand towns from coast to coast boasted a Church, a Maple, a State, et cetera, but if her store hadn't been located in Northbrook, where they met, she would have been more specific about location when she invited him to come over and browse.

Brewster threw his car into gear and cut through the city to the Edens Expressway. Then he headed north, driving past mile upon mile of fifties-style ranch homes in the city's earliest bedroom communities until the landscape transformed to the semi-rural look favored by the far northern suburbs. At Willow Road, he exited west.

Like many former Chicagoans still clinging to their toddling town, he hadn't bothered to learn much about his new suburb despite having lived there for several years. He didn't even know street names in the local area, other than those nearest his home. So where was 918 Church?

He had a map somewhere.

He slowed, popped the glove compartment open, and rummaged through the mess, finding his owner's manual, registration, a few oil-change receipts, some energy bars, and what looked like an old hot dog wrapper. But no map.

Gas stations had maps. Better yet, the people working the counters probably knew the local street names. He spotted a Shell and started turning into the lot when he noticed a tall steeple off to the left—the logical location for the street he wanted. He drove over and found an old church next to a small strip mall. The sign at the nearest intersection made him feel like a genius.

*Church Street.*

He checked out the strip mall. Diner, bookstore, dry cleaners, convenience store, card shop, but no Rag Thyme. This just got better and better. He completed the circuit around a horseshoe-shaped parking lot, then found an address above the door of a women's clothing store—*1329*. Four blocks off. He left the lot and headed west.

The area quickly changed from commercial to residential, but all hope wasn't lost. Some businesses spilled into the housing. A small Cape Cod along the tree-lined street had been converted to a tarot card reader's shop. Half a block farther down, a raised ranch now served as a law office. He parallel-parked and got out to look for the store.

And just like that, he spotted Carla sashaying away from him down the sidewalk. Her sandal heels clicked the pavement, her hips swayed, and her tight skirt flashed a purple and pink zigzag for the angels to behold.

"Carla!" The echo of his shout still rang in his ears when he realized his mistake. This woman's hair seemed wrong, sweeping too long over her shoulders and cut differently.

Two young girls raced out of a driveway all knobby knees and ponytails, shouting "Mommy!" in unison. They wrapped their arms around the woman's legs and spun her.

Now face-to-face with Brewster, the woman fixed him with a quizzical stare.

One of the girls looked up at him with gleaming eyes. "We found a rabbit!"

"Under the porch," the other squealed.

He tried to fight past the ache of disappointment and fake something resembling enthusiasm. "Wow."

"Yeah!"

"Can I help you?" The woman flashed a smile, friendly enough despite his intrusion on one of those cheerful, domestic moments that worked best without the presence of annoying morons.

What had he been thinking to jump all over the first dark-haired woman who happened to strut down the street in a pair of heels? He gathered himself and tried to act like a guy who had a clue. "I'm looking for this shop." He fished Carla's card out of his shirt pocket and held it up for her.

"That's a cute store name."

"Do you know where it is?"

"No. Sorry."

"Not even a hint?" His cheeks burned. Enough already. Why not go door to door, ringing bells and begging for clues?

The girls tugged their mom away, but before disappearing into the house, she turned back. "Wait!"

At last, a glimmer of hope! Good-bye burning cheeks and hello beating heart.

"The addresses don't go that low here. Are you sure you've got the right suburb?"

He couldn't be sure of anything except the air rushing out of his balloon.

*Same day, different town*

Carla worried her fingers over Brewster's business card for so long the edges frayed. She forced herself to set it down on the little desk in her bedroom and think about something else. Her mom popped into her head. She'd be stopping at the store for lunch on Wednesday. Maybe they could chat about insanity.

She pulled up a chair and booted up her computer.

A Google search of *schizophrenia* yielded a ton of hits. She opened one and found a list of possible symptoms.

Voices in the head? Nope.

Blackouts? Uh-uh. Well, maybe kinda.

Delusions?

Oh hell, what was the point? The science of mental health didn't come anywhere near explaining what had happened. Her hour with Brewster DeLay was no delusion. *She still had his card.*

She picked the thing up for the thousandth time. The night earlier, she'd been too distracted by his smile, his blue eyes, and a carefree muddle of sandy hair to read more than the motto, *Words escape me,* when he handed it over. She hadn't focused on his impossible address.

Northbrook, Illinois, was one hell of a long distance to walk from Syracuse, New York!

She'd been born on Friday the thirteenth. When she was young, the brattiest kids seized the opportunity to call her a witch.

So what had she done this past night, gone for a ride on her broomstick?

# Chapter Twelve

*A day later, at midnight*

**CARLA OPENED HER EYES** and gazed down a grimy stairway into a manmade netherworld. Vertigo lurched her stomach. She steadied herself with a hand on the railing.

Hordes of commuters swept up from below, jostling her in their haste to make meetings, dinner dates, shopping excursions, Broadway shows. Others hurried against the flow—down to the subway—their subterranean passage to a different place where they might escape the smell of exhaust and street-vendor hot dogs and garbage all mixed together, the constant clatter, the buildings rising to dizzying, vaguely ominous heights, and the waves of yellow taxis clogging the streets.

She'd seen this movie before, and she nailed the opening scene for what it was, the beginning of a recurring nightmare. She was dreaming, caught in a subconscious loop that had been torturing her for months. But hope throbbed in her chest, for with newfound awareness came an exciting idea, the possibility of rebellion. She wouldn't head down the stairs this time. She'd seize control and turn away, perhaps buy one of those street-vendor hot dogs or go shopping at Macy's. Anything but go near a train.

Carla tried to turn right...and her body went left. She wanted to back away from the stairs, but her body plunged forward. Hope flat-lined into despair, and defeat signaled its triumph by shoving a cloud across the sun, shadowing the scene into a more appropriate nightmare scenario.

As if trapped in someone else's head, she stared out the eyeholes but had no control over the reflexes. Her zombie body took a step down on its own, followed by another, again and again, bent to the task of reaching the station below. The street noise diminished, replaced by the deafening roar of a subway train in the tunnel. Always such a racket! In the suicide dream, she never escaped it.

She reached the gate, dropped a token into the slot, and passed through to a shorter flight of stairs down to the platform. Dampness chilled her bones. The station's grime brought to mind a bat cave littered with scattered patches of human guano—cigarette butts, spit, wrappers, and a few unidentified, oily-looking spots.

Presuming the pattern in earlier renditions still held, she did have choices. Each dream had minor variations. She could pause on a bench if she wanted, but a gum-chewing jerk in a hooded sweatshirt usually sat beside her, invading her space by leaning too close.

Instead, she selected the straightforward script and stepped up to the edge of the platform, beyond the yellow safety line. She looked down at the cold steel rails of track, then across to the same billboard ads she'd seen dozens of times—perfume, clothing, shows. Those encased in plastic were cracked, the ones papered onto the wall were peeling, and all had been tagged by street artists who somehow got away with it, despite the threat of an occasional transit police patrol and the seemingly constant presence of waiting passengers.

A high-pitched screech signaled the approach of a train from within the dark recesses of the tunnel. Carla would have slumped her shoulders if she could, resigned as she was to her doom.

Someone's shadow approached from behind. A man.

"I don't understand why you'd stand so close to the track," he shouted. "You told me you wouldn't." He settled a hand on her shoulder with a gentle, familiar touch.

He soothed her. He was someone she loved. But for the life of her, and her life *was* at stake, she couldn't remember who he was.

"Do you think I have a choice?" she asked.

He slid his hand down to grip her forearm. "I hoped you did."

The line of an oft-repeated script rose to the surface. She tightened her lips to prevent the words from escaping.

"Let's go," he said.

She clenched her teeth but couldn't prevent the death sentence from vomiting out of her mouth. "I want you to push me in front of the train."

"You're talking crazy, Carla."

Yes, crazy. She screamed to erase her words, but the deafening train drowned her cry. Its lead car burst out of the tunnel and into the station with a grinning skull tagged to its front window by an underground artist with amazing talent.

The man tugged her arm toward safety.

Carla couldn't stop herself from twisting out of his grasp, losing her balance, and falling to the tracks. The train leapt up to her in an instant, its horn blaring, and its brakes showering the platform with sparks.

And then...

The smell of forest, earth, and grazing animals, the blinding sunlight, and the white noise of crickets ushered Carla into another world entirely. Back on her feet, heart racing, breath coming in gasps, she revolved in a slow half circle, sweeping her gaze from forest to glen to her thatch-roofed cottage before sinking to her knees. Her crossbow fell from her hands.

Once again, death in the subway served as a portal from one dream to the next. Hadn't it? If not, what just happened? Perhaps a wormhole in the cosmos allowed her to exist in more than one reality at the same time. That idea had great appeal over the more likely possibility. She was a crazy woman, a schizophrenic, a mishmash of personalities competing for a single body—the Carla who ran Rag Thyme in Syracuse, the Carla who asked a familiar but anonymous man to help her commit suicide in a New York City subway station, and this Carla who lived in a place known as Sanctimonia, where she guarded the far boundary of her village grounds against raiders.

No, not Carla. Her name was Maynya in this place.

Collectively delusional? She couldn't discount the possibility each of her personalities imagined their surroundings, creating scenes and then thinking them real, including another Carla who traveled hundreds of miles in her sleep only to awaken in her own bed and find physical proof of the journey—a man's business card impossibly in her hand. *A card she might have hallucinated, too.* After all, where was it now, at this moment?

A hare bounded out of the woods, raced across the meadow, and entered the forest on the other side. *Each of her worlds had unique rules of order.* In Sanctimonia, new things happened. Every episode followed a chronological path, always picking up where the last left off—she could remember walking out of her cabin earlier to stand in the meadow—and the randomness of events prevented her from guessing the future. But the subway nightmare chased its own tail, returning to the same beginning, then building to the identical climax each time, with only minor variations in between.

And what about free will—something she possessed in Sanctimonia but not in Manhattan? Did she follow a script in Syracuse, too? She couldn't remember.

Any place not Sanctimonia slipped into the shadows, leaving her with only one reality she could be sure of. She was Maynya. Her other name and peculiar language scattered like fragments of a fractured dream and evaporated into a sky marred by thick black smoke billowing from deep within the forest.

"*Flamma!*" She scrambled to her feet and ran toward the village.

The foliage on her right crackled, but not from flames. The fire was on her left. These had to be men, unschooled on how to steal through the trees in silence. She spun, reaching for the knife in her belt.

Two of Virtus's barbarians emerged from the woods.

How could she have let them trick her with fire? Any simpleton could have recognized the diversion for what it was. She glanced over her shoulder at the crossbow she'd left behind. Too far away to be retrieved. She ran away from it, away from the men, as well, cutting an angle across the meadow toward the trees on her left.

The barbarians loped after her, hoisting a net between them, as if trolling for some creature of the sea. They gained on her with every stride. Their shouts, their footfalls, their labored breath came closer and closer.

She clenched her fists, gritted her teeth. She'd bite, scratch, kick. These animals would *not* get the better of her.

The net caught her.

She went down, face first into the ground. Stars burst in her head.

And then...

Carla wobbled on her feet, nearly swooning from the shock of yet another scene shift. Bright daylight had been swallowed by blackest night, and the rural landscape of Sanctimonia fell off a cliff, replaced by a familiar semicircle of tract houses in a suburban cul-de-sac. She knew this place. A captivating imaginary man had let her into his home recently and poured tea.

She got out of the street and climbed Brewster's stairs, closing her eyes when she reached the porch and leaning forward until her forehead pressed against the wood of his front door. Perhaps by relaxing, she'd soften this door to the contours of her pillow and transport herself back to her Syracuse bedroom, where she'd wake up. The very idea eased her pounding heart and slowed her breathing.

The door didn't get any softer. She choked a sob, pushed back, and turned to the neighborhood behind her.

The street ending at the cul-de-sac stretched through the darkness toward a mysterious point of origin. She couldn't see beyond the pale illumination of a halogen lamp halfway down the block. What had happened the last time, after she left this house? Where had she gone? She couldn't remember.

Carla had a notion to follow the street into the gloom. She wouldn't have been surprised to find the end of the earth waiting out there.

Unlike the subway station, she had choices here. She could take off. Hit the road. Find out what truly waited at the end of that street. But her strongest urge was to play the hand dealt. She'd been delivered to this house again, to an alluring man who earlier reached through a displacement of space, depositing his business card in her hand when she awakened. This man was important.

She pressed his doorbell.

The opening chords of Beethoven's Fifth chimed, and a light switched on somewhere in the house. Soon, the echo of footsteps approached, a brighter light came on, and the door cracked open. Brewster poked his head out and gazed at her for a long moment before breaking into a grin. "Remind me to never complain about my doorbell again."

"Are you still having a fight with it?"

"More like a mild disagreement." He unlatched the chain and opened the door wider.

Brewster's easy smile brought out his handsomeness despite the tousle-haired, sleepy-eyed appearance of someone who'd been jarred awake. Light, wavy hair sprang out all funny on one side of his head, and the shirt he'd obviously just thrown on showed the wrinkles of a previous day's wear. He'd only buttoned the thing halfway, teasing her with enough skin to draw her gaze lower. He'd failed to close his jeans properly—her heat welled up when she noticed his belt hadn't been buckled—and he'd left his feet bare.

Who established the rules in this place called Northbrook? To hell with her wormhole theory, maybe *she* was the puppet master here! She didn't want this particular scene to be real. She needed a place where she could plunge into a pool of wanton desire and forget all the rest.

She pressed against him before he could utter another word. Their lips met and he responded at first, brushing his lower one against hers like a magic man.

But he slowed down. He stopped. He took a half step back. "I know this'll sound nuts, but I can't shake the feeling you're a figment of my imagination."

"A what?"

"I'm dreaming, right?"

Maybe if she smacked him one, they'd both know the answer. "You certainly can't be *my* dream or we'd still be kissing."

He tried to put his hands on her arms. She shrugged him off, but his bewildered expression seemed so much a mirror of the chaos inside of her, she lost her resolve to stalk away.

"You disappeared into thin air last time," he said.

"Oh, that."

"There *was* a last time, right?"

Who knew? She wasn't even sure there was a *this time*.

"Don't leave," he said.

She reached past him and tentatively touched the door—still hard, still not her pillow. "Why shouldn't I?"

"Because you're special."

"You don't know me."

"Can we work on that?"

"I'll need something stronger than tea this time."

Brewster motioned toward the darkened houses scattered around the cul-de-sac. "Me, too. Maybe after a couple of stiff ones, we can come back out here and put on a little show for the neighbors."

"I have my doubts whether neighbors even exist in this scenario." Carla gazed at the sky, searching for an extra moon, a green Big Dipper, the Southern Cross, a square planet.

# Chapter Thirteen

*Back inside for something stronger than tea*

By THE TIME BREWSTER came out of the kitchen with a bottle of wine, Carla had settled onto the couch and kicked her shoes off. She'd found the bowl of chips on the coffee table and now munched away, staring over her shoulder out the picture window behind her.

He paused to enjoy her in profile—brooding expression, dark, shaggy hair, a funky silver earring hanging like tinsel from a milky lobe—until she noticed him and turned.

"Cheers." He filled two glasses and handed one over.

"How did you know I like white wine?" she asked.

He didn't for sure, but, "Who doesn't?"

"That's too glib an answer." She glanced over her shoulder again. "Maybe our lives are scripted."

"Then I should thank whoever wrote yours for bringing you to my door."

Carla's smile brought a twinkle to her eyes.

"Here's to predestined midnight visitors," he said.

They clicked their glasses, and he joined her on the couch. Their shoulders touched and lingered, easing his concern he might have cast a shadow on their fledgling relationship by breaking off the kiss in the doorway. She provided further evidence of forgiveness by lifting a foot and running it a few inches up his leg, under the cuff of his jeans.

"I don't quite know what to make of you," she said.

Her touch renewed his desire, but he kept his hands to himself. Carla presented a perplexing combination of forwardness and skittishness. She'd seemed ready to bolt after mugging him on the porch, and she *had* taken off by disappearing the night before in her best rendition of a *Twilight Zone* episode. "I'm having a little trouble figuring you out, too."

That was all the talk for a time, but they shared a language of touches, gazes, and smiles to communicate an easy sensuality and comfortable bond transcending the questions hanging between them. Eventually they drained their glasses, and he poured more wine.

"I need to explain myself," she said.

"Do you know the secrets of the universe while you're at it?"

She gazed behind them, into the moonlit neighborhood. "I'm afraid my world defies comprehension."

"Join the club."

Carla set her glass on the table. "Imagine yourself dreaming but fully aware. You're the man behind the curtain, the puppet, and the audience all at once."

"Got it," he said.

"Some totally hot woman comes along and—"

Hmmm. This hypothetical was hitting close to home. "Anyone I know?"

She poked his arm. "Shut up. I'm trying to tell you something."

Brewster would have liked to close the lids over her mirthful eyes and press his lips to each one, but he needed answers to the questions buzzing in his head. "I'm all ears."

"You and this woman are alone at her place. You know from her words or her body language or simply the context of the situation she's available to you. You take her, right?"

The question had double meaning written all over it, but what response was she looking for?

Carla offered no help. She folded her arms and waited.

"Well, see, there's this whole *I'm Catholic* thing to deal with." A punt at best. He almost motioned to the crucifix on the wall but didn't want to overdo it. Catholic or not, he hadn't been a saint all his life when it came to women. Lately, though, he'd sworn off his previous ways.

"Don't waffle. I'm describing something happening to you *in a dream*, Brewster. Religion doesn't count, because none of this will be happening in the here and now. You're in a dream, you know you're dreaming, and the most desirable woman in the world comes along. What do you do?"

"Bust into tears?"

"Don't make me kill you." She leapt off the couch and paced in front of him, sloshing her wine with each step. Then she stopped and polished it off, returned the glass to the coffee table, and fixed him with a stare from eyes suddenly vulnerable. "Now you know why I came on to you."

He tried to follow her logic, but the heat of the earlier moment must have fogged his brain. "Because I'm dreaming?"

"No, you impossible man. I thought *I was*." She headed toward the kitchen but paused in the doorway and turned. She didn't seem annoyed, just unaccountably determined. "I'm not a slut. I swear to God, if you're sitting there thinking I'm—"

Had he been thinking that? If not, why were his cheeks burning? He held up his hands. "Easy, girl."

She came back and poked his arm again. Hard. "Don't call me girl. Carla works just fine if you can't think of anything more endearing to say. Now come on." She grabbed his wrist and tugged him off the couch.

"Where are we going?"

"I noticed a laptop on the kitchen counter last time I visited this imaginary place. There's something I need to show you."

A minute later, they stood side by side at the counter. Carla fiddled with the mouse and danced her fingers across the keyboard until she came up with a website and opened a cam shot of somebody's bedroom. A sleeping woman appeared on the screen, sheets pulled up to her chin, dark hair splayed across her pillow. Sections of newspaper lay scattered about, as if she'd been reading when she dozed off.

The scene wasn't zoomed in enough for Brewster to get a good look at her face. "Whoever that is, she sleeps well in god-awful brightness."

"I had to leave the lights on so we'd be able to see her."

"Wait. You were in the room with her?"

"In a manner of speaking, yes."

She zoomed in.

*Carla* was the woman in the bed. He blinked. "Why did you film yourself like that?"

"Wrong tense," she said. "I'm *filming* myself. You're watching a live webcam."

"Right." God. How strong was that wine?

"I mean it. There I am in my bed and here I am standing with you."

"I could use the idea in a novel."

Carla grabbed his arm. Got in his face. "Act shocked... surprised...scared." Her wide-eyed expression combined all of the above.

As for his, what could he convey but confusion? Did she really expect him to buy into some supernatural explanation instead of the obvious? They had to be viewing a recording, not a live feed. "Shouldn't there be a time and date stamp on the bottom of the screen?"

"The camera app is new. I spent half an hour just figuring out how to get it to do this much."

A little voice in Brewster's head told him to shut up, play along, and keep the sexiest woman he'd ever met amused, but he couldn't stop his brain from shooting a bolt of cynicism out his mouth. "So, where's the proof of what you're—"

"Look at the bed! I spread the newspaper so you could see the date and location. I'm sleeping in Syracuse, New York at the moment."

Carla's doggedness over something this ridiculous made his skin crawl. He grabbed the mouse and zoomed in on the paper.

*Syracuse Post Standard?* "Wait. Last night, you said you walked here from Sanders Road. That's here in Northbrook."

"No, I came from Sanders Creek Parkway in East Syracuse, eight hundred miles away."

Yeah, but the date on the newspaper was from 2012—a year ago. She'd recorded herself then, not now. Ha ha.

Carla shifted from foot to foot, arms hanging limp at her sides, far closer to tears than laughter.

He tapped the date on the paper. "I don't get it, Carla. You filmed this a year ago."

"What?"

If she truly believed she was in two places at once, what did that make her? Delusional? Insane? No way. Wildly eccentric maybe, but no worse than that. Just a woman in need of a steadying hand, especially after a couple glasses of surprisingly strong wine. In fact, he was beginning to feel tipsy himself. "Look at the wall calendar over the sink."

"What are you talking about? I—" She gaped at the calendar for a long moment, then turned and headed out of the kitchen.

"Where are you going?"

"I've had too much to drink."

Bingo.

"The bedroom's upstairs, right?"

He came after her. "Yeah, but—"

Carla reached the stairs, wobbled, and slumped against the bannister. "We're not having sex. We just met. I'm not a—"

"Shh... I know." He wrapped an arm around her waist. "Easy."

"It's called bi-location." She'd lowered her voice to a whisper, and her eyes took on the reverence of a nun in church.

"What?"

"Being in two places at one time. I looked it up."

He helped her climb the stairs.

"I've done a lot of research lately," she said. "Bi-location, schizophrenia...maybe I need to add a subject."

"Sorcery?" With all of this commotion, they'd completely

neglected the obvious question. How the hell did she vanish the night before?

"Time travel."

Huh. What better bow to tie around disappearances, reappearances, and chiming doorbells in the dead of night? For a stomach-churning moment he almost went along with it.

But he shook his head clear of the fuzzies and returned to planet earth.

Carla stopped him at the guest bedroom doorway. "You're catching me at a bad moment. If you plan on trying to tuck me in, that's as far as it goes. Treat me like a..." She trailed off and leaned against him.

"I could slip a pea under your mattress and treat you like a princess."

She kissed his cheek, and he eased her into the room.

Carla climbed into bed fully clothed. She rolled to the wall.

Brewster pulled the sheets over her shoulders. This woman needed protection. From what, he couldn't guess. But premonition, instinct, a strong hunch, or whatever shouted at him to watch her back.

Keeping watch *would* have its advantages. Just being in the same room with Carla buzzed him more than a bottle of wine. He crept toward the chair by the window to take his sentry post.

The hardwood floor creaked beneath his feet.

"Where are you going?" she asked.

"Just over here."

"Spoon up behind me, and I'll share my secrets."

"Now you're talking." He came over and climbed in with her, respecting the dress code by keeping his shirt and jeans on. He shaped his body against her backside and settled a protective arm across her shoulders.

They rested together for such a long, quiet moment he thought Carla had drifted off. But she eventually started speaking in a soft voice, first about nothing—the legions of ladybugs appearing out of nowhere every October, the weather, the sharpness of the crescent moon she'd seen in the sky while standing on his porch. "Would mankind have evolved into a savage people if the moon were red instead of white?"

"Are you suggesting we *aren't* a savage people?"

She didn't argue the point, rambling instead about her shop and its scent of strawberries. Carla explained she didn't sell berries of any kind, but the fragrances of different herbs combined into that singular aroma, and she even noticed the scent in her dreams sometimes.

She shifted around and faced him, eyes gleaming out of the shadows as she spoke about the mystery of dreams and what they might mean. She worked her way up to the description of a specific nightmare she'd been having—her struggle with a mysterious man in a subway station and her inexplicable urge to jump in front of a train.

"The last time I had the dream, I thought it might be from a previous life. But that makes no sense. Everything in the scene is modern." She shuddered. "Let's face it. This is my subconscious telling me I'm suicidal."

He ran his fingers though her hair. "No, you aren't. We could probably interpret that dream a hundred different ways."

"I pay good money for a professional to tell me that. You need to come at this thing from a different angle." She pulled a pillow over her head.

Brewster lifted it away. "You're seeing a shrink?"

"I was afraid my minister would bring in an exorcist. Anyway, I'm sure you've noticed how crazy I am."

"Not really. You're eccentric and free-spirited."

She giggled. "So, you think I'm a modern-day Tinker Bell?"

Good. He'd eased her mood. He ran his fingertips up and down the warm flesh of her arm. "Tinker Bell had a mean streak. I'm thinking more along the lines of a forest nymph."

Carla went quiet.

"What?"

"You called me a forest nymph."

"Uh-huh."

"Then listen to this." She bounded past him, out of bed, and paced the room, describing her passage from the suicide dream to a woodland where she existed as someone named Maynya. "The forest dream comes with its own language."

That little tidbit sent a tingle down his spine. "Sometimes I dream in Latin," he said.

She stopped pacing. "You and I weren't thrown together by accident, were we? Not many people dream in tongues."

Brewster swallowed. As creepy strange as the world had gotten lately, it hadn't redefined itself until that moment. Carla stood as living proof his Latin dreams didn't have a logical foundation. Yes, as a child, he might have overheard his language-professor dad spouting some Latin when preparing lesson plans, but *she* hadn't been there.

His head swam. He shifted up to the edge of the bed to clear his vision.

She came down beside him, gripped his hand, squeezed tight.

"Weirded out?" The shakiness of his voice certainly betrayed his own anxiety.

"I have been for a long time. But now I've got this... vulnerability. What happens when I get swept away again? What if I forget we ever met?" Her voice cracked. "Or you forget me?"

"No way."

She touched his nose with a fingertip, smiled, and got back in bed, this time facing him, not the wall. "You bring to mind a line from *Anne of Green Gables*. Ever read it?"

He eased down beside her. "I'm not sure a guy should admit that."

"We're *kindred spirits*," she said.

He gazed into her steady eyes, basking in the warmest glow he'd ever experienced.

"Tell me what happened last night, from your perspective," she said.

"You raced for the door like Cinderella and disappeared, but instead of a shoe, you left your card behind."

"That's when I woke up."

"I looked for Rag Thyme today," he said.

"It's fourteen hours east of here by car...and a year ago." Carla rolled. "Spoon with me some more."

They'd both had too much wine. A complete loss of inhibition lurked only one wayward touch away. He shifted closer but took care to put his hand somewhere relatively safe—on her arm. And he stayed on topic. "Let's compare notes about our dreams."

"Tell me your life story, instead," she whispered.

"Which one?"

"The one where Latin *isn't* spoken."

"I'm a wannabe with a big mortgage." In the darkness of the room, in a world gone so wacky that possible embarrassment was the least of his fears, he manned up and told her everything. Bad career choices, failing finance companies, struggling Russian truckers, unpublished novels, and his theory that life was like a running game in football, requiring its players to keep pounding away, pounding away, until finally, by the third or fourth quarter, holes would open.

She took his hand. "You're a brave man."

"Nah. Just some random clown who dreams in Latin. What about you? What's your story?"

She went quiet for a long moment. "I've been falling through cosmic wormholes lately. My soul keeps drifting away from my body."

The fear in her voice shook him as much as the haunting imagery. He scrunched closer and paced his breathing with hers to form an alliance against shared anxiety.

"I like your touch," she said.

"Same here." Their remarkably easy bond triggered his fear of bad luck, and his mind raced to memories of the failed relationships he'd glossed over while telling Carla about himself. He'd always suffered the effects of too much ambition, only rarely allowing himself to feel content. For the ambitious, anything other than purpose and accomplishment was a distraction. As a result, he'd been labeled too serious or humorless or—

worst of all—boring by the various girlfriends who'd had enough of him sooner or later.

Beth Holiday, the most recent of his flings, was a high school English teacher who had enough starry-eyed cheerfulness in her own disposition to carry the both of them for six great months but not quite enough to keep her from bolting to Denver when an opportunity to teach creative writing at a private college presented itself. She left with kind words and sage advice, telling him to find someone who needed a hero. He'd kill two birds with one stone that way. The woman would fulfill his romantic needs while simultaneously satisfying his inner need to save someone.

He hadn't followed Beth's advice, choosing instead to go it alone after she dumped him. Playing the role of somebody's hero would have required long-term commitment and plenty of energy, but his job at Crestview Finance sapped everything he had.

Now, though, he lay beside a woman who needed a champion and offered an elixir of beauty, creativity, humor, and intelligence in return. In comparison, his career came across as a cold-hearted, passionless bitch of a mistress. The time had come to put a good relationship ahead of a lousy job. "Are you seeing anyone?" he asked.

"I'm seeing you." Carla's soft answer came with no small hint of pleasure. She intertwined her fingers with his.

"I have to warn you, I've been called selfish and boring and a workaholic and—"

"I'm seeing you," she insisted, "for as long as you'll have me."

Brewster squeezed the hand of a damsel in distress who thought she lived eight hundred miles and a dozen months away. "And I'm seeing you, for as long as you'll put up with me."

Carla wasn't eccentric or a little off or downright crazy anymore. Brewster cast his lot with heaven-sent. He couldn't freeze time at this moment of contentment forever. Sooner or later, whatever forces had swept her away a night ago might do so again. But he took comfort from the notion any wormholes hovering nearby had already proven to be benevolent. They'd brought her to his home twice so far, and they surely wouldn't end a game unfinished. Otherwise, the first two visits would have been pointless.

If Carla wanted to see him for as long as he'd have her, the wormholes would be there at the ready.

The gentle hum of arousal crept over him. He sensed heat in Carla as well, but a hero would want her to feel protected, not craved. So he controlled his urges and surrendered to the sandman, ready to drift away whenever and wherever, as long as the forest nymph breathing contentedly at his side came along for the ride.

But she didn't.

# CHAPTER FOURTEEN

*Across the portal, in Virtus*

QUINTUS LASKARIS EASED HIS horse around a clump of scrub brush baked brown by the sun. He'd likely be skirting these patches of thirsty vegetation for a few more days, until he reached the somewhat wetter capital city of Dubris. Then, should he continue into the woods, he'd cross the Sanctimonia border. Thoughts of fiery Mystic women and the hard-drinking, story-telling men of that territory tempted him sorely. He enjoyed their company far more than that of his own brutish lot. But border saloons were rife with the king's spies. Albus wouldn't be amused to hear about any side trips to consort with the "enemy."

Meanwhile, well outside his ruling brother's reach, a trinity of more immediate scourges shaped Quintus's day—drought, dust, and danger. A little ahead, Bertramus and his band of six soldiers had already pulled up short. "I smell trouble," the lieutenant said. He pointed east.

Quintus squinted toward the horizon. Anything greater than a mile out faded into the same dusty haze that had turned everyone's blue uniforms gray—capes, shirts, trousers, and boots all gone to chalk.

Winds gusting across the scorched earth stirred up an earthy powder he could taste. He longed to rinse the bitter flavor from his mouth, but he'd stolen too many swigs from his canteen already. Rationing would be the word until they came upon the next creek.

"I don't smell a thing." Quintus hoped Bertramus hadn't jinxed them by bringing up the possibility of trouble. Although the region was notorious for its dangers, the first day and a half of their journey had proven blessedly uneventful. They hadn't skirmished with any of the hostile gangs of fugitives, bandits, or indigenous savages who favored the area for its general lack of soldiers. Despite their side trip to fetch Quintus from his border patrol, Bertramus's principal orders were to root out these scoundrels. Thus far, though, they'd come across only a few dry-land farmers—peaceful folk for the most part, if somewhat crazy. No sane man could expect hardy crops to spring out of the cracked earth. Quintus admired their pluck.

"One o'clock." Bertramus continued pointing east.

Quintus could barely make out a distant hint of smoke at a slight angle from the path they'd been following. The time had come to say his good-byes and move on. These other soldiers had been assigned peacekeeping duties, whereas he'd been summoned to see the king. But he couldn't abandon this small troop to face an unknown danger, could he? In a skirmish, one extra gun might make all the difference. Besides, why hurry to visit a brother he despised, whether he'd been summoned or not?

He stayed with the men.

They advanced with caution, using undulations in the land as cover. When they rounded the last hill, they had their weapons at the ready, the soldiers with rifles in their hands and Quintus with a pistol. As a scout and occasional spy, he traveled lightly armed. Now, approaching the unknown with only six bullets in his chamber and a relatively short range of fire, he prayed he could count on the soldiers as good marksmen.

But the time for shooting had already come and gone. They rode up to the smoldering ruins of a cabin where the bodies of a homesteading couple lay outside, riddled with arrows. The man had been scalped.

"They were unarmed, by the looks of it." Bertramus shaded his eyes and gazed toward a fenced area south of the cabin. "Bound to happen sooner or later. I'm surprised these fools survived long enough to plant their crops."

Quintus longed for the ability to stave off emotion and make such a callous comment. He'd seen plenty of death in his thirty years, more than enough to harden the hearts of most men, but his remained too soft. As usual, he couldn't stop his thoughts from straying down a path littered with pointless empathy. Had the couple been happy? Had they been living their dream? What of their parents who'd eventually hear the sorry news from the soldiers? And what of those others whose lives might have been touched by these two? Homesteading was the best means for taming a forbidding land, but this couple had found death doing it.

He escaped the heart-wrenching carnage and wandered to a brook some hundred yards away. An irrigation canal had been scooped out, and he followed it to the fenced plantings—a row of corn waist high, a small field of wheat, another of soy. The wind triggered rippling waves across the unburned plots. The region's warring indigenous tribes never touched crops, focusing their wrath solely on settlers and their dwellings. Perhaps the savages considered the isolated pockets of splendor in a fallow land akin to hallowed ground.

He closed his eyes and tried to imagine a world where one might carve out a homestead in peace. But he saw only two bloodied corpses.

Bertramus came up, stooping to fill his canteen in the clear canal water. "The northern tribe hates settlers."

"They see these plains as their land," Quintus said.

The bearded man stood, took a swig from his canteen, and wiped his mouth with his sleeve. "You and I share a history. How many battles have we fought side by side?"

"Counting saloon brawls?"

Bertramus split the dust at his mouth with a wide grin. "Whatever they were, you fought with conviction. Don't go soft on me now. You'll be traveling alone, across *their land,* the rest of the way."

"And you'll be traveling?"

The lieutenant jerked his chin to the north.

The possibility of action tugged Quintus like a magnet. "I can lend a hand in a fight."

"I doubt we'll catch them."

"If you do, you and your soldiers could use the help. I've never known the northerners to travel fewer than two dozen strong."

Bertramus took another pull at his canteen, then squinted at the sky as if looking to God for an answer. "I have my orders, and you have yours, no matter how unmilitary the reasons behind them."

Quintus knelt and washed the dust from his face with blessedly cold water. He gulped straight out of the canal before filling his canteen. When he stood, he found Bertramus lingering rather than helping his men dig the graves. "Tell me why I've been summoned."

The lieutenant shook his head. "You know how Albus loves his little surprises."

"Give me a hint."

Bertramus tried to turn away, but Quintus stopped him with a hand on his shoulder. "You and I are old friends."

They locked eyes for a long moment before the lieutenant relented. "You've been summoned to a wedding."

"Summoned from the front for *a wedding?*"

"Not just any wedding. *Albus's* wedding."

Quintus stalked away. Either that or strangle the man.

"Where are you going?" Bertramus asked.

"I saw a hoe in the field. It'll make a good club."

"I'm only the messenger."

"Then here's your message. Tell Albus you never found me." Quintus shaded his eyes to look west across the baking prairie. One day's ride and he'd be back where he started. Two days and—

"We shoot deserters, Quintus."

"Even the king's brother?"

Bertramus slung his canteen over his shoulder and headed toward the men. "Act surprised when Albus announces his wedding, or I'll be the one getting shot."

Quintus turned east and sighed. Given his blood ties, he could have been stationed wherever he wanted, but he'd chosen a distant scouting assignment to escape Albus. He and his brother had always been like oil and water. The situation had worsened when birthright crowned Albus king and elevated the man's ego to the clouds. Still, maybe his brother had turned a new leaf.

*Marriage.* He'd never expected Albus to grant any maiden the honor. In the past, the man had taken and discarded woman after woman without regard to the virtue he'd ruined each time. Perhaps a visit *was* in order.

Several hours after bidding the soldiers farewell and continuing his eastward trek, Quintus again enjoyed a cold splash of water. He'd come upon a spring-fed fountain within the square of a ramshackle town. He used cupped hands to drink his fill.

He'd packed his military cape in his saddlebag earlier when the sun had grown too hot. Now he unbuttoned his shirt, stripped it off, and lowered his upper body into the pool. After a long moment, he lifted out and felt human again.

A scream pierced the all-too-brief moment of peace. He hurried to a group of eight ragged monks who'd formed a circle around a golden-haired angel of a young woman dressed in a floral shift and silver sandals.

The zealots surrounding her had murder in their eyes.

He'd come across their kind in other settlements, men who carved out a station by terrorizing the local populace into following an ancient creed of purity and sacrifice. Like the others, these men had shaved their heads, and also like the others, their long robes probably concealed the scars of self-scourging.

The woman quaked in their midst with fists clenched, chest heaving, and terror in her eyes. "I've done nothing!"

He worked his way into the circle and nudged the man on his left. "What's this all about?"

"It's about traveling gypsies whoring in our god-fearing town!" The monk sprayed Quintus's face with his angry words, then bent to a small pile of stones he'd gathered at his feet. A quick glance around the circle revealed similar stashes collected by the others.

The irony of fate never failed to amaze him. Two law-abiding settlers might have been spared a flurry of arrows had he and the others arrived an hour earlier. But no, destiny decided he should risk his life saving a gypsy, instead. Backing away wasn't an option he could consider. Any man unwilling to protect a maiden was no man at all.

He took three long strides into the center of the circle, wrapped an arm around the woman's waist, and turned with her, slowly, looking each man in the eye. "Who among you hasn't lusted for a woman? According to your creed, the thought is as great a sin as the deed, is it not? Maybe you should stone yourselves."

Fear—a welcome friend—made his voice tremble. He'd always known a dose of it during battle and perhaps he'd stayed alive for that reason. Fear could keep a man from underestimating his adversary and getting his fool head knocked off. Although Quintus had a weapon, these monks, all larger men, had him surrounded and could strike from his blind sides. The element of surprise might be counted on to freeze them at first, but he couldn't rely on them to stay that way for long.

The giant of the group, a bear of a man, leered at him with dark eyes bulging above too sharp a nose. His barrel chest heaved with each breath as if trying to burst free from the dusty robe constraining it. "You won't enjoy our answer, sinner."

The others shifted closer, stones in hand.

Quintus pulled his pistol from his belt and aimed between the man's eyes, struggling to hide the shadow of worry from his.

None of the monks were armed as far as he could tell, but if they sensed any weakness in his resolve and chose to fight, eight stones thrown in unison would surely take him down. "What's your answer now?"

The big man worked his jaw on a wad of tobacco. He shifted his glance back and forth to the men on either side of him, but the fight had gone out of their eyes.

The other monks started backing out of the circle.

Quintus released the woman. "Watch my back."

"They've eased away. I'll gather my things and—"

"Stay put." He left her standing there, stepped up to the giant, and pressed his pistol against a bead of sweat on the man's forehead. Those other monks in his range of vision had dropped their stones. He heard additional stones falling to the ground behind him in a series of soft plunks. Quintus could only hope the group would remain more frightened than he was. "I'm on the king's business."

The man sneered. "Hasn't the king enough whores of his own?"

They locked eyes. A crow squawked somewhere in the distance. Gusts of wind sent a tumbleweed rolling up against the stone fountain. Finally, the giant wavered. "Take the whore and leave."

The woman rushed up from behind, grabbed Quintus's free wrist, and whispered in his ear. "I'll need my belongings."

"You can buy new things in the next town." He kept his eyes fixed on the giant. The battle could still shift if the others saw the opening and came to life.

"Please!" She pointed toward a makeshift tent some distance from the fountain.

The silly fool seemed bent on getting them killed, but he couldn't disregard the urgency of her plea. Women had always been a great mystery to him. Every trinket in their possession served some vital if incomprehensible purpose.

"Let's go." He shoved his adversary forward, then raised his voice to a shout. "The rest of you can move on. I have more than one bullet left in this gun, in case you're wondering."

The three of them—Quintus, the woman, and a bear of a hostage—marched to the woman's tent. The others scattered, but he didn't trust them not to rally for an ambush. He gripped the pistol so tightly his hand ached.

The woman disappeared within the folds of her tent and came out a few moments later with far less than anyone should have bothered retrieving.

The monk laughed. "You sell your flesh for these simple things?"

"Shut up." Quintus held his pistol to the man's head and waited an eternity for the woman to stash her things into a pack, fold the cloth tent, and stuff it in with the rest. Then he backed with her to his horse and got out of town as fast as he could.

After two miles riding behind him in silence, the woman eased her clenched grip around his waist. "My name is Adala."

"Quintus."

"I've dodged death before."

He doubted she had. Her voice still trembled.

"But never through the courage of so handsome a soldier."

He cringed at the compliment—most likely the opening gambit of a gypsy's campaign to get her fingers into the money pouch at his hip.

"I can repay you for saving me." She slid a soft hand from his neck down into his shirt, tightening her other arm around his waist to stay steady on the horse.

He refused to be stirred. "Have you considered a worthier occupation?"

"Don't be like those monks."

"I'm nothing like them."

"You assume the worst of me, just as they did."

"Tell me the best."

"I sing, I serve wine, and I sketch. Which would you prefer?"

"Let's be honest with each other, Adala." The all-important belongings she'd retrieved from her tent consisted of no more than a pitcher, a sketch pad, some charcoal, and three pencils— hardly as marketable as the charms beneath her dress.

Adala turned stony silent until they reached a fork in the road. "I'm heading south," she announced.

She'd almost been killed earlier when trying to fend on her own. Quintus arrived at the same decision he'd made in the town. Every woman deserves a champion, no matter her station. "The capital is two days east. You can sing to me and pour wine from your empty pitcher to pay your fare."

She scrambled off the horse. "I've been to the capital."

"Suit yourself. The town of Portus lies two miles south. Go pitch a tent and sell your charms."

She glared at him. "There's a brook nearby. Do you hear it?"

"What if there is? My canteen is full."

"Is it filled with wine?" Adala turned on her heel and strode toward a row of low bushes.

*Women and their mysteries.* He dismounted and followed her.

They came upon a shallow creek snaking a bubbling path around scrub brush and scattered rocks. Adala knelt on its bank. She filled her pitcher and held it up with both hands. "Drink and doubt me no longer."

Quintus noticed a butterfly tattoo on the underside of her wrist. The marking stirred a vague memory he couldn't place. He'd seen this image on another woman's neck, hadn't he?

"Drink!"

He accepted her offering, but an inexplicable whiff of wine stopped him short before he brought the pitcher to his lips. The liquid inside was far too golden to have come from the stream. "What manner of sorcery is this?"

"A superstitious man would call it witchcraft, and a religious man the hand of God."

He set the pitcher on the ground beside her. "I've seen these tricks. You spiked the water with powder from a vial."

Adala stood, lifted her head, and laughed at the burning sky. She planted her feet wider, raised her arms. "Search me for the empty vial."

"Save the chamber games for your customers."

Adala was on him in an instant, slapping him hard enough to ring his ears. "Save the insults for your whores." The fury in her eyes said he'd misjudged her from the beginning.

Both of his cheeks burned although she'd struck only one. "I apologize."

"No need." Adala rummaged through her pack and pulled out the sketch pad he'd seen earlier. She tossed it to him. "Behold the mistress who turned me into a whore for a single night."

He flipped through the drawings but found nothing notable—landscapes, flora, a few sketches of men and women.

"Are you familiar with the bridal pool in the capital?" she asked.

"Who isn't? The sale of slaves fills the king's coffers."

"Do you know how harshly these women are treated before they're sold?"

He clenched his fists. He'd been powerless to stop the ruthless debaucheries of his brother's rule. "Where are you going with this?"

"Keep turning the pages."

He flipped one more and froze at the sketch of a woman he'd seen before. But where? An overpowering sense of déjà vu buckled his knees.

"Her name is Maynya," Adala said.

No. He knew the maiden by another name.

But how could the recent, intoxicating companion in his endless series of midnight dreams be real?

"She'd been suspected of helping other brides escape," Adala said. "So they put her in the stocks for a day and a night without food or water."

The charcoal likeness of the strikingly beautiful woman spun his mind like a top. *Her name is Carla.* He shivered.

"I waited till after dark. Then I let her drink from my pitcher."

Maybe the blazing sun had finally taken its toll on his brain. He forced his gaze up from a drawing he'd mistaken for an imaginary siren.

Adala had gone soft, too, judging by her crazy jabber. "The guards would never allow such a thing."

"Soldiers can be bought."

"What are you saying?" He blinked, and the pendulum sway of his dizziness steadied.

"I'm saying I surrendered my virtue to help a saint." Adala snatched the sketch pad. "That guard was the only *customer* to ever set foot in my chamber."

The tears in her eyes tore at his heart. "I've misjudged you."

"Yes, you have. My sketches are the charms I sell, and sometimes the wine, but only to men I can trust." She stuffed the pad back into her pack. "If the monks knew of the illusions Maynya taught me, they would've burned me at the stake for practicing witchcraft."

"You trusted *me* with your wine."

"I wanted you to know you risked your life to save someone better than a whore." She lowered her gaze to the ground. "Perhaps my pride will get me killed one day."

"It might if you try any tricks in Portus. You won't find many trustworthy men in these frontier towns."

"No illusions, then."

"You mean vials of powder?"

"Believe what you want."

"I don't buy your notion of saints, either," he said. "They've been few and far between, in my experience."

Adala turned away. "Surely you'd agree Maynya is one of the few and far. Her mere sketch brought more life to your eyes than I could."

Quintus didn't know what to say. He hadn't intended to reveal his inexplicable feelings for a woman he'd never met, nor had he picked up on Adala's attraction to him. In a gesture he hoped was spurred more by generosity than guilt, he reached into his pouch and came out with a fistful of coins. "You'll need money for provisions."

"I'm quite good at barter."

"Take some bread at least."

"Save it for Maynya. No doubt she'll be in the stocks again when you reach the capital, if she's still alive."

"*Servo is pro Maynya.*" Save it for Maynya.

Brewster shot up in bed, fully awake, but with Adala's words still ringing in his ears. Lately, the memories of his Latin dreams had been lingering. This time, he clung to enough detail to realize the storyline didn't match Carla's. She'd told him about life in a woodland, not bondage in Virtus's bridal pool. Her shadow world was completely different than the one he'd just seen.

He turned to Carla. To where she should have been, sleeping beside him.

And he found an empty side of the bed. Not even an indentation on her pillow.

Gravity might as well have doubled. He lacked the strength to stay upright.

Something small and metallic pressed against his back. He rolled over and found a two-headed silver coin with a chain hole near the top. The identical sides displayed a centurion surrounded by a ring of Latin words. *Somnium. Virtus. Spiritus.*

Virtus? Carla might have been having dreams about a forest existent, but she'd left a coin behind with the name of *his* imaginary homeland. He racked his brain for a logical explanation but failed. No matter. He could chew on that one later. For now, he closed his fist around the coin, closed his eyes, and tried to bring it back.

But the wormholes didn't surrender their prizes so easily.

# Chapter Fifteen

*Back in Syracuse*

CARLA SQUIRMED ON A stool at the checkout counter of her store, flipping through a stack of bills she hadn't found a way to pay. Sales were half what they'd been a year earlier, and she hadn't brought in enough cash to cover expenses. Most shoppers were too worried about putting food on the table to buy anything as superfluous as a stuffed bunny. One domino falls and brings down the others. She understood economic theory well enough to know her store teetered straight in the path of those dominoes.

She'd taken steps to seize control of the situation, having set plans in motion to cut expenses, carry less inventory, and borrow a bit more from the bank. While the unpaid invoices still brought a tingle of unease each time she went through them, she didn't panic anymore—not over her business, anyway. No, her anguish had a new, more frightening focus. Her pinball bounces from one reality to another had been increasing, as had her worry she was losing her mind.

Earlier that morning, she'd fished Brewster's card out of her purse and tried calling him, only to get an out of service message in reply. He'd told her the card carried his new cell phone number, so it should have worked. Directory assistance for a

Brewster DeLay landline in Northbrook, Illinois, hadn't panned out, either. On the other hand, if she and Brewster were separated by a year...

The haunting possibility he didn't actually exist, other than in a crazy corner of her subconscious mind, nearly brought her to tears—and not only from fear of insanity.

They'd clicked, big-time. This funny, kind, tender, honest, intelligent man, this kindred spirit who dreamed in Latin, this fellow vortex traveler had triggered a hum in her soul and an ache for much more. She wanted him in her life.

Carla tried talking herself down from the ledge, reminding herself Brewster had to be real or she wouldn't have his card.

And now he had her coin, a talisman her mother had given to her when she was a child. Carla had awakened before Brewster did. She'd run her fingers through his hair, kissed the tip of his nose, and pressed the coin into his palm. Then she woke again. In Syracuse.

The act of giving served as additional proof, didn't it? The talisman truly was gone in the morning—not in the drawer of her bed stand, where she remembered seeing it the night before. But tentative confirmation of her sanity brought little joy. She missed Brewster. Hard.

Carla paid the few invoices she could afford and stuffed the rest into a drawer. Browsing through her collection of merchandise often lifted her spirits, so she headed to the window display up front.

"Hello, sweeties." She ruffled the curly heads of two oversized rag dolls. Raggedy Ann and Andy sat in little yellow chairs, ruling over a collection of toys scattered on the floor— soldiers for him and the Seven Dwarfs for her. She'd made the figurines out of wax and painted them with loving care.

The two dolls kept watch out the window, taking in the sidewalk, a row of meters hosting too few parked cars for a shopkeeper to survive, a street almost devoid of traffic, and three stores on the other side, the bakery, the fudge shop, and the ice cream parlor. Word had it those owners were in the same straits as she, barely hanging on, but they kept a stiff upper lip and always greeted her with a smile, offering a free cupcake or a piece of fudge or a scoop of vanilla-chocolate swirl whenever she stopped in. She'd given some of her miniature waxed toys to them for their kindnesses. And she'd taken delight when the shopkeepers put them on display, lining up the little figurines on table tops or counters and one time even in a window, gathered around a giant plastic ice-cream cone.

She turned away and wandered down the aisles of her store, first passing a display of eggshell ornaments—they conjured the memory of her tenth Christmas, when her mother surprised her with a tabletop fir tree to hang them on. Next, she walked alongside shelf upon shelf of handmade dolls and cuddly animals, followed by an aisle lined with candles and wax figurines, and finally the section reserved for consigned goods and herbs provided by others, mostly single moms hoping to scratch out a few extra dollars.

When she reached the back of the store, the little bell up front tinkled. She rushed over to greet a rare customer but ran out of steam when she identified her visitor. She tried smiling to hide her reflexive disappointment over a lost sale that never existed.

"You can't fool me. I know that look." Her mother breezed into the store wearing one of her trademark twentysomething outfits—in this case a floral skirt topped with a short, midriff-baring blouse tied closed at the bottom. Turquoise reigned supreme, coloring a winter coat left open despite the cold, her blouse, the bow twisted around her ponytail, and a pair of heels rising an inch higher than seemed reasonable.

She'd dressed the same way a week earlier when accompanying Carla to a local fundraiser dance. A man chatted them up in what had to be a misguided attempt to get laid, claiming mother and daughter might pass for identical twins, especially since one dressed somewhat older than her peers and the other much younger. He went on and on about various shared features unsullied by any generational differences, from their classically curved frames to the dimples when they smiled, their matching high cheekbones, the hint of green in their hazel eyes, and the auburn shadows in their raven hair. Her mother ate it up, but Carla couldn't back out of the scene fast enough.

"I'll smile wider if you buy a stuffed bunny," Carla said.

Her mother shook her head. "We've talked about this before. Why not stop worrying over rent and move home with me for a while?"

"Mother, please."

At thirty years of age, running home was so not an option. She'd as soon give up her apartment and sleep in the back of the store.

They chose the window booth of a corner restaurant for their lunch. A youngish hunk of a waiter brought menus. When he walked away, her mother stared after him a couple beats too long. Carla couldn't let that pass. "Would I find your picture in the dictionary under midlife crisis?"

Her mother laughed, then fixed her with a stare, the sharp kind capable of piercing a daughter's soul. "I think we'd find yours under brooding."

"Wrong letter. Flip forward a few pages to the Cs and look under crazy."

"Everyone feels that way at times."

"Just once, I'd like to be part of the great *everyone*. But there's good news! Lately I've been having doubts about my insanity."

Her mother didn't show the slightest amusement at the clever play on words. "There's nothing wrong with you."

Carla escaped out the window to watch the chill winds of autumn swirl dead leaves across the sidewalk, but the waiter soon pulled her back to the restaurant by setting an iced tea in front of her. She met her mother's eyes again. The woman pursed her lips around a straw and sipped her drink, beating her down with an overly concerned stare.

"I've been seeing a counselor, Mother."

"A shrink?"

"Not so loud." She would have loved to flee out the window again, but a lifetime of mother-daughter exchanges foretold that an explanation would be extracted sooner or later. The longer she held out, the noisier the conversation might get. "I've been having nightmares about asking a man to kill me."

She cringed, expecting an outburst, yet her confession was met by silence. Working up the courage to meet her mother's eyes took awhile.

But her mother displayed neither shock nor scorn, only her trademark, head-tilted, half-smile expression of curiosity. "How are your waking thoughts?"

"I'm not suicidal." As if a simple denial could prove such a thing, even to herself.

Her words hung in the air like the bloodied blade of a guillotine, until her mother leaned forward with the sharp stare of a coconspirator. "You're merely having dark sexual fantasies!"

With impeccable timing, the comment filled a brief void in the restaurant's general clatter. Heads turned in their direction.

"Mother, do you not have an inside voice?"

The waiter returned. He set their lunches down and caught Carla's eye. She had to admit her mother had targeted a suitable subject for leering. Either this dark-haired Adonis inherited his muscular frame from the gods or he was bent on setting the record for frequent visitor points at the gym. Under different circumstances he might have stirred her, too, but only one man could accomplish such a thing at the moment. She averted her gaze until the waiter left, fighting the urge to reach into her purse and fondle Brewster's card.

Once they were alone again, her mother shot a glance around the restaurant and then leaned forward, like some character in a spy novel. "All right, Carla, here's my inside voice. The women in our line have been blessed with amazing dreams."

Carla caught her breath. "And you waited until now to tell me?"

"You've never said anything one way or the other about yours, so I assumed the trait stopped with me."

"So what do you mean by amazing?"

"They seem every bit as real as this lunch we're having. Conversations with actual people, journeys to other worlds—"

"*You've* visited other worlds?" Carla accidentally brushed her sleeve into her salad, but who cared about French-dressing stains at a time like this?

Her mother slumped away. "Not lately. Somehow, I've outgrown the ability to do that."

"But you remember it happening?"

"I remember having two lives, one here and one somewhere else."

"In the forest?" Carla barely heard her own whispered words over her pounding heart.

"I'm not sure. The point is, I'm not crazy and neither are you." Her mother turned her attention to a bowl of chicken noodle soup.

Carla didn't know whether to press the matter further or wait until a time when they might have more privacy. Her mother was perfectly capable of bouncing an exclamation of surprise off all four walls of the crowded restaurant if their notes about dreams matched. She decided to come at the topic from a different angle, a dream her mother would know nothing about. "I've started seeing someone."

"Good. You're more stable when dating."

"I'm quite the handful otherwise, huh?" Although she'd been dwelling on her mental health for months, the comment still stung.

Her mother set her spoon down. "I was teasing."

"Do *you* like being teased?"

Her mother reached across the table, patted Carla's hand, smiled. Her eyes gleamed with genuine interest, perhaps even pleasure.

Carla forgave her.

"Tell me about this new man."

"His name is Brewster DeLay."

"That's no ordinary name!"

"He's no ordinary man. He writes novels that don't sell, and he's failing at his day job, but you'd think he was on the top of the world. I love his attitude. He's always positive, funny, caring."

"Handsome?"

"Uh-huh."

Her mother broke eye contact and looked down at her hands. "You think I'm shallow for asking."

"No, Mother, I think it's time to get real. I've given my talisman to a man I only meet in my dreams."

"The coin?" Her mother's hushed question was spoken so sharply it managed to turn a few heads.

"Shh. Didn't you hear the weird part? I've given an heirloom away to a shadow."

Her mother turned to the window and stared with thousand-mile eyes. "You've given the talisman to someone special. I suppose that's how it was meant to be used."

English didn't seem to be working. "He and I haven't actually met in the traditional sense of the word."

Her mother took her by the hands. "What are you talking about? I see true love in your eyes."

And Carla had true love in her heart, but she was setting herself up to be crushed when the wormholes or whatever snatched Brewster away. "He might not be real!" She pulled her hands away. "We've only met in my dreams and not very often."

"There's something so sweet about love at first sight."

"Mother, have you been listening to me?"

"Have *you* been listening to *me?* I'm sure the place I visited in my dreams was real. Yours must be, too!"

The notion was amazing, dizzying, validating. Terrifying. A chill ran down her spine. "What if the *train* is real?"

A shadow crossed her mother's face.

"You think it might be?" Carla asked.

"No. I just… Did you ever get a sudden fright for no reason? I thought I remembered something, but I didn't."

"Well, here's a reason for *me* to be scared, mother. I'm in a lot of trouble in another world. Two men are chasing me and—"

"But you found your hero!"

"He can't help. He's in a different place entirely."

"Is he?"

"Are you suggesting he isn't?"

Her mother went at her salad, took her time chewing a forkful, thinking the question over, perhaps. "Everything ties together somehow."

Carla tended to tune her mother out when she got going down this path. With any encouragement, her mother would start talking about crystals or pyramids, witchcraft...as opposed to the likely conclusion they both suffered from some form of genetic instability.

The waiter returned to freshen their drinks. "Hey, are you sisters?"

"Don't even go there." She shot a look at her mother, fully ready to put her fork to good use if any more flirting went on.

The waiter wandered off, leaving them to brood in silence.

Eventually, her glass-half-full mother brightened. She motioned out the window. "Look at that! I can't remember ever seeing lake snow this early."

Carla turned to the window and lost herself in a swirl of white. The squall dissipated as quickly as it came, leaving a dusting of powder in its wake, then a burst of windswept leaves, then no sign she'd seen any snow at all. She wouldn't let herself dwell on the possibility she'd imagined it. "I've been thinking about getting away for a few days to sort things out. Can you watch the store for me?"

"Now you're thinking straight! The cabin would be the perfect escape for you. Remember how your father used to take us there to celebrate the first blizzard?"

"I was just a little girl."

"Don't ever let go of that." Her mother's smile didn't quite hide the tinge of sadness in her eyes.

Carla had been planning a trip to Manhattan, but the thought of a brief detour to the Tug Hill Plateau carried plenty of appeal. She loved the nature walks and antique picking the area afforded. Not to mention a quiet evening or two in the cabin, where she could sew new dolls for her shop. She'd been neglecting her craft.

Her mother fished in her purse, came out with a key, handed it over. "Stay as long as you like."

Carla closed her hand around it. "Just for a couple nights, but I'm driving to Manhattan after that."

A shadow crossed her mother's face again. "Why so far?"

"A subway keeps calling my name. Elaine is big on facing down fears."

"Elaine?"

"She's my thera— She's a friend of mine."

"Manhattan isn't safe. I've told you this before."

"Yeah. Way too often."

Her mother crossed her arms.

Time for a white lie. "Okay, I'll just go to the cabin."

"Promise?"

"Mother."

"What?"

"When you visited, you know, other places, in your dreams, did you ever come back with anything?" The very act of asking such an incongruous question in a commonplace setting disoriented her. The couple across the aisle might have been deciding which movie to see, and the businessmen behind them could have been closing a deal. A baby's fuss could be heard from the other side of the restaurant. She closed her eyes against the sensation of being out of body, as if looking down at the booth from the ceiling.

When she reopened them, her mother's probing gaze stole into her soul again. She found refuge in her purse, pulled Brewster's card out, and slid it across the table. "This makes him real, doesn't it?" Her voice cracked.

Her mother handled the card as gently as a Communion host before handing it back. "You and I have a gift, Carla."

"You need to tell me more about it."

"The talisman you passed on? I woke up to find it in my hand one day."

"What?"

"A girl gave it to me in a dream."

Carla replayed the words in her head twice before she could trust she'd heard them. Her stomach tingled. If a coin could emerge from a dream, kick around in the waking world, and then disappear into an entirely different dream years later, her ideas about wormholes, time travel, and alternate realities had now become far more likely than any self-diagnosis of dementia. Yet, if she were sane, the whole universe must have gone crazy. "What's happening to us?"

With a slow shake of the head, Carla's mother said it all. Neither of them had any idea. "What's wrong with having a little extra God in our lives?" she said.

Carla grimaced. Not everyone could share so cavalier an attitude. Barbarians were closing in with a net. A subway train was barreling too fast into a station. "Who was the girl?"

"We ran into her in a park when you were three. She was the typical blonde-haired, ponytailed girl you'd find on a thousand middle-school playgrounds. First she visited our waking lives and then she popped into my dream. Abbie or Addie...no... Gabby. Gabriella, I think. I never saw her again after that."

# CHAPTER SIXTEEN

*Nine hundred miles west in his Chicago office*

**BREWSTER FRITTERED HIS TIME** staring out the window, gazing at the paintings on his office wall, and halfheartedly flicking spider mites off his desk. He'd been in a fog since staggering into the building earlier that morning.

Somehow, the Virtus dream had settled into the area of memory reserved for actual events. Although only seven hours had passed from when he and Carla drifted off together to the point he awakened alone with her coin in his hand, the disorienting recollection of a two-day trek through scrubby desert had gotten lodged between those bookends.

This thing scared the hell out of him.

He reached into his wallet and examined the coin. Why not leave a damn note instead? *Dear Brewster, catching a wormhole back to Syracuse. See you soon.* Would he see her soon? The possibility he wouldn't plunged through his stomach like a bad taco.

A ringing phone pulled him back to a world where people were expected to get some work done. He slipped the coin back into his billfold and tried answering with something resembling enthusiasm. "Brewster DeLay."

"We've got problems." Charlie Hanson's whine grated through the receiver.

Brewster suppressed a groan. "What's up?" He made a mental note to check caller ID next time he got the crazy impulse to answer his phone.

"Are you managing that place or what, Brewster? You people burned through one hundred thousand dollars cash last month. We're almost out of dough up here."

As the chief financial officer of Parker Investments—a sorry mess of a holding company that owned not only Crestview Finance but several other stumbling businesses—Charlie certainly had the authority to lodge a complaint. But the man had forfeited all right to straight answers by failing to attend a single strategy session. Ever since the recession began sucking the life out of Crestview, Charlie had avoided brainstorming meetings like the plague. He kept his hands clean by steering clear while Brewster struggled alone against an avalanche of loan defaults.

"Are you there, Brewster?"

"What do you want me to say?"

"You couldn't have sounded more positive when we met with the bankers a week ago."

"How did you want me come across? They're scared enough."

"Not only them."

No kidding. Brewster took a deep breath. "It's no big deal, Charlie. Most of our customers wait until month-end to make their payments, and the last two days of September happened to fall on a weekend. You'll see a huge Monday deposit in our October numbers."

"Can I count on a better month?"

"Uh-huh." If he tried taking another deep breath, he might have choked on the lingering cloud of false optimism he'd just exhaled into the phone. Who knew what could be relied upon anymore? Try as he might, Brewster couldn't account for, let alone predict, the company's monthly cash flow with any degree of precision. Money came in from fees on new deals and from customer payments on old ones. It went out to cover payables, expenses, payroll, and amortization of Crestview's whopping bank loan.

*Amortization.* Therein lay the problem. The bank pulled loan repayments out of the company's accounts at the end of each month. The complex formula determining amounts due was supposed to be driven by the number of days since last payment, but it seemed inconsistent. He'd grown suspicious nervous bankers had started cheating to get their money back quicker. Whenever he thought Crestview had finished a halfway decent month, the unsolvable amortization formula bit him in the ass.

None of this ever mattered in the good old days. The company's cash hadn't been any easier to predict, but it tended to grow from one month to the next. Nobody worried over unexplained fluctuations.

"Just break even for a change," Charlie whined. "That's all I'm asking."

"You can take it to the bank." The false assurance rolled off Brewster's tongue nice and smooth. Poor Charlie needed a dose of comfort wherever he could find it. In addition to Crestview, the man had the failing performances of several other recession-ravaged companies to worry about. Parker Investments had demonstrated an uncanny knack for buying the wrong businesses.

Brewster ended the call, shifted his gaze to a print on the wall, and pictured himself sitting beneath the willow tree depicted, a thousand miles away—ideally with Carla snuggling beside him. That thought brought the dream back, the water turning to wine, and the sketch of a dead ringer for Carla, named Maynya. Frontier-rugged or not, the world he'd been dreaming about offered plenty more potential than this one. He could imagine himself a hero there.

Why had breathing become so difficult all of a sudden? He headed out of his office in pursuit of open spaces, but he had to scurry through the even more claustrophobic bullpen area first. Everyone's quiet stares said it all. Heather and her staff didn't need to pore over the numbers the way Charlie had. Having lived and breathed loan defaults every day, they could smell pending disaster.

At least when he escaped to the lobby, Ronda managed to lift his mood. The eternally optimistic redhead always cast gloom to the wind. This time, she'd arrived in the office wearing a frilly pink-and-white skirt-and-blouse combo—a nice contrast to the others who tended to dress darker as times got harder. She glanced up from the reception desk with a friendly grin before returning to the task of polishing her nails.

"You look like a slice of strawberry shortcake," he said.

Ronda reshaped her smile into a comic pout. "Are you harassing me?"

"Kinda."

"We could call the police again. If I'm lucky, they'll arrest *you* this time."

"That's why I'm lamming it."

"Good. Send us a postcard from wherever."

Outside, nature grabbed Ronda's relay of cheerfulness and ran with it. The intoxicating, early-autumn scent of burning leaves served as an antidote to his malaise. He lifted his gaze heavenward, where a phalanx of geese pointed an arrow to the south, honking across the sky. He almost forgot his problems.

"Excuse me."

The unexpected voice shot directly into his nervous system. He jumped and spun in tandem, almost giving himself whiplash in the process.

"Sorry, I didn't mean to startle you." The woman smiling at him must have come out of that Honda in the visitor space. But she might as well have stepped out of a gothic novel, given the world's craziness lately and the nature of her costume. A lacy black dress spread an aura of midnight all the way to her ankles, and the red silk scarf looping around her neck hinted at vampires. The woman's thick mass of raven hair billowed in the breeze and brushed against a rose-and-thorn tattoo high up one arm.

In the past, such haunting beauty might have melted him into the pavement. The old Brewster might have rallied and risen back up, responding with a good line. But he'd lost his moxie.

What could he blame but a stolen heart? Not only had Carla opened the floodgates for disturbingly vivid dreams, she'd reprogrammed his desire reflex to switch off in the presence of anyone but her.

"Are you Brewster DeLay?" the woman asked.

His answer depended on whether she came with accomplices. He stole a visual sweep of the parking lot. One couldn't be too careful in a country where legions of busted truckers focused their wrath on the dastardly finance company that still had the gall to expect monthly payments during the toughest of times.

He didn't notice any signs of danger. Her Honda was empty, and the only other vehicles in the lot were clustered, as usual, at the far corner of the building. His employees liked having getaway cars at the ready in the event the opportunity arose to sneak out the back exit and head home early.

"Yeah, I'm Brewster."

She extended a hand. "I'm Kara Danahey."

He lingered in her soft, warm grip and studied her eyes for any signs of malice.

"You helped my boyfriend yesterday, and I wanted to thank you."

"Who's your boyfriend?"

"Igor Tesfaye."

He flinched. "Oh. We found an error in his contract and set it right."

Judging by her sharp, probing eyes, she wasn't buying the error story. "I appreciate what you did, but…"

"Would you believe me if I said we don't actually make any money in this business?"

"Neither does Igor."

"Touché." Back in the days when lenders and truckers shared the fruits of a strong economy, a seemingly never-ending series of successful transactions fed Brewster's desire to make a positive difference in people's lives. Recent times had proven those earlier successes to be time bombs, exploding into defaults and reversing each well-intended loan into a cruel joke. He looked away from this secondhand victim, unable to come up with anything positive to say.

"Thanks again." She turned and headed back to her Honda.

"Wait. You came here just to thank me?"

Kara glanced back at him. "Why not earn good karma wherever I can?"

Brewster almost let her get away. But as Kara bent for her car door, he realized she might have been present when the mystery girl called on Igor.

"Hold up. How about I buy you lunch and earn some karma of my own?"

They picked a bar and grill a few miles down the road and sat in a booth near the back. The dim atmosphere heightened Kara's gothic appearance, bringing out the darkness of her hair while paling her skin to a shade bordering on translucence.

He sipped his coffee while she teased hers, stirring a sugar cube into it, pausing to steal a drag from a cigarette, and then stirring again.

"Igor isn't a dress-for-success kind of guy," she said. "You probably wrote him off as some sort of deadbeat."

"If he is, he's got plenty of company in our customer base."

"He's a poet, you know."

"I'm impressed. We don't have many deadbeat poets."

The joke won a rueful grin. "Poetry and trucking go hand in hand," she said. "Each leads to heavy drinking."

"Funny you should bring that up. Igor mentioned a young girl who told him to find me. But he said he'd been drinking at the time so I wasn't sure—"

"A girl?"

"Yeah."

She averted her gaze.

Brewster burned his tongue on his coffee. "She's real?"

"Define real. Igor sees the girl in his dreams."

"Oh." So there it was. Clearly, the trucker's vanishing visitor lived in the bottom of a vodka bottle.

A waitress set their food on the table. Kara turned her attention to a bowl of soup, stirring it, scooping some onto her spoon, blowing it cool, tasting it, and frowning. Did she ever actually eat or drink?

"Your boyfriend and I have something in common," he said. "I'm a writer, too. Novels, though, not poetry."

"Are you published?"

"Nope. The agents and editors have written me off as some sort of deadbeat."

"Hah! A man with a sense of humor."

"I try."

Kara looked down. "I might as well come out and tell you Igor can't afford the truck. I could have killed him for buying the thing." She spoke into her coffee rather than meet his eye. "We went over all the numbers this morning—how many loads he'll get, how much he'll make on each one, what his expenses will be, and so on."

It was Brewster's turn to look away. Train wrecks always made him queasy.

"Can we give you the keys and call it even?" she asked.

"Hold on." While the math wasn't pretty for his typical customer, the numbers were just as bad for Crestview. If Brewster took the truck back, they'd probably lose five grand, minimum, after reconditioning expense and the commissions they'd have to pay some dealer for reselling the thing on consignment. "How upside down is he?"

"We'll be short at least three hundred a month. That's after living expenses. I bring a check home, but my hours keep getting cut."

"What do you do?"

"Cashier at a bookstore. I should have stuck with waitressing. The tips were better."

"You just can't get away from the world of literature, can you?"

"Funny man. I wouldn't call it literature, though. Airport bookstore. The stuff is mostly trash." Kara sipped some coffee and went quiet.

That should have been the end of it, but a ridiculous, outside-the-box idea popped into his head. He took a bite of his hamburger, chewed and thought, chewed some more. "Suppose we waive the interest."

Kara set her cup down hard enough to slosh coffee onto the table. The glimmer of hope in her eyes tugged at his heart. "Would the payments go down much?"

"I'm guessing as much as four hundred a month. If that keeps us from getting the truck back, we're happy to do it."

"Wow! I can't believe your generosity."

And he couldn't believe he'd come up with such a great idea. By cutting interest—the company's perceived lifeblood—he'd actually found a way to avoid a loss, or defer it, anyway. Yeah, they'd miss out on interest income by collecting lower payments, but that shortfall wouldn't add up to the five thousand bucks they'd otherwise lose on the truck for at least a year. Maybe by then, the economy would be better.

He dove into his burger with gusto. When he paused for breath, he caught Kara staring at him with love in her eyes.

"You're one of the good guys," she said.

"Uh-uh. I'm being totally selfish here."

She reached across the table and settled a hand on his. "Igor has your back from now on." She flashed one of the Latin words from Carla's coin—*Somnium*—tattooed in black ink to the underside of her wrist.

Brewster almost choked on his burger. "Can I call in the debt right now? I've been meaning to look up that word in a Latin dictionary."

She flipped her wrist over, revealing the tattoo more clearly. "Dreams."

"Wow." Of all the coincidences. But should he believe in coincidences anymore? He pulled Carla's coin out of his pocket and slid it across the table.

She lifted the coin, looked it over. "Roman? This must be worth a mint."

"Who knows? It isn't for sale."

"Family heirloom?"

He shook his head. "Someone gave it to me last night."

Kara went silent for a long moment. She stirred her coffee, added more sugar, glanced at the coin again. "Do you feel manipulated, Brewster?"

"Huh?"

"The words on this coin. *Virtus.* That means virtue maybe? *Spiritus.* That one's easy. Spirit. *Somnium.* Dreams. You were confused about *that* one. What are the odds you'd meet somebody who had the same word on her wrist?"

He tried to process that. Couldn't. "I'm not following. Manipulated by whom?"

"Somebody scary strong." Kara grabbed her purse and started sliding out of the booth. "This mystery girl Igor keeps talking about... She didn't tell him her name, but I should have put two and two together."

"Wait. I thought you said she came to him in a dream."

"She did." Kara slung her purse over her shoulder, glanced at the door as if she had a bus to catch, looked down at him. "And we wouldn't be here talking if she hadn't. Sorry, Brewster, but I'm not good at following somebody else's stage directions."

Great. The world's craziness had seeped into every aspect of his daily life. He couldn't even have a simple lunch with someone without something nutty happening. "But she was a dream!"

"Dreams are real, Brewster. That girl..." Kara's eyes flared. "Real. I have to go talk to Henry."

"Who?"

"A crazy uncle of mine. He knows more about Gabriella than I do. Thanks so much for offering to help Igor." Kara hurried out of the restaurant.

# CHAPTER SEVENTEEN

*Later that day, in Virtus*

THE BACK OF QUINTUS'S neck prickled. He slowed his horse and glanced behind him. Dust kicked up from the road, perhaps a league back. He tightened his grip on the reins.

He rode a mile east, turned, and waited. The small dust cloud didn't appear again until a few minutes passed. Whoever was trailing him came on foot, not horseback. That ruled out a soldier. Unfortunately, anyone else could well be hostile—a savage, or a monk, perhaps—maybe a thief. Might be more than one.

One solution would be to outrun whoever approached, but the day's shadows had grown long, and the immediate location was the best he'd seen all day for making camp. A bend in a creek cradled a bushy oasis just north of the trail. Rather than give that up, he waited to get a better handle on who he might be up against.

Quintus swatted at pesky flies and dwelled on the folly of traveling alone without a partner to help keep watch after dark. He hadn't gotten much sleep the night before, even without immediate danger. Now, he had possible hostiles to worry about. And a vulnerable woman to worry over. He cursed his poor judgment in not convincing Adala to travel with him. If she didn't want to go all the way to the capital, she still could have ridden with him for quite some distance before splitting away at Navio or one of the other satellite towns when they got close.

After several minutes peering through his spyglass, he made out shapes in the shimmering distance and breathed a sigh of relief. A solitary man leading a pack mule didn't pose the threat he'd feared. The rumor of a silver find earlier that summer had lured scores of prospectors into the frontier to chase their fortunes. Most gave up after a few weeks in the baking sun. More than likely, this traveler had been cut from the same cloth, a harmless man just looking to go home.

Let him. Quintus dismounted and gathered dead brush for a fire. He'd built a decent pile by the time the man and his mule arrived.

The gaunt stranger did wear the garb of a prospector. Rough leather trousers, a weathered shirt, and a wide-brim hat shading his prickly growth of beard. He owned the proper tools and weaponry, too—a pick-axe for digging and a rifle for shooting game. His shifty eyes were a worry, though. "Snared a rabbit back yonder, but I ain't got no fire," the man said.

Quintus kept his mind on his pistol and flexed his shooting hand, just in case. "I've got bread and beans. That'll do for my meal."

The man guffawed—a deep, throaty laugh that made him seem more trustworthy. "Ain't no soldier gonna win battles living off bread and beans."

Quintus set to the task of starting a fire with flint and stone. Sparks flew on the sixth attempt, and the dry kindling caught right away.

The man trudged past him, leading his mule to the creek. A few minutes and one rifle-shot later, he returned with a rucksack draped over one shoulder and a rabbit carcass over the other. "Name's Gaius. We'll skin her up and share a king's meal, eh, partner?"

"Call me Quintus."

"I'll be happy to call you whatever gets me a go at that fire."

Quintus gave in against his better judgment and decided to share camp with the man, the thought of cooked rabbit being the main selling point.

Gaius rustled through his rucksack. "Got a pan in here somewhere, for the beans, if you ain't got one."

"Uh-huh." Quintus carried his own. What seasoned traveler wouldn't?

"Picked up some other things, too, this morning in Portus, but mostly things a man ain't got much use for."

A prickle of concern raced down the back of Quintus's neck. Portus lay well off the beaten track for prospectors, most of whom kept to themselves like hermits.

Gaius chuckled. "Drawing supplies. Worthless junk. The pitcher might fetch a price, though."

*Adala.* Quintus's blood ran cold. He had his pistol out in an instant.

Gaius dropped his rucksack to the ground and raised both hands. "Whoa there, partner."

"We aren't partners."

"What are you waving that piece at me for?"

"Tell me again how you happened to come across that *worthless junk* of yours."

"Steady." The man eased his arms down. "Ain't never told you in the first place."

"Tell me now, then."

"Saved a woman from crucifixion. Her pack was my reward."

The grip of the pistol went slippery in Quintus's hand, and a bead of sweat stung his left eye. He'd let Adala walk to Portus on her own, knowing full well the dangers of the frontier. "How exactly did you save her?"

"I shot her between the eyes. She would have suffered on that cross for two, maybe three days. They nailed her hands and feet, man." Gaius was talking too fast to be believed.

A wave of dizziness blurred Quintus's vision. "Who crucified her?"

"Monks."

"And they let you just walk up and shoot her?"

"Shot her from a distance with my rifle."

"Then how did you get in close enough to steal her pack?"

Gaius wouldn't look him in the eye.

Quintus needed every ounce of willpower to keep from shooting Gaius cold. But he couldn't take down an unarmed man. "What other tales do you know? I've heard plenty of stories about women being raped and murdered by thieves out here."

"Hold on now. I won't camp with anyone doubts my word." Gaius bent to his rucksack and rummaged inside again. "You can have her things and I'll be on my way."

"Keep your hands where I can see them!" Quintus tried to stay focused despite a wave of guilt nearly buckling his knees.

Gaius pulled a gun out of the rucksack and dove to the side all in one motion. Quintus dove as well, and each got off a shot.

For a long moment, Quintus lay on the ground, waiting for some sign he'd been killed—a bright light in the sky or maybe a smile from Adala. She'd be a fellow ghost if he were dead. But the thought of her being murdered as a result of his negligence brought such a pain to his soul he knew he couldn't be a corpse. Remorse was a unique curse reserved for the living.

He scrambled back to his feet, staggered past Gaius's dead body, and stared with welling eyes at the simple belongings spilling out of the rucksack—a sketch pad, pencils, some chalk, and a pitcher.

Brewster awakened in a sweat. Recognition of his time and place should have eased his pounding heart—his own bed late at night—but his anxiety heightened even as the dream faded. Quintus's failure to protect Adala stirred deep worries over Carla, a *real* woman suffering from her own Latin dreams, not to mention nightmares about suicide. She needed a champion.

He glanced at the clock on his nightstand—almost the witching hour. Wow. Both of her visits had come around midnight, and he hadn't thought to set the alarm for the next one?

He hurried downstairs, but the glow of a streetlamp out the living room window didn't reveal any drop-dead-beautiful visitors stepping through wormholes into his cul-de-sac.

He collapsed onto the couch and groped for a reality check. He'd always been a practical man. So how could he now cast science aside in favor of the belief wormholes had reshaped the world into funhouse-mirror shapes?

By watching Carla disappear, that's how. And, more recently, by getting stuck on something she'd told him during the second visit. She'd mentioned her hometown. He hadn't paid the snippet of information much mind at the time, the time-travel story being the larger issue. The wine had gotten to both of them. But he'd performed a Google search later, and he did find a Sanders Creek Parkway in East Syracuse. Either Carla was delusional and thought she resided hundreds of miles away—to the point of knowing specific street names out there—or she was sane and lived on the other side of a portal.

He'd tried researching a store named Rag Thyme again, calling directory assistance to check within the Syracuse area, but he came up empty. That supported the delusion theory, only he still couldn't explain her vanishing act or the word on her coin matching Kara's tattoo.

He glanced over his shoulder to look out the window again. No Carla.

Wait, what was that? He shifted around and leaned over the back of the couch, almost to the point his nose pressed against the glass.

Only a deer. He kept on staring and tried not to blink. He didn't want to risk missing the reappearance of a woman he'd fallen in love with, whether or not they'd both gone crazy.

# Chapter Eighteen

*The Tug Hill Plateau in Upstate New York*

CARLA AWOKE WITH THE glare of sunlight in her eyes. She shot an uneasy glance around the bedroom for clues where she might be. An old family picture hung from the wall from when she was a little girl and her dad was still alive. A dressing table that had been there forever held up her suitcase. She'd awakened in her mother's cabin.

Relief barely had a chance to take a foothold before she realized with no small measure of disappointment she hadn't had a single dream last night—yes, a reprieve from the nightmares but also an evening without Brewster.

If a sigh could echo off the walls, hers did. The change of venue from Syracuse must have cut off whatever psychic connection she and Brewster had, casting her adrift in a sea of loneliness.

She rolled away from the window and closed her eyes, willing to repeat her subway nightmare or endure whatever mayhem waited in Sanctimonia just to spend a little more time with the man fate had surely thrown into her life for a reason. And even if destiny never schemed, even if her encounters with Brewster had been nothing more than two lucky spins on the random wheel of alternate realities, she still wanted him. He fit her like a glove.

No. Far more than that. How could she give short shrift to

their burgeoning relationship with a mere cliché? Even the most fleeting thought about the man quickened her breath.

If recent "dream" events were what her mother had confirmed—true interactions rather than the isolated fantasies of her subconscious—she was willing to endure another round with the barbarians to reach Brewster again. Twice she'd been vulnerable and twice he'd given her what she needed, hospitality the first time and tenderness the next.

Unfortunately, dreaming was no longer an option. Sunlight flooded the room, bouncing its rays from one wall to another, leaving no corner where she might scurry and hide. When she tried pulling the sheets over her head, asphyxiation picked up where nature left off.

Her cabin retreat wasn't getting off to a good start.

She crawled out of bed and stood in the middle of the room, staring at nothing, until she summoned enough energy to shower and dress. The day stretched ahead as an agony of endless time to be endured until another night might come along, one that simply had to bring a visit to Brewster's neighborhood.

She headed into the only other room, a tight living space merging into a dining nook and kitchenette. Stale memories permeated the cabin and sprinkled its trappings like dust, coating the old couch and upholstered chairs, the throw rugs thinned by time, the vases filled with cat's-eye marbles, and the magazines scattered about for rainy days. She turned toward the fridge, but a billeted army of half-finished rag dolls ambushed her from their makeshift barracks on the dining room table. The few finished ones scolded with silent demands for her to stuff and sew their friends together. She shuddered and kept going, found a yogurt, wolfed it down, and escaped outside.

A gulp of crisp country air helped. She took another, spread her arms, gazed at a clear blue sky, and circled in a slow three-sixty. That did the trick. She got into her car and headed toward the nearest village with something resembling vigor. She wasn't quite ready to paint the town, but she'd be damned if she'd let depression paint her.

Carla spent the morning in the local towns, shopping for antiques and making small talk with gabby storekeepers, many of whom she'd known since early childhood.

"Your head barely came over that counter the first time your parents brought you here." The comment by an old woman selling leather goods triggered the fond memory of a gumball machine that used to stand sentinel in the doorway of her shop.

Later, in a haberdashery, the bearded owner came up to her while she tried on a hat. "What happened to that fella on your arm last time?" His question summoned a twinge of longing for the missing fella's recent replacement, Brewster.

"The weather's picking up tonight." Almost every shopkeeper expressed that notion one way or another, stirring a tingle of anticipation each time. The dusting of snow in Syracuse the day before had ushered in a remarkably early brush of winter. Heavier squalls were expected to blow off the lake and across the plateau later in the evening when the wind shifted.

She hoped so. A snowstorm's ability to hide the world's worries beneath a pristine blanket of white had always enchanted her.

She enjoyed lunch in an old diner with a wonderful outdoorsy atmosphere, shopped some more—mostly just browsing—and later spent an hour or so hiking a trail half-hidden by fallen leaves near the cabin. She zoned into a fantasy of Brewster at her side. Her vapory breath became his, and the frozen twigs crackling beneath their feet comforted her.

Just before twilight, Carla found her way back to the cabin. She took a stab at working on the dolls until the confinement of lonely spaces pressed down on her again, forcing her attention to a bookshelf for possible diversion. She went over and flipped through a few dog-eared paperbacks, but she'd read most of them during previous stays, and the others just didn't pull her in. That didn't leave much. The cabin had never seen a TV, having always been intended as a place where one might take a breather from modern life. In this case, she would have welcomed the distraction of a bad sitcom. She'd left her laptop home, another device that might have helped her while away the time, but she wasn't on speaking terms with the thing after nearly being driven up a wall setting up the software for her silly webcam two nights earlier.

*The webcam.*

A question tickled the back of her mind but not loudly enough to make its concern be heard. She went back to the dolls and eventually got lost in her craft. The project kept her busy and worry free until the evening wore on to a late enough hour for a woman to go to bed without feeling guilty she had no life—not that such a notion should have concerned her in any event. She had more lives than she could handle!

Carla retired to the bedroom and had a shivering fit once she undressed. The wood-burning stove struggled gallantly to heat the place, but sweaters and heavy blankets had always been the rule. She slipped a cotton nightgown on, added a terrycloth robe, got back into bed, pulled the covers to her chin, and gave herself up to the stream of random thoughts that invade a person's mind when all other distractions have been removed.

*The webcam.*

Presuming she'd traveled a year forward in time to meet Brewster, how had they been able to see the live feed from her apartment? Did she somehow snatch the man from his date on the calendar and flip the pages backwards twelve months, or did her camera shoot its signal through a time warp? She puzzled over the mystery until she reached the pre-dozing stage when clarity makes one final burst before giving things up for the night. The answer came in a flash.

The morning before, after being swept out of Brewster's bedroom back into her own, Carla awakened to discover the power had gone out at 2:32 a.m. according to the clock on her nightstand and the microwave in the kitchen. The webcam went down along with everything else, and the last signal it sent must have frozen on her website. Evidently, that image hadn't refreshed for a full year!

Why would she leave the camera off for so long? On the

other hand, why not? That stupid camera and its interactive website had been too sophisticated for her simple mind to handle, and she didn't care to play with it ever again.

But wait. Did fate now preclude her from turning the webcam on again if she did get the notion to try? The possibility sent a tingle of dread down her spine, although she couldn't quite put her finger on why a simple metaphysical question might trigger any emotional response at all.

Rather than spiral into a chasm of unanswerable questions and escalating anxiety, Carla steered her thoughts to a more whimsical mystery. Assuming she'd been bouncing out of her dreams and into one alternate universe after another, how did she always arrive fully clothed? She'd recently read a novel about a time traveler, and he always showed up naked wherever he went. And who was in charge of costuming? She usually came dressed for the occasion—a summer outfit in Manhattan, a peasant frock for Sanctimonia—but not always. In her two meetings with Brewster, she'd been suited up like some dark-haired slut Barbie not available on any toy store shelf she'd ever seen. She had to admit the brazenness had been titillating, but a vague sense of manipulation unnerved her as much as the earlier question about trying to change her fate.

A draft hummed into the cabin in a spooky, Halloween sort of way. Carla's mental meanderings had left her vulnerable to the kind of fear a dark, lonely atmosphere was great at creating. She cuddled the blankets around her like a cocoon and rolled toward the wall, defeating any possible attempt by the window to trick her into mistaking the shadows of rustling tree branches for dreadful creatures of the night.

Once again, Carla knew she was dreaming. Her amazing, newfound omniscience thrilled her with its possible implications. She was building up to something. Perhaps the time would come when she could break the shackles of a forced script and overcome her body's refusal to forge an alliance with her will. Maybe that time *had* come.

But no, one of her legs moved, then the other, taking her the wrong way again, steering her down the despicable flight of stairs in the midst of bustling Manhattan. Frustration throbbed her temples from a corner of her brain so distant she might as well have been watching through the lens of a telescope. She repeated her death march into the forbidding cavern of the subway station. Once there, she engaged in the same brief verbal sparring match with the mystery man lurking behind her. The same train exploded into the station. She screamed and fell toward the tracks once again.

A flash blinded her. And then, for the length of a breath, a sweet intake of country air, nothing more happened. The train's roar still rang in her ears and its headlight brought spots to her eyes, but she'd cheated death again by escaping to a different place. Something had snatched her away, a force more powerful than she could imagine, preventing her from falling to the tracks and meeting an inevitable fate that still hadn't occurred in all these many iterations of the same nightmare.

A burst of inspiration eased her pounding heart and calmed her labored breath. For the first time, she considered whether the theme of her dream might be redemption rather than death. Perhaps if the reel ever played to the end, the man would latch on to her arm and save her from falling.

Carla tried to keep hold of this amazing notion and redefine her plight as a mere test, a gauntlet of sorts with a frail spirit at one end and a stronger one at the other. Then, a second flash revealed the folly of any attempt to tie a tidy bow around her dark wanderings. Another existence announced itself—softly at first, through the scent and tickle of grass at her face—then harshly. A net raked the exposed skin of her arms and legs where the fabric of her frock had bunched. The cruel hemp tightened, and bright sun glared into her eyes from the wrong angle, coming straight at them rather than from above her head. She'd been taken down and now lay on her back—the defenseless, desperate, doomed, and, above all, disappointing prey of hunters who simply couldn't be allowed to win. But they had.

The two barbarians brought shade, bending over her to leer, guffaw, and even defile her with spittle before taking up the net and dragging her toward the woods. She screamed, hoping to alert those who needed to be spared, and then groaned, remembering her village lay well out of earshot.

"Quiet." One of the men kicked at her, and his partner joined in, grunting with the effort and bringing explosions of pain to her back and sides. She curled into a ball and tried to cover her face. A glimpse of her abandoned crossbow lying useless where she'd left it shamed her. She'd failed her charge of watching for invaders. They'd caught her by so swift a surprise she hadn't had the opportunity to light a signal flare and stall them with arrows until reinforcements might arrive. Families lived in the village around the meadow's bend...children. She prayed these savages had stolen through the woods on their own and didn't serve as scouts for a larger raiding party.

A final kick between her shoulder blades forced a choking gasp out of her. She writhed on the ground, helpless to fend off any additional blows.

Thankfully, the barbarians must have vented their urge for violence. The beating stopped. They gathered the net and began dragging her again.

Carla hadn't lost her omniscience yet. She was able to distance herself from the terror and escape into a safe corner of her mind. A voice of logic rose above the clamor of pain and anxiety. She'd been whisked out of the subway to Sanctimonia, but her memory of another life, a calmer one in Upstate New York, lingered. At least for the moment, she maintained enough clarity to raise questions.

Would she be aware of these multiple personalities if she were crazy?

No, not according to any clinical literature she'd ever read. And she had her mother's confirmation of duplicate worlds in the form of the talisman the woman had received in a dream.

Okay then. Presuming sanity, how sound was the back-to-back nightmare theory as opposed to the notion cosmic wormholes had sprung into action, bouncing her from one time and place to another? The subway scene's repetitive cycle bore the closest resemblance to a dream, but even that horrid play came choreographed with sights, sounds, scents, and touches far too sharp for her simple subconscious to conjure.

Carla staked her money on wormholes. Her soul had hit the spin cycle again, beginning the circle from one reality to another, then a third, a fourth, and hopefully home. Better yet... Brewster's engaging smile flashed through her mind. She wished herself into Northbrook and clicked the ruby-red slippers of hope. A dream might allow such a thing, enabling her to flee a desperate situation. On the other hand, a wormhole in charge of her wanderings and ultimate fate wouldn't grant leave until it was ready. A wormhole would take its own sweet time.

Grass gave way to rougher ground, announcing her cosmic puppet master's decision to torture her a while longer, scraping and bruising her as the barbarians dragged her into the woods. "Please give me leave."

Her plea to the mysterious higher power torturing her soul elicited a laugh from one of the bastards who'd snared her. He must have imagined himself the target of her appeal, and her blood boiled at his audacity. She'd *never* humble herself before a barbarian. No. A prisoner should remain quiet and steadfast, steeling herself and clinging to anything dear for strength while keeping an eye out for the moment the tables might turn.

Carla closed her eyes and summoned the shimmering mirage of Brewster. He touched her cheek but soon faded and dissolved, along with her omniscience, leaving her baffled by the brief lift of spirit. She knew only one reality. Her name was Maynya and she resided in Sanctimonia, body and soul, both of which would undoubtedly soon be ruined.

"Help me get her out of this net, Phineas." The barbarians had dragged her up against a tree.

She looked across at a boot, then up at the heathen who wore it. His metal-plated vest reflected a hint of sunlight filtering in through the forest canopy. The man's partner came over and leered down at her. Both of the monsters were heavily bearded and tattooed. They stank of sweat.

She put up a fight, curling her hands into claws and hissing until one of them grabbed her by the hair and brought his face so close to hers their noses touched. "It's all the same to me whether you go along with this or we nail you to one of these trees and leave you here to die."

Maynya guessed that wasn't true. These men had been looking to steal a woman and sell her in the market, not kill her. But wrong decisions are often made in the heat of a moment, and her captors seemed fully capable of making one. Otherwise, they wouldn't have beaten her in the meadow, potentially causing enough harm to reduce whatever value they hoped to get for her in the market. She needed to focus them on their greed. "I'm sorry," she said. She tried to keep her tone soft. "I won't fight anymore. Let's not damage the prize."

"Do you hear that, Emil? This whore thinks she's a prize." The dark-haired speaker, Phineas, smirked and kicked at her again, sending a glancing blow to her side. Then the two invaders wrestled their net off her, reigniting the rope burns already marking her legs.

The heathen named Emil, the shorter and lighter-haired one, clamped a thick hand onto Maynya's throat. He squeezed until tears welled in her eyes, then shifted his grip to her chin and forced her up. She scrabbled to keep pace with him. Her back scraped against pine bark, ripping the upper part of her garment. Once he had her on her feet, he pinned her against the tree, choking the breath out of her. Phineas came up beside his partner and moved a rough hand between her legs. Only the blessed but woefully thin fabric of her frock protected her from complete violation.

One of the barbarians ripped her top down the middle. Her breasts came free. The fiend settled warm hands on them, bringing a chill to her soul.

She had to think fast. "I'll fetch a better coin if left a virgin," she said.

Phineas guffawed. "You have too many years in your eyes. Where I come from, even a girl of sixteen would be hard-pressed to make such a claim."

Maynya's stomach turned at the suggestion these two men would take a girl that age and the awareness they most certainly had. "A proper woman saves herself for a husband," she said.

"And what does a proper whore do? We'll spare your honor if you get on your knees and show us."

"I'm not a—"

A slap brought stars and knocked Maynya to the ground. Both barbarians loosened the ropes binding their trousers. She fought her fury back as the bastards exposed their pitifully small mastheads. From somewhere within, a voice of compromise tried to save her. *Take what's offered and gain control over these creatures. If you bite, they'll kill you.*

# Chapter Nineteen

*From agony to ecstasy to fear*

THE BARBARIANS SHIMMERED, FADED, and disappeared. The ground hardened beneath Carla's knees, and the rays of sun filtering through the forest faded to near darkness, eased by a glow off to the left. She turned toward a streetlamp and choked back a sob. She'd fallen through the wormholes to a different place, a better place, the only place she wanted to be.

Her heart remained two steps behind, pounding with rage, but she knew from experience how to steady herself. She rolled onto her side and took deep breaths, quick at first. Then slower, slower still, until she calmed so completely she could have drifted off. She stared through half-lidded eyes at a neighborhood in its own state of rest. Every window was dark, and not so much as a single porch light joined the streetlamp's lonely battle against the midnight pall. The ghost-town atmosphere reminded her of the notion she'd had the last time she visited. Did anyone live behind those suburban walls, or was she gazing at the backdrop of a cosmic stage where only Brewster performed?

Perhaps she'd found heaven, and he was the gatekeeper. If she could pull herself up from the pavement, she'd hurry to that doorbell, ring a chord of Beethoven, and, when Brewster came to the door, ask him to keep her safe forever.

No. She couldn't kid herself. Yins always follow yangs in the true cycle of life. Sooner or later, she'd be whisked back to Sanctimonia and forced to pick up where she left off. In any event, she wasn't about to lean on anyone, and above all, she'd never ask this special man to help her play the coward. The scuffle with barbarians had momentarily made her weak. She wouldn't have that.

She needed a weapon, something to keep hidden up her sleeve when she found herself kneeling before her captors again. The good side of her wanted it for defensive purposes, but the corner of her heart smoldering over the audacity of two barbarians to do what they'd done and plan what they planned... that side longed to castrate the bastards.

Carla tried to get up and search for a shard of glass or a stick she could sharpen to a point, but a wave of dizziness took her down. She stared into the sky from flat on her back and looked to the Big Dipper for answers. The organized pattern of stars served as a reminder she had her paths confused. Northbrook didn't point backward to Sanctimonia. She'd progressed forward to Upstate New York after each of her two previous visits. Whatever weapon she might fashion wouldn't be needed in Syracuse or her mother's cabin on Tug Hill. Besides, she didn't know how to bring anything from one reality to the next. Brewster's business card had come from his world to hers on its own without providing any clues about its methods. She needed to fit the pieces properly if she wanted to take control of the jigsaw puzzle her world had become.

As lucidity took hold, so did her self-awareness. She lifted her head enough to see her skimpy outfit. She'd been costumed for a whorehouse again, this time in the flimsiest of black negligees. She wrapped her arms around herself and considered her next move. Hiding behind a bush and waiting for a wormhole to Syracuse crossed her mind, but not if it meant missing her man.

A twig snapped, and she jumped.

"Are you all right?"

*Now she was.* Brewster came out of the shadows, knelt beside her, and settled a gentle hand onto her shoulder. That simple, caring gesture triggered a low hum in her soul and drowned out whatever embarrassment she might have suffered over arriving underdressed for just about any occasion but one.

The handsome, light-haired hunk of a wonderful man had dressed more modestly than the last time. He'd buttoned his shirt, buckled his belt. She supposed she could forgive him for that. "Here I am, eating the pavement again," she said. "You always see the worst of me."

"There is no worst of you." He ran his fingers through her hair, then shifted his hands beneath her. "You're trembling."

"I've had too many thrills in one night for a simple girl."

"How about one more? Roll a little closer and hang on."

She melted into him, wrapping her arms around his neck.

He rose to his feet and brought her along for the ride.

"Macho man," she said.

"Yeah, right. I think I just broke something."

She almost laughed, but an echo of her earlier trauma ambushed her with a pang of humiliation. She lost the context of the moment. "I would have fought them, but they wrestled my knife away."

"Who?" He swung her around and started carrying her toward his house.

The sudden motion snapped her out of it. "I'm just talking crazy."

"Your voice is sexy when you're crazy."

She cuddled tighter against him. "And when I'm sane?"

"I better not touch that."

Brewster got her into the house, took her to the couch, and sat, bringing her down on his knee. "Besides, what makes you think I'm not the crazy one?"

She kept her arms around his neck and leaned into his shoulder. "Then what am I?"

"A figment."

She loosened her grip enough to push away and study him. He seemed serious until he winked at her. She poked his arm.

"You're a traumatized figment by the looks of you," he said. "I should carry you upstairs and put you to bed."

"So you can have your way with me?" The notion of sleeping with Brewster, sizzling in its own right, had even greater appeal as a possible means of erasing the sordid forest scene from her mind.

He gave her a long, appraising look.

She bit her lower lip. For the second time in two visits, she couldn't have come on to him more blatantly, and in this case, she regretted laying her cards on the table without knowing what hand he might show. She didn't think she could handle any kind of rejection at the moment.

Brewster set her mind at ease by looking her up and down, letting out a low whistle, and busting into a grin. "I'll try to control myself, Carla, but honestly, you're making me dizzy."

She followed his gaze down her skimpy, dark-as-the-night negligee. He had heat in his voice behind the humor, and she'd seen it in his eyes. She sat half-naked on his lap, he was making no attempt to hide his desire, and the raw electricity of the situation continued fueling her own arousal. Heat surged into her from every point of contact between her body and his. "The dark-haired slut Barbie has returned."

Brewster drifted his fingers down her arm, tuning her buzz a notch higher. "Not that there's anything wrong with that."

"Would you believe this isn't necessarily my own costume choice?"

Her question chased him away. He turned to the picture window behind the couch. "I was sitting right here, watching the street when you appeared out of thin air. How much more magic does a man need to see before he stops denying something weird's going on? I'm ready to believe anything at this point."

"Let's believe it's God or His angels. There's comfort in that."

He nodded, stroked her hair again.

Carla stared with him into the shadowy night. The streetlamp spotlighted the urban stage she'd been trotted onto for him. "How late is it?"

"Past midnight."

"And you were just sitting here staring out the window?"

He turned to her but still had a thousand-mile look in his expression. "You didn't show up last night."

"Yes, I did, I—" Wait. Maybe their year-apart lives weren't in perfect sync. No matter. She shifted a hand to his face and kept it there until he returned his gaze to her. "We've cast a spell on each other, haven't we?"

"After only two dates."

"Remind me to send my puppet master a thank-you note."

"Your what?"

"Don't you feel we're being marched through the paces?"

Brewster scrunched his forehead. "Somebody else said that recently. But hell, I'm not complaining at the moment." He closed his warm hand over one of hers.

Carla kissed his cheek. "Neither am I." She went for his thick, beautiful hair, ruffling it at first, then grabbing a handful and tugging. "Last time we locked lips, you said we were moving too fast."

"That had to be a fit of idiocy. I'm thinking seizure."

"How do you feel now?"

"Why fight destiny?"

She yanked his hair a little harder. "Try a more romantic line, mister novelist."

"You have gorgeous eyes."

"That's better."

"And you have an old soul."

"Hmmm." She pecked his cheek.

"And that silky hair of yours—"

"Good enough, handsome. It's time to carry me upstairs."

Brewster frowned down at the couch. "Okay, but…could this cushion be any softer? We're lost in it."

She giggled. "Now I'll discover how my man handles adversity. What would Prince Charming do?"

"Poof."

Too funny. She waggled a finger in his face. "No, that's the fairy godmother, and she's in a different story."

Brewster put a hand under his chin in a perfect imitation of the thinking man. "Maybe Snow White and Prince Charming could try bouncing up at the same time."

"Like this?" She lurched up, came back down on his lap, started laughing, and almost couldn't stop.

He rolled his eyes. "You're punch drunk, aren't you?"

She stifled one last giggle. "I might be trying a little too hard to get lost in the moment."

"No, hey, you might be right on track with that, but we don't want to damage the goods here, Snowy. Let's try it *together* on the count of three."

Carla wrapped her arms around Brewster's neck and leaned into him as he counted and lifted her from the couch on cue.

"You're my hero," she said.

"I've been keeping your charm in my pocket for strength."

"I've been keeping thoughts of *you* in mine."

He carried her up the stairs. A wave of renewed heat rushed through her when she caught a glimpse of the bedroom doorway, and it burst into a bonfire as they neared the bed, but she came to her senses in the nick of time. "Set me on my feet, Prince Charming."

Brewster stood her on the floor. He shifted his hands to her sides, brushing a delicious whisper of silk negligee against her skin.

She tried to stay focused. "Brewster." Her voice came out hoarse and throaty.

His soft eyes melted her, but she pressed on. "I'm nearly thirty years old. I know that's a long time to wait, but I've been waiting. For the right man. After only two dates, is it too much to ask that we wait a little longer?"

He nodded. "Say no more."

She glanced at the bed. "I want you to stay with me. The way you did the other night."

Brewster moved his hands to her face, leaned in, kissed her nose. "Your wish is my command."

They got into bed together again. They spooned again. And she lost herself in the joy of having a man who cared more about her than his own primal needs.

Carla awakened with her back to Brewster. He'd draped his arm over her, and she closed a hand on it, ready to fight whatever force might pull them apart.

They were one. She basked in the glow of him.

She knew with all her heart Brewster was her destiny. She might get whisked away to Syracuse or Manhattan, Sanctimonia, even Pluto, but she'd always find her way back. Wormholes be damned. She could simply get into her car and... She froze.

Brewster jolted awake. "What's wrong?"

She couldn't answer.

"You look like you've seen a ghost."

"You're a year in my future," she whispered.

"I'm having a little trouble wrapping my mind around that idea."

"It's true, Brewster, so tell me this. Why didn't you already know me the night of that thunderstorm? I've a notion to come and visit you right now, a year in your past, but you don't remember me ever doing that, do you?"

"Is that a trick question?"

The room brightened and went into a spin. Brewster's essence sifted through her fingers like sand. "No!" She groped for him but came up with nothing more than pillow. "Oh no, please don't pull me away now!"

Her plea came too late. She'd already moved on.

# CHAPTER TWENTY

*The next day...or a year earlier?*

A GRAY BANK OF clouds rolling in from the west threw a shadow across the interstate, spurring Brewster to turn his car heater up a notch. The approaching squall stalled at that point, as lake-effect snowstorms sometimes do, and the landscape's personality split—bright on the right side and shaded on the left—until he reached the County Route Two exit near Pulaski, New York, and headed off the highway.

Those last few miles had been surprisingly lonely. True, the Tug Hill region wasn't renowned for its population, but Brewster couldn't recall driving *anywhere*, not even the dusty stretch of desert road he once traveled out of Phoenix on the way to Vegas, without coming across so much as a single long-haul trucker, let alone any cars. The air in his car nearly crackled with electricity, adding to his unease and reminding him of the time he rode his bicycle along a path that crossed beneath a power line. What the hell was going on?

He tried to fight out of a mental fog and remember why he'd driven to Upstate New York in the first place. *Maybe he was dreaming.*

Brewster followed the county road east, getting some distance ahead of the sluggish squall before slowing at an old filling station.

A couple pumps stood sentry outside a listing shack of a store—a smaller version of a gray abandoned barn he'd passed a mile earlier. He was driving on fumes and decided not to risk running out of gas by holding out for a more modern station. He turned into the lot, parked alongside one of the pumps, and got out of his car.

An icy gust of wind blasted him in the face and ripped a newspaper out of a stand near the building. Most of the pages went airborne, but one section spread apart and hugged the pavement, rolling and dancing like tumbleweed. The front page flew up and pressed against the side of a trash can long enough to flash its headline—*Watertown Daily Times* on top and *Heavy Lake Snow Coming*—before blowing away.

Brewster caught a glimpse of something else, lettering above the headline, but the print was small, and the paper took off before whatever he'd seen could register, except in his stomach. He shrugged off the tingle as one of those random, unaccountable fits of foreboding. They come out of nowhere and leave just as quickly without ever revealing their cause.

He shoved one hand into his pocket and used the other to fumble with his credit card until he got it into the payment slot the right way. Then he punched his zip code twice into a touchpad before it registered and started the pump. Next came the hard part, waiting in the cold. Rather than heighten his misery by watching the gas dribble into his tank one grudging tenth gallon at a time, he stared into space and tried to zone out. Another gust of wind tore into him. He glanced down at his appallingly thin clothing. Light jeans? A flannel shirt? A windbreaker? How could he have done this to himself?

Gas pumps worked fine on their own. He abandoned this one in favor of the dilapidated building, thinking hot chocolate but willing to settle for a donut or candy bar and a minute or two in the warmth. He tried the door. *Locked.* He stepped back and looked around. Somebody had used a blue marker to scribble a message on a cardboard sign taped to the window. *We're hiding from the butterflies. Back in thirty minutes!*

"There's no one here." A girl's voice came from behind.

Heart attack time. He'd been alone, hadn't he? He spun and came face-to-face with some twelve-year-old kid who must have crept up on him from around the corner of the building. The girl could have passed for an ice skater in a Courier and Ives print, bundled up in a white down jacket, with hands kept warm by blue wool mittens. Her matching snow hat hid most of her blonde hair except for a couple loose bangs in front and the lower portion of a ponytail in back.

She smiled like a portrait. "I'm Gabriella."

That name. *Where had he heard it recently?* He tried to return the smile, but the entire situation had gone from weird to creepy. "I'm Brewster."

"I'm keeping an eye on the pump for them."

Brewster wrapped his arms around himself. He looked over the girl's shoulder at the locked door. "Geez, couldn't they have let you watch from inside?"

She shifted from one foot to the other. "I like standing out here."

"No, you don't." But what could he do about it? Thirty-year-old guys weren't supposed to pal around with somebody's teenage kid. Still, the poor girl was freezing. "Why not wait in my car until they get back?"

She shook her head. "You know the rule about staying away from strangers."

"Rules don't apply in cases of frostbite."

"If I get too cold, I'll just head home."

He looked across the road at a boarded-up, ramshackle house.

"See? It isn't far," she added.

The wind gusted harder, chilling him to the bone. The slow-motion pump had probably gassed up his car by then. "Okay. Nice meeting you, Gabriella."

"Thank you."

Brewster started to head away but stopped when he saw that window sign again. "Hey, what's with that message?"

"The one about butterflies?"

"Yeah."

Gabriella gazed up at Brewster with an intense, Children-of-the-Corn expression, bubbling a wave of foreboding straight through his stomach. The wizened look in her eyes didn't fit the mold of any twelve-year-old girl he'd ever met.

"That refers to the butterfly effect," she said.

"Huh?"

She glanced around with a furtive expression before leaning toward him. "A single butterfly can flap its wings and change the course of weather forever."

"Okay, I guess I've heard of that." But the sign's weird, out-of-context message and the girl's odd behavior raised the hair on his arms.

She pointed to a newspaper holding its own against the wind, somehow still in the stand although the door had blown open. "You're the butterfly, Brewster. I can't let anyone see you flapping your wings here."

"*You can't let…?*"

He could almost see electricity crackling out of her eyes.

He tore his gaze from the scary kid and turned to the paper. The date made his skin crawl. *October 2012?*

He hadn't seen any traffic on the interstate. He didn't belong in Upstate New York. And he certainly had no business falling backward in time. "I'm… I'm dreaming, aren't I?"

"Yes, but you've stepped out of your dream into the real world. There's a difference."

"I don't get it."

"No matter. You were driving in the wrong direction. I can't seem to get things to happen the way they should anymore. You'll find Carla down there." She pointed to a side road heading south.

The girl started fading.

And he remembered. *Gabriella.* Igor Tesfaye's girlfriend nearly spat the name out just before hurrying out of the restaurant. "Wait! Tell me what's going on."

She shimmered like a mirage. "This isn't the right time for the telling."

"What about Carla? Where is she?"

"Just down the road." Gabriella motioned with a barely visible hand. "Go spread your wings."

Two blinks later, she disappeared.

Brewster put about five miles' distance between him and the station before the shock wore off. At that point, a dozen questions popped into his head, none very lucid and most along the lines of the one he finally shouted aloud. "What the hell is going on?"

He reached down and pinched his leg, hard, but that didn't wake him up. It didn't bring him back home, either. He still sat behind the wheel of a car that had no business being in Upstate New York let alone a year earlier than the night he'd fallen asleep. He tried to open his eyes wider. Nothing changed.

Clearly, he'd be stuck in this hiding-from-the-butterflies scene for however long he was meant to stay. He almost followed the urge to turn around and head toward something he'd be sure to enjoy—the snow squall still looming in the near distance—but Gabriella said he'd find Carla down the road, and rebellion wouldn't get him there.

The squall had been creeping after him ever since he left the station. He glanced in his rearview mirror at an apple grove he'd passed a few minutes earlier. Shadowy curtains hung like cobwebs from the threatening sky and swallowed the trees as he watched. Up ahead, enough sunlight still peeked out of broken clouds to paint a field of pumpkins a bright shade of orange while greens, golds, reds, and yellows poured out of nature's palette to color the autumn leaves blowing onto the empty road.

The juxtaposition of images seemed far too striking to be part of a dream.

A squirrel burst out of a clump of bushes and raced across the pavement. The critter looked up at the car, did a quick three-sixty, and hurried away, but a beat too late. Brewster swerved to avoid it. His passenger-side wheels hit the shoulder, and the rougher surface vibrated through the shock absorbers, jostling him and again bringing the dream idea into question.

Not only that, he'd experienced icy-cold weather in the lot. A sensation that sharp sure wasn't coming out of his pillow.

He caught a whiff of skunk. He kept his eyes on the road and groped his hand across the dashboard to find the air circulator button. Dreaming, huh? Not hardly. This was more along the lines of what Carla talked about the night they lay together, baring their souls. She said she'd been falling through wormholes from one reality to another. She thought her soul had lost connection with her body and had begun taking flight. She'd also been dragging the fear of insanity around with her like her own shadow, but thanks to this wraith or witch or angel or whatever Gabriella was, Brewster could now put that diagnosis to rest. After all, he'd just stumbled across the same kind of wormhole, and maybe not for the first time. Had he been *dreaming* in Latin or *living* in some Latin-speaking universe at night lately?

The realization this might not have been his initial fall through the looking glass was a little more than he could handle while driving. He needed to chew on something else, too—the hint of manipulation prickling the back of his neck. He glanced again at the approaching snowstorm through his rearview mirror, then slowed his car, pulled to the shoulder and switched the ignition off.

Dreams and reality. Dreams and manipulation. Kara Danahey had touched on both combinations during their lunch. Presuming dreams were real and he was being manipulated by someone *scary strong,* as she put it, he needed to reexamine what had been happening to him at bedtime lately.

Carla's disappearance hadn't been the only bizarre event the evening they first met. His Virtus dreams had become sharper. The last two about Adala had been so vivid he could still tap into the memories as if they'd been real events. And labeling this little road trip a dream was definitely out of the question. An actual snow squall crept ever closer from behind, not some subconscious fantasy. The sudden chill in his car came from switching the ignition off, not from forgetting to pull the blankets up to his chin.

The brain-teasing manipulations of time and space were like the squares of a cosmic Rubik's Cube. He gave it a few simple twists in his mind and came up with a solution that seemed to match all the colors. He and Carla had been swept into a supernatural whirlwind, and whatever barriers separated one dimension from another had been flattened by the relentless storm. The two of them blew from here to there like the spits of snow now blasting past his car, landing for a moment in one place only to lift and move on to another. Somehow—and here was the weirdest aspect of the whole mess—he and Carla had been falling out of their dreams and into the waking world with their trappings in tow—clothing, a placeholder card, a coin with *dreams* spelled in Latin, and, incredibly, an entire automobile.

That last trapping was the real mind-bender. He hadn't been in his car when he fell asleep. He'd been in bed with Carla. He remembered finding her in the street, bringing her inside, carrying her upstairs, and discovering the rapture of pure love. They'd whispered endearments back and forth until she dozed off.

Or had *he* been the one to fall asleep? Yeah, he must have been. And when he did, his grip on the cosmic grid faltered. The maelstrom swept him away and dropped him into the wrong coordinates of a world with a broken calendar. This all might have been plausible in a universe frequented by wormholes, except he came fully equipped to hug the road—in a car, an actual automobile, a rental, by the looks of it, transportation to a gas station where he noticed the date. That sure smacked of manipulation, and he had a good idea who was behind it. Gabriella. She even spoke like a puppet master, didn't she?

*"I can't LET anyone see you flapping your wings here."*

The sense of foreboding he'd suffered in the lot still clung to him like stale smoke. He couldn't shake the notion Gabriella might be the villain in this fantastic story they'd fallen into. Yet this wizard-child behind the curtain might have been the one to bring Carla into his life. If so, he'd need to take the pitchfork out of her hands and paint a halo over her head.

Was she good or evil? The imminent squall provided an encouraging clue. In a world shifting off its axis and twisted by a girl evidently able to spin time and place like a top, anything might have come raining down on Brewster's shoulders, from tidal wave to nuclear cloud to volcanic ash to a trillion white butterflies fluttering their wings. But no. She brought snow.

*And he'd loved snow all his life.*

The squall overtook his car, sweeping all deductive reasoning aside and letting primal emotion hold sway. The same anticipation and wonder he'd been experiencing since childhood. He fixated on a nearby junkyard as the most extreme example of what he was about to witness. Every old, tired, flawed, rusting, tossed aside, and just plain ugly thing in that lot, everything from broken cars to worn-out mattresses to obsolete washing machines would soon be hidden beneath a sanctifying blanket of white.

Snow had been casting a spell on him since the day in his childhood when a storm blew into Chicago and closed the schools for a week. That blizzard swept a roaring metropolis back in time to a quieter age. All modern modes of transportation stalled, leaving everyone to trudge from here to there on foot, dressed in heavy coats, bright scarves, and ski caps, gazing at the glittering wonderland and commenting how amazing it all was. Nature had granted furlough from schools, jobs, and all the other dreary obligations that can crush adults and children alike beneath the weight of relentless responsibility.

He'd longed for a repeat of that magical blizzard through every subsequent winter. Sadly, perhaps because older eyes see less magic, he never enjoyed another storm quite like it. Still, each snowfall he witnessed always did bring a thrill.

The squall bellowed with gusts so strong the weather-stripping at his windows hummed in musical accompaniment to the swirling madness outside. He stared at the scene until there was little left to see. A nearby line of trees became chalky, then vanished altogether. Closer in, a speed limit sign faded away. Even his hood ornament blurred and disappeared behind the veil of white.

Brewster had never seen one of these Lake Ontario squalls before, but the fury he witnessed was no great surprise. As a boy, he'd read every newspaper and magazine account of blizzards he could lay his hands on and learned that lake-effect storms tended to be the most impressive of the lot, particularly east of Lake Ontario where the rise of Tug Hill can strengthen a snowfall's intensity. Four inches or more could accumulate in as little as a half hour, three feet in a day. That was no urban legend, but word didn't get around much about the magnitude of these storms. South and east of Watertown, where the fiercest blizzards raged, the population was too scarce to capture the attention of network news—just a scattering of hamlets whose citizens took nature's wild winter displays in stride.

*And* whose citizens probably stayed off the roads when newspaper headlines screamed warnings about incoming storms. Citizens hiding from the butterflies. What better scene if the puppet master didn't want him to be noticed?

Snow flew at the car from all directions. The relentless, thick fog of giant flakes danced, tumbled, and skidded across the hood, refusing to cling except where his motionless wiper blades formed a windbreak and built two miniature drifts. Similar buildups whitened the weather-stripping of his side windows. He switched the ignition back on to warm the car. Good for the moment, but suppose he ran out of gas and the blizzard buried his car in a drift? He'd read accounts of people stuck in their cars for days. But just as he shivered from the realization a little too much snow might not be a good thing, the storm abated.

Shadows of the tree line reappeared. Perhaps the squall had contracted into itself like a roiling sea, gathering for the next wave. Yet for now, a hint of sun peeked through the clouds off to the left, still shaded enough for him to stare right at it. He did for a long moment, then glanced in his rearview mirror and discovered an amazing sight.

Someone had parked no more than sixty feet behind him—just a pitcher's distance to home plate—and gotten out of their vehicle in the height of the storm. The heavy snow had apparently hidden the woman from view initially, but the squall had diminished enough to lift the curtain and reveal her, twirling beside her car with arms outstretched and head lifted. She danced like a ballerina. Or a pagan in the midst of a mating ritual. A mystic summoning spirits. The wind lifted her snow-covered hair and splayed it in all directions.

She shadowed and disappeared behind one last heavy burst of snow before coming back clearer as the most beautiful sight he'd ever beheld.

*Carla.*

He scrambled out of his car, slipped on two inches of snow that had fallen in ten minutes flat, and nearly went sprawling. He steadied himself, took in the clean smell of winter, then exhaled a cloud of breath back into the brittle silence. His shoes got wet and his feet turned instantly cold. He rushed toward her, but she kept on circling as if in a trance. She looked gorgeous as ever, although dressed in an ordinary outfit for the first time since he'd met her—jeans and a peacoat, blasted white and showing only hints here and there of the darker colors beneath. The squall had transformed her into a snow angel.

He took in her flushed cheeks, solemn eyes gazing upward, and the expression of rapture on her face and decided she qualified for automatic beatification. "Carla!"

His voice must have broken the spell. The world's widest smile spread from her lips to her eyes. "Brewster?"

With heart thumping in his ears, he wrapped his arms around her, sending fluffy snow airborne from her coat and hair. As it settled, he could almost hear the chiming tinkle of fairy dust. "You must be freezing!" he said. "What are you doing out here?"

"I'm celebrating the first blizzard of the season." Her soft, breathless voice warmed his ear.

"You're celebrating—"

"Hold on." She pushed back a step. "What are *you* doing here, Brewster?"

"Dreaming?"

She stared at him long and hard.

He could have told her trying to figure things out would be fruitless.

But eventually…first with a twitch of her lips, then a renewed smile, and finally a mistiness in her eyes, she came up with an answer. "Oh, you beautiful man! I'm not crazy after all, am I?"

"Not unless we both are."

# CHAPTER TWENTY-ONE

*Refuge*

**THANKS TO TOASTY AIR** bathing Brewster from the heating vents, the storm out the windows of Carla's car transformed from a brutal endurance test to soft entertainment. Carla sat frosty-cheeked beside him, and together they watched windblown white sheets perform pirouettes across the hood. As he held one of her hands in his—a warm hand, despite her recent dance in the snow—he tried to trace his steps backward to figure out how he'd landed in such a wonderful place. The effort dizzied him as though he'd risen too suddenly from a prone position.

"Do you know where we are?" Carla asked. A mind reader.

"Upstate New York?"

"Okay, when?"

He hesitated. To answer would be to admit the universe had twisted into shapes he could never understand. "Yeah, I know that, too. Two thousand twelve."

"So what do you think of my time-travel delusion now?" She focused the soft, gray-green eyes of a kindred spirit on him.

"I don't know the definition of delusion anymore."

Carla leaned her head on his shoulder. "Do you know the definition of a dream? Mine have become so much sharper since we met. It's like you flicked a switch in my mind. I remember every detail."

He closed his eyes and summoned the image of the red-bearded lieutenant riding beside him as they crossed the hot scrublands of Virtus on horseback. "These aren't dreams at all, are they?"

"No," she whispered. "They're real."

*Real.* Because somebody had flicked a switch in the universe, igniting a black light that made everything look different than it had before. "Carla, I met a creepy kid who implied she's behind all of this. Have you dreamed about a Gabriella?"

She tightened her hold on his hand. "She's the girl who never ages."

He caught his breath. Gabriella hadn't just gotten around, she'd left an impact. Igor Tesfaye dreamed about her, the trucker's girlfriend feared her, and now Carla spoke of her in a reverential tone. "Can you elaborate?"

"Pilgrims journey for hundreds of miles to hear Gabriella's teachings. You don't remember her from your visits to the other side?"

"No." But another image floated to the surface of his addled mind—a crude church huddling in the shadows of a town's fortress walls. Something bad had happened to its builders. Luckily, his memories of Virtus were few and far. They often dragged sadness with them.

But Carla's mood was brighter. She looked up at him with a gleam in her eyes. "Listen to this. Two days ago, my mother mentioned something I didn't remember. She and I met a girl named Gabriella when I was three. We met her in Syracuse, on *this* side. My mother says Gabriella came back to her later in a dream and left the Roman coin I gave you."

"When you were *three?*" Evidently, the wormholes spinning him and Carla out of their dreams had been building momentum for ages. He reached into his pocket and closed his hand around Carla's coin. *Somnium.* Had Gabriella been stalking Carla, in and out of *dreams*, for almost thirty years? "I'm not ready to fix a halo over that girl's ponytail quite yet."

"Saint or not, we should definitely drink a toast to her." Carla opened the console between their seats.

Somehow she'd managed to defy the laws of physics by cramming a small thermos into a space already overloaded with enough clutter to fill a woman's purse and then some—lipstick, tissues, dental floss, sunglasses, first-aid kit, needle and three spools of thread, a paperback, and a packet of unmentionable womanly stuff that had every chance of striking Brewster blind. He averted his eyes until she drew him in again by unscrewing the thermos and releasing a cloud of steam. The chocolaty scent summoned the image of roaring fires on cold winter days. She filled the cap to the brim, took a slow sip, and lifted her eyes heavenward.

They passed the cup back and forth.

The drink warmed his hands, the steam bathed his face, and the taste of chocolate and marshmallows sent him straight to paradise. He let Carla have the last of it. "I'd toast Gabriella with a little more gusto if she'd brought us together from the same page of the calendar. Why a year apart?"

Carla polished off the drink, screwed the cap back onto the thermos, and stowed it away. When she turned to him again, she wasn't smiling anymore. "I think she's doing it to save my life."

"What?"

"Hear me out." She switched the wipers on. Crescents formed on the windshield with each swipe. The storm filled them in, and the blades repeated the process. Again. And again. An impasse between technology and nature. "I live in Sanctimonia over there, and you're from?"

"Virtus."

"Two nations perpetually at war. I need saving there, too, believe me, but we're too far apart." She turned to him. Her eyes had moistened. "We're worlds apart here, too. You're from 2013, and I'm from 2012. Why? Because I don't think I'm still alive in your world."

*Alive* could have had a dozen possible meanings, but the tremble in Carla's voice narrowed the options, sending a chill down Brewster's spine. "What are you talking about? Sure, you—"

She pressed a finger to his lips. "I don't do well as a puppet on a string. Do you think I'd just sit on the sidelines for an entire year, waiting for Gabriella or wormholes or whatever to drop me into your neighborhood the few times they got the whim? No." She motioned to a travel bag in the backseat. "I'd pack my things and come calling on the Brewster DeLay who lives in 2012, *my* year. But if I did, the Brewster who lives in 2013, *your* year, would have known me when I wandered into his neighborhood during that thunderstorm."

He racked his brain for a counterpoint. "Wait. Maybe we have a fight and break up."

"Think that'll happen?" Her gaze reflected the same, deep, misty-eyed love swelling his own heart and soul. "Maybe a subway train kills me before I get to Northbrook. That's what Gabriella has been warning me about, I think. She brought the *2013,* lonely version of Brewster DeLay into my life to nail the point home."

The notion sank to the pit of his stomach like a rock.

But Carla smiled. She leaned over, whispered in his ear. "I have a plan."

"If it involves us staying safely in this car forever, count me in."

"Not forever, but we *will* take a little drive in it." She put the wipers on high and threw the car into gear. "You and I are going to Manhattan *together.* We'll go into a subway station together, we'll sit on a bench together until a train goes by, and I won't die. *Then,* I'm going to kiss you good-bye, drive to Northbrook, and meet Brewster DeLay in *my world,* 2012. We'll be changing my future and your past, thanks to Gabriella."

He shook his head. For two puppets on a string, that plan held equal doses of logic and risk. "Why go to Manhattan at all?"

Carla hit the gas. "Because the best way to end a nightmare is to defeat its monsters."

They'd driven south of the snow country. The pavement had dried and become much more manageable, but Carla slowed the car. Her face had gone pale.

"Want me to take over?" he offered. "You look tired."

A tear ran down her cheek. She wiped it away with one hand, turning the wheel with the other. "You're shimmering, Brewster."

"What do you mean?"

She pulled onto the shoulder and stopped.

He tried to shift over and wrap an arm around her.

"Wait," she said. "I have something in my glove box for you."

Brewster popped the button. A snow globe fell into his hands, heavy as a paperweight.

"I bought it in Pulaski," she said. "Shake it for me?"

He shook the globe, creating a blizzard that blurred the log cabin within.

"Isn't it beautiful?" Carla's voice cracked. "Take it back with you, Brewster. If I don't make it, you'll have something I loved."

"If you don't make it?"

The bright, sunny day turned to midnight black. Brewster shuddered. He'd realized what Carla meant by *shimmering*.

The wormholes had hold of him again.

"Don't go down to Manhattan alone, Carla."

Everything went black.

# Chapter Twenty-two

*Three hours later*

**"I CAN DO THIS."**

Alone.

But she could do it.

Carla stood at the top of the subway stairs. The sun's rays cut through the cold air to energize her while scattered clouds puffing across the turquoise sky spared her their shadows, casting them on the other side of the street. Luck seemed on her side, and her earlier sadness dimmed like the remnants of a broken dream.

No reason for sadness anymore. She had a plan. For happiness. She'd exorcise her demons alone, down in the subway, glued to the bench until the first train swept by. Then she'd go after Brewster in *her* year.

Two thousand twelve.

Time to roll. Passengers exiting the station brushed past her, just as they had in her dreams. City smells of exhaust and street-vendor hot dogs came at her again, along with the clatter of jackhammers and the impatient horns of taxicabs painting the traffic with their signature splotches of yellow. All seemed the same except for the mood. A pall of gloom no longer shadowed her world.

She headed down.

At the halfway landing, she bought tokens from a machine and smiled at a transit officer standing at the cashier's booth. He'd been chatting up the woman inside the cage, but he paused for a moment to flick a wave at her. Who says New Yorkers weren't friendly?

She approached a turnstile, glanced at a ponytailed girl struggling to get past the bar in the next aisle, and stifled a laugh when she noticed the reason. "Honey, that doesn't take pennies. You need to use a token."

"Oh." The girl looked up at her—a cute thing, perhaps twelve or thirteen, blonde, bright-eyed, all sheepish smile and red cheeks. She thrust thumb and fingers into her blouse pocket, as if a treasure trove of tokens waited inside, but she came up empty. She shoved a hand into the slit pocket of her skirt and failed again. Her smile faded.

"I've got extra ones." Carla had purchased them as souvenirs, but she could certainly spare one for the poor kid. She fumbled in her purse, glanced up, shrugged. "They're in here somewhere."

The girl stared back with the strangest unsettling eyes.

Carla shuddered. A sudden urge to be done with the transaction set her heart pounding. She came up with a token and held it out. "Here."

Their hands touched. The world went into a spin.

She clapped her free hand onto the railing between aisles to keep from collapsing to the floor. She couldn't break eye contact with the girl. Two bottomless orbs probed her with a cold, appraising stare in total contrast to the innocence portrayed by the girl's simple dress, her blushing cheeks, and that ponytail with its cute little bow.

*Gabriella.* But the halo Carla had earlier pasted over the girl's head didn't fit. Gabriella's eyes held no kindness.

Carla screamed, but no sound escaped her lips. The transit officer off to the side kept flirting with the cashier. Neither he nor the woman showed any sign of noticing her silent plight.

Not one other soul stood on the landing. No one climbed up

the stairs from below. Nobody came down from above. How had a Manhattan subway station gone empty in the middle of the day? Where the hell was everyone?

"Don't be frightened." The girl who was so not a girl summoned a childlike gleam to her eyes, fading the horror-show agelessness she'd flashed moments before.

Carla tried to snatch her hand back, but her puppet master clenched it with an iron grip.

The bars of their turnstiles went into motion, ushering them through. Tokens be damned.

"I can sweep your fears away like so much dust," Gabriella said.

"Please, no. I don't want—"

The buzz of the creature's touch intensified, and Carla's immediate terror evaporated, along with every other fear, large and small. All the nagging worries she wore like a shawl on her shoulders even on the best of days sprouted wings, took flight, and left her staggering in an emotional vacuum.

A single question swept in to fill the void. "Why is all of this happening?"

"I'll explain everything by the tracks."

They floated down the vacant stairs together, hand in hand.

She and Gabriella settled onto a bench in the middle of the subway platform, fifteen feet from the tracks on either side. A train approached on the left, first with noise, then wind. A rat scurried from a rail to safety beneath the platform moments before certain obliteration.

Carla would have shuddered at the sight of the rodent if she had any emotion. "You want something of me, and I'm guessing I don't have to agree."

"Yes," Gabriella said.

"Give my emotions back, or you'll get nothing."

"You're better off not—"

Carla started off the bench, but Gabriella touched her before she could get away. Sheer terror churned up a wave of nausea that almost had Carla retching.

"You asked for your emotions," the creature said.

Carla closed her eyes long enough for her heart to calm and stomach to settle. When she reopened them, her nightmare of a puppet master still sat beside her. There'd be no avoiding or dancing around this creature. "I get it now. You want to murder me, Gabriella. That's what the subway dreams have been leading up to."

"Murder you?" Gabriella patted Carla's leg as if she were the doting adult and Carla the child. "No, my dear, I'm trying to piece you back together. Your soul is split between two bodies—yours and Maynya's. One must die for you to reach your full potential."

"Keep your hands off me, you vile thing."

The rebuke elicited a gasp, as if Gabriella actually thought of herself as good. "Look, I'll freely admit I made a mistake splitting the world in two. But the end justifies the means." She looked down, scuffed the cement with the tip of a shoe. "This has all been for the greater good."

"As defined by you?"

Gabriella's face contorted into an expression of fury for the briefest of moments before returning to angelic innocence. "As defined by God."

Gabriella's obvious struggle with her feelings would have been comedic under different circumstances. Apparently, even powerful puppet masters had anger-management issues. Her eyes moistened. "At first I thought God turned his back on me."

"*At first?*"

"Yes, but this amazing line of begats *must* have been His doing. We've gone well beyond the bounds of statistical probability. After a hundred generations, one couple still straddles both worlds, you and Brewster. Or should I say Maynya and Quintus? You are God's grand gift of forgiveness for my conversation with Herod—not one messiah but two."

Carla couldn't follow. She tried to get off the bench. Failed.

"Still, you're right to think me a monster, Carla." Gabriella averted her gaze and, for a long moment, said nothing more. Finally, "By killing the baby Jesus, I denied Maynya's world its savior. The people of Sanctimonia, Virtus, and every region beyond their borders live in moral bankruptcy, thanks to me. But your twin can save many of these souls if you help her."

Carla's skin tingled. She took a deep breath and replayed the word in her head. Your *twin*. She knew everything about Maynya—a selfless woman living in a pristine forestland, a guardian who protected fellow villagers with bow and arrow, and a soon-to-be victim of rape, or worse. "How do I help her?"

Maynya looked up from her knees at the dark-haired barbarian, Phineas, and his scraggly-haired companion, Emil. The two bastards held their penises in their hands, as lewd an offering as she could imagine. She'd never compromise her chastity by servicing them in the debauched manner they proposed, not even to save her life. "I'll bite them off."

Phineas kicked her in the side of the rib cage, sending her tumbling to the ground. She struggled to rise and accept death in the manner befitting a guardian, but the sharp pain from the blow defeated her.

"We took eight of these whores to the wagon already," Phineas said. "That's all the bride master asked us to fetch."

"But this one was served on a platter!" Emil said.

"Bad meat, I say."

The voices came at Maynya as if mere whispers in the wind. The swooshing sound of a sword yanked from its sheath soon followed. She took a deep breath and readied herself for passage to the next life.

A flash of light brought stars to her eyes.

Had death arrived? No, a cracked rib from the kick to her side wouldn't torture a dead woman, would it? And would she still smell the sharp scent of forest pine?

A shadowy presence pulled her to her feet. Maynya gaped at her *other self,* the woman in odd attire who previously existed only beyond a curtain of dreams. A bolt of light shot out of this woman's chest, this *Carla's* chest, and into hers. *"We're one now,"* came a voice that wasn't a voice. More like an echo within her head.

Maynya fell to her knees, still bathed in the bolt's lingering glow. "How can I be one with…a saint?"

The vision dissolved with an aura of finality that stole her breath away. Had the woman she'd always known but never knew, the sister in her dreams, a woman named Carla, died? A staggering pang of loss pressed harder than the grief she'd suffered after her mother's death years earlier.

She closed her eyes, readying herself again to die.

Another flash. This time in her head, bringing with it a vision of rats.

A clatter rose in the near distance, a multitude of squeaks so great in number they combined into a shriek. She reopened her eyes.

A single rat ran at Phineas from behind a tree. He kicked it away.

Another came.

And another.

The shriek grew louder. A great swarm of rats, thousands, came at the men from every direction.

"Fuck! They're all over me!" Phineas lost his footing, fell to the ground, and skittered like a crab until he backed into a tree. He swatted the closest rodents away, but scores more followed.

His partner, Emil, turned heel and ran.

Maynya scrambled to her feet. Phineas twitched beneath her, shouting, swinging…at nothing. She aimed a kick with as much strength as she could manage and got the man squarely in the balls.

He doubled over. His scream rang in her ears.

She shot a hurried look around. Emil had headed back toward the meadow where she'd been captured. She'd have to go the opposite way, deeper into the woods, closer to the Virtus border.

She hurried away, gasping at the fire in her ribs where she'd been kicked.

A half hour later, Maynya still ran. She stirred up the fauna as she passed, chasing chattering birds to the treetops. A chipmunk got under foot. In sidestepping it, she tripped over a gnarled root and went sprawling. The sting in her palms and knees joined forces with her ravaged rib cage to bring tears to her eyes. She staggered up, pressed on, using reddened hands to fend off low-hanging branches swiping at her face.

She'd covered a good three miles during her flight, but for all she knew, the barbarians might be fast on her heels. Whatever she'd done back there, she had no way of knowing how long it might last.

What *had* she done? *Witchcraft?*

She shuddered.

No, the flash of light from Carla's passing had somehow awakened an amazing ability. Like an infant grasping at a rattle for the first time with no knowledge how, Maynya had unwittingly groped inside two men's minds, found their fears in the shadows, and shaped them into life-sized rats. Were the creatures real? If so, she could do wonderful things when she learned to harness the power. Perhaps she might read hunger in a starving child's mind and conjure food.

On the other hand, what if she never learned to harness Carla's gift? Suppose she lost herself at an inopportune time and created an illusion in front of her own people? The Mystics would surely think her a witch and brand her chest with a W. They'd throw her across the border into Virtus, where the barbarians would crucify her.

She started running again.

A clearing came into view through thinning trees. Maynya gasped. She'd gone too far, clear across the border between Sanctimonia and Virtus.

"Help!" A woman's voice rose from the meadow, spurring a flock of sparrows into noisy flight.

The chattering birds swarmed, cut into the forest, and dove toward Maynya before fleeing deeper into the woods.

Had she conjured them, as well? No, they'd come on their

own, chirping a warning to save her from whatever danger loomed.

"Over here," the woman cried. "Come open the latch."

"No. Leave us be." The voice of a second woman rose above the first.

Maynya ignored the sparrows. She hurried out of the trees to help.

Eight women stood captive in a wooden cage fitted onto a flat carriage. They sported the long black braids and signature floral dresses of fellow Mystics. Horses had been hitched to haul them away.

"Hurry, before the barbarians return!" A wide-eyed young woman of perhaps twenty gripped the bars at the back of the cage, the swell of her belly stretching the fabric of a faded dress. "My child can't be born in this awful place."

Maynya bunched her fists. Did the cruelty of barbarians know no bounds? Someone's pregnant wife had been stolen for sale as a bride to another man.

"Please!"

She glanced around, creeping forward. "Where are your captors?"

One of the women pointed toward a cabin in the near distance. "They're settling accounts with our own border guards."

Maynya stopped. "Our people wouldn't do that."

The woman spat. "Sentries are corrupt on *either* side of the border. Ours will trade anything for coal, even women, apparently."

"Just let us out," the pregnant one screeched.

"No!" The other shot a fierce gaze at Maynya. "We're bridal stock now. You know what could happen to you."

Maynya knew she'd hang if caught trying to save anyone, but she'd cheated death once already. She examined the cage's latching mechanism, a heavy wooden bar lowered into a metal grip. The captors hadn't padlocked it, apparently judging it impossible to open from inside the cage.

"Be gone while you still can," one of the women said.

"Go home," said another.

"Leave us be."

"They'll kill you."

Could she ever find such inner strength as these selfless Mystics? They'd probably fought like hellcats to avoid capture. All were bruised and bloodied. Dresses torn. Braids in disarray. Yet now that they'd been caged, they wouldn't think of endangering her life to regain their freedom.

Maynya knew without a doubt what course she must follow.

A shadow of grief had been clinging to her from the moment she'd been touched by her imagined sister. She choked back a sob and glanced over her shoulder to bid a silent farewell to a land she might never see again. "Did they count you?"

"Aye," a woman said. "They know we are eight."

"Then eight you'll stay." She struggled to lift the latch, gritting her teeth against the pain in her ribs until she pulled the lever all the way up. She swung the gate open and motioned to the pregnant woman. "Climb down."

"No," a woman said. "We told you—"

"Silence!" She didn't know where the power in her voice came from. Her cry stilled everyone in the cage.

The pregnant woman jumped down and started to run, but in the wrong direction. Maynya caught her by the arm. "Are you able to climb a tree?"

"Y-yes."

"Hurry into the woods, find a tall one, and stay hidden until nightfall. Then go home. Is that understood?"

The woman nodded.

"You must latch me into this cage first." She climbed into the makeshift prison and pulled the gate closed. "We'll be eight again."

# PART III:

# THE RAPTURE

# Chapter Twenty-Three

*Virtus, nearing his destination*

THE GREAT DESERT'S SCRUBBY nothingness gave way to an increasing number of shacks and lean-tos. Quintus Laskaris had gotten within a few miles of the capital at last. But the end of his journey did little to lift his spirits.

He dismounted beside a stream. While his horse took water, he pulled Adala's sketch pad from his pack and gazed at the beautiful stranger who teased him with vague longing every time he examined the drawing. Who was she? Why did the striking image evoke a reaction?

He set the pad aside and regarded the simple clay vessel Adala had been killed for. He'd been grinding his teeth all day over this. The poor woman had nothing of value in her pack when the thieving bastard Gaius took her life.

What a kingdom his brother ruled! Yet the nation across the western border was little better. The inventors of an amazing machine, a *locomotive,* practiced slavery, killed innocents in the arena, and slaughtered prisoners captured in battle, just as those in Virtus did. And the Mystics to the east? He'd heard tales of this tribe's complicity in the capture of their own women to be sold as brides in Virtus, not to mention their branding of witches.

Oh, to find a people as noble as the pilgrims he'd met three years earlier! Worshipers of the one true God, disciples of a girl who never aged. Perhaps one day he'd cut across the border to Sanctimonia and track this Gabriella down. If she'd share with him the secrets for tolerance, kindness, and peace, he'd abandon his station in life and devote his final years to a higher purpose.

Quintus looked down at his feet. Who was he kidding? Gabriella would find him wanting. God would, as well. He could have protected Adala, but he hadn't.

He dipped the pitcher into the rushing brook and brought it to his lips. Gritty desert water filled his mouth.

Unsanctified.

So unlike Adala's wine.

Brewster shifted up and glanced around the bedroom. A tall oak dresser stood in exactly the right place, a foot from his window, across from his closet, and all in his Northbrook home. He sagged back down against his pillow.

If Carla had driven to Northbrook to change his past, something would be different by now. She'd be sleeping at his side. Loneliness wouldn't be sucking the oxygen out of the room.

Two days had passed since their amazing meeting in the snowy wilds of Upstate New York. Had the cosmic merry-go-round stopped spinning for good?

No way. Either she'd visit him or he'd be whisked back to her again, and soon. To believe otherwise would be to believe an ordinary suburban existence complete with too much house, an unfulfilling job, and an unsuccessful stab at a writing career was all fate had in store for him. That couldn't possibly be the destiny of a man linked to a woman as extraordinary as Carla or teased by a ponytailed imp who could twist time and space like a pretzel.

So…despite the pang of separation and the still unanswered questions about dangers looming at subway stations, the Virtus frontier, Sanctimonia, or wherever a puppet master might send either one of them next, he dragged himself out of bed to give life another shot.

A wonderfully hot shower breathed buoyancy into his soul. Afterward, he emailed Heather to let her know he'd be coming to work late. That way, he could take his time with breakfast, maybe enjoy a walk around the neighborhood, and perhaps finish off with a pilgrimage to the very spot in the street where he first met the woman of his dreams.

After a round of bacon and eggs, Brewster headed out of the house and down the block. The weather had turned colder, reminding him of the icy wind he'd endured hundreds of miles away and a year earlier. Or two days ago, depending on how he looked at it. Falling leaves paint-gunned the lawns in a variety of autumn colors. He caught a whiff of burning brush, a seasonal ·fragrance saying trick or treat. And so did the decorative pumpkins on streetlamps and stencils of witches and goblins in a few windows. Someone had even constructed a pirate ship and manned it with skeletons. Halloween loomed in the near future.

Or did it? He rounded the corner and came upon a house already decorated for Christmas. The sharp change in weather worried him. He couldn't be sure whether he'd just finished touring a pre-Halloween neighborhood or one not fully dehaunted during the limbo of time stretching from that holiday to the big one. He didn't even know the proper year.

With Gabriella and her wormholes always lurking, Brewster couldn't simply assume anymore which page of the calendar *or even which calendar* he might have stumbled into. As he neared his house again, the dizzying sense of disorientation compelled him to seek reassurance, and fast. He snuck onto a neighbor's porch and stole a quick peek at a newspaper waiting on the welcome mat. Whew. No less authority than the *Chicago Tribune* verified he was fine—right where *and when* he was supposed to be.

He glanced up at his own porch a few houses down. A policeman flanked by two other guys stood at his doorstep.

Brewster swallowed. Maybe he wasn't as fine as he'd been thinking.

Trespassing didn't seem a good strategy anymore, so Brewster left the house he didn't own and ambled over to the one he did, sizing up his three visitors along the way.

The cop was the same freckle-faced, starry-eyed young man who'd issued a warning several days earlier when Brewster cheated around a corner despite the no-turn-on-red sign in clear view on a lamppost. The friendly kid seemed like he'd just graduated from the local police academy and probably hadn't seen any real action yet. Grizzled veterans, like the crew-cut, stony-eyed men now flanking this kid—plainclothes cops for sure—never gave warnings when a ticket would do. Not in his experience, anyway.

Tough as they seemed in some respects, those other two men could have won a Laurel and Hardy look-alike contest. The one on the left was shorter than average, red-faced, and about fifty pounds overweight. His thinner and taller pal on the right seemed to be favoring his side. The poor guy moved his hand to the appendix area and grimaced, first while chatting with his companions and then when all three of them trained their sights on the time-traveling clown they'd apparently come to see.

Brewster climbed his porch. The three cops shifted over to make room for him.

"Hey." He tried sounding nonchalant, but the presence of police on his doorstep burned his cheeks, even though he hadn't done anything wrong.

"Brewster DeLay?" the local cop asked.

"That's me."

"I'm Officer Fred Burton of the Northbrook Police. These two gentlemen have flown in from New York City to ask some questions about an accident out their way." He motioned to the short, heavy guy. "This is Detective Ethan Jones." Then he nodded toward the slim, wounded soldier on his other side. "And this is Detective Samuel Barnes."

Brewster shook hands all around. He didn't have a clue about any accidents, but his mouth had gotten twitchy over the news that two detectives had traveled all the way across the country to give him the evil eye. Could he come across any guiltier?

The nearest neighbors damned him, too, and why wouldn't they, what with the police on his porch and all? Emily Saunders, a gray-haired retiree living on the other side of the cul-de-sac, rushed out of her garage with rake in hand, no doubt foraging for gossip fodder. She made an unconvincing show of clearing the leaves from the perfect vantage point in her lawn to stare at his porch. Another neighbor watched from a few doors down, until Brewster turned in that direction and the man ducked inside. Didn't these people have a life?

The wind gusted. The thin cop tightened his jacket.

Brewster leapt at the opportunity to get his embarrassing guests out of view. He grabbed a ring of keys out of his pocket and fumbled one into the door lock. "Come on inside where it's warm, fellas."

Brewster offered coffee, but all three men declined, so he steered them away from the kitchen and into the living room. They grabbed the couch—fat cop, rookie cop, thin cop lined up in a row of solemn faces and probing eyes—leaving him to sit in a chair in front of them like a kid dragged into the principal's office. Only worse. These were cops staring him down, not Sister Mary Josephine. He tried not to fidget, racked his brain for a reason he'd attracted the attention of the NYPD, came up with the city's status as a well-known target of terrorism, and settled on a conclusion that set his knee bouncing.

Crestview Finance loaned money to truckers, *and a big rig could haul a huge bomb.* His staff was supposed to use various loan application screening techniques to weed out identity thieves and other lowlifes, especially the dangerous ones whose names popped up on watch lists. He hoped to hell his team had been following the protocol. Still, even if a terrorist had slipped through the screen and financed a truck with Crestview, Brewster hadn't heard about an attack in the recent past. Also, the FBI would have come, not the police, and they would have tracked him down at his office, not his home. Wouldn't they?

The Northbrook cop spoke first. "Mister DeLay, I'm just going to fade into the background and let these other two gentlemen talk." He'd already done a pretty good job of that, having sunk into the cushions in the middle of the couch between the out-of-town heavies. The poor kid didn't have any room for his elbows and knees.

"What's this all about?" Brewster tried to control a knee threatening to twitch again.

"We're looking into an accident from a while ago," the bigger cop said. His glare left no doubt whose fault the accident might be.

"This is probably no big deal," the guy's gaunt pal added, apparently assuming the good-cop role.

"An accident?" Brewster cursed the tremor in his voice. He reminded himself he couldn't possibly have caused an accident a thousand miles away. But these two New Yorkers had damned intimidating stares.

The bad cop leaned forward and scowled. "Let's cut to the chase."

"Okay."

"Were you in New York City last year?"

Whew. This had to be a case of mistaken identity. "I haven't been east of the Skyway in ages."

"The Skyway?"

"A bridge. It goes from Chicago to Indiana."

"And you haven't gone east of there."

The big cop's expression had disbelief written all over it, but these guys had the wrong man. Brewster's twitchy knee steadied. "Look, I run a company that finances trucks. I used to travel east for dealer visits, but times are tough and—"

"Pulaski, New York. It's right on the inscription." The skinny cop couldn't keep his hands to himself. He'd found Carla's snow-globe on the coffee table—the one she'd hoped Brewster would carry home through a wormhole.

And he had.

The cop had turned it over, base up. "This has a date from last year stamped right on it. Are you sure you haven't been out east lately?"

Brewster gripped the arms of his chair. Having three cops barge in on him and insinuate his involvement in an accident was one thing, but picking his stuff up, especially that particular item, crossed the line from annoyance to outright violation.

A measure of anger also stemmed from the embarrassing realization he'd been caught in a lie, although he hadn't intended to tell one. His mind-boggling trip to Tug Hill seemed in retrospect to have little connection with any real time or space. He might as well have gone to the moon, and he hadn't made the connection he'd actually traveled east when asked the question. Brewster looked the cop in the eye—Barnes or whomever. "A friend gave that to me. Would you mind setting it down and telling me what the hell you guys want?"

All three of them kept their calm. The good-cop-turned-bad returned the globe to the coffee table, the Northbrook cop stayed squished in the middle, and the bad-cop-still-fat spoke up. "Look—"

Barnes cut his partner off with a wave of his hand, then turned to Brewster. He flashed an easy smile, leaping onto the good-cop saddle again. "Can I call you Brewster?"

"Whatever."

"Brewster, we can clear this whole matter up in the blink of an eye. We're investigating an accident that occurred on October twenty-third of last year, in New York City. If you can provide proof you weren't there at the time, we'll apologize for bothering you and be on our way."

"Or I could ask you to get out and come back with a warrant." Whatever tremor Brewster had heard in his voice before was now replaced by the steely tone of an insulted man. He reached for the cell phone in his pocket. "Who's your boss?"

The Northbrook cop sprang to life, clasping his hands over his pressed-together knees and leaning forward. "Yes, you could ask us to leave, and we do understand your right to do that." The second those words escaped his lips, Laurel and Hardy turned to glare at him from either side with a silent but obvious *speak only when spoken to* instruction.

Enough of this nonsense. Brewster went ahead and pulled out his phone, opened the calendar, and scrolled backwards twelve months. An office appointment on the date in question would chase all three bozos back to their circus.

He hit pay dirt. October twenty-third of the previous year happened to fall on a Saturday. He'd been on a weekend trip out of town that day—a trip supported by all kinds of documentation and proof, from travel itineraries to hotel registers to... He fought the urge to taunt the cops with a victory dance but couldn't keep from busting into a wide grin. "I met with an agent that day, in Seattle."

"An agent?" the bad cop asked.

"Yeah, I was at a writers' conference, and I met with a woman to pitch a book I've been working on."

"I thought you financed trucks."

These cops were really getting on his nerves. "Don't you have any hobbies? Now do you want to hear this or not?"

All three men fished little notebooks out of their pockets and flipped them open.

He provided the details of his trip, scrolling through old emails and notes to come up with names, addresses, phone numbers...the whole nine yards. The cops seemed friendlier after that—even the fat one—and Brewster stifled the urge to pump his fist or do anything else that might win a yellow flag for taunting, having lifted the burden of false accusation from his shoulders. When he finished divulging all pertinent information, he waited for the three intruders to say something in apology and leave.

The Northbrook cop actually did start getting up, but the gaunt one stopped him by settling a hand on his shoulder. The heavy cop spoke again. "You're probably wondering what this is all about, huh?"

"Well, I—"

"And our apologies for barging in on you like this," his partner cut in, embracing the role of good cop with gusto.

The willingness of two New York detectives to tell a story he probably had no business hearing stirred Brewster's suspicions, and even brought the hint of a twitch back to the surface. He'd been watching old Colombo reruns on TV lately while on the treadmill at the health club. Peter Falk always closed in for the kill by pretending to leave and then stopping mid-stride to turn back. *"Oh, one more thing."*

But Brewster was an innocent man, a guy with an alibi, and someone sufficiently relieved to act magnanimous. Not to mention a man now burning with curiosity. "I've got to admit you guys have me wondering why you strayed so far out of town over an accident. Are you sure you don't want some coffee?"

The body language of all three men said they might.

"I picked up a blueberry pie at the grocery on the way home from work yesterday," he added.

The four of them sat at the kitchen table. The kid from the Northbrook PD faced Brewster, and the two New York cops flanked him on either side. Brewster dug into his pie and listened to the heavy one, Jonesy, bitch about how accidents and suicides that got reclassified as homicides a whole frigging year later were a royal pain in the ass, because the evidence at the scene gets totally obliterated and even the forensic stuff scooped up by the cops before the stomping feet come along can get lost or mishandled or tainted. "You don't wanna know how often that OJ Simpson stuff happens." And the witnesses get on with their lives, unable to remember a goddamn thing anymore.

"What sort of accident was it?" Brewster asked when a pause in the man's diatribe gave him a chance to work in a question.

The cop rolled over him and kept on going, but his rant became more focused. "If that ain't bad enough, here's a case dumped in our laps because of a couple goddamn dreams."

Dreams? The taste of pie went flat in Brewster's mouth. He stopped chewing and listened up.

"The operator had a blackout just before it happened. Train almost jumped the station."

"It did stop, but a little too late," Barnes, the thin cop, chimed in.

"Ain't that a bitch?" Jonesy said. "At the time, the operator claimed this woman was standing alone out there, but he checks in with a different story last week and says he remembers it better, because he just had a dream about it."

"Slow down," the Northbrook cop said. He caught Brewster's eye. "We're not following you."

Jonesy ignored him and plowed on. "Then some chick who'd been on a train heading the opposite direction, and who'd made herself scarce after the thing went down, comes into the precinct house three days ago and says she glanced out her window when it happened. She saw a man standing with the victim, too. Wanna guess why she came in?"

Brewster gazed into the cop's unreadable eyes. An accident, *dreams,* two cops flying all the way from New York City to talk to him. His hands were getting sweaty. He didn't have a clue where the cop was going with the story or what he was even talking about, for that matter, but the answer to the guy's question was an easy guess. "She dreamed about it?"

"Damn straight." The cop frowned at his empty dish, then motioned to the last corner of pie in the tin. "Hey, mind if I finish that off?"

Brewster didn't trust his voice enough to try answering. He shrugged.

The heavy, plain-clothed cop slid his plate aside, grabbed the tin, and put his fork to work.

"Were you born in a barn, Jonesy?" his partner asked. "Use your own plate."

The big cop grunted and ate.

Brewster turned to the skinny cop... Barnes. "I'm really not following this story."

Barnes grinned, deepening the hollows of his cheeks. If anybody needed another slice of pie, this guy was the poster child, but he'd hardly touched his plate. "Here's what Jonesy is trying to explain in that half-assed story-telling style of his. We're investigating a case from last year. A woman jumped, fell, or got pushed onto the subway tracks in Manhattan and—"

All of a sudden, Brewster couldn't hear anything over the ringing in his ears. He was pretty sure he dropped his fork with a clang, because all three men gave him an odd look, and the piece of silverware wasn't in his hand anymore. He'd just been with Carla, *a year ago,* and she'd been planning a trip to Manhattan to purge herself of a subway suicide nightmare. *He told her not to go alone.*

Now he told *himself* not to leap to the obvious conclusion or bust out crying or lose it in any way. Nervous breakdowns were best suffered alone. He needed to keep cool, speak coherently if called upon, get these cops out of the house as soon as possible, and then collapse. "Sorry," he said.

"Hey, no problem," the Northbrook cop said. "It's your china." That brought a laugh out of the other two, but suspicion lurked in their sharp eyes.

The heavy cop, Jonesy, had almost finished demolishing the rest of the pie. He picked up the thread of the story. "Think the dreams are weird? That ain't all. This chick buys it in one of the busiest subway stations in America, and there isn't one other person on the scene at the time."

"Granted, the accident didn't happen during rush hour, but still," Barnes added.

Something about that heightened the buzz in Brewster's head. He placed his palms flat on the table to keep them from trembling.

Jonesy shook his head. "The security cameras in the station went down. Some kinda malfunction. I guess we wouldn't be here if they'd been working."

"But the cameras outside didn't show anybody going into the station for a good five minutes before the accident," his partner said. "Plenty of people came up the stairs, but nobody went down, except the victim."

"The cashier was on a landing one level above the platform," Jonesy added, "so she didn't see nothing, either. Neither did the idiotic transit cop flirting with her at the time."

Brewster averted his gaze from the Northbrook cop sitting across from him, begged himself not to faint, and refused to even blink for fear he'd see a sign reading *We're hiding from the butterflies* the instant he closed his eyes.

"The station drained out before the accident," Barnes said.

"Like rats chasing tail outta the sinking ship, only it wasn't sinking yet," Jonesy added. He speared the last remnants of the pie.

"There was a bus accident a block away at the time," Barnes added. "That drew the crowd away. I guess most people would rather look at carnage than take the subway on home."

The thin cop reached into his shirt pocket and pulled out an all-too-familiar business card. He laid it on the table for all to see. *Brewster DeLay, Words escape me.* "They found this card in the victim's purse."

Brewster took the card and flipped it over, praying to read a punch line—the *gotcha* at the end of a sick practical joke—but he came up empty and let the thing slide out of his hand. "Why—" His mouth had gone dry. He couldn't choke out another word.

Barnes scooped the card up and slid it into his shirt pocket. "So...we have a woman alone in a subway station, standing near the tracks."

Bewilderment, incomprehension, and even a vague sense of betrayal twitched one of Brewster's eyelids.

"A train comes along and almost doesn't stop," the thin cop continued, "because the operator has a blackout from a mild heart attack. He comes to and hits the brakes but not in time to avoid this woman who is now on the tracks."

"No witnesses but the operator," Jonesy said. "And he claims at first the woman bought it without any help."

"But he changes his story last week, and a witness from a passing train comes forward and corroborates," Barnes added. He gazed intently into Brewster's eyes. "We showed them some pictures, and they both identified you as the man standing with that woman."

Brewster couldn't even begin to process what he was hearing. He wanted to open his eyes and wake up. "Wait. How do you have my picture?"

"Facebook," Jonesy said.

"But you say you have an alibi," the Northbrook cop chimed in.

Barnes sighed and broke into a gentle smile, back in the role of good cop. "Brewster, this woman's name was Carla Summers. She had your card in her purse. You knew her, didn't you?"

Knew her? He still did. And that was the thing. A large part of the emotion trying to filter through his shock was grief, but a voice of logic—or denial—kept whispering that if Carla really did die a year ago, somehow she'd cheated death to interact with him after the fact, meaning she was still alive. Unless—his cup-all-the-way-empty voice argued—she'd been visiting him in her time-traveling dreams *before* she died, and those dreams ended the day the train took her out.

Could he prevent that? What if he took another spin through the wormholes and told her to drop Manhattan from her itinerary? Carla had thought she could change his past and her future. Maybe *he'd* be the one to let the butterflies out of the jar.

The thin cop's friendly expression faltered into a frown. What had he asked?

Brewster tried to focus. "I knew Carla, but I didn't know about…" He couldn't finish.

"We have forensic evidence," Jonesy said, "strands of hair on her coat."

Brewster reached into his back pocket. "If I give you my comb, will you guys hit the road?"

# Chapter Twenty-Four

*Alone with his thoughts*

**BREWSTER STARED OUT HIS** living room window as a spectator in what had to be somebody else's unraveling life. The cops lingered on the sidewalk in full view of his nosy neighbors before getting into an unmarked car. All in all, a pretty good show for Emily Saunders, who still dragged a rake across the same patch of grass, bent on seeing the final act through to the end.

Finally, the three faces of death sped away with scythes in tow.

Brewster collapsed into a chair and turned a misty gaze to the spot in the street where Carla had appeared at the midnight hour of a magical night. Three cops had just rewritten history into a horror story, claiming she'd already been dead for a year.

He fought the overwhelming sadness fogging his vision by using a coping mechanism honed from many stressful episodes at work. He closed his eyes, relaxed his arms on the chair rests, took deep breaths, and drifted away. Only with a calm spirit could he sift through the chaos of bewilderment, disorientation, grief, and anger setting his entire body into a jittery tingle. Every problem had a solution, every story two sides, every thesis an antithesis. He needed a new angle to rally his hope around.

Carla had been run over by a subway train in a real-life

enactment of a recurring and obviously precognitive dream. That cold piece of information had to bite the dust, and he went to work building the case for denial.

Exhibit A—He'd touched Carla's face, gotten lost in her eyes, savored the spicy fragrance of her perfume, kissed her lips. She couldn't have been dead. Wraiths didn't melt in a man's arms. Yes, he and Carla visited each other through wormholes that might have clamped shut when she wandered too close to the subway tracks, but...

Exhibit B—A paranormal connection transcending the barriers of time and space brought him and Carla together, and the super being behind such a miracle had to have a plan in mind. Derailing the cosmic merry-go-round before the end of the ride didn't fit the equation, and in any event...

Exhibit C—Didn't Gabriella's comment about the butterfly effect at the Tug Hill gas station imply the past could be changed?

He sprang out of his chair and paced the room.

The twelve-year-old girl with thousand-year eyes tipped her hand with that sign in the window about butterflies. Clearly, she wanted the past left alone, and witnesses posed a problem for her. If a tree falls in an empty forest, it creates no sound, and fate continues its predestined course. But if others observed and reacted to an event such as Brewster's time-traveling Tug Hill visit, the course of human history might have been altered.

Suppose someone had seen and interacted with him? The encounter would have created ripples. A brief pause for conversation at the gas pump could have prevented some stranger from reaching a predestined point farther down the road at the proper time to discover his soul mate, thus triggering a chain reaction of sweeping consequences. A marriage might have been erased, a child unborn. As Gabriella said, a single butterfly can flutter its wings and change the course of weather forever. Or history, for that matter.

But no, he had it all wrong. Gabriella couldn't have cared less about the ripples in other people's lives. Her only concern was the possibility a random bystander might slow *him* enough to prevent his appearance at the right place and time—parked on the side of the road when the love of his life came along to celebrate the snowstorm.

Carla had been the victim of his butterfly wings, the woman needing to be stalled. She'd been on her way to Manhattan without him, but first the snow squall slowed her and then he did, delaying her arrival on the subway platform to just the right moment—the instant a train operator suffered a heart attack, blacked out, and barreled into the station too fast. By flinging Brewster into Carla's path, Gabriella committed murder as surely as if the little bitch had pushed the woman onto the tracks herself.

And that wasn't all. The puppet master framed him. The train operator and another witness said recent *dreams* refreshed their memories regarding a certain man standing beside the victim.

Brewster balled his fists. But with anger came confusion, a host of questions without clear answers. Why frame a man with an alibi? Surely a little vixen able to plant dreams into minds could have poked around in his head and learned he'd been somewhere else the day Carla fell to the tracks.

And why frame him at all?

Above all, why did she want Carla to be killed?

Brewster stopped pacing. He refocused his gaze out the window at the very spot where Carla first entered his life. They were meant to explore the world hand in hand, as soul mates, kindred spirits, two peas in a pod, Romeo and Juliet—no, that ended badly—Prince Charming and Tinker Bell, two butterflies fluttering their wings as one.

He couldn't let destiny slip away without a fight. Battle lines were forming, storm clouds brewing, and puppet masters could go to hell. He'd suit up in the armor of love and determination, find his way back to the past again, and make a few changes.

Big ones.

Because he could never, ever let Carla go.

His cell phone rang. He ripped it out of his shirt pocket and flipped it open, ready to roll. "Yeah?"

"Where the hell are you?" Heather's voice came at him in a near screech, from the office, in the real world, where business transactions still happened whether or not the rest of his existence had been turned upside down.

But couldn't they happen later? "Didn't you get my email about coming in late today?"

"No. I haven't been granted access to my computer yet."

That didn't make any sense. Among her many duties, Heather acted as the supervisor who controlled system access at Crestview for everyone, obviously including herself. "What are you talking about?"

"The holding company went down."

"I'm not following."

"Charlie Hanson committed some kind of fraud. The banks are taking over every company Parker Investments owns, including ours. Their auditors are crawling through the files right now."

He tightened his grip on the phone.

"So, we need you here, Brewster, and—"

"Wait. Let me think."

Something about those files triggered a half-formed germ of an idea, but it couldn't quite work its way through the turbulence in his mind. He swept his gaze around the living room. When he settled on the snow globe Carla had given him, the idea came closer to finding a voice. He bent to the coffee table, took the sphere in his hand, and shook it. The snow puffed up in a cloud, then settled back down on the little cottage—insulating Carla's safe haven beneath a pristine blanket of white once again.

Brewster needed to dream his way back and talk her out of that Manhattan trip. But he couldn't count on a wormhole assist by Gabriella this time. She'd done him wrong once already. The task of harnessing the amazing, time-and-space-bending energy of dreams rested on his shoulders alone.

Only he didn't have a clue how to tackle the problem.

And yet, he'd recently met someone who wore dreams right on her wrist. *Somnium.* And who knew Gabriella.

The time had come to join forces.

"Heather?"

"Are you coming?"

"Yeah, but listen. Has Igor Tesfaye signed his new loan documents yet?"

"Who the hell cares?"

"If the bank is running the company now, we need his paperwork in the files before they have a chance to renege on the deal."

"You're always the Good Samaritan, aren't you, Brewster?" Heather's voice was getting ever more shrill. "People are worried about their jobs at the moment. Why not try focusing on that instead of some trucker?"

He took a deep breath. "Actually, the man's a poet."

"Are you sitting at home sniffing glue? I need help here."

"Calm down. We'll work something out with the bankers. I'm on my way."

"Hallelujah."

"Meanwhile, get Tesfaye down there and tell him to bring his girlfriend along as a witness."

"She doesn't need to come. Any one of us can—"

"Just do what I said, Heather." Brewster ended the call and hurried out of the house.

He got into his car and backed out of the driveway without shooting a second glance at the police cruiser parked just outside the cul-de-sac. Parents had been complaining about speeders lately, and the cops had responded by increasing their presence on neighborhood streets. When this one pulled out and started following him, Brewster's main concern was to stick to the speed limit and avoid cheating at stop signs. Not until after he'd driven from Shermer to Willow, then east to the Edens Expressway and onto the southbound entrance ramp did his hands start getting sweaty. The cop had tailed him all the way.

Once on the highway, Brewster cut across three lanes of traffic from the far right to the far left. The cop tagged along, gliding from lane to lane until settling between him and another car. A mile later, Brewster switched back to the right lane but failed to shake his new friend. His grip on the steering wheel had gone white-knuckle. Then, two separate police jurisdictions executed a perfect tag-team maneuver at the Touhy Avenue exit. The Northbrook squad car peeled off the highway, and a Chicago cop swung on.

Brewster wasn't a mere citizen caught in the ticket-quota sights of a local cop anymore. Somehow, he'd become a hyperventilating, high-profile person of interest throughout the county.

So this was the game now, huh? Those New York City cops hadn't called on him for a touchy-feely interrogation topped off by coffee and pie. They'd had every intention of arresting him on the spot and plenty of cause to do so. Wacky circumstances or not, two separate witnesses put him at the scene of a possible murder, and a business card in Carla's purse suggested a relationship with the victim. If he hadn't had an airtight alibi, he'd probably be sweating it out under a bare light bulb at the nearest holding pen. He'd earned a reprieve, but the cops couldn't be expected to let him out of their sights until they checked out his story.

He pulled off the highway at the Foster Avenue exit, headed west toward his office, glanced in the rearview mirror, and still saw the tail. He tried talking himself off the ledge with the assurance the cops were sure to stop following him as soon as they confirmed his alibi—most likely a matter of placing a few phone calls or calling on a person or two. Deep down, though, he knew better.

In the heat of the earlier moment, Brewster had seen no problem in producing his comb as evidence of his innocence. He hadn't been with Carla at the accident scene, and in fact, he'd never been in a New York City subway station in his life. But that comb now looked like a boomerang fully capable of flying back at him with the opposite of his intended result.

Disassociation had been the problem. Twice during his police interrogation, he'd failed to think of the Tug Hill incident as a real event. First he told the cops he hadn't been out east, and later he forgot the forensic evidence he'd left in his wake. Hairs on Carla's coat? They'd hugged, leaned against each other, shed hairs all over each other for sure. When the police mined his comb for a DNA sample or whatever, they'd learn without any doubt their person of interest had been with the victim shortly before her death. What then? His inadvertent lie about not traveling east would have guilt written all over it.

And how strong was his Seattle alibi, really? Brewster shrank deeper into his seat. Nobody out there could confirm for certain they'd met *him*, presuming they remembered anything at all a year after the fact. The clerks at the airline, hotel, and rental car counters, the attendees at the writers' conference, and even the agent had never seen him before. An accomplice could have gotten away with posing as a writer and flashing forged identification whenever necessary.

Would the literary agent recognize Brewster if called to a witness stand? At least two dozen writers had pitched their novels to her during the conference, and the woman might have attended a dozen other conferences since then. No wonder that fat cop had been talking up forensics! Jonesy had probably figured out that an accomplice could have filled in for Brewster in Seattle—some unknown person of interest number two.

Brewster almost drove over a curb. He tried harder to keep his tingling hands steady, stay on the road, and avoid sidewalks whose stray pedestrians—a group waiting for a bus here, a homeless person holding up a cardboard sign there—managed to go through life in blissful ignorance about the hazards of being in two places at one time. After a few miles of strip malls and grocery stores, he completed his nerve-racking drive by turning down the street spilling into Crestview Finance's parking lot. The cop gave up the chase at that point and pulled over, clearly banking on the certainty Brewster would eventually need to head out the same way he came in.

A sawhorse blocked the driveway, and a security guard post had been stationed beside it. Brewster parked, stepped out of his car into the brisk autumn air, and tried to enjoy maybe his last breaths of freedom.

Enjoy. What a laugh. Carla was dead. He had only the sketchiest of ridiculous plans to rescue her. And on top of that, he'd become the target of a perfect frame with no way to explain the situation without coming across as a guy practicing his insanity plea.

# Chapter Twenty-Five

BREWSTER STEPPED AWAY FROM the lobby window. He wouldn't bring Igor Tesfaye and his girlfriend to the office any quicker by waiting with his nose pressed against the glass. Meanwhile, Crestview's workforce, *his employees*, stood every chance of losing their jobs if he didn't do something quick. That meant putting time travel on hold and dealing with the present.

He took a deep breath and headed into the conference room, settling into a seat across the table from Steve Franklin. The uninspiring, gray-haired banker had arrived in the standard power outfit—dark suit, white shirt, red tie—befitting his position as senior vice president of First Collateral Bank. His army of similarly clad minions had conquered the place in a blitzkrieg of intimidation, using steely eyes and intimidating, handheld computer gadgetry to win the battle without firing a single shot.

Word had it Steve would oversee Crestview Finance until the bank figured out whether keeping the company afloat or letting it sink represented the least loss. How fitting! The man had a reputation for being a least-loss kind of guy, a fence straddler who'd somehow scurried up the bank's corporate ladder without possessing any real talent. Recessions came and went, retirements, layoffs. Whether by luck or nimbleness, Steve had never had his name connected with a big loss, and whenever the music stopped playing, he'd always managed to grab a bigger chair.

Such a man would probably lean in a bad direction. Any move other than the liquidation of Crestview presented downside career risk for a guy who loved working the safest angles. Steve knew all about the company's struggles with trucker loan defaults—he'd been Crestview's banker for years—and he certainly hadn't been given any reason to believe these problems would go away.

Only the dog and pony show of a lifetime might change the man's mind. Tall order, but Brewster was ready to step up and give it his best shot. Anyone planning to battle the cosmos by turning back the clock and changing history couldn't settle for half measures. If he wanted to be a hero, he had to play the part.

Someone had ordered donuts. The pastries waited on a platter in the middle of the table, serving as a centerpiece for the opponents to talk across. A blonde underling in an unflattering business suit came in, sat beside the banker, and readied herself with a ballpoint pen poised in hand and a blank legal pad waiting to be scribbled upon.

Steve spoke from his notes, droning on about this and that until Brewster caught the end of something important. "...keeping you in your present position until we sort everything out. You'll report to me."

Brewster swallowed. "Actually, no, I'm not staying on."

The banker set his reading glasses aside and glanced up at him. "Abandoning the sinking ship?"

"It isn't sinking." Brewster pulled some spreadsheets from his folder and walked the man through as patient an overview as possible, given the constraints of a racing heart and a wall clock ticking a steady reminder that his remaining hours of freedom might be best spent elsewhere. Igor and Kara were due any minute.

The presentation had plenty of detail—bankers loved that— but the plan was simple. A tough recession had knocked most of

Crestview's competition out of business. Therefore, conservative lending practices in an easier market—two other concepts bankers adored—could now transform the company from a loser to a big winner.

He shoved the folder across the table and looked the guy square in the eye. "You can turn this mess into a home run."

Steve pored through the spreadsheets, sliding page after page over to his blonde assistant, who scribbled notes on her pad. Finally, he set the last document aside. "If you believe in this, why are you leaving?"

Because Brewster had dreams to follow, a woman to save, and a fledgling writing career to pursue. If he never got published, he'd take a stab at consulting or teaching, and if all else failed, he'd be perfectly happy spending the rest of his life helping Carla stuff ragdolls after he'd snatched her from the jaws of a subway train. Actually, if he found a way to turn back the clock, who knew how broad the butterfly effect might be? Maybe Charlie Hanson wouldn't commit the fraud that brought the wrath of First Collateral down on their heads. Brewster's stomach fluttered. The world was his oyster.

"I'd like to pursue other opportunities," he said. "We have another manager here who's perfectly capable of following this plan." He motioned to the papers spread out between them, one of which had gotten too close to the pastry tray and picked up a jelly stain.

The assistant stopped scribbling, chewed on the tip of her pen, turned to her boss.

Steve shook his head. "What do you mean? I can't—"

"You've met Heather Cummins. She knows this business inside out. She's damned smart, a hard worker, and a complete slave to policy and procedure." Compliance had always been a prized trait in the banking world.

Brewster leaned across the table to close the deal. "Here's the best part. Heather's a player. If there's a problem, she won't come whining about it. She'll fix it for you. *Every time.*"

The gears in the banker's head started turning in a more

favorable direction, judging by the hint of a smile on his face. Brewster could easily guess his thought process. Heather might be valuable in more ways than one. She'd do all the heavy lifting and keep Steve out of the day-to-day decision-making. If things went well, the banker would find a way to grab the credit and bask in the kudos. If Crestview's new business plan tanked and caused good money to be thrown after bad—money Steve's bosses wouldn't be happy about losing—Heather could take the fall as scapegoat.

The banker picked a donut from the platter, took a bite out of it, chewed, swallowed, and finally spoke. "I'd rather keep you."

If only. But the time had come to move on. "That's not gonna happen."

Steve motioned to the spreadsheets. "Does she understand the lending approach you're proposing here?"

"She's the one who came up with it."

Steve stared into space. "I'm remembering something unconventional about her appearance."

"Heather? No way."

"Maybe I'm thinking of somebody else."

Brewster pushed away from the table. "Heather's a straight arrow. Hell, I'm pretty sure she votes Republican. I'll send her in."

He left the conference room and found the architect of Crestview's new business plan in her office. Heather sat at her desk, busy as usual and dressed conservatively in blouse and skirt—nothing unconventional in her appearance, from just below the butterfly tattoo on her neck, anyway. He came in and closed the door behind him. "You're the new boss."

The brunette dynamo, tamer of problems, handler of any situation that might come her way, looked up at him with Bambi eyes. "What?"

"I'm quitting."

The same expression flashed across her face he'd heard earlier on the phone—equal measures of anger and panic. "That's it, huh? Things get a little tough and you just walk away. People here have families, babies—"

"Look, I can't explain my reasons for leaving, but we both know you can do my job in your sleep."

"No, I can't."

"Yes, you can, and I'm just a phone call away if you ever need advice." Presuming he stayed out of jail. But he refused to let his mind go there. "Undo your ponytail and let your hair down. That'll make you look a little older."

"Older?"

"More mature." Brewster bid a silent, sad farewell to the tattoo on her neck. "The man's an old-school creep. The only symbols he wants to see are dollar signs."

"Fine." She reached behind her head and unbraided her hair.

"It's a small price to pay, Heather. That guy's dying to have somebody turn this company around for him. You'll be a star."

"Yeah? Who'll get the credit?" Heather was nobody's fool.

"Who cares? Just march into the conference room, say yes to as many questions as you can, and ask for a raise at the end."

The prospect of higher pay worked wonders on her frown, almost turning it into a smile.

"That's right, a raise," he continued. "Then you can move your stuff into my office and put your feet on the desk."

"You mean after I kill you?"

He knew she'd be fine once she plunged into the job. Heather had come up with a solid business plan, and she was tough enough to see it through. She had no qualms about saying no most of the time, perhaps the single most important characteristic for somebody tasked with the responsibility of making proper loan decisions. If Brewster had said no a little more often, the company wouldn't have needed a turnaround plan in the first place.

He swept his arm toward the conference room. "Go get 'em."

Heather started away.

"Wait. Where's my trucker and his girlfriend?"

"In your office."

Brewster swallowed past a lump in his throat as he turned to leave. He'd just taken his first tentative step off the grid, leaving no small portion of his self-definition behind. Unless he succeeded in changing the past, he might never find his way back.

But he'd done something fantastic just now. He'd found the courage to turn his back on the false god of a poorly earned paycheck by stepping down. Heather was capable of rescuing a fine team of employees from the unemployment line. He hadn't been.

Maybe he didn't have a spring in his step as he walked out of Heather's office, but he had no problem holding his head high.

He went into his own office, closed the door behind him, and smiled at a scruffy poet-trucker and his raven-haired girlfriend. "Thanks for waiting. I'm hoping you can help me with something."

Igor Tesfaye extended his hand. "We have your back, my friend."

"Thanks." Maybe the two of them could find a way to pull Gabriella's knife out of it. He shook Igor's hand and turned to Kara Danahey.

She looked down at her shoes. "Sorry about stalking out of the restaurant before."

"No problem. I was hoping we could resume the conversation, though."

Kara's eyes narrowed into the same scared-rabbit expression they'd assumed before she bolted two days earlier. "About dreams?"

He glanced at the *somnium* tattoo on her wrist, weighing how much to say. Despite her intimidating getup—black dress, deep red lips, overshadowed eyes—Kara had assumed the body language of a skittish deer. "Yeah, dreams. And a girl named Gabriella."

"I went straight to my uncle Henry last time you and I met. He's strong enough to deal with Gabriella. I'm not."

Igor winked at him. "The man is fierce. If you need magic, Henry's the right guy."

Judging by the look Kara gave Igor, she would have turned him into a toad if *she* knew any hocus-pocus. "*Gifts* like my uncle's have been misconstrued as magic for centuries. Let's not paganize God's blessings." She shifted to the door and grabbed the handle.

Brewster couldn't let her get away again. Misconstrued or not, some form of magic was exactly what he needed. "Come on. Just another coffee down the street. I won't bite."

The trucker settled a hand on Kara's wrist. "We have this man's back, love. Remember?"

# Chapter Twenty-Six

*Lamming it*

A SQUAD CAR STILL lurked along the curb just beyond the company parking lot. Brewster scrunched as low as he could get in the back seat of Kara's car until they got well past the cop.

His two new friends didn't seem to notice. Kara had her eyes fixed on the road. Her boyfriend, Igor, gazed out the passenger window, muttering in English mixed with Russian curses about a prolonged DOT safety inspection of his truck. The rig sat waiting its turn in some shop, leaving him unemployed for the day, whereas in Mother Russia, a few rubles pressed into the right palms would have avoided such a headache.

Not all problems could be solved so easily. Brewster doubted rubles by the truckload would keep him off the fugitive list once the police learned he'd bolted from the office building for good. He didn't have any intention of returning for his car.

Another step off the grid. He wiped a bead of sweat from his brow.

They stopped at the same bar and grill where he and Kara had lunch a thousand years earlier. Once inside, they grabbed a booth in the shadows of the back wall, and Igor continued his rant against American trucking regulations until a waitress came along. They ordered drinks, the waitress returned with them, and the trucker quieted, shifting his attention to a vodka martini.

Kara ignored her coffee. "Dreams and Gabriella are a bad combination," she said.

"No argument there." Brewster glanced from face to face. Could a hard-drinking Russian's quirky girlfriend possibly help a man rewrite the past? He had nowhere else to turn. "Let's forget her for a minute and focus on *somnium*. My girlfriend, Carla, and I have been hooking up in our dreams."

That got a grunt out of Igor. "Hooking up? Kara tells me you're a writer, but this expression of yours is a cliché, no? Trust your own words better." He speared an olive and popped it into his mouth.

"You're missing the point, love." Kara lit a cigarette, gazed through the smoke at Brewster, waited.

Although he might have tried putting a sane spin on his tale for an ordinary audience, Brewster skipped the fluff with these two. Kara had an uncle with "gifts," and she dressed like the type who believed crystals could heal. As for her vodka-chugging boyfriend, Igor had earlier come to the office demanding a refund based on what a girl told him in a dream. "Suppose I said Carla fell asleep, stepped out of her dream, and came into my house, one year and nine hundred miles away."

Kara tapped her ashes into a saucer. Igor grabbed another olive. Neither said a word.

Maybe they'd misheard. "We're traveling through time! Carla and I have been bouncing back and forth between last year and this one."

The trucker took a long, forlorn look at his drink and sighed, clearly reluctant to spend a moment away from it. "Haven't you ever visited your past in a dream?"

How to get through to these people? "You mean in fantasy? Yeah, I guess. But this is real."

Kara glanced at Igor and nodded. "Last time we met, I told you *all* dreams are real." She and her boyfriend made a good tag team.

Brewster stilled his twitching knee and took one more try. "Let me elaborate. I close my eyes in my bed and step into Carla's life, literally. When I wake up, I find *physical objects* she gave me in the dream. And the same thing has been happening to her."

"Then I'd say you're blessed," Kara said.

"Blessed?"

She scattered her coffee steam with a puff of breath. "This is us when we dream. Our souls leave our bodies and mingle in the World of Mortal Dreams, a timeless dimension shaped by the imaginations of every man, woman, and child who ever lived."

Igor fluttered his hands upward and whistled like a bird.

She grabbed a menu and swatted her boyfriend with it. "Don't always make it so hard to love you, funny man." Then she glanced around, leaned across the table, and lowered her voice like a spy spilling secrets. "Traveling from one time and place to another is commonplace when we sleep, but the ability to *leave* the spiritual dimension and rematerialize in the waking world is a rare gift called dream walking. You're blessed!"

"There's that word again." But Brewster's pulse quickened. She'd implied exactly what he'd been hoping to hear. Other people stepped out of their dreams, too. He just needed the handbook. "How do I do this dream walking thing again?"

"You don't know?"

"It just happens."

"Then let it happen."

His temples throbbed. "What if it doesn't anymore?"

"Good question." Kara puffed a ring of smoke, watched it dissolve, dropped a sugar cube into her coffee, watched *that* dissolve, and puffed her cigarette again. "Then I guess it's over."

He clenched his fists. "It can't be over. Carla and I have had a bridge between our dreams all our lives. For as long as I can remember, I've been visiting a scrubby wasteland that seems like a stage set for a Mad Max movie. Carla's been traveling to a woodland called Sanctimonia. And every one of these dreams, hers and mine, are in Latin."

Kara's eyes widened. *"Somnium."*

"That's one word. We're talking an entire lexicon of the language, which neither one of us could begin to translate when awake. If dreams are real, we're alive over there. This can't be over."

Igor set his martini down. "Conflict. Confusion. This is where Gabriella comes in, no?"

Although the ice had been broken, Kara didn't run away this time. She stayed put in the booth, smoking for all she was worth. Her cigarette shook in her hand, but she didn't leave.

Brewster took a deep breath. "The cops came to my house this morning and told me Carla died in a subway accident a year ago."

"Brewster, I'm so sorry, I—" Kara crinkled her forehead. "Hold on. Did you say a year ago?"

"Uh-huh."

"But you've been seeing each other?"

"Yeah."

She snuffed out her cigarette. "After she died?"

"According to the cops, after I killed her. They think I pushed her in front of the train."

Kara and Igor exchanged an open-mouthed glance. They turned to him and spoke in perfect harmony. "Why would they think that?"

He'd lost them. Kara seemed ready to bolt again, this time with the trucker fast on her heels.

"I've been set up! A week ago, two witnesses dreamed they saw me standing next to Carla on the platform. Somehow those dreams triggered false memories of an actual event." He spread his hands. "*That's* where Gabriella comes in, I think."

"Gabriella." Kara spat out the name. "Fallen angels can manipulate dreams in ugly ways. If she's messing with you and your girlfriend, you both better run for the hills."

"I can drive you there when I get my goddamn truck back," Igor said.

She glared at him. "Does this really strike you as the time to crack jokes? Remind me to leave you at home next time."

"Back up." Brewster locked eyes with her. "Did you just say Gabriella's a demon?"

"No. She's an *angel* who fell but wishes she hadn't. That's what my uncle thinks, anyway. Fallen ones are always trying to win their way back into heaven, and they think nothing of dragging us mortals into their twisted schemes."

That did sound like a puppet master, all right.

Kara grabbed a pen out of her purse and started scribbling on a napkin. "Henry's not really my uncle. He's an extraordinarily old man, and I'm one of many in his long line of begats. Do you follow me?"

"Like a great-granddaughter?"

"Add a few greats."

Igor pressed his lips together and nodded, in total solidarity with his girlfriend.

And why not? If some people could spill out of their dreams into the wrong time and place, why couldn't certain uncles with "gifts" live for a century or three? The scribes who wrote the Old Testament probably wouldn't argue against either count.

Kara slid the napkin across the table. She'd drawn a map of the interstate heading north, a county road in Wisconsin, and an X west of Kenosha labeled *Sacred Heart Cemetery*. "Henry has always been overly protective of me, so I normally take his warnings with a grain of salt. But he had deep worry in his eyes when he told me to steer clear of Gabriella."

"But I'm not involving you. I'm just trying to find out how to—"

She flicked her hand at the napkin. "I'm out. If you want to take your problems to Henry, he brings flowers to his late wife Sarah's grave every morning. That's the only place I know where to find him."

"Can this guy help me?"

"What are you trying to do?" she asked.

"Change the past."

She snatched the napkin back. "Leave the past alone."

A snippet of hope took a roller-coaster dive through Brewster's stomach. Kara wouldn't have admonished him if changing the past was impossible, would she? He grabbed the napkin and shoved it into his pocket. "Look, if he's the unapproachable type, maybe you guys could come along and—"

Kara shrank away.

"Just to introduce me."

"Brewster, bad things can happen when Gabriella gets involved. My best place is on the sidelines, keeping a low profile, and making a normal life with Igor." She turned to the trucker, shrugged, and smiled. "Well, it's a life, anyway. Visiting Henry would drag me deeper into whatever this is."

"Okay. You say I'll find him at that woman's grave?"

"Every morning."

But the morning was long gone. "Tomorrow, then."

"Use the word *vagrant* when you approach him. That's our code word."

"Why?"

"Because if Henry thinks some random stranger is interrupting his visit with Sarah—"

Igor smacked his glass on the table. "Thunder! Bolts of lightning! Witchcraft!"

Kara turned to the trucker, eyes burning with all of the above. "Remind me again why I left a perfectly good boyfriend to take up with the likes of you?"

The trucker flashed an easygoing smile. He took both her hands in his. "Tomorrow is my hedge against boredom. Come, my gypsy, and tell me *your* future instead of mine. What dreams will flit behind those hazel eyes? What colors will please you as you gaze at the rising moon?"

She softened instantly, caught in the spell of the out-of-context poetry he'd cast on her.

Brewster slid out of the booth. Tomorrow was his hedge against boredom, too. He needed to break a fallen angel's spell if he ever wanted to gaze at the rising moon with Carla again.

# CHAPTER TWENTY-SEVEN

*Meanwhile, ninety miles north, in Kenosha*

HENRY STODDARD TRUDGED ACROSS weedy grass into the farthest corner of a forgotten cemetery until he reached the stone that marked his late wife's grave. A wilted bouquet of roses at his feet sagged over the mouth of a clay vase. He set them afire with a sweep of his arm and watched them burn across the darker colors of the spectrum. The remains drifted away in a puff of green smoke.

He waved again, and fresh flowers burst out of the vase. "Presto, darling." He bent close enough to take in the fragrance, then straightened and stepped back, gazing at his handiwork and basking in the memories of his finest days with Sarah.

The flowers, of course, were a simple illusion. Who could afford new ones every day? Nevertheless, he knew in his bones she'd been enjoying his ritual of love and remembrance, day after day, month after month, for all of these years. More years than he cared to count or remember.

"I'm sure she does." The easily recognizable voice came from behind—an annoyance dogging him for centuries. Gabriella came around to face him. The ponytailed, blue-eyed imp of an angel sported her typical plain summer dress, this one

233

a faded green-and-yellow plaid. Innocence served as the perfect camouflage for her duplicitous nature.

"Still," she added, "Sarah resides in a different realm now, where the concern is for the collective rather than the self. She spreads her love among many."

Henry clenched his fists. One after another, his darkest emotions roared in his ears like thunder—anger over Gabriella stalking him in his most private of moments, a keen sense of violation she'd pick a thought from his head and turn it on him, and fierce jealousy over the suggestion his Sarah shared with others the love she once held for him alone. He spun around. "Weren't you angels created to spread joy?"

"How can I? God took my harp away." She pouted. As if on cue, a gray cloud blotted the sun, casting a long shadow across the graveyard. This wasn't the contrite Gabriella, the misguided angel who sometimes tracked him down at his castle for consolation and encouragement whenever her schemes went awry. He'd have to deal with the bad side of her personality this day, a mischievous creature who couldn't resist the urge to create chaos.

"You'll never get your harp back," he said.

"I get no appreciation for the good things I do."

"You only make things worse with all of your meddling." Henry tried to scowl her into humility. He didn't expect much luck.

She met his comment with stony silence.

He waited for her to make the next move.

A hummingbird fluttered from grave to grave. A crow cawed from a nearby tree. From just beyond the woods at the edge of the cemetery, a steady whoosh of highway traffic marred the atmosphere of forgotten history he enjoyed most about Sarah's cemetery.

"Let's not wound each other," she said finally.

"You started it."

"I was simply telling you something a friend should tell. We are still friends, aren't we?"

*Friends?* He had a bone to pick with her. Kara Danahey tracked him down just the other day with a convoluted story about dreams and schemes, ending with an annoying punchline—Gabriella. The back of his head tingled. "Stop that."

She giggled. "What?"

"Stay out of my mind, *friend.* And tell me what in the world possessed you to bother my Kara."

"I'll get to that in a minute." Gabriella took his hand. Her small fingers disappeared within his larger grip, their softness conveying the harmlessness her overall image suggested. Yet, for a moment, his willpower faltered from the strength of that simple touch.

He yanked his hand away, and the urge to do whatever she wanted evaporated. "If you want to take me somewhere, just ask. I'm not in the mood for your rudeness."

"I want to show you something."

"Give me a hint."

"It's a little beyond the trees."

"You lead. I'll follow."

They headed into a narrow grove not yet flattened to asphalt by the creeping civilization on the other side. The highway noise grew louder, but as they closed in on it, he redefined the sound as rushing water in an area he thought to be dry.

Henry slowed. He didn't care for surprises at the best of times and certainly none orchestrated by this annoying brat.

"Just a little farther." She led him deeper into the grove until they reached a clearing.

An unforgettable sight hovered ahead—the curtain of smoke Gabriella dragged to his castle decades ago. The plume roared like a waterfall and rushed almost as fiercely, but from bottom to top instead of top to bottom. Each end curled into itself like the ends of a scroll, one emerging out of nowhere and the other disappearing into the same thin air.

He reached toward it, thought better, pulled away.

"What are you afraid of?" she asked. "You put your hand through the smoke the day I brought it to you."

"I did?" Henry shoved his hand into the plume, up to the wrist. Despite its appearance, the smoke was cool to the touch.

"Step through it for me, Henry. Everyone else who tried has been scorched, but you seem fine. It's God's will."

"God's will?" Henry guffawed. "When have you ever been right about such a thing?"

"Impressive-looking gateway, though, isn't it?"

An unusual one, to say the least. "Have you considered theater choreography?"

She sighed. "It's a little late for me to change career paths."

"A pity. I was hoping to spare the world."

Gabriella bent to pick a turned dandelion, the type gone puffy white and ready to wreak havoc in a frenzy of procreation. She puffed her cheeks, exhaled, and sent the parachutes scattering. "Sparing the world is a slippery slope. Who knows whether the butterfly effect would create flowers or weeds?"

"Try practicing what you preach." Henry pressed the palm of his hand deeper into the smoke. A hole opened, parting the column like the Red Sea. He slid his forearm through to the elbow, then shifted around, but he couldn't see his hand come out the other side. "Happy?"

Gabriella bounced from foot to foot. He'd never seen her so agitated. "I'll be happy if you step across to the other side," she said.

"No."

"Please, Henry. I have a message from God for someone." She revealed a folded piece of notepaper hidden in her fist.

"Deliver it yourself."

She stomped her foot like a petulant child. "Don't you think I would if I could? I can't get more than a hundred yards beyond this gateway."

"Pity, that. We're at an impasse then, aren't we?" He peered through the roiling cloud at a shadowy landscape on the other side. Intriguing, but not enough for him to risk life and limb. He headed away.

Gabriella came after him, grabbed his sleeve. "Wait. A damsel in distress needs saving, and you'll just leave?"

"I prefer the damsels who know how to save themselves." He shrugged her off, took a few more steps.

"Do you still read the Bible, Henry?"

The inexplicable randomness of Gabriella's question was suspicious enough to stop him. "I've been known to riffle through the Psalms."

"I love Genesis," she said, "especially the begats."

He turned to her.

Whatever friendliness she'd been pretending earlier had drained out of her expression, leaving nothing but an ageless stare in its wake.

"You've lost me, Gabriella."

"You know how it goes. Adam begat Seth. Seth begat Enosh. Farther down the line, Irad begat Mehujael. Noah begat Shem, and on the begats progressed from century to century." Gabriella moved a hand to her chin in mock puzzlement. "Now here's an interesting question."

"I'm all ears."

"Who did Henry Stoddard begat?"

The girl's babble was taking a bad turn. He caught a whiff of blackmail.

"As I recall," she continued, "you and Sarah begat a girl named Rachel. She married a man, and they begat Grace. Nearly three centuries of begats continued, until the magical day when one lucky couple begat Kara Danahey."

"You stay away from her." He clenched his fists so hard the nails bit into his palms.

Gabriella stared him down during the long, pregnant pause. "You wanted to know why I've been mixing her up in things? Leverage, Henry. God's message *must* be delivered. Who knows what trouble I might involve Kara in if I don't get my way?"

He had the urge to grab Gabriella's ponytail and swing her like an Olympic hammer, but he knew, despite the illusion of her inferior size, he'd fare worse than David without a slingshot against a hundred Goliaths. He needed to come up with a nonviolent way of gaining the upper hand.

"There is no upper hand."

This annoying creature refused to stay out of his head! "What's my Kara to you?"

"She's nothing to me, just a minor character in the opening scene of a play. You're the messenger I'm looking for."

Henry tried to think past the red tide of anger threatening to explode his head. Perhaps a favorable bargain could still be struck. "I have it on good authority an angel can never tell a lie. Not even a fallen one."

Gabriella flashed her sweetest little-girl smile. "This is true."

"If I do what you ask, will you leave Kara alone and stay out of her life *forever*?"

"Yes."

"And all you want me to do is deliver a message to someone."

"Yes again."

"Can you assure me I'll return unscathed and—"

Gabriella laughed. "I'm surprised at you, Henry. I'm sure you'll be fine on the other side, same as here. Just use your illusions to render yourself invisible until you locate Maynya, let her have the note, and hurry back."

A hand of smoke curled out of the portal, beckoning him to enter.

"Will I be walking into yesterday, today, or tomorrow?"

She shrugged. "Time waxes and wanes from one dimension to another. A man might dream for a second about living a full day."

"In English, Gabriella."

"Sanctimonia and Virtus are approximately today, give or take."

He glanced over his shoulder at Sarah's grave. His stomach fluttered.

"Don't worry, Henry, you'll be back tomorrow with fresh flowers."

"I better be. Where will I find this woman who was so unfortunate to attract your interest?"

"Go west through the woods until you reach a clearing. She's in the capital's bridal pool, last I heard. Ask around. It shouldn't be far."

"What does she look like?"

Gabriella planted the image of a hauntingly beautiful dark-haired woman in his mind.

"I told you to stay out of there."

She pouted again. "I'm just being helpful. You did ask."

He started into the portal.

"You forgot the note!" Gabriella rushed up and handed it to him. "By the way, they don't speak English over there."

"I didn't expect they would."

"I'm sure you'll understand a word or two. You still remember some Latin, don't you?"

# CHAPTER TWENTY-EIGHT

*Across the portal in Virtus*

MAYNYA TRUDGED UP THE hill one grueling step at a time, dragging the cross on her shoulder. After twelve long months of harsh captivity, she'd been singled out as the first bride to perform a macabre new wedding ritual.

A woman placed her life in the hands of her husband in marriage. The life-sized crucifix symbolized his right to kill her at will, without reprisal—an overly barbaric notion even for the horrid rulers of Virtus.

A hundred more paces until she'd reach the top. Soldiers would help her plant the cross into the ground, and she'd be done with it. She considered herself lucky, having heard rumors the king suggested far worse when he first came up with this idea. She shuddered. As further evidence of a bride's willingness to sacrifice for her betrothed, he wanted a hand spiked into the wood. Or a foot. The versions varied. But the king's advisors had argued a new husband wouldn't want his bride damaged on such an auspicious day. Or so the story went.

She didn't doubt such cruelty had been contemplated by this awful ruler.

Soldiers lined Maynya's path on either side, all smartly dressed in their blue uniforms, brass buttons, and well-placed caps. Many peasants had joined their ranks, dusty and shabby in comparison. The throng included gentry, as well, the men wearing wigs and lacy-sleeved topcoats, the women in their finest silk with smiles painted on their faces. Excitement gleamed in their eyes, perhaps even inexplicable pleasure. She couldn't understand the betrayal by her own gender.

She turned her attention to the other members of the bridal pool, dozens of women in long purple dresses—a faddish color choice thrust upon them by the bride master—and with hair brushed to a shine. Most had dark tresses, the signature of captured Mystics. A few others sported blonde locks and even red—women stolen from lands she'd never traveled. The brides had taken great care to look pretty, and Maynya could barely hold back tears over the thought of their motivation.

An attractive bride might fetch a high bid at auction, bringing great pride to everyone in the pool. This propaganda drilled into everyone's heads by the bride master wasn't the true reason behind the pains the captive women had all taken to present themselves so well. No, these fellow inmates clung to the superstition that a pretty, well-groomed bride might catch the eye of a kindly man, one who wouldn't be inclined to beat her on a regular basis.

Halfway up the hill, Maynya paused to gaze at the plume of smoke rising from the foundry's great chimney, careful not to linger long enough to feel the sting of a cane against her thigh from one of the two hulking, big-boned matrons walking with her on either side. The cloud of soot drifted to the edge of the forest and beyond, perhaps far enough for a free Mystic to see from a vantage point deep in the woods of Sanctimonia. She'd been transfixed by the smoke every day for a full year now. The sight of its unimpeded drift never failed to trigger a pang of homesickness. The path in life she'd chosen a year earlier, when she traded places with a pregnant prisoner, would probably preclude her from ever seeing her homeland again.

She looked away and moved on.

As heavy as the burden of homesickness might seem, another

sorrow pressed down on her heart with greater weight than the cross on her shoulder. She'd enjoyed the company of an invisible sister in Sanctimonia. The mysterious companion of her dreams vanished on the day her captivity began. The memory still triggered aching sadness. Maynya could no longer travel to a remarkable world by night and view a different life through her other half's eyes.

She seldom dreamed anymore at all, literally or figuratively.

"You go, Maynya!" The cry of a bride spurred her onward. The only joy she now found was derived from the company of these poor souls. They'd been drawn to her from day one as if they were her own children, even though many were her age or older. She sang to them, she combed out their hair, she whispered encouragement, and above all, she helped them plot their escapes. Thirteen brides had gotten away during this single year of her captivity. She'd used illusions most times, and she'd also taught others how to cast their own. Some few other Mystics in the pool had similar gifts but needed instruction on harnessing their powers, a knowledge that had come to her by instinct.

The cross scraped through the thin shoulder fabric of Maynya's wedding dress, stinging its way across a welt, a reminder of the price she'd paid for helping these cherished women. Although she'd never been caught in the act of aiding a slave's escape, suspicion had been directed her way more than once by angry guards seeking a scapegoat. Just a week earlier, a flogging forced the bride master to throw aside the open-backed gown he'd originally planned for this momentous wedding in favor of something less revealing. He'd beaten her for spoiling his plans, nearly causing the need for a veil over her face. But the bruises had mended.

Maynya distracted herself from the pain by gazing at her onlookers and imagining happy lives for each bride. Then she met the eye of a soldier whose intense return stare nearly buckled her knees. She almost thought she knew the man. Yet such familiarity couldn't be possible. She'd been cloistered away from the men of Virtus for a full year except for two failed, unconsummated, and very brief marriages. The bride master had beaten her bloody the second time. No man enjoyed refunding money less than he.

The soldier's lingering gaze could only be born from lust, and she cursed the mother who would raise a boy to grow up so arrogant and presumptuous he'd look at another man's bride in such a manner.

Maynya lost her footing and stumbled to her knees, triggering a wave of murmurs, groans, and even cruel laughter from the throng. She blamed the soldier for distracting her, and she despised him all the more.

The damnable dolt was at her side in an instant. His cap fell from his head when he bent to take her arm, revealing a mass of wavy blond hair. She turned away from the man's handsomeness, but somehow the light touch of his hand stirred her heart, even though she held nothing but scorn for any and all barbarians.

One of the matrons flanking her scowled at the soldier. "Let her be! She must rise on her own and finish the task."

Maynya found herself in league with a captor—a rare occasion indeed!

"Do you not know who I am?" the soldier asked.

The second matron pulled her companion aside, but not far enough to keep Maynya from overhearing her harsh whisper. "He's Quintus Laskaris, the king's brother."

The king's brother! Maynya almost laughed at the cruel game. One man had set her on a path to role-play her own crucifixion. Now his brother came to her aide, no doubt with the design to further her humiliation. She spat at the man's feet and tried to shrug his hand from her arm. "Leave me be."

Even if she were wrong, if the soldier acted with noble intentions, she had no need for a hero. She could have used her gift for illusion to escape from Virtus at any time from the moment she'd taken the pregnant woman's place in the cage a year earlier.

These brides needed her as their champion! A true guardian could find no nobler role. She'd been flogged, beaten, bound in the stocks without food and water for as many as two days at a time. She could certainly survive this latest trial without assistance from a soldier with lust in his eyes.

"Let me carry the cross for you," he said.

"Do you see those brides?" she retorted. "You'll be too busy pillaging to make the same offer when the next woman's turn comes. My sisters will never find the strength to carry a cross if I don't do this for them." Maynya struggled from her knees and resumed her trek.

The persistent fool came after her. "Drink from this then, and I'll hire a soldier to offer water to each bride who follows your footsteps up this hill until I convince the king to stop this awful show."

She would have spat at him again, but the pitcher he offered was so familiar as to flutter her heart. She knew the moon-and-star pattern painted around its girth. Another bride had sculpted this very clay! The woman, Adala, later paid the price of her own virginity to quench Maynya's thirst during a dark hour. In return, Maynya taught Adala a water-to-wine illusion and eventually helped the young woman escape the bridal pool. "How do you have this?" she asked.

The man regarded Maynya with such remorse in his eyes a tingle of dread swept down her spine. She struggled to find her voice. "Please tell me Adala isn't—"

"I should have been there to protect her." He scuffed the dirt with his boot.

At that moment, she understood how anyone might turn cruel if provoked enough. She held pure malice in her heart for this barbarian. "Did you love her?"

"We barely knew each other. I'd already fallen in love with the sketch of a woman I can never have."

"Then find someone you *can* have." Maynya moved on without drinking. She couldn't have swallowed for the lump in her throat.

*And in Chicago...*

After bidding good-bye to Kara and Igor, Brewster headed to a bank across from the restaurant and withdrew as much cash as the ATM machine would allow. He pocketed a paltry five hundred bucks and tried not to dwell on the futility of living off the grid. He couldn't use any more plastic or he'd get tracked down. Maybe a buddy would let him sleep on the couch for a day or two when the cash ran out. After that he'd be out of luck.

The wormholes sweeping him into this impossible situation simply had to whisk him out. And fast. He didn't possess enough street smarts to evade the law and live underground. The transition from business executive to a homeless man reliant on someone's uncle Henry, on dream walking, and on a hard reboot of history had him dragging his heels, hoping for divine intervention.

He headed down the sidewalk into an older part of town, following a street lined with pawn shops, tattoo parlors, saloons, and numerous boarded-up storefronts. But he couldn't find the Greyhound station. He thought he'd seen one in the general vicinity during better days, but who pays attention to such a thing when speeding through a bad neighborhood on the way to a cool party? Maybe the station had closed...another worry not to dwell on.

Construction sawhorses blocked the direct route, forcing him to wander down streets gone even seedier. He stepped around broken glass and the occasional vagrant sleeping off a bender—each one giving him a shuddering glimpse of his own possible future—until coming upon another dead end. More sawhorses stood in his way as part of some massive construction project zigzagging through the stretch of broken-down territory he needed to travel.

Maybe they were building a big bus station. He'd gone crazy enough to laugh.

He caught two thugs eyeing him from a doorstep across the street. The men swapped a paper bag of booze back and forth, the loud beat of hip-hop music pumping the world full of anger as they plotted his murder. Not the best guys to be bothering with a request for directions. Nor were the arguing couple whose shouted curses and crashing bottles wafted out the open window of a tenement building not yet demolished by the construction project. Brewster turned back, hurried around a corner, and took his chances with a different forbidding street. He avoided eye contact with anyone unsavory—virtually every person he came across—until finally breathing a sigh of relief when he stumbled onto a thoroughfare far too busy for any mugger to stalk in broad daylight.

A young woman with spiky purple hair emerged from the shadows of an alley and clattered up to him on four-inch heels. Her short, tight skirt and translucent blouse betrayed an age-old profession even before she opened her mouth to ask the trademark question. "Want a date?"

He never failed to marvel over the irony of a modern world still caught up in a bad bargain dating back to biblical times. Thousands of years of evolution hadn't taught his kind a simple truth. Sex without emotion leaves a man hollow. Fall in love, get married, *then* melt into each other. Not before.

"I'm just looking for the Greyhound station," he said.

The hooker shook her head. "You shouldn't wander on foot in bad neighborhoods. There aren't enough of us to keep an eye on you."

The incongruous motherly advice rendered Brewster speechless for a moment, but she winked and smiled, no doubt having merely taken a weak stab at a joke. He unclenched his fists.

"The bus station is around the corner." She pointed it out and, in doing so, revealed a butterfly tattoo on her forearm identical to the one Heather sported on her neck.

Brewster no longer trusted coincidences as random events. Again he found himself at a loss for words.

"Come on. I can see you want some." This hooker definitely had the moxie for her trade, but something about her seemed off. She'd dressed the part, even going overboard with the makeup—chapter one in the hookers' handbook—but she hadn't been able to hide the deep intelligence in her eyes.

"No, I'm just... Let me ask you something. What's the story behind that butterfly?"

"This?" She traced a red-nailed finger across the black-and-gold body of her symbol. "Rebirth. Resurrection."

"So, it's like a newborn Christian thing?"

"Uh-uh. I'm strictly old school."

A car pulled to the curb and honked. The hooker sauntered over to chat up the driver, pausing just a moment to glance over her shoulder at Brewster. "Be careful which way you go. The roads have gotten twisty lately."

"Wait!" That purple-haired woman was no hooker. He needed to buy her a coffee and trade notes about wormholes, but the unexpected puzzle piece in a world holding precious few had already gotten into the man's car and sped away.

Brewster had no choice but to resume his original plan. He found the Greyhound station and caught a bus to Kenosha.

*A few hours later*

Kara's napkin map proved right on target. After getting off the bus, Brewster walked three miles to the X, Sacred Heart Cemetery, and found Sarah's grave in a neglected section where hundred-year-old trees shaded a weedy stretch of forgotten plots. The weathered marker was the only one decorated with a wreath. Someone had also left a dazzling bouquet of blue roses.

He bent to examine the stone's faded inscription—*A rose always blooms for my beloved Sarah*—and the date—*1676 to 1756.* He swallowed. Henry Stoddard's wife had been dead for over three hundred years?

Brewster dropped to the stone and closed his eyes. They were useless, anyway. He couldn't trust what they saw anymore.

# Chapter Twenty-Nine

*Meanwhile, in Virtus's capital*

ANOTHER STRANGE DREAM SHATTERED into shards, leaving Quintus groping for his own name.

He'd been visiting the impossible world in his sleep for as long as he could remember, a land of amazing machines, fantastic weapons, and dazzling women. Each time, he experienced the journey through the eyes of a man named Brewster. He usually awoke without emotion, but this latest turn in the story had him sweating. A wonderful woman had gone missing, presumably dead. Now, not only Brewster, he— *Quintus!*—ached with longing. Imaginary or not, this Carla had found a way to pounce out of his sleep-addled head and seize his soul.

He'd fallen for someone in a dream, a dream, nothing more than a dream. He'd fallen for... His heartbeat quickened. He shook the cobwebs and realized he'd come across the spitting image of this woman in the waking world. She was the slave Adala had sketched! And earlier today before his nap, he'd met this defiant woman dragging her cross up a hill.

Were Maynya and Carla the same—one the body and the other the soul? He rolled over and groped through the rift between reality and fantasy. On one side, daylight streaming in from a window tried to tickle his eyes open. And on the other? The dream hovered just beyond his desperate reach.

"Quintus?"

"Halt!" He shot a hand to the knife sheathed in the leather belt at his waist but came to his senses before lashing out with it. By all the gods, had he been at the front so long the voice of a harmless maidservant would stop his heart? Even worse, Teasha had stolen in on him, and he hadn't been aware of her presence until she'd spoken his name—not a good sign for a soldier who prized his life.

Too much dreaming threatened to get him killed. He blinked the last wisps of Carla's image from the backs of his eyes, leaned with an elbow on his cot, and gazed up at neither a doomed woman from an imagined world nor the real-life forced bride who refused his pitcher of water.

Teasha beamed at him. She was easy on the eyes, a shapely brunette with a flair for fashion, to the extent possible for a slave. In this case, she wore a captivating turquoise dress—he wondered whether someone's curtain had disappeared in the dead of night—and an improvised necklace made of dried flowers. Best of all, her personality matched her looks—quirky, carefree, and full of good humor. She'd shown a quick wit when he flirted with her earlier.

Why not defeat his sour mood by teasing her again? "You've changed your mind, dove? Come to lay with me?"

Her smile evaporated. She swept her arm toward the window of his bungalow and the palace beyond. "I see through this façade of yours, Quintus. Unlike those others, you respect a woman's virtue."

He threw his blanket aside and shifted off the cot, but she blushed at his near nakedness. He slipped behind a changing screen. "In this kingdom, the man who respects virtue is labeled either fool or traitor." He grabbed his trousers from a chair.

"Then your brother sent for a fool."

"Ah, him."

"Albus will see you now."

He reached for his shirt. "Let him wait. We're on the subject of virtuous men and women."

"Idle chat about rare creatures is more important to you than the wishes of your king?"

"Idle chat about *one* of them is." He stepped from behind the screen. "I came upon a raven-haired slave lugging a cross up a hill this morning. Whom did I see?"

Teasha crossed her arms. "Even the fool who respects virtue has the wandering gaze, does he?"

"A beauty as proud as this one would catch any man's eye." He went to his dressing table, unlocked the drawer, and considered which weapons to choose. The knife at his belt was too puny an arsenal. He pulled out a pistol to holster beside it and a second knife to hide against his calf. As he bent to sheath it, Teasha's skeptical gaze bore into the back of his neck. This slave had to be part Mystic, able to read a man's true motives no matter which words he utters. "You think I should bring more?"

"We slaves are told not to think."

He couldn't help but chuckle at her wit. "What would you say about a man who fell for a woman before they'd ever met, just by chancing upon a sketch of her face?"

"We're not supposed to speak much, either."

"Now this woman is troubling my dreams."

A mischievous gleam intensified the sparkle in Teasha's eyes. "Maynya troubles every soldier's dreams. This is why we find hope in her."

"Hope?"

She motioned her hands to signify flight…escape.

Quintus gasped. "Have you gone soft? Trust no one with such treasonous ideas. Not even me." He headed toward the door but paused to glance over his shoulder at the pretty fool. "And this Maynya was carrying a cross because…?"

"Albus will marry her this very day."

The news buckled his legs. He settled back onto the cot and waited for his racing heart to slow.

His brother had summoned him to a wedding, and Maynya had been carrying out a macabre wedding ritual on the hill. He should have put two and two together. But why did the woman's bonding with Albus stab into his heart? Adala's death must have unhinged him. He couldn't imagine a more ridiculous fit of infatuation than the one he now suffered.

Teasha set a hand on his shoulder. "Is something wrong, Quintus?"

"I wouldn't know where to begin." He brushed past her.

Quintus shaded his eyes and hurried past the ripe odor of livestock in a nearby pen. The afternoon had grown chillier despite a bright sun. The notion of returning for his cloak and another whiff of Teasha's lemony perfume almost tempted him back to the bungalow.

He wrapped his arms around himself and continued across a vacant marching ground separating the last dwelling at the edge of town from the palace, a ridiculously presumptuous name for the makeshift wooden building housing the royal chambers.

Albus and his bands of thieves—no better term for the marauders—had been cutting through tribe after tribe, taking their land, raping their women, and stealing houses, roads, monuments. They'd never found the skill to build anything of substance on their own. The most impressive structure in the area, a foundry he'd noticed when Maynya struggled up the hill, had been constructed by the latest fallen ones, a hardy tribe of laborers who now stoked its fires night and day as slaves.

Quintus, too, had often led bands of soldiers who might have been likened to marauders by the innocents who strayed across their path. Yet he saw a critical difference. His men faced a greater power, an army bent on pushing the natives of Virtus east to the sea—a tribe boasting frightening inventions, such as the fierce metal beast, the *locomotive*, he'd seen at the western border. Quintus and his men served as defenders, not invaders.

Even on those rare occasions when they managed to seize a territory instead of surrendering another slice of their own—Virtus crawled like a snake, shrinking in the west as it expanded to the east—they allowed the defeated men some measure of freedom, and they left the women unharmed. He'd kill the soldier who so much as thought about touching a woman against her will. Just ask Gaius, the bastard who took Adala's life.

The reminder stirred more ice into the wind. Quintus hurried to the door of the palace.

He nodded to three soldiers standing checkpoint, but he surrendered only his visible weapons. The fools didn't frisk him. Then he strode across a great room crowded with scoundrels, rakes, and whores, the profiteers of war. Many sat drinking at a long table, echoing randy songs and raucous laughter off the walls. Others made merry at a piano, while a few had already begun unlacing maidens' bodices in the hall's shadowy corners. Any excuse for an orgy. In this case, the inexplicable wedding of a king and a slave.

He slowed to endure one more inept soldier's careless search before passing through a door to the next chamber, a quieter one, a war room where maps had been tacked to the walls and spread across a large table in the center. At the far end of that table, he found Albus on a high throne, puffing his chest. The normally slovenly man had dressed like a dandy this day, his dark hair wrapped into a diamond-speckled braid, a purple, star-studded robe thrown over his shoulders, a jeweled crown set upon his thick head, and gold chains cascading from his neck.

The maidservant attending Albus seemed as young as Teasha, nineteen at best, but far less innocent. She'd painted her lips, shaded her eyes, and unlaced much of her bodice. She swayed her hips when she started forward to greet him.

The king waved her off.

She scurried out the door with barely concealed excitement, no doubt eager to dive into the debauchery on the other side, body and soul.

Alone now but for a soldier at the door, the two men stared each other down. Three years had passed since Quintus had last seen his brother, but he had no interest in exchanging niceties. "You've pulled me from the front so I might serve as a guest in a sham of a wedding?"

"Best man, Quintus, best man!" Albus leapt off the throne and rushed over to embrace him. "It's so good to see you!"

Quintus endured his brother's liquored breath.

After the hug, they stepped back and gazed at each other in silence. Words had never passed easily from one to the other. Quintus noticed hints of his brother's earlier physical charms— an ever-youthful face, dark, curly hair, eyes capable of melting a princess—but the steady creep of sloth had already compromised the man's handsomeness with an extra chin and too large a gut.

Albus was the first to turn away. He shook a fist at the soldier standing guard. "Get out! Can two brothers not share a moment alone?"

The guard hastened out of the room and shut the door behind him.

"You need better help," Quintus said. "These soldiers don't have your back."

Albus clapped a hand on his shoulder. "I have my own back, plus a brother at my side now, and the grandest of plans." He lowered his voice and for good reason. Walls within the shifty kingdom had many ears. "I'm defeating Maynya in this *sham of a wedding*."

Another pang troubled Quintus, thickening his throat to the point he almost couldn't speak. Though no less irrational, his emotions were becoming harder to shake off. "You're defeating a *wench*? A simple slave?"

His brother scowled. He started pacing the floor with hands clasped behind him. "A simple slave? Why, yes, she was captured and thrown into the marriage pool a year ago. I suppose, by that definition, she's a *simple slave*." He raised a hammy fist and spread two fingers. "Twice Nigellus sold her, and twice he had to take her back the next morning, paying full refund each time!"

Quintus had trouble suppressing a smile at the news the bride master had gotten the worst of a transaction. Nigellus had long been renowned as a cheat and a poacher, but Albus blindly trusted him despite the carnage he'd caused. Along what should have been a peaceful northern front, several Mystic raids had been triggered as retaliation for this man's thefts of women, leading to death and destruction on both sides of the truce line.

Albus waved his arms. "We promise satisfaction or money returned. This woman gave no satisfaction, only the scratches of a lioness and bite marks…not to mention the nightmares. One of her unfortunate husbands hanged himself two days after he brought her back."

The reference to nightmares gave Quintus pause. The unpleasant dream Teasha interrupted had been another in a long line, some good, some bad, and most occurring well before he ever saw the sketch of Maynya or met her in the flesh. She hadn't cast the evil eye on him to disturb an afternoon nap. They had a history.

"Thirteen escapes!" Albus railed. "Each time, *this simple slave* was rumored to be the planner, the ringleader, the instigator, *the witch behind the schemes!* We put her in the stocks, we flogged her in the square, we beat her to within an inch of her life, and now the peasants are riled up. They complain we're abusing their saint!"

Quintus's heart drummed with pride, not so much for Maynya's actions but the fierce determination he'd seen in her eyes, despite the tortures she'd endured. What had she done to him? She'd steered him like a siren into a shipwreck of emotions.

Albus grabbed a vase of flowers and threw it against the wall. "I wanted to burn her alive. We should have nailed her to a cross and lit a bonfire!"

Quintus's heart pounded harder. "I saw her dragging a cross up a hill."

"I'm toying with her! Phineas advised against anything worse."

"Phineas?"

Albus had another vase in his hands. He stopped short and turned. The rage in his features eased. "You've been gone too long, brother. Phineas serves as my head of state now."

The appointment would have served as a slap in the face if Quintus cared. Phineas was no more than a common raider, one of a dozen thieves who stole brides from Sanctimonia when they weren't too busy scheming to steal from the palace coffers.

For centuries, fractious tribal states scattered across this vast continent shared a single trait. They embraced command structures based on bloodline. Quintus was the second son. He should have been appointed head of state, his brother's right-hand man, the moment their father died three years earlier. But Albus had chosen to leave the position vacant until what, he found the least suitable man?

No matter. Quintus's second greatest desire—after this perplexing Maynya/Carla infatuation—was to steer clear of this madhouse of a palace and get back to the army at the earliest possible moment.

"Maynya has a following," Albus said. "Our foolish peasants worship the ground she walks on, and Phineas says the death of a martyr might incite their revolt."

"He provides good counsel then. Look what happened in Barcavia a decade ago."

Albus arched his brows. "Ah, but I have a plan. Shall I tell you the story of the magnanimous king?"

The ugly gleam in the man's eye sent a chill down the back of Quintus's neck. "Save your stories for Phineas."

"Oh, but you must hear this one! The king became smitten with a saintly slave, married her, and shared his kingdom. Then one day, the poor bastard suffered a grievous loss. His lovely wife died in childbirth."

Quintus tried to control the twitch in the hand closest to the knife at his calf.

"Do you know what the unwashed masses did? They worshipped the widowed king like a god, rewarding him with devotion for making their beloved queen's final days such happy ones." Albus dropped the vase he'd been holding, scattering fragments across the slate floor in a hundred directions. "Beautiful things break so easily."

Quintus's keen awareness of his knife intensified. The temptation to end this man, Abel rising up against Cain, nearly overwhelmed him.

To hell with the masses. How had a mysterious woman managed to clutch *his* heart with so strong a grip he'd kill his own brother to save her? The western front would have to wait until he discovered the answer. "Allow me to stay a fortnight or two, Albus. I'd enjoy watching this fairy tale of yours play out."

Albus elbowed him. "I knew you had a hint of mischief inside of you. We are brothers after all."

"So they say."

"From the moment I first heard about this proud filly, I've wanted to break her in my bed. You can have a go at her, too, if you like."

The bubbling blood in Quintus's veins drowned the simple moral code he'd followed all his life. He'd never lied, stolen, cheated, or plundered. He'd never committed murder. Not until now.

He bent for his knife, but two soldiers burst into the room before he could whip it out of its sheath and plunge the cold blade into his brother's heart.

"The ceremony is beginning," said one.

"You're needed at the tent, sire," said the other.

Albus grinned. "I've prepared a sacrifice to make this occasion all the more auspicious, brother. We recaptured one of the women Maynya set free."

# Chapter Thirty

*Waiting for her groom*

**DUSTY WIND FLUTTERED THE** upper folds of the wedding tent like a billowing sail. Maynya looked beyond toward the foundry's plume of smoke. The breeze blew it straight north toward the forest. She closed her eyes, imagining the ability to spread wings and soar to the highest branches.

But she landed where she'd been standing, flanked on either side by two matrons. Each had a firm grip on one of her arms.

Maynya gritted her teeth and accepted her role yet again. She could never leave the brides abandoned without a champion. She scoured all fantasies of flight from her mind and focused on her immediate goals. Get through this ceremony. Play the gracious bride to the masses. Find some way to avoid sex with her horrid husband without getting herself beaten to death in retribution.

Her pudgy fiancé, warlord of a pitiful state, stood flanked by his soldiers at the tent's opening. He stared at her with brooding eyes. No hint of warmth, even on their wedding day.

She flinched.

The king broke eye contact and went inside. Guests followed him in, few of whom she recognized. Slaves didn't mingle with royalty. After the wedding she might come to know some of these people, but she doubted for very long. She had no delusions about the length of her remaining life.

She shifted her attention to a soldier lingering outside the tent flap. Unlike her despicable groom, this man held kindness in his eyes. They'd met ever so briefly when he came to her aide with a pitcher of water during her trial up the hill.

She'd rejected him. Had she made a mistake? Her temples pounded.

Something about this man summoned the faintest whisper of a memory, from another life, perhaps, one most certainly brighter than this one, but...ending in darkness? Yes, that was the sense his return gaze inspired, and then something else, recognition so overpowering her legs trembled to the point of collapse. She loved this man. He'd provided shelter at his home, frolicked with her in the snow, and told his life story in the quiet of his bedroom.

What was his name? Surely he'd find a way to stop this wedding.

Oh Lord, what was the man's name?

Hers came to mind, instead. "I am Carla!"

The soldier's face became a mask of confusion.

A blow to her face came hard and swift. "You speak in tongues now, you fool?" The maiden on her left, a dark-haired, middle-aged woman glared at her the way a mother might scold a wayward child. "You Mystic witches bring your own troubles down on your heads with your foolhardiness."

Maynya saw stars. Her cheekbone throbbed. "I am not a witch." And she said so in the correct language this time. *"Ego sum non a veneficus."* What dialect did she babble before? What came over her?

"Woe betide any witches in *this* kingdom," the matron said.

Two of the bridal pool women began crying. Maynya met their eyes and tried to smile reassurance. The effort might have failed. Elsewhere, angry peasants muttered behind their hands. She avoided their gazes so as not to encourage a rebellion, one the capital's heavily armed soldiers would surely put down in an instant. Finally, she settled her attention on the gentry, not one of whom seemed bothered that the king's bride had been slapped hard enough to bring tears. These wealthy women despised her, and the men no doubt wished they had fresh brides of their own to beat.

She scanned the crowd for the soldier again. Couldn't find him. He must have gone into the tent with the others.

Maynya's disorientation intensified. The sun seemed to pale. The ground wobbled beneath her feet.

Another man caught her attention. Deeply tanned, dark-haired, and handsome, he stood taller than any in the gathering. She tried to gauge his age, at first thought him young, but recalculated upon studying his eyes. This man was well advanced in years despite his vigor. She had trouble unlocking her gaze from his until he did it for her by ducking into the tent.

A flutist began a wedding ballad, and the matrons led Maynya inside. One of them released her arm, freeing her to slip a hand into a slit pocket of her gown. She touched a few possessions she'd brought for luck—a goose feather, a tiny doll whittled from wood, and a quatrant—the two-faced coin serving as currency in Virtus.

Guests crowded on either side of the aisle, a mishmash of indistinguishable faces, too many in such a small space, sucking the air out of it. She struggled to breathe, her temples pulsed, and a gust of wind pounded against the tent as if in response. She tried to focus on the groom waiting twenty paces ahead, but her blood ran cold at the sight of the bound sacrifice on the altar behind him. Not the traditional pig or goat. No, far worse than that. A young, red-haired woman in a white shift twisted against her bindings. A gag muffled her cries.

"Abelia!" Her stomach lurched. She'd helped this poor girl escape two days earlier. Maynya shot desperate glances around the tent. Surely someone would put a stop to this. Then she saw the soldier who teased her memory outside, the man named...
*"Brewster!"*

The soldier froze. He stared at her with as perplexed a gaze as anyone could summon—the same tortured confusion she must have reflected back to him from her own eyes.

A blow came hard across her face again. "Be still, woman, and thank the gods you aren't the one on the altar."

The matron's tone threatened greater violence. She wielded a bamboo cane in her free hand.

The soldier clenched his fists and stepped forward, clearly ready to do battle with matrons large and small. But another cry from Abelia distracted his attention to the king, Maynya's groom, who stood several feet to his left. The glare he cast in Albus's direction seemed capable of destroying the man on the spot.

She could only hope.

The king pulled a long, curved dagger from a scabbard at his waist and approached the bound victim. Maynya opened her mouth to shout again, but the cry caught in her throat when she noticed the soldier gripping a knife in his hand as well. He took a step toward Albus with murder in his eyes.

None of the onlookers made a move to stop him. Perhaps they thought the soldier and the king acted in league, planning to kill Abelia together. But Maynya knew better. This soldier was a good man.

The matrons dragged Maynya forward. She dug her feet into the ground and struggled to stay rooted to the spot, her temples pulsing and heart pounding in sync with the flute. The king's dark-haired, forever frowning sister glared at her. *Orelea.* A sadistic woman who'd earned the name Lady Sting among those slaves who'd gotten in the way of her whip.

Maynya looked away, only to fall under the spell of a tall stranger's eyes, the vigorous older man she'd noticed outside the tent. He nodded.

As the wind gusted stronger against the tent, a surge of strength boiled up inside of her, stoked by a fire blasting from her very soul.

At the altar, the king raised his arm to plunge his knife into the heart of the purest woman she'd ever met.

The soldier closed in on him from behind, his own arm raised.

But he stopped and gaped at an impossible transformation.

Maynya shuddered. She couldn't have caused what just happened, could she?

During a few eye-blinks of time, feeling like an hour but perhaps lasting no more than a second, Albus had turned to stone, inch by whitening inch. First his head, then an arm, then the other. His torso, his legs.

A powerful gust ripped the canvas overhead, dislodging a timber and sending it swinging down in an arc toward a man turned into a statue. But not stone after all. The pillar of *salt* that had once been King Albus exploded into a cloud of white dust as the heavy wooden beam struck it down.

Shouts and screams rose throughout the tent.

"By all the gods!"

"This is sorcery!"

Pandemonium took hold. The torn canvas flapped wildly, women shrieked, men yelled. Then the wind stilled as suddenly as it had erupted.

"Maynya's a witch!" Orelea's shriek rang across the broken tent. "She killed Albus with her black magic!"

"No, I—" The hollow echo of Maynya's voice cut off her words mid-sentence. Everything had stopped. The people stood frozen, their faces locked into expressions of fear, anger, panic. Stone-cold silence hung in the air.

She wrestled her arms away from the no-longer-clenching hands of the matrons. She swung around. Those behind her stood as motionless as those in front. What had happened? A scream welled inside of her and blasted its way out, echoing across the stillness of the broken tent.

Sudden motion silenced her, the tall stranger in action. He navigated around frozen guests and rushed toward the altar, glancing over his shoulder to shout at her. "Get out! Run while my spell lasts."

She hurried after him. "Is she... Will she be..."

The man bent to the task of sawing Abelia's bindings open with a knife. "Is this woman someone to you?"

"Yes."

"She fainted. I'm sure she'll be fine." He hefted the slave over his broad shoulder. "You're Maynya, yes?"

She nodded.

The stranger thrust something into her hands. "An angel named Gabriella has you fixed in her sights. Best stay clear of her."

"Why? My people worship the ground she walks on."

"She's a schemer."

Maynya's temples had stopped throbbing, but her ears rang. She ignored the crumpled papers he'd given her and motioned to the soldier, the man one who'd somehow stirred her heart but now stood frozen with the others, his knife poised for the kill, his eyes staring at the fallen king with icy contempt. "I need to help this man!"

"Run, I tell you!" The stranger turned away and carried the girl toward a torn-open side of the tent with great strides.

"Wait! Help me free the brides."

"What? You heard the woman. These people will tear you limb from limb when my spell ends."

"But you have the power to stop them. You turned the king to salt!"

The man swung toward the small pile of white salt near the altar. Most had scattered in the wind. "Don't play games with me. I've never seen the devil's power glow so fiercely in anyone's eyes as I did in yours when all hell broke loose."

"No, I'm not a... I didn't—"

He stepped out of the tent.

"At least tell me your name."

He slowed again but kept his back to her. "Henry Stoddard."

"Be kind to Abelia, Henry Stoddard. She's a saint."

"All of you women are, except when you're sinners. Damsels in distress, indeed." The man loped away in the direction of Sanctimonia. "I'll rescue this one," he shouted. "You save yourself."

Despite the stranger's urgent tone, his spell showed no sign of breaking. Everyone remained frozen in the positions they'd assumed when the miracle occurred, the myriad of expressions in their faces ranging from anger to fear to wonder and even hope in the case of the bridal-pool women. Those standing closest to the fallen king had been dusted white as if by a flurry of granular snow.

Quintus stood among the others.

She prayed he wasn't dead.

# Chapter Thirty-One

*Running from a bad situation*

HENRY HURRIED THE UNCONSCIOUS woman beyond the ruins of the great tent. He didn't trust his powers of hypnosis in Gabriella's strange parallel world. Yes, almost everyone seemed to react to his spell as intended, freezing in place like statues. *Yet Maynya hadn't.*

Why?

He slowed, gasping for breath, and waited for his heart to stop pounding. How had he gotten the notion in his head an old man might play the gallant knight? He should have given the message to Maynya and taken off alone.

Once in the woods, he set the woman down and knelt beside her. "Wake up."

Her eyelids fluttered.

He shook her shoulders. "You're free. Wake up and be on your way."

The woman opened her eyes—beautiful green eyes. She clutched his arm and babbled in Latin.

Henry eased out of her grip and stood. "I'm rusty. Don't you speak English? The other one did."

The woman said something unintelligible again, tried to stand, but collapsed down to her knees. She moved the back of her hand across her forehead as if fighting a migraine. In doing so, she revealed the tattoo of a butterfly on the underside of her wrist.

"They picked an insect lover for their human sacrifice, eh?"

"Have you no sense of symbolism?" She spoke English this time.

Good. At least they could communicate. "I'm Henry."

"Abelia."

Having been abandoned by the mysterious Henry, Maynya staggered alone through a tent full of human statues. Her greatest urge was to race away, unlock the gates to the bridal pool, and set the women free. Only about a dozen of them stood frozen in the tent. Scores more might be unguarded now within their wood-fenced compound near the palace.

But Henry Stoddard had handed a fistful of papers to her before carrying Abelia out of danger, and the ink on the pages began a seductive dance, drawing her eyes to the wriggling words, pulling her with a hypnotic rhythm she couldn't fight. With no choice but to read what had been written, she sank to her knees.

> *Maynya,*
>
> *A year ago, the Mystic ruler, Sylvanus Graccus, happened upon my cabin in the woods. I made arrangements with him to leak the location of a certain witch named Maynya to his border guards. Those superstitious soldiers then revealed your whereabouts to barbarian slave traders from Virtus, in the hope these fiends would seize you, thus ridding Sanctimonia of a dangerous conjurer.*
>
> *The plan worked, as you know all too well.*
>
> *I offer no apologies for my action, nor do I ask for gratitude in return. You had reached the age of thirty, and the time to send you on your ministry had come. You are the messiah for my fallen people, thanks to the death of your sister, Carla.*

What? Maynya's hands trembled so badly she could scarcely read more of Gabriella's scrawl. In a brief fit of insanity a few minutes earlier, she'd imagined herself to be this Carla, even to the point of speaking in a strange tongue. Yet how could she trust the words of Gabriella, someone who had just admitted a terrible betrayal?

She cast the pages aside, or tried to, but they clung to her fingers like a spider's silky threads to a fly. The written words wriggled again, demanding to be read.

*Carla was your other half in a different world. When she passed, your gift for casting illusions was born. You've thrived since then if I can believe half the stories. But word has recently reached my lonely cabin of a plot against you by the warlord who rules your terrible new home. A soldier named Quintus Laskaris can protect you from danger, I think.*

*Yes, Maynya, the warlord's brother. He has a psychic connection with a man who loved Carla very deeply. I brought those two together, but that's another story.*

*Find Quintus. He may be the key to greater power.*

Maynya's head swam. She'd never desired power. But this soldier, Quintus, stirred knee-buckling emotions of love, loss, and longing in her soul. If he could somehow also conjure more Carla moments, like the one she'd had earlier...

The papers heated, nearly burning her hands.

*But whether you find this man or not, I need to share a message from God I almost overlooked. Twenty-eight years ago, during a shared precognitive dream with Carla's mother, I hurried down a stairway after the man possibly responsible for Carla's death. In my haste, I rushed past these words pasted on the wall: Exodus, return engagement, October 4.*

*I closed my eyes a month ago, and God brought the dream to me again. Do you know what I missed the first time?*

*Perhaps you're familiar with the Bible. I've taught it from my cabin for many years. Exodus 10:4. "If you refuse to let them go, I will bring locusts into your country tomorrow."*

*I have no use for locusts. God's message must be meant for you. Do with it what you can.*

*Yours,*

*Gabriella*

Locusts? Maynya shoved the useless note into her pocket and gazed up at the statue who'd been Quintus, still frozen and perhaps dead along with all of the others in the tent. *Dead.* Her stomach churned. Maybe if she touched Quintus, or kissed him? No. Mystic fairy tales wouldn't save the day.

Someone's hand gripped her forearm from behind. "You'll burn at the stake for what you've done!"

Maynya gasped. She tried to twist away from the king's sister, Orelea, a woman no longer frozen.

Henry found himself squeezing Abelia's hand as they trudged through the woods together. He pulled his away. By all that was holy, he wouldn't fall for this wisp of a woman, no matter how achingly pretty and red-haired she happened to be. He needed to find his way back to Gabriella's cabin and, hopefully, the portal of smoke. This funhouse mirror of a duplicate world made his skin crawl. "Tell me again how Maynya knew English."

"She channeled subconscious memories from the other half of her soul."

He swept a low-hanging branch from their path. "And how do *you* know English?"

Abelia's intoxicating green eyes glittered with the hint of mischief. "I never told you, and you won't like the answer when I do."

"Try me."

"I picked the language out of your head."

He stopped walking. "So, you're just another fallen angel."

She shifted her hands to her hips and stared him down, the picture of innocence—bare feet, peasant dress, freckled cheeks. Abelia didn't have any of the ageless guile he'd so often seen in Gabriella's eyes. Perhaps he'd misjudged her.

"You did misjudge me," she said.

"Are you rooting around in my head again?"

She kicked dirt at him. "I'll root where I want, you old fool. You insulted me! Fallen angel, my ass!"

Henry doubled over with laughter. This Abelia had moxie.

Abelia stormed past him, swatting branches out of her way with such fury a few caught fire.

"Wait up!" He hurried after her, choking back a guffaw. "And stop burning things!"

"Apologize to me."

Fallen or not, these angels were a greater trial than he could bear.

"You're only digging a deeper grave for yourself," she said.

A broken branch near his feet burst into flames. He cursed and stamped it out. "If I apologize, will you spare this forest?"

"Apologies should be unconditional," she said.

"I'm sorry. You're not fallen. You're just a regular angel who happened to get herself into a jam. If Maynya hadn't turned that man to salt, he would have—"

Abelia burst into tears.

Oh, not this. Why did angels have to be so damned sensitive? He came up beside her, hesitated, then gave in, draping an arm across her shoulders.

"I did it," she said between sobs.

"You did what?"

"I transformed the king into a pillar of salt!"

"I think he deserved it, Abelia."

She sniffled and looked at him with tears running down her cheeks. "We're supposed to observe, protect, and love. I turned a man to salt!"

He shrugged.

"What would God say, Henry?"

"Good job?"

She broke into a moist-eyed smile. "You're just trying to cheer me up."

"You acted in self-defense."

"No, I didn't. I'm invulnerable."

Henry guffawed. "Not from where I'm standing. You were out cold for half an hour."

"You try turning a man to salt. Then tell me whether that doesn't sap every ounce of energy you have."

He took her hand. "So why do it?"

She sniffled. "Are you trying to start me crying again?"

"It doesn't make sense is all."

"I needed to protect the soldier."

"And if he hadn't gone after the king?"

"I would have pretended to die when the king stabbed me."

Henry had trouble following the logic but hesitated to question her motives further for fear her story would become all the more muddled. Unfallen or not, this red-haired beauty of an angel seemed as great a schemer as Gabriella. "Abelia, who exactly do you angels observe, protect, and love?"

"Chosen ones."

"Such as Maynya?"

"Not only her. The soldier, too."

"But we left them behind."

She gave his hand a gentle squeeze. "God spoke to me."

Right. He'd heard *that one* before. Still, he couldn't stifle his curiosity over what yarn Abelia might try spinning next. "What did He say?"

"Go with Henry."

"Excellent. We old men are always on the hunt for groupies."

Abelia snatched her hand away. "He didn't tell me what a trial you'd be."

They approached a break in the woods. The cabin came into view through thinning trees. He breathed a sigh of relief when he saw the portal of smoke still waiting beside it. "Do you know of this Gabriella?" he asked.

"I do."

"Then tell me. Who is *she* observing, protecting, and loving?"

"No one," Abelia said.

"Because?"

"Where did you get the notion she's an angel?"

He'd gotten the idea from Gabriella. Good Lord, how gullible had he been to believe anything that schemer might say? "What is she then?"

"The multitude."

"The what?"

"It's complicated."

# Chapter Thirty-Two

*Back at the gravesite in Kenosha*

**FALLING.**

Falling.

Brewster came to a sudden stop. He gasped for breath, risked opening his eyes, saw the steep drop beneath him, and clamped them shut. He couldn't be floating in the air.

"Actually, you are," a woman said from below.

"Stay out of other people's heads, Abelia," her male companion muttered.

He reopened his eyes to the same harsh reality, hovering facedown, some twenty feet above Sarah's grave.

"Closer to thirty," the woman said.

"You can't stop yourself, can you, Abelia?" the man retorted.

Damn. He should have taken Kara seriously when she warned him about her curmudgeon of an "uncle." The man glaring up at him had to be Henry Stoddard, a tall, dark-haired, brooding sort, unassuming in appearance but for the jagged lightning bolt crackling upward from his outstretched arm.

"Let him down." The barefoot red-haired beauty tugged on Henry's sleeve.

Brewster thanked his lucky stars the lunatic had brought this Abelia woman along.

Stoddard shrugged her off. "Why were you sleeping on my wife's grave?"

"I zoned out." After the homicide cops' bombshell about Carla, followed by the police tail, the bank takeover at work, and random women popping up everywhere with butterfly tattoos, the eighteenth-century dates on Sarah's gravestone must have finished the job, shorting the circuits in his befuddled mind. He remembered getting woozy. Maybe he'd fainted.

"Tell Henry the safe word," Abelia said.

"Huh?" Brewster could barely remember his own name, let alone some safe word. A sparrow chirped overhead. He waved off its attempt to light on his head.

Abelia's gentle voice tickled the back of his mind. *"Vagrant."*

First levitation, then telepathy. If Igor Tesfaye's girlfriend had told him half what to expect from this lunatic and his pals, he would have steered clear of Kenosha and taken his chances with the cops.

*"He isn't a lunatic,"* the woman whispered in his head. *"He's a blessed man with trust issues. Use the secret word."*

"Vagrant!"

The lightning bolt faded.

Brewster floated down, landing on his knees beside the grave where the dates on the marker flabbergasted him all over again. *1676-1756?* This Sarah hadn't walked the earth in over three hundred years, yet her husband was still alive and…

He scrambled to his feet and groped to introduce some sense of normalcy to yet another rip in the fabric of time. Smiling as best he could, he shook hands with Abelia, then tried to do the same with Henry, unsuccessfully. He plunged ahead with a greeting, anyway. "I'm Brewster DeLay. Kara said I might find you here."

Henry folded his arms. "Don't tell me she dumped a perfectly good poet for the likes of you."

Great. He'd definitely scored points already. "We're only friends. She said you could help me."

"If this involves Gabriella, you can be on your way."

Abelia stepped between them. "Henry, I wasn't entirely straightforward about my reasons for coming through the portal with you."

Henry gave her a long, hard look. He shook his head. "Here I thought I'd found Virtus's version of a Russian bride."

"I came as *God's* version of a messenger."

"Doesn't He believe in email?"

"Go tweet Him and ask." She turned her back on the crusty guy and took both of Brewster's hands in hers.

The world went into a slow spin. A kaleidoscope of images converged into a forest scene. The air grew damp and piney. Brewster looked down at a kneeling woman in a prairie dress and two bearded thugs holding their dicks in their hands, each dressed like a nineteenth-century frontiersman.

The woman glared at the taller one. "I'll bite it off."

The man unsheathed a sword, but Brewster barely registered the motion. With heart leaping to his throat, he gaped at... "Carla!"

"No." Abelia's gentle voice drifted to his ears from a thousand miles away. "Her name here is Maynya."

The cosmic whirlpool latched on to Brewster again, sweeping him through its spiral and depositing him into a subterranean corner of the modern-day world—windy, acrid, chillier—a subway platform. A roar rose from somewhere within the tunnel, and the tracks hummed from the vibration of an approaching train. The lead car burst into the station.

A woman lowered her head, ran forward, leaped in front of it.

He caught a glimpse of Carla's tight-lipped expression a moment before impact.

His knees went wobbly.

Once again, the wormhole snatched him away.

"Open your eyes, Brewster," Abelia said.

"No. You're killing me."

"You need to see the cause and effect."

The thick forest atmosphere closed in on him again. Although he kept his eyes shut tight, she somehow projected the images through the lids.

As one of the frontier men lifted a sword to kill Maynya, the shadowy outline of another woman swept into her from above. The two merged as one, and thousands of screeching rats raced out of the brush from all directions. The other thug shouted and ran, leaving the man with the sword to fend off the rodents alone. He fell to the ground, lost his weapon, and skittered backwards until a tree trunk prevented further retreat.

Maynya kicked him in the balls and fled.

The scene faded. Brewster staggered back, but Abelia held fast to his hands. "Carla and Maynya shared a dormant power for casting illusions. When Carla killed herself, Maynya gained the ability to harness it—in this case, bringing the rats. One woman died so the other might live."

He clenched his fists. "That's great, but I need to go back and stop Carla from jumping in front of that train."

"Because you love only her and have no feelings for the other half?"

A new series of images burst before him, carrying the vague familiarity of remembered dreams—the bodies of two murdered settlers outside their burned cabin, a confrontation with bloodthirsty monks, and a woman, Adala, producing a sketch done in chalk. Brewster's heart swelled with the identical love at first sight the soldier experienced upon glimpsing Maynya's portrait. *As if he were that soldier.*

"The two of you share the same soul," Abelia said.

"No. He's an alter ego my crazy imagination kicks up when I'm dreaming, especially lately."

"Don't deceive yourself. You know you never dream." Abelia's soft voice warmed his mind like a blanket. "You shift between realities. These memories have become more vivid recently because you share a blessed bond with Carla. Her aura has been pulling the two halves of your soul closer together."

The lighting dimmed. Brewster found himself in a wedding tent. And he knew everything that had happened as if he'd been there all along.

"You *were*, Brewster," Abelia whispered. "Or should I say Quintus?"

In a sudden burst of motion, the frozen wedding guests sprang back to life. Orelea grabbed Maynya by the arm and pressed a knife against her throat.

"Cut the witch apart!" someone shouted.

"Burn her at the stake!" cried another.

"No," Orelea hissed. "The king should decide her fate!"

All heads turned, but not to Albus. That cruel ruler had been rendered into salt.

Everyone looked to *him* for direction—the dead king's brother. Long live the king. He'd become Quintus, as he had in every Latin-speaking dream since his boyhood. Except this time, he was also Brewster—two sets of memories sharing a single head.

The back of his neck prickled. He was no leader, just a soldier born with the wrong blood in his veins. If he found the courage to say what these people didn't want to hear, they'd probably kill Maynya anyway and turn on him, as well. That thieving raider, Phineas, already had murder in his eyes. Whose direction would the other soldiers follow, the deceased king's head of state or his disenfranchised brother?

Abelia released his hands.

The world brightened. He'd returned to the cemetery.

Henry Stoddard's psychic companion had tears running down her cheeks. "If you go back and prevent Carla's death, Maynya won't be alive in that tent. She'll have died at the hands of the two barbarians a year ago, because she wouldn't have been able to conjure the illusion to scare them off. Brewster, Maynya might be the messiah the people of Sanctimonia, Virtus, and all the lands beyond need so desperately."

"Wait. Let me process this."

"You and Quintus love her!"

"What do you mean me and Quintus? We're the same guy, right?" This concept of duality was as dizzying as if she'd swept him into the wormholes again. He never dreamed? For his entire life? His self-identity went beyond businessman and writer to include somebody who mixed it up with crazed monks?

She nodded.

A shiver of dread ran down his spine. He'd shared Quintus's emotions in the tent—the man's fear and uncertainty. *His own* fear and uncertainty. Did Abelia realize the full scope of the sacrifice required to ensure success against the angry mob? "You've shown me that if a host body dies, the two half souls converge, making the survivor stronger."

A shadow of worry creased her forehead. "You shouldn't draw conclusions beyond the need to leave Carla dead."

"The premise is true, though, isn't it?"

Abelia wouldn't meet his eyes.

A half-baked notion had his hands trembling. "You want Maynya to live, but she's gonna die in that tent if Quintus doesn't rescue her. Do you really think he's strong enough?"

"He's a warrior. We have to let things play—"

Beads of sweat stung his forehead. No way could he summon the courage to kill himself, even with the absolute certainty that rather than die, he'd simply be shifting all of his awareness to a different head. But if he was with the woman he loved, doing it together with her... "Send me back to Carla."

Abelia's eyes widened. "You don't know what you're asking!"

Brewster closed his hands into clammy fists. "Yes, I do." He turned to Henry. "Did you see the visions Abelia gave me?"

Henry scowled. "She came to bring *you* a message. I'm only the fool who risked his life bringing her here."

Abelia lifted to the tips of her toes and planted a kiss on Henry's cheek. "Don't be hurt. Brewster may be the reason I came through the portal, but he isn't why I might stay."

A slow smile brought some humor to his eyes. "Another schemer."

"And you're a brute, but you rescued me rather than worrying about your own skin."

In a different time and place, Brewster might have been drawn in by the odd couple's mating dance, but how long could his burst of courage last before he dissolved into a quivering mass of jelly? "Henry, I need you to send me into the past."

Henry's smile faded. "Presuming I had such a gift, why would I use it?"

"To set things right in Virtus. Don't you see the destiny aspect here?"

"Maybe I should introduce you to my friend Gabriella. The two of you think alike."

"We've already met."

"Then take your request to her. I'll have no hand in changing history."

This guy was maddening. What could Abelia possibly see in him? "You've got it all wrong. I'll be *choosing*, not changing." Clearly events had multiple versions. The subway suicide he'd just seen conflicted with the story two witnesses told the cops about his involvement in Carla's murder. And now he had a third iteration in mind, one that had sent his pounding heart into overdrive. He directed his plea to Abelia. "This *is* all about choice, isn't it? Otherwise, why would you have shown me anything?"

She again averted her eyes. "I'm a messenger, not a sage."

"Then what's your message? I need your help, Abelia. Do the right thing."

She spread her hands and looked into the gap between them as if searching for a speck of an answer in sifting sand. "You think I know right from wrong? I've already turned a man to salt today."

Stoddard swept an arm toward the roses decorating his ancient wife's grave. "Don't worry, Abelia. If heaven casts you aside, I know an old man who might need a hand with his gardening."

"Thank you." Some life returned to her eyes. She reached a hand to Brewster's forehead.

Before she touched him, he noticed the butterfly under her wrist. "I've seen that tattoo everywhere lately."

Abelia's smile faded. "I'm part of a sisterhood. We're supposed to bring grace, but I've carried only death this day."

She settled her palm on his flesh, and the world went black.

# Chapter Thirty-Three

*Swept into 2012 Manhattan*

BREWSTER STRUGGLED AGAINST THE worst case of fog-brained jetlag he'd ever experienced. He wobbled on his feet and clutched a lamppost to keep from falling.

A wave of yellow taxis racing down the street quickened his pulse. He'd made it, right? The aroma of street-vendor hot dogs in a nearby stand sure screamed Manhattan.

A man dressed in a business suit and sneakers hurried by, nearly elbowing him into the traffic. "Watch where you're going, creep," the man said.

An icy wind clinched the deal. Early autumn had been unusually cold a year earlier. He and Carla had danced in the snow on Tug Hill.

The low rumble of a train sounded below. The station had to be nearby. He spun around. Sure enough, a stairway led down. A row of newspaper machines displayed the front pages of *The Wall Street Journal, Daily News,* and *New York Post.* They all showed the same date, October 23, 2012.

Did Romeo tremble like this before drinking the poison?

And where was Carla, down in the station or still approaching? A neon sign flashing the time and temperature from across the street didn't do any good. The cops hadn't said anything about Carla's time of death.

Or had they?

The immediate area sure seemed empty. That businessman who elbowed him had been the only person on the sidewalk. He turned to a commotion a block or two down—emergency lights, a crowd of gawkers.

Barnes, the skinny cop, had mentioned a bus accident occurring when Carla died.

Brewster leapt to his feet and hurried down the stairs.

At the first landing, he saw Carla and Gabriella floating—not walking, floating!—hand in hand on the other side of the gates. They'd started down a second stairway.

"Wait!" He ran up to a turnstile and tried climbing over the bar. "Carla!"

"Hey!" A man's voice came at him from off to the side. "Hold it right there, buddy!"

He turned to a uniformed conductor standing at a nearby cashier's booth. "I'm with that woman!"

"Pay your fare or I'll call the cops." But the man barely moved. All bark and no bite, he seemed more interested in chatting with a pretty blonde through the bars of her cage than worrying about a misdemeanor. He muttered, "Must be another dumb tourist," to the cashier in a loud enough voice to carry.

Brewster held his breath and reached into his pants pocket where his wallet should have been. Who knew whether anything he'd been carrying in the cemetery had come along for the ride through time? He found the thing, whispered thanks to Abelia, and ran to a token machine on the wall.

After three attempts to hurry a bill into a slow-motion slot, he managed to coax some tokens out of the machine. He raced back to the turnstile.

"Doing it right?" the man yelled.

A knee-buckling flash of insight nearly had him fumbling the tokens to the floor. The conductor and cashier stood as living proof the events in a Manhattan subway station on October 23, 2012, were fluid.

The homicide cops hadn't mentioned any witnesses seeing

him on the landing, only the operator of the train down below and the passenger of a second train passing through the station in the opposite direction. Certainly, anyone in the vicinity would have been interviewed. These two should have provided their accounts, *and they wouldn't have waited a year to do so—* further proof he and Carla could rewrite the script however they wanted.

He whipped through the turnstile and ran down the stairs to the platform.

The love of his life stood weeping beyond the yellow safety line with her arms wrapped around herself.

"Carla!"

"Brewster?" Tears streamed down her cheeks.

He gathered her in his arms. How much should he tell her? What did she already know?

The clamor of a train rose from deep within the tunnel.

She pushed away. "This isn't how my dream goes. You approach from behind. I never see who you are."

"Nothing's set in stone anymore."

"Oh dear God, I hope not. Gabriella told me I have to do a terrible thing."

*Gabriella?* The mere mention of her name frayed his nerves like nails grinding across a chalkboard.

The train grew louder. The tracks hummed.

Carla started to speak, sobbed, closed her eyes. When she reopened them, her expression had transformed to steely resolve. "She explained how I could only save Maynya by dying. And *I'm* Maynya. So I won't be dying at all, will I?"

The beam of the approaching train brightened the station.

"I want you to push me in front of the train, Brewster." Her voice shook.

*No.* He'd jump with her. They had the perfect opportunity to escape this world and, in doing so, save Quintus and Maynya.

A torrent of voices roared through his mind. Speaking English. Speaking Latin. His father's voice. His mother's. Quintus's. His own voice as a child. Every priest and minister he'd ever known.

They shouted snippets from all the lectures, admonitions, warnings, *and sermons* that had shaped his moral fabric.

The voices went silent. Did he imagine them? An impossible ray of sunshine flooded the dank tunnel and bathed him in its warmth before rushing away so fast it had to be imagined, as well. His ears rang. His knees shook.

What was happening? He clenched his fists. "I won't do it."

"No?" She wobbled.

Brewster grabbed her by the arm before both of them fainted onto the tracks. "You want me to push you because you'd never kill yourself. Suicide is terribly wrong and you know it. Guess what? So is murder."

Carla's lower lip trembled. She broke eye contact and looked down at her shoes. "I'm fallen."

"No, you aren't." He took her in his arms again. "You're trying to save Maynya however you can. We'll find a better way."

"This is the only way!" The girl's shout came at them from behind.

Before Brewster could react, something shoved him forward. A force against his back far more powerful than any girl could muster. He lost balance, still holding Carla, and fell to the tracks with her.

The train burst into the station.

The brakes screeched.

The world went dark.

# Chapter Thirty-Four

*Limbo—a world without time*

**ALIVE OR DEAD?**

Heaven or hell?

Brewster tried breathing.

The sweet scent of lilacs sent him soaring. He drew another breath, savored it, took in one more.

Birds chirped. The voices of a woman and child came at him.

He landed. The sensation of cold stone beneath him cracked the mood, allowing worries to creep into his brain like spiders. What had become of Carla? What happened to Maynya in the wedding tent? He opened his eyes.

A Japanese girl of perhaps twelve sat on a marble bench, and a woman he'd met, Abelia, knelt before her on the flagstone path with head bowed, as if she were the child and the girl a scolding parent.

He sat on a bench of his own, facing them and the stone wall behind them—a garden enclosure, judging by the idyllic scene of flowers and ponds visible through an unusual circular entrance.

Closer to him, the two across the path contrasted like a princess and a scullery maid—an exquisitely garbed girl lording over a red-haired penitent dressed in a simple shift. The child sat straight-backed and proud in a blue-and-white kimono. Her dark hair had been fixed in a bun to bare a delicate neck. A blue mosaic butterfly rose from the bone holding the hairdo in place.

Most likely, he was dreaming.

If so, what about Carla? And Maynya? Timelines had reached a climax on each side of a portal, waiting for him to step in and set a new course. But he failed, didn't he?

Wavy motion drew his gaze to the garden again. A fountain bubbled just beyond the wall's round opening. A willow tree waved droopy branches in the breeze. The images shimmered and blurred from the dance of butterflies—hordes of them—in the gateway.

The nearer scene proved vague, as well. A conversation between woman and child seemed loud enough to hear, and certainly close enough, yet so distant he might as well have been viewing a stage act from the last row of the highest balcony. He strained his ears to make out the words.

"What were you asked to do in Virtus?" the girl asked.

Abelia sighed, long and deep. "Bring grace to Maynya."

"But what *did* you do?"

Abelia reddened. "I turned a man to salt."

The girl caught Brewster's eye. She shook her head.

Abelia had wanted him to save Carla. And he was ready to try again. He'd return to the subway station a thousand times if that's what it took to set things right.

Brewster tried getting up but remained on the bench. His pulse raced. His mouth wouldn't open and let him speak.

The interrogation continued.

"Afterward, what were you asked to do in the cemetery?"

"Show Brewster why he shouldn't change the past."

"But what *did* you do?"

"I'm sorry, Mother." Abelia's voice trembled.

"Tell me."

"I helped Brewster change the past. Sometimes circumstances require improvisation."

"Not on my watch," the girl said.

Or Brewster's. He tried saving Carla, but she'd fallen under the wheels of a train, anyway. He couldn't have let such a thing happen.

The girl folded her arms. "Why is obedience such a challenge for you?"

Abelia sniffled. "I'll try harder next time."

"Is there anything you've done lately I'd be pleased to hear about?"

Abelia stared at the flagstone at her knees as if searching for answers in the cracks. She glanced up with a teary-eyed smile. "I learned a new language today. English!"

The girl laughed, but not with the mirth of a child. Her chuckle carried a combination of surprise and wisdom, like that of a professor who'd heard the right answer from his worst student. "Sometimes I forget how young you are." She leaned close enough to place her hands on Abelia's shoulders. "Spend some time with Henry Stoddard. Perhaps his steadfastness will rub off on you."

Abelia jerked back. "But we didn't get along! He still pines for Sarah."

"Make a pest of yourself. Sleep in his garden until he takes you in."

"I could be sleeping out there for months."

The girl made a shooing gesture with her hands. "Go."

Abelia rose and headed toward the garden gateway. The butterflies parted to let her in. She paused at the entrance. "Mother?"

"Yes?"

"You aren't clipping my wings, are you?"

"Oh no, Abelia. I'm delighted with the way things turned out." The girl flashed a smile.

Abelia beamed. "How long should I stay with him?"

"Stoddard? Give him a hundred years and we'll see how things work out. Mind you, he's grumpy. I don't want to hear about you turning him to salt when things don't go your way."

"No, Mother. I would never again—"

"Go!"

Abelia disappeared into the garden.

The girl focused her attention on Brewster, drawing him out of the balcony and into the orchestra section. He blinked, but he couldn't dissolve the fog from his brain. This girl's eyes stirred up a better buzz than a double martini. What had he been worried about moments earlier? He'd lost the thread of his thoughts.

"My name is Asura Ito," she said.

Did he have a name anymore? What if he'd died beside Carla, and this little meeting was a final reckoning? What if he'd been stripped of everything but the pain of his failure? Stripped even of his own identity?

"Who would you like to be?" she asked.

Easy answer. "Quintus."

She arched her brows. "Why?"

"So I can be with her."

"Carla? Maynya?"

"I guess they're the same, right?" He tried to sit taller. Better posture stood a chance of clearing the fuzz from his head. And maybe he could take control of what might be the most important interview of his life. *Or of his death.*

Asura straightened more, too. Checkmate. "I know all the secrets," she said. "Would you like me to share any with you?"

"Are you God?"

She grinned as wide as the Cheshire Cat. "Think of me as a varsity squad leader. In business speak, perhaps you'd call me a VP of Communications. I spin the tales."

In business speak, a VP was only halfway up the corporate ladder—like the banker who'd swooped into Crestview Finance. He slumped. Where had he landed, in a Purgatory of wannabes? "So we aren't in heaven then, huh?"

"We're neither here nor there."

"What happened to Carla?" Speaking her name brought on another fist-clenching fit.

"Gabriella triggered her rapture."

His heart thought that sounded good, but his knee started twitching. "I don't know what you mean, Asura."

"Carla and Maynya are omniscient now, thanks to Gabriella's little shove."

He drew in a breath. "So *she's* the one who pushed us onto the tracks."

"Who else?" Asura shook her head. "That poor, confused girl can be amazing at times, but she disappoints far too often. The same can be said for all of mankind, I suppose."

Philosophy lessons could come later. Metaphysics first. "I don't follow what you mean by omniscient."

Asura held out a hand. A pair of monarch butterflies left the garden entrance, fluttered over in swoops and curls, and perched on her index finger, side by side. "Carla's and Maynya's essences live in Maynya's body now, sharing two sets of thoughts and memories. The twins are now one."

"They're both happy then?"

"Rapturous."

Could he believe that? His bouncing knee needed proof. "And they're safe?"

"One of them is. You and Quintus do need to rescue Maynya, though."

He caught his breath. The knee had been right to worry.

"What else would you like me to share?" she asked.

"How will this turn out?" His last rescue attempt hadn't accomplished much. But why waste questions on cause and effect in a world with untrustworthy realities? "Never mind. The more I learn, the less I know."

"Well, *I'm* always curious." Asura headed into the garden. She came back with a red-and-blue ball in her hands. "Let's play a game while we talk."

She settled onto the bench again and bounced the ball across the path. "Why did you consider killing yourself, Brewster?"

The act of catching the ball almost distracted him from hearing her. When he did, his reaction grew from the bottom up, lurching his stomach before heading north to his mind. "Just for a second, I thought about jumping with her, but I came to my senses."

"Voices in your head? Flashes of light? Some things can't be allowed to happen."

"You mean you were the voices? What've you been doing, toying with us all along?" He bounced the ball back. Hard.

Asura handled the rebound off the flagstone with ease. She kept her composure for the most part but revealed a hint of anger by narrowing her eyes. "This game involves answering questions, Brewster, not yelling accusations at me. Why did you consider killing yourself?"

He fought against a lump in his throat. "Quintus needed whatever extra strength I could give him."

"You would have sacrificed your own life for your brother?"

"And for Maynya." He nearly dropped what he found himself holding. Through some crazy breach in the time-space continuum, the ball rested in *his* hands instead of hers. Its color had changed to match Asura's kimono, blue as the sky with puffy streaks of white.

"Do you remember the story of Abraham and Isaac?" she asked.

"I'm having trouble remembering much of anything."

"Abraham agreed to kill his son Isaac because he thought God wanted that. But God stopped him. He'd merely been testing the poor man."

Several more butterflies fluttered out of the gateway. They circled Asura's head like a halo. "You passed your trial, Brewster."

He gripped the ball tighter. "Okay, I get it now. This is a dream, right? Wake me up. The last thing I need is some manipulative—"

"Suppose I say you can save both Carla and Maynya and spend the rest of your life with both of them?"

The possibility knocked the wind out of him. But he didn't dare let himself believe in promises by a girl fully capable of destroying him with a simple comment such as *I'm joking. You are, in fact, asleep.*

"Bounce the ball back. Didn't your parents ever teach you how to play a game?"

The thing had turned to crystal. Despite arms turned to jelly, he somehow managed to get it back in her hands.

"I have one condition," she said.

He cringed.

"Don't worry. I'm letting you off easy, although even *considering* suicide is a great sin. Do you remember how I gave dreams to two witnesses so they'd remember seeing a murder?"

"*You* did that?"

"Of course. Gabriella lost control of this game long before you were ever born. You can't imagine how many dreams I've had to plant in her head to keep her on track."

She tossed the ball to him. This time, it changed into a globe. The markings seemed like a child's handiwork—crayoned outlines of green continents and blue oceans, with the coloring straying over the lines in places. Names had been scrawled beneath oddly shaped territories where the United States should have been. Sanctimonia and Virtus filled much of the area where Texas belonged.

"Brewster will confess to Carla's murder and live in solitary confinement without appeal. A scribe needs peace to write a proper gospel. That's my condition."

Just as he feared, she'd pulled the rug out from beneath him.

He closed his eyes. Counted to five. Reopened them.

Dream or real, she remained on the bench across the path, waiting for an answer.

"How exactly does that get me closer to Carla and Maynya?"

"Because you'll be Quintus. Sometimes you'll *dream* about being a man in jail."

"And during these dreams?"

"You'll be a happy man, omniscient, fully aware of your life with Carla and Maynya. Think of it as walking the earth with heaven in your pocket. Carla and Maynya are heaven to you, aren't they?"

"They're everything."

Asura leveled a steady gaze on him. "Do you agree to my condition?"

Yes or no? Up or down? Of course he'd agree. He nodded.

The globe transformed into Albus's head, grinning up at him. He bobbled it to the path.

"My angels will help when they can," Asura said, "but don't delude yourself into thinking you're out of danger. The devil never sleeps."

The king's head reformed into a red trident, wriggling along the flagstone like a snake.

# CHAPTER THIRTY-FIVE

*An eye-blink later*

QUINTUS GRABBED ONE OF the broken tent's remaining posts to prevent a wave of dizziness from toppling him to his knees. A hole in his memory had swallowed whatever happened from the moment his brother exploded in a white puff. He must have blacked out. Perhaps the beam struck him a glancing blow before scattering the pillar of salt that had once been King Albus.

The swiftness and finality with which fate—or the heavens?—obliterated Albus set Quintus's hands trembling. The world had changed in mysterious ways. Where had the bound woman on the altar gone? Why was he still breathing? He'd thrown away his life in a futile attempt to stab his own kin and perhaps spare the woman from certain death, knowing full well the soldiers would take him down.

Somehow, he'd survived, and the struggling redhead had disappeared.

A clamor rose off to the right, beneath a torn fold of tent where sunlight now flooded its golden rays onto the woman who'd stolen his heart. His tremble eased, giving way to tense muscles and a quickened pulse.

Orelea pressed a knife against Maynya's throat.

"Cut the witch up!" someone shouted.

"Burn her at the stake!" cried another.

"No," Orelea hissed. "The king should decide her fate! What say you, Quintus?"

Everyone turned to him for direction. With pinched faces and clenched fists, shouts of "Tell us the verdict," and "We'll put her down," they left little doubt what answer they wanted to hear.

Distracted by emotions stoked to a bonfire, he couldn't at first understand why a sister who had habitually treated him with disdain would now grant him the right to choose Maynya's life or death. The vague realization he'd inherited power came slowly. "Release her!" Panic spurred his cry, not entitlement.

"No! She's a witch!" Orelea held her knife so tight against Maynya's throat a thin line of blood trickled down to stain the upper bodice of the widowed bride's wedding dress. Always a woman who disregarded those wishes not to her liking, his sister had reverted to form at the worst possible time.

In contrast to Orelea's crazed expression, Maynya maintained a singular focus on Quintus, gazing at him not with fear in her eyes but a pressed-lip purpose he couldn't decipher.

He glanced around the tent, desperate to find an ally. The knife in his hand would do little good against an angry throng bent on vengeance. Whatever authority he now possessed hadn't slowed Orelea from taking matters into her own hands. The others revealed similar disregard in their scowls. Having been away for several years, he'd lost whatever bond he might once have had with these people.

Did Acanthus remember the comradeship they'd shared during boar hunts back in happier times? The sandy-haired soldier averted his gaze.

Or Titus…surely, he—

No. This once fellow carouser scalded him with burning eyes. Whatever lingering friendliness he possessed had disappeared into the deepening furrows of his forehead.

Quintus flinched. If his friends offered no support, what help could he expect from an enemy? His fist-clenched rivals seemed ready to drag him next to Maynya and skin them together.

The dark-bearded brute, Phineas, moved a hand to the sword sheathed at his side. This furious man would no doubt rally the soldiers to—

Wait. Quintus came up with an idea. He squared himself and spoke in as regal a tone as possible under the heart-pounding circumstances. "Phineas, we'd like a word with you."

Albus's right-hand man marched over with head raised high, already campaigning in posture for the throne he coveted. "Who are you to make commands? Your brother held you in contempt."

Quintus willed himself to stop shaking as he draped an arm over Phineas's caped shoulders and led him around the altar, away from the others, where they could speak with some privacy. "At least half this kingdom will follow my command, friend. Tell me now. Wouldn't you want them to stand down?"

The parry deflated Phineas's puffed chest. He squinted into Quintus's eyes, no doubt searching for the lie behind the words he'd just heard. "Speak more plainly."

"I'll take Maynya and be on my way. The kingdom is yours." But could he do that, leaving the palace in worse hands than Albus's? What would become of the slave brides?

Maybe his uncertainty showed. As they stared each other down, the narrow-eyed distrust in Phineas's expression failed to dissipate.

"And I'll have your support?" Phineas said.

"Only up to a point. I won't serve in your army." More than likely, he'd come back with a band to *fight* the army, but he tried to hide the notion from his expression.

"I wouldn't have you," Phineas barked. "Tell everyone I'm the rightful king, and you can leave with any whore in this tent *except one*."

Quintus offered his hand. "Are you saying we have a bargain?"

Phineas glanced at Maynya, who still held steady despite Orelea's knife. "No. You don't get the witch until we finish with her. You can bury her broken bones before you leave." But he spoke with enough of a tremor in his voice to reveal a shadow of fear lurking behind his bravado.

Quintus pressed the advantage. "Where's your birthright? Once these people calm down, they'll remember tradition and turn on you, unless the king's true successor endorses you."

Maynya's deeply focused stare raised the hairs on the back of his neck. He was missing something. What had she just mouthed to him?

Still holding the blade with one hand, Orelea twisted Maynya's arm behind her back with the other. Maynya winced but repeated her silent message.

He read her lips—*rats*. What was the context?

Phineas sneered. "She dies, you leave, and I rule. That's the only bargain I'll strike. The soldiers are behind *me*, Quintus."

Quintus raced his mind for associations and came up with a simple one—rats and fear. Might Phineas be afraid of rats? He'd heard rumors about an incident some time ago.

Only a great show of confidence could carry the moment, combined with a bluff. The day a captive bride could save herself by conjuring anything at all would be the day the sun rose in the west. Quintus spread his hands. "I'd try killing Maynya myself if I didn't think she'd summon every *rat* in the kingdom to sink their teeth into my flesh."

The worry lines in Phineas's forehead deepened.

Quintus closed in for the kill. "I'm offering to rid you of a burden as a gesture of peace between us. If you let me take Maynya alive, you'll never set eyes on her again."

Phineas shot a look of pure hatred toward Maynya. He took Quintus's hand in a rough grip and shook. "Tell my people who their new ruler is. Then get that whore of a witch out of my sight!"

Quintus raised his arms. "Everyone!"

The muttering mob quieted. Gentry, visiting princes, merchants, and their women, all dressed in wedding finery but contorting their faces into murderous scowls. They couldn't be trusted to wait long.

"Albus chose wisely in selecting Phineas as his successor," Quintus said. "I am a mere soldier cut in the wrong cloth to serve as your king."

The small group of brides in attendance lowered their heads. They must have thought he'd betrayed them.

With strengthening resolve to return for them after resolving the immediate crisis, Quintus pressed on. "I'll rid this witch from your hands and step down in favor of a worthy ruler, my good friend Phineas."

He stepped into the gathering with bated breath. The soldiers and gentry shifted aside to let him pass, but he met fierce resolve in Orelea's eyes.

"You won't have her," she hissed. Orelea cut an inch-long gash along the side of Maynya's neck, painting the tip of her blade red.

Maynya stared into Quintus's soul with no hint of pain or fear, only adoration intense enough to buckle his knees. The love she radiated seemed to crackle the air. "Brewster!"

Why did she address him so? This woman had baffled him from the beginning, capturing his heart when he first saw her portrait, later rejecting his offer of water on the hill, and now speaking another's name even as he tried to save her life. He drew a deep breath, perhaps one of his last. His love for Maynya was so overpowering he was ready to die for her.

"Bring on the rats!" Phineas shouted. "We're a hundred strong to fend them off."

Good God! Quintus had been a fool to think he could trust this snake. He again shot his gaze around the tent, but his only allies were a huddled group of defenseless brides.

Phineas stalked toward him, waving his arms like a wild man. "You all saw! He tried to stab Albus. That witch has him under her spell!"

Quintus crouched, tightening his grip on his knife. Fool or not, he had every intention of going down with a fight.

A merchant shook an angry fist. "Conspirator!"

Two soldiers elbowed the man aside and came forward with blades in hand.

"Conjurer!" A third advanced toward Maynya with unsheathed sword.

Someone grabbed Quintus from behind. He spun around.

At that moment, Orelea's piercing scream nearly startled him into dropping his knife.

As the hand on his shoulder fell away, a collective gasp rang in his ears. He glanced at his sister in time to see her blade curving away from Maynya's neck. It slithered like a snake, then stretched to the length of a sword before plunging into Orelea's shoulder. She collapsed.

Bzzzzz. What was that roar, ten million insects? Or did he simply over-amplify the rush of adrenaline in his ears?

No, this had to be real. Others shifted their hands to their ears. Maynya began twitching. Her eyes rolled. Her head tilted back.

A black cloud of insects tore into the tent—thick-bodied, ugly locusts. They poured through the torn flaps above, across the entranceway, ripping new holes in the flimsy lining.

Everyone yelled, swatted, ran, fell. Orelea twitched on the ground. Phineas covered his face with his cape.

Only the brides held steady. The swarm stayed clear of them.

Maynya staggered backwards. Quintus wrapped his arms around her to arrest her fall.

"Don't worry about me, Brewster," she rasped. "Free the other brides caged in the compound...beside the palace!"

*Brewster?* That odd salutation tickled his memory but failed to awaken it. Perhaps in her excitement, Maynya had spoken a lover's name. The notion she had someone else in her life turned his stomach to the point he almost retched.

Quintus rebuked himself for letting his selfish needs slow him in the heat of battle. He took Maynya's hand and headed for the opening of the tent, pausing just a moment to glance back at the few brides inside. "Follow me!" He had to shout above the insects to be heard.

The locusts parted to let them pass.

Outside the tent, pandemonium reigned. Swarming locusts blotted out the sun. People ran in circles, waving their arms in self-defense. Women screamed. Horse-drawn carts overturned.

A bright flash of lightning set a secondary tent ablaze. Thunder shook the ground.

Quintus tightened his grip on Maynya's hand and turned to the forest.

"Not that way," she said. Whatever magic she'd created left her pale and unsteady. She faltered against him, trembling.

The brides poured out of the tent and gathered around them.

Maynya rallied, straightening and pointing toward the trees in the distance. "Chrysanta, Jillian, Johanna...all of you others, run to Sanctimonia! We'll free your sisters and send them on your heels."

Each of the women hurried up to hug her. A moment later, these dozen prospective brides in their flashy makeup and colorful dresses with hair fixed just right in the hopes of finding kind husbands who wouldn't beat them...these rescued maidens kicked off their shoes and scampered away in bare feet, like a group of traditional Mystic women chasing down a turkey to make a feast for their men.

Quintus stared after the women until they'd put a good distance between themselves and anyone who might have followed had the locusts not proven to be the greater distraction. Then he directed his gaze to the empty marching field he'd tramped across seemingly a hundred years earlier for a meeting with a tyrant of a brother now turned to salt. The thick cloud of buzzing insects obscured the palace from view.

Sadness for the lost soul of his brother thickened his tongue. They'd been friends once, in their early youth, before corruption began eating at Albus like a cancer. But he couldn't slow himself with these thoughts. "How long will this last?"

Maynya must have sensed his grief. She gave him a moment before answering. "God willing, this will last until every slave is freed, my love."

The endearment warmed his heart.

They walked into the chaos together, hand in hand. The locusts spilled apart like the red sea for the legendary Moses.

Maynya stroked Quintus's hand with a thumb. She had love in her eyes.

Her obvious fondness lightened his step. Still he needed to

raise a question that would otherwise gnaw away at him like a different form of cancer. "Whose name did you speak earlier?"

She stopped, stepped in front of him, settled gentle hands on his face. Her eyes welled. "You don't know him, do you?"

"I'm not sure."

She wiped a tear from her cheek. "A man died for me in another world. I want to thank him with all my heart."

"Any good man would die for you in this one."

Maynya's face seemed to blur ever so slightly, fading the shadows of a hard life from beneath her eyes. The same woman, and yet different somehow, softer, more forward, kissed his cheek. "*Quintus,* darling, if you ever even think about dying for me again, I'll kill you."

For the briefest moment, the thick swarms of locusts transformed into windswept snow—something he'd rarely seen in Virtus. He knew this woman by another name. What name? His foggy brain could only summon his own.

"What's wrong?" she asked. "You've gone pale."

He closed his eyes and reopened them…to locusts…and Maynya. The moment had passed. His fellow soldiers had a saying for trauma-induced hallucinations. "The angels lost their grip on my soul."

"Cast your lot with me, then." Maynya grabbed his hand and led him toward the lusterless wooden palace of a dead ruler who'd lost *his* soul to demons. A barred-window building just to the east held brides in need of a champion.

## Chapter Thirty-Six

*Within a federal correctional facility several months later*

HEATHER STRUTTED INTO A visitor area beyond the partition of bulletproof glass. She settled into a chair across from Brewster and grabbed the phone.

If not for his head-over-heels love for Carla, his former office manager's new look would have gotten a rise out of him. She'd dyed her hair from brunette to auburn and gone with a shorter cut, one leaving the black-and-yellow butterfly in proud display on the side of her neck. On top of all that, her short skirt and tight blouse had him averting his eyes to stay out of trouble. He groped for some small talk like a lifeline. "How are things at Crestview?"

"Tesfaye's behind in his payments already."

"No surprise there."

"Makes me miss the old debtor's prison days." She fished a cigarette out of her purse. "Mind if I smoke?"

"The guards might."

She lit up anyway.

Brewster had already deduced a simple formula—butterfly tattoo equals Asura minion. But he still couldn't get used to the concept that the heavens had a soft spot for chain-smoking office managers. "This sisterhood of yours? You aren't anything like Abelia."

"She's just a kid." Heather took a slow drag, exhaled, and glanced around at the other convicts lined up across the glass from their moms, wives, girlfriends, molls. "How are your buddies treating you?"

"Knock on wood, they've been steering clear of me in the showers."

"I'm seeing to that."

Whew. He could have floated off his bench from *that* morsel of good news. Here he'd been worrying about his luck running out sooner or later. "So, what's the story? You've been my guardian angel in this gig all along?"

"I'm just another slave working for the Asian bitch."

The slur took his breath away. "You're not talking about—"

"Asura. She wants me to leave Crestview now that you moved on."

"Do you have a choice?"

Heather watched a smoke ring drift to the ceiling. Judging by her reddening face, her signature version of counting to ten wasn't working. "I told her to stuff it."

"You said that, huh?"

"Bet your ass! This idea we can be moved around like chess pieces with no voice in the matter is so Dark Ages. I'm spreading grace at work. Employees rely on me for their livelihoods!"

He'd agitated her. Good. Prison time tended to be short on entertainment. He folded his arms, leaned back, let her vent.

"So Asura says, 'Fine, keep financing losers who can't afford their trucks.' Those were her exact words, Brewster."

"I seriously doubt that."

"Okay, so I'm paraphrasing." Heather glanced around, leaned forward. "She isn't necessarily on the A team, just so you know."

He caught his breath again.

"Never mind. I'm just venting. Call me a problem employee. Anyway, Asura wants me to edit your journals when I'm not too busy with my day job."

Perfect. That meant a never-ending stream of visits. Prison time could get a little lonely.

Not that he was complaining. He'd never been more content. In fact, he regarded himself as downright blissful. He'd traded a stressful career in an unforgiving world for the simple life of an inspirational writer. Thoreau would have been envious.

Besides, he had Carla/Maynya in his pocket, always just an eye-blink away, as Asura had promised—part of his days spent with the woman he loved and part working on a masterpiece. Better yet, he spent far more time in that reality than this dream, as far as he could tell. Or were they both realities? His head still spun when he tried to sort it all out.

Heather snuffed her cigarette and leaned forward again, all business now. "Let's title your series *The Gospel According to Quintus.*"

"That's a mouthful."

She waved him off. "We'll go small press with this. The best religions start with a whisper. At least Asura and I are on the same page about *that*."

"Wait. I thought the idea was that the world needed a new Gospel. Christianity stays in place, right?"

"Yeah, yeah."

"Hold on, Heather. I'm not writing a damned word if you're planning to change—"

Heather held up a hand. "Fine. We'll follow Asura's wishes. *Again*." She glanced over her shoulder at a door in the back. "Anyway, I brought a visitor."

If only. He let out a sigh. "You know the rules. I'm allowed just one per day."

"I make the rules here, dear boy."

The lights flickered, and the low buzz of conversation up and down the partition ended. Prisoners, visitors, and guards froze mid-sentence with mouths open and body language locked in place. Liquid spilling from a visitor's tipped glass hung toward the floor like a crystal waterfall. The wall clock stopped.

He'd seen some weird stuff since his meeting with Asura, but Heather had been relatively low-key until recently, no doubt trying to ease him into the shock she was somewhat more than a working stiff. "Um—"

"Wait here." She left her chair and slipped out of the room.

The dark-haired woman entering a minute later seemed thirty something at first, but when she came closer, he realized a shaggy haircut, halter top, short skirt, and great diet had chased quite a few years away. Then she got close enough for him to see the family resemblance. He swallowed.

Carla's mother stepped around immobilized visitors like they didn't exist. She grabbed the chair, lifted the phone, and grinned, motioning toward the frozen convict in the next slot. "Hocus pocus."

He grinned. "Heather's a card, isn't she?"

They stared at each other, and an awkward silence stripped the veneer of humor away. Tears welled in her eyes.

"I am so sorry," he said.

She mustered a smile. "Your friend over there did a weird little mind meld on me. I know everything that happened now. Carla died before you ever met her."

"Yeah, but maybe I could have—"

"You tried to rescue her. That's what matters."

That he did. Still, he couldn't prevent the lump in his throat over the fact this woman might still have a daughter in real time if he'd caught sight of Gabriella before the little witch had a chance to push them.

Her expression turned dreamy. "I've started getting glimpses of Carla's other half when I sleep. More Heather?"

"This sisterhood thing is pretty cool."

"Yet here you are languishing in prison. She can freeze everyone in this room, but she can't get you out?"

He glanced around at surroundings grown no less drab by their familiarity. Dirty, barred windows high up near the ceiling grudgingly allowed some sunlight but not enough to bring life to the olive-green walls, the worn tile flooring, or a row of prisoners who'd lost the luster from their eyes. "The party line is I can do my best writing here, since I won't have many distractions."

"And your line?"

"Judging by what Heather told me a few minutes ago, maybe I could have stood up for myself and cut a better deal."

"Is it too late to try?"

"Six-and-a-half years is the deal." The frozen wall clock showed no inkling of spinning backward, and he was fine keeping it that way. A gospel needed to be written. A religion reignited. Crafting such a powerful tome could be no rush project.

"You're two heroes, Brewster."

"Uh-uh. The only star in my story lives across the portal with Maynya."

And he shared that man's happy life whenever he closed his eyes.

"Wake up, sleepyhead."

Quintus squinted up at the overly sunny afternoon. Maynya had knelt beside him.

She smiled. "I've married a lazy man."

He rose from grass as soft as a hammock and looked past her at the tent city of followers, perhaps a thousand pilgrims strong, maybe more. The town of Portus lay five miles distant across the sun-baked prairie. They'd carried their message to its inhabitants these past few days, swelling their ranks with new believers.

Success should have energized him, but he'd grown weary after so many days wandering, so many days scavenging for food, so many days gathering new followers from the scattered settlements stretching the long distance across Virtus's frontier. He'd stolen a nap.

"I remembered something as I awoke," he said.

Maynya's eyes lit up. "A vision from the other dimension?"

"Maybe, but I wasn't in prison. I think this happened earlier."

"Tell me."

"I found you dancing on a road, in a snowstorm. You beamed like a child on her name day, and you called me a beautiful man."

Her smile spread wide as the sky. "Who was this beautiful man?"

"Booster?"

She ruffled his hair. "Sometimes I think you pretend to remember less than you do, just to get a charge out of me."

Sometimes he did.

She stood, reached down, and tugged his hand until he came up beside her. "I have a surprise for you, *Booster*."

Maynya led him to a ragged, makeshift tent pitched among the many others. Had he seen this one somewhere before? The recollection stirred his emotions as much as the dream he'd just had. He struggled to quell a leaping heart. His terrible act of negligence during his journey to the capital couldn't possibly have gone undone.

Yet a woman reached her arm from within the tent to pull the flap open, and she did have a butterfly tattoo on her wrist, just like—

Adala stepped out of the tent.

"Look who wandered into our camp," Maynya said.

Quintus gaped at the golden-haired, water-to-wine magician turned...ghost? He couldn't find any words.

Adala brushed the back of his cheek with a warm, soft hand no wraith could ever possess. "Did you really think a simple highwayman could smite me down?"

"I don't know what to think anymore."

Adala winked. "If men would leave the thinking to our gender, we'd all be better off, eh, Maynya?"

Quintus motioned to the half-filled wicker basket visible through the open flap of her tent. "We think better with full stomachs. I see they've already recruited you to help with the scavenging."

"Yes, but I've only managed to scrounge five loaves of bread and two fish," Adala said, "hardly enough to feed so many. I'm sure you can come up with something, though, Maynya, can't you?"

Maynya motioned toward one of the tents. "We have a store of food in there. Let's not forget who is God and who isn't."

When the late-afternoon shadows grew long, and a thousand bellies swelled from a bountiful feast of fish and loaves, Maynya climbed a low hill to behold her following, a rabble of villagers, deserting soldiers, escaped brides, and some monks who'd seen the light. A pair of doves cut across the sky—a favorable sign. Then a swarm of monarch butterflies darted out of the shrubbery alongside the stream—even better.

She raised her arms until the horde of pilgrims grew silent.

"I want to share with you a sermon once preached by the Son of God."

She motioned to the women her locusts had rescued, a small group of unwed brides who'd chosen to make new lives for themselves in the wilds of the prairie instead of scampering after their sisters to the forests of Sanctimonia. "Blessed are the poor in spirit, for theirs is the kingdom of Heaven."

She gestured toward a follower whose husband had drowned in a flood. "Blessed are they that mourn, for they shall be comforted."

Then she turned her attention to Quintus.

Maynya, the Sanctimonia guardian-turned-prophet, and Carla, a simple shopkeeper killed by a train, gazed together at the man they loved. They swallowed. Tears stained their cheeks.

Each woman had found joy.

# EPILOGUE

*Hiroshima: April 12, 2020*

GABRIELLA KNELT AT THE edge of the azalea garden and busied herself with a planting. When she finished, she set her spade on the ground, wiped her hands in her apron, and looked up at the empty sky, praying to a voice she couldn't remember ever hearing. After over seventy offerings, decades of visits, perhaps the gardeners would relent. Her tulip deserved to stand tall among the other flowers.

"I suppose it should."

Such a familiar voice! She spun around to face a girl who hadn't died after all. Somehow, history had refreshed itself in a wondrous way, as if a door opened to reveal long-absent colors, elusive sounds, shy fragrances. Amazement and joy combined to steal Gabriella's breath away.

Asura, the girl who knew all the secrets, looked little different than on the day the pilgrims flocked to her garden from miles away and butterflies danced in the circular entranceway. She still kept her dark hair in a bun adorned with pins, she reflected the sky with her blue-and-white kimono, and she revealed nothing in her stoic smile. The enigmatic child had returned.

Gabriella grabbed Asura's hands and gazed into deep, ambiguous eyes. "Why did you wait so long to come back?"

Asura pulled away. "How long would *you* hold a grudge over the premature death of an only son?"

Jesus had been her son? The implication nearly sent Gabriella to her knees in supplication. But perhaps she'd misheard. Self-absorption often compromised her senses, a flaw she'd come to believe might be as bad as her pride. "Are you... You can't be God."

"I might have been, for all you knew. But let's not dwell on my definition. Consider me a girl in hot water, just like you. God isn't happy with either one of us at the moment."

Gabriella turned away to hide tears welling in her eyes. "My few mistakes were made with good intentions."

In the stony silence that followed, the horseshoe-shaped white cenotaph in the near distance mocked her, a memorial lacking Asura's name for good reason.

She choked back a sob. "You goaded me into going to Herod, with your talk about pebbles and boulders, the butterflies in the gateway, and the way you let your shadow burn into the bench. What could a proper angel do but read the signs and act accordingly?" Her voice shook. She'd spent many years considering iterations that wouldn't have included betrayal of God's only Son.

When an immediate response didn't come, she turned to face Asura again, half fearing her guilty conscience had summoned a mere hallucination. During the early aftermath of the bomb, she'd seen Asura in crowds, shadows, pool reflections, clouds. She'd mistaken the voices of random children as Asura's. She'd chased butterflies across meadows into woods where the girl might have been hiding.

This time, so many years later, Asura proved to be no mirage. She remained standing, but with arms folded and an unhappy frown on her face.

Or pity? Gabriella's stomach lurched at the thought anyone might feel sorry for her.

"Suppose you *aren't* a proper angel?" Asura said.

She flinched. Why so harsh a verdict for a single transgression?

Okay, perhaps she'd committed more than one, but not many. When measured against the decades gone by, the count had been relatively small.

Gabriella stammered an unintelligible response even she couldn't understand. She lowered her gaze, traced some dirt with the toe of her shoe, and dared to look up again, only to find the same expression. But she'd misinterpreted it. Asura's hint of a frown didn't suggest sadness or pity.

Far worse.

*Disappointment.* She gulped. "I can work at becoming better. I'll be magnificent! Henry Stoddard thinks I might be young for an angel. There's still hope for me."

"Suppose you aren't an *angel* at all?" This question came sharper, carrying the sting of a slap.

Gabriella gasped. Did Asura plan to strip her of her wings? She should never have spoken to Herod. Why had she interfered with Carla's fate? Or Brewster's. Or…or…

The list went on and on, widening the gap from a minor lack of propriety to some serious mischief indeed. But Asura had her all wrong. Didn't she? She stomped her foot. "I am *not* a demon."

"Nor were you ever an angel." Asura settled a gentle hand on her shoulder.

Gabriella shrugged her off. "What would you have me be then, some immortal freak?"

Asura reshaped her frown to an almost smile. More pity? Sympathy perhaps? "I'll have you be what you are, Gabriella, *the multitude.* You are the echo of every man, woman, and child who ever walked the earth. This is the reason you can pass so easily from mind to mind and memory to memory. They are all you, in a sense. You are the sum of everything good *and bad* in this world."

The multitude.

Not an angel. Not a demon.

Gabriella's eyes moistened. Surely not from tears. The strong never cried. No. Asura's disturbing term had been so ridiculous as to bring on an allergy. "You're saying I'm nothing. Just a shadow."

Asura flashed the kindest smile. "I'm saying you're unique. Come walk with me."

Gabriella had enough of the reunion. She tried to stalk away...but smoke stopped her at every turn.

The portal between realities, while always an annoyance, had at least been consistent in its behavior, shadowing her, serving as a singular gateway. Not anymore. It duplicated itself again and again like an amoeba gone wild. She swung away from one iteration only to have another shift in front of her. A third positioned itself to her right. A fourth materialized on her left.

She threw up her hands. "Enough!" She could only flee Asura's awful revelation by passing out of the Christian world into what...yet another broken civilization begging for a messiah?

Asura gripped her shoulder from behind. "Mankind needed a fresh gospel, Gabriella. Heaven knows the old ones have been ignored lately."

"So this was all about rebooting religion? You played me like a pawn from the beginning."

"No. I don't micromanage any more than God does. You made your own choices." Asura sighed. "I suppose if He did micromanage, we wouldn't have gotten ourselves into such a fix to begin with."

"You mean He would have stopped you?" Gabriella turned to face the beautiful porcelain doll she'd once hoped to protect. "If I am the multitude, what are you, Asura? Tell me that much."

Asura looked down. "A messenger? I suppose we all should speak less and listen more." The portals disappeared, and she walked away.

Gabriella hurried after her. "Where are you going?"

"My home."

They walked in silence, leaving the garden and passing the various landmarks of Hiroshima Memorial Park—the cenotaph, the fountain, the skeletal ruins of the Industrial Promotion Hall, and, impossibly, a low garden wall with a unique, circular stone entranceway. Marble benches waited across a flagstone path from each other. Gabriella's knees wobbled.

She and Asura sat across from each other, positioning themselves as they had so many years earlier.

Asura's smile spread to her eyes, bringing a deeper blue to the sky.

Gabriella struggled not to cry.

"You've walked the earth in confusion throughout your long life. Perhaps you'd have made better choices if you hadn't been alone." Asura motioned toward the gateway, and a girl stepped through.

Gabriella gaped at her own profile. In reflection? As a mirage?

"She's real," Asura said. "Meet your twin."

Sorrow fluttered away on the wings of a thousand butterflies. A blonde-haired, ponytailed girl now stood among them.

"Your act duplicated every man, woman, and child on earth at the time of Herod," Asura said. "And what is the multitude if not all of them? Meet your clone."

Gabriella rushed up and wrapped her arms around her double. "Where have you been all this time?"

Her double grimaced. "Gaul."

"Gaul?"

"It's a hopeless place, and I'm powerless there. I only have a cabin. This invisible wall keeps me from—"

With heart in throat, Gabriella could barely find the voice to respond. "I know the feeling."

"I've been searching for a messiah among the rabble," her sister said.

"No need," Gabriella said. "I've got that covered."

Asura brushed past them into the gateway. "I have a ball in the garden. Shall we chalk the path for another game? Maybe we'll get it right this time."

TERMINUS

## *Did You Enjoy The Multitude?*

Please do this writer a solid, by hopping onto Amazon and leaving a reader review. The process is simple:

(1) Type *The Multitude* in the search box.

(2) Click the cover picture.

(3) Scroll to the bottom and click Write a Review.

(4) Write a bit about your travels through time in space with Gabriella, Carla, Maynya, Brewster, and Quintus. You don't need to write much. Some reviews are only a few words in length. Others are longer. Just do what feels comfortable to you.

(5) Once you're finished, while still in Amazon, maybe you'd like to read the other novels in the Gabriella Trilogy? You'll find excerpts of *Faulty Bones* and *The Witch of the Hills* on the following pages.

Thank you!
J.M. Fraser

*Excerpt from*

# FAULTY BONES

## by J. M. FRASER

ONE DAY, RUNNING ON empty and down to my last few dollars, I run into a friend of a friend who introduces me to another friend, who tells me about Hal, who knows some guy named Philippe. A French guy. Philippe has a scam going. Counterfeit chips.

Enter Philippe. We're at his joke of an apartment, and I'm sitting across from him at an ancient Formica table with wobbly legs, in a kitchen so old the appliances are colored yellow and green. Not white or stainless steel like the kind I'd buy if I could ever build up a bankroll large enough to cover anything more than a poker buy-in and the next meal. We're talking hard times all around, and that shouldn't make any sense to me, given the fact Philippe is supposed to be a successful counterfeiter and all.

But I'm a little too desperate for cash to worry about that. Besides this man's nationality has captured my entire focus, distracting me from all else, cuz for a poker player, there's nothing more important than the initial read. Ironic, huh?

Anyway, Philippe isn't French. He's an everyday, balding, older guy with tattoos all over the muscled arms bulging out of his dirty T-shirt. He looks like another Joe or Bob or Hank. A former seaman or retired cop who let himself go in his declining years. Until he opens his mouth to speak.

"What can I help choo weef and how much woudchoo pay me?"

Yep, he's Russian through and through, not only based on his accent, which I won't try to pathetically imitate anymore, but also the *give something to get something* attitude, especially the way he emphasizes the word *pay,* dragging it out slowly, the same way he'd undoubtedly prolong my torture if I fail to return every penny I'll ever owe him, notwithstanding the fact I'm a woman, and a pretty one at that. Uh-huh, that's a brag, but I work long and hard at taking good care of myself. We're talking six miles of roadwork a day, minimum. I eat the right foods, barely any at all, and thanks to the unfailing wisdom of my late mom, I brush my hair to a shine at least once a day. She always said what a man finds the most appealing in a woman at first glance sits north of her forehead. My mom insisted on that, so don't believe anyone who claims they're a tits man or a legs man. That all comes after the initial impression.

I know all about reads, believe me.

I gaze into Philippe's eyes, cool as can be, and I silently count to twelve before answering, just to convey how unintimidating I find his subtle menace and the overall dire situation I may be getting sucked into. Who in their right mind goes to a man who isn't only Russian but undoubtedly mobbed up, to get involved as a mule for his dastardly counterfeiting enterprise? Yes, my right knee is beginning to tremble in its hiding place under the table and out of view, but I command it to hold steady. *Not one inch of my body* can even hint at the absolute terror causing my heart to pump a thousand miles per hour.

Otherwise, I'm sunk with a guy like this. He'll have me for breakfast if that half-empty bottle of vodka at his elbow hasn't satisfied his appetite already.

"I don't like the feel of you," I say in a steady voice, "so let's just say I came for a visit, and I choked down a nice glass of vodka with you, but now I'll be on my way."

That's what's known as a bluff, folks.

I start to rise from my chair, but quick as an eyeblink, he has me by the wrist with a powerful hand. Anyone...*anyone* would scream at this point, but I've commanded all body parts, including my throat, to behave, so I merely whimper, and then I bust out crying.

*Faulty Bones* is available now on Amazon.

*Excerpt from*

# THE WITCH OF THE HILLS

## by J. M. FRASER

**A TINY SHAPE EMERGED** at the shimmery point in the distance where highway squiggled into heat mirage. Brian squinted but couldn't make it out. Fence post?

Eastern Wyoming had so much to offer.

The distance closed fast, and the figure turned into a girl with her thumb out. A stiff breeze scattered dark hair across her face and ruffled her long country dress. She held her ground where the shoulder met the pavement, as if daring the next semi to take her down. Spunky, unconventional, interesting, the hitchhiker represented everything Brian had been hoping to find on his first-ever road trip alone.

As foot on the gas became foot off the gas became foot on the brake, the possibilities raced through his mind.

Together in the car, the two of them could crack jokes about the boring scenery. Bluffs, scrub brush, coal trains. *Let's stop and take a picture of those wicked telephone poles.*

They could swap life stories. Matching sets, most likely—parents, school, part-time jobs, rules, rules, rules, but also a vision of a promising future, a light at the end of the tunnel, the day when they might be old enough to start making the rules themselves or at least wouldn't have to follow every stinking one of them.

Maybe they'd stop for gas and have a moment, looking at each other but pretending not to look, and then catching each other's eye, holding that gaze, and, and, and—

And with all the wishful thinking, he almost blew past this glistening can of soda in the desert, this cheeseburger in a sushi bar. Brian braked harder and cut over from the fast lane.

The girl allowed him some room to get off the road. She was cute up close. A smile would have helped, but cute nonetheless, in a scraggly-haired, brooding sort of way.

So far, so good. He lowered the passenger window, imagining the best possible exchange. Something like…

*"Want a ride?"*

*"You bet!"*

With that in mind, he spoke his line to perfection.

She gazed at him a beat too long for somebody following the best possible script. And she crossed her arms. Bad signs. A car roared by, buffeting them with draft. She waited for it to muscle past them, waited until silence hung heavy in the air. "Not with the likes of you," she said.

*The Witch of the Hills* is available now on Amazon.

# About the Author

**J.M. FRASER** is a businessman and writer. He's living the dream with his better half, Mary, in the suburban prairies west of Milwaukee. When not doing whatever it is that they do, they spend as much time as they can with their two daughters, Carolyn and Natalie, and a cute little grandson named Colin.